C000063805

*The Girl from Norfolk with
the Flying Table*

The Girl from Norfolk with the Flying Table

LILIE FERRARI

MICHAEL JOSEPH
LONDON

MICHAEL JOSEPH LTD

Published by the Penguin Group
27 Wrights Lane, London w8 5tz
Viking Penguin Inc., 375 Hudson Street, New York, New York 10014, USA
Penguin Books Australia Ltd, Ringwood, Victoria, Australia
Penguin Books Canada Ltd, 10 Alcorn Avenue, Toronto, Ontario, Canada m4v 3b2
Penguin Books (NZ) Ltd, 182–190 Wairau Road, Auckland 10, New Zealand

Penguin Books Ltd, Registered Offices: Harmondsworth, Middlesex, England

First published in Great Britain 1996

Copyright © Lilie Ferrari, 1996

All rights reserved.
Without limiting the rights under copyright
reserved above, no part of this publication may be
reproduced, stored in or introduced into a retrieval system,
or transmitted, in any form or by any means (electronic, mechanical,
photocopying, recording or otherwise) without prior
written permission of both the copyright owner
and the above publisher of this book

Set in 11/13.5 pt Monotype Bembo
Typeset by Datix International Limited, Bungay, Suffolk
Printed in England by Clays Ltd, St Ives plc

ISBN 0 7181 40788

The moral right of the author has been asserted

In memory of my mother

CONTENTS

CHAPTER ONE

Love Me Do – 1962

POSY PINK. DAISY PINK. Pink Meringue. Pearly Pink. Cissie wasn't sure. It felt like a Daisy Pink sort of an evening, but perhaps you shouldn't wear lipstick in church at all. She had no one to ask, no one who would take that kind of a question seriously. Peggy would throw back her head, laugh that throaty cigarette laugh and say why not Satan Scarlet, or Devil Damson? Mike would give her the pained, puzzled look he reserved for moments when he thought Cissie was just being plain difficult, and then he'd retire to his shed and ponder the mysteries of teenage girls over his pipe. Cissie sighed, absent-mindedly twiddling a frond of red hair. She was completely alone.

Downstairs Mike was fiddling with the radiogram, and the sound of his Dave Brubeck long-player floated up. Cissie stared at her reflection, dissatisfied. No lipstick, perhaps, but then she looked so pale. Perhaps the red mohair beret?

'Baby's asleep, finally.' Peggy was leaning in the doorway, holding a glass of wine. She was wearing a tight dress of some shiny green material, and long earrings. Cissie stared at her mother's reflection in the mirror and was unable to prevent a slight frown of disapproval flickering across her face.

'What's the matter?' Peggy looked down at herself, uncertain. 'Don't you like it?'

'A bit tight, Mum.'

Peggy crossed the room to examine herself in Cissie's dressing-table mirror, crouching slightly behind her daughter, squinting at herself, critical.

'Oh, I don't know. I've seen Marilyn Monroe in tighter things.' She straightened up, doubts forgotten. 'I came up to see if you want a drink – get you in the mood.'

'No, thanks. Maybe some lemonade.' Then, seeing the expression on her mother's face, 'I'm *fifteen*, Mum!'

Peggy sighed. 'I don't think you'll get arrested for drinking a glass of wine. If this were France –'

'But it isn't.' Cissie pulled a hairbrush through her hair. 'Anyway, I'm going out.'

'Out? But it's Sunday evening! You never go out!'

'I'm going to meet Bennett. In the village.'

'But I thought Bennett had to go to church on a –' Peggy stopped. Here goes. Cissie's heart sank. 'Cissie! You're not going to church!'

Cissie's mouth set in a line. 'It's a special service tonight. Because of the crisis.'

Peggy started to laugh, that rich sound, the one that made people tell Cissie that her mother sounded like Lena Horne (a *coloured* woman, for heaven's sake). Peggy crossed over to the window and opened it, so that she could flick her cigarette ash outside, and a cold blast of October wind swept the room.

'Mum!'

Peggy slammed the window shut again, ignoring Cissie's reprimand, and turned to face her daughter again, smiling.

'Didn't they have a special service last week? And the week before? Didn't stop the Bay of Pigs, did it?'

'You've got lipstick on your teeth.' Cissie wished her mother would get out of her bedroom, but Peggy was sipping from the wine glass, warming to her subject, waving her cigarette.

'What language are these prayers in, Cissie? That fat vicar – speaks Russian, does he? Or Spanish?' Cissie concentrated on her hair, tugging at a knot rather too savagely and making her head ache, trying not to listen to Peggy. 'Do you think Castro's going to hear him? Or Kruschev? Or Kennedy?' Peggy was persisting. 'Or does God act as a kind of conduit, passing the prayers of Polston Wood down the line to the Kremlin and the White House?' She let out a snort of exasperation. 'Honestly, Cissie – you're the limit.'

2

'Go on, say it – I'm a foundling. That's what you always say when you're drunk.'

Peggy stopped smiling, hurt. 'Do I?' She stared at Cissie, her mouth slightly open, as if she were momentarily short of breath. Then she crossed back to Cissie and leaned over her again, squeezing her shoulder, the scent of her perfume suddenly making the air heady. 'Well, I'm not drunk now, and I certainly don't think you're a foundling, Cissie. You're far too much like me.' She studied their reflections in the mirror, their faces close now, comparing their blue eyes, the similar line of their noses, the same characteristic fullness of their mouths, one pale and unadorned, the other a rich, unnatural scarlet. Peggy's hand, with its chewed fingernails, came up and rubbed at her front tooth. The red mouth curved upwards in a smile. 'I know you'd like to think you're nothing to do with your awful mother,' it said, '– sorry to disappoint you.' The pale mouth smiled, reluctant, in reply, and Dave Brubeck suddenly got very loud.

Peggy straightened up. 'Good God!' she said, brisk again, 'I said conversation level, not lip-reading level!' she hurried away, calling to Mike to adjust the volume, leaving Cissie as she always left her: flustered, angry, affectionate.

Perhaps just a little Peachy Pink . . .

Downstairs, where Cissie descended a few moments later, the kitchen had been transformed into a bar, with rows of glasses set out on the table, and bottles ranked in rows behind. Oliver was sitting at the table, changing the fuse on a plug. He looked up at Cissie as she appeared at the foot of the stairs.

'Not coming to the party, I hear,' he said. Oliver was Cissie's step-brother, an alien creature from London, twenty years old, who hardly ever came to the house in Norfolk, and when he did, hardly spoke. Cissie ignored him and wandered into the living room. She didn't like Oliver, she thought he was sinister. Always appearing when you least expected – or wanted – him to, always somehow critical in his silence, always watching, never speaking. Cissie wished he would stay in London.

This room too had a tidy, unfamiliar look, with the family's odd assortment of chairs lined up round the walls and a great empty space in the middle ready for dancing. Mike's mother (who was mysteriously always referred to as 'Mill', even though Cissie knew this was not her name), was spread out in her usual armchair by the fire, puffing on a cigarette.

'Like a girl getting ready,' she said, seemingly in the throes of profound thought. Cissie ignored her, helping herself to some peanuts on display in a paper party plate on the sideboard. Mill watched her, disapproving. 'The room,' she said. 'Like a girl ready for a party – all different, all fancied up, but still the same underneath. Leopards and spots and all that.' Mill was fond of repeating homilies, proverbs and sayings, but never quite remembered how they fitted together.

'Girls getting ready for parties don't stink of Woodbines,' Cissie said, then fell silent, feeling cruel. Mill smoked Woodbines all the time. But Mill ignored the implied insult. 'Well, this one certainly will,' she said, comfortable, reaching out with a fat arm to rescue her own packet from the mantelpiece. 'Couple of hours, she'll have lost her virginity, never mind smelling of Woodbines.'

Peggy heard this as she came in. 'Mill, try not to spend all evening sounding like someone out of *Cold Comfort Farm*, will you? And Cissie, if you eat all the peanuts you'll be sick in church.'

Mill turned to look at Cissie, her eyes round with surprise, her head wreathed in smoke. 'Church?'

'Cuban crisis,' Peggy said, by way of explanation. Mill tried to repress a snort of derision and failed.

Cissie headed back towards the cupboard under the stairs in the kitchen. 'I'm going,' she called. A small black bundle immediately materialized from under Oliver's legs at the table, and began to leap at Cissie's knees, panting. 'No, Toulouse,' she pushed the dog away. 'Not you.' He retired, hurt.

As Cissie pulled on her coat, Peggy and Mike appeared together. Cissie buttoned her coat and avoided their eyes, as they stood there in the doorway, so comfortable together, Mike's arm resting on his wife's shoulder, Peggy leaning into him, as if they had been born like this – linked, permanent.

'Hat?' Peggy asked. 'It's cold out there.'

4

Cissie shook her head. 'It's not far.' She was ready to escape. 'I don't know what time I'll be back, Mum,' she said. 'I'm going to Bennett's afterwards.'

'We'll still be up,' Peggy said.

'I know.' Cissie wanted to say, 'Yes, and drunk,' but didn't. She was only too aware of how she sounded. Miss Prim, Mike called her when she told him off about playing his records too loudly or swearing. 'Yes, Mother,' Peggy would say drily, when her daughter sighed over her mother's outfits or begged her not to turn up at the school in black woolly stockings.

Gloves, scarf. She was ready. She opened her mouth to say goodbye. 'I thought your friend was going to come – Jude. To the party.' Mike said.

Cissie stared at him, aghast. 'Who said?'

'She did.'

'What – Jude?'

'She phoned up earlier, when you were out with the dog. I mentioned the party – she said she'd be here.' Mike wandered over to the table and took the plug Oliver was holding out to him. 'Thanks, son.' He headed back towards the living room, but then paused, seeing Cissie's face. 'Did I do the wrong thing?'

Cissie's face closed down. 'Right,' she said, abrupt. 'In that case I'll be back. With Bennett. Don't know what time. And don't play my records.'

And she hurried out, ignoring the reproach in Toulouse's eyes, slamming the kitchen door behind her, and wincing in the sudden icy wind that whistled maliciously round the side of the house and almost overbalanced her.

Sod, sod, sod. She stamped down the icy path, her cheeks hot with anger. Always something, always people interfering! At the front gate, which sagged on its hinges, its peeling sign with the word 'Brigadoon' only just visible in the dark, she turned to fasten the catch and saw suddenly in the lighted windows of the living room how her home must seem to other people. There was Mill, large and overpowering in something black and sequinned, puffing away on her blasted Woodbine and staring glumly into the fire. There was Mike, wearing the usual corduroys and faded shirt, pipe on the go, sorting through a pile of records. There was Oliver, intent, dark hair falling over his face, doing something to a lamp in the corner. And there was Peggy, beautiful Peggy, standing alone in the middle of the room, her green dress catching the firelight so that the sheen on it glimmered, her dark red hair piled up untidily on her head. She was swaying slightly, as if dancing to an unheard tune. There they were, then: the Lovelock family, at home in Brigadoon, expecting guests. Cissie turned away and began to tramp towards the village.

This may be the last time I do this, she thought, head down, hunched against the wind. She wondered what happened when an atomic bomb went off. Did you just burn to a cinder where you stood? Did you see the mushroom cloud before you died? Perhaps, she thought, you simply saw the cloud and died of fright before the awfulness happened. What was it called? Fallout. Nuclear fallout. Mike had brought a sketch home from the art school last week; it was supposed to be a joke, one of his students had done it. It showed the market-place in Norwich, with its striped awnings and its buckets of flowers and its rows of neat vegetables, and the church of St Peter Mancroft to one side and City Hall behind; only it was all leaning drunkenly to the left: everything – people, church spire, trees, town hall clock – all sagging away under the weight of a great burst of mushroom-shaped red to one side, where the Guildhall ought to be. Cissie hated that picture. The others had laughed, thought it clever, telling. She had nearly been sick. How could they laugh? Everything she knew, everything familiar – all blown away, all melted, or flattened, and they laughed.

She felt tears welling in her eyes. I might never see them again, she suddenly thought. Kruschev may be pressing the button right now, this minute, and those nuclear bombs are rushing this way . . . She peered across the dark fields in what she supposed to be the direction of London, looking for a glow in the sky which might indicate mass conflagration: nothing. Only the familiar rustling shadows of the trees along the roadside, and the lights of the village ahead. She trudged on, imagining the moment when Peggy and Mike, dancing at their party, saw the great burst of flame as a bomb flashed through the orchard at the back of the house and ignited the cabbage field. For a second they would catch each other's eyes, anguished – just a second they would have before they died, and in that second, a little, bleak voice inside Peggy's head would be saying, 'Cissie! I've left my Cissie to die alone on a windy road while I'm in here, in the warm with the Lovelocks –'

'I'm going to die without my daughter . . .' Cissie-being-Peggy murmured, brokenly. Her footsteps echoed on the road, a comforting, regular sound. The fantasy stretched, slightly out of control. The bomb had only killed her, no one else. Miraculously, Brigadoon had escaped the blast, and now, in this grey post-nuclear dawn, the Lovelocks were gathered, their party clothes in tatters, their faces hollow, round the grave of the one they had so neglected, and their tears of regret flowed down ash-covered faces, their broken sobs filling the choking air. A tear, warm in the corner of her eye, slid satisfyingly down the side of her nose.

Someone was coming towards her, she could just make out a round figure, head down, walking steadily. Her heart jumped: this was it, then. Not the atom bomb, but a madman from Polston Wood Mental Hospital, axe under his coat, looking for youthful flesh. She kept walking. So be it.

'Cissie?' It was Bennett, of course, hurrying out of the dark to meet her, her round face, framed by a headscarf, made ruddy by the cold. 'You sure you want to do this? We'll have to sit with the Germans.' She linked arms with her friend, reassuringly bulky in her maroon school mac.

'I'd rather do anything than be at home,' Cissie said. Bennett, not understanding as usual, merely laughed. 'I'd rather do anything than sit with the ruddy Germans,' she said. 'Maybe we should swap lives. Did your mum actually let you leave the house wearing lipstick?' The relaxed attitude of the Lovelocks never ceased to amaze Bennett, and in particular Cissie's sheer good fortune in having a *laissez-faire* romantic novelist for a mother.

They had reached the outskirts of the village. Together they passed the village shop and headed towards the Methodist hall, down a narrow lane between two bungalows.

'Can you get away afterwards?' Cissie asked.

Bennett looked at her, surprised. 'I thought you were coming back to mine to do homework.'

'It's Jude. She rang up, and Mike invited her to the party.'

'What party?'

Cissie grimaced to herself in the darkness. All she had wanted was to get out of the house, put up with a couple of hours in church, then go back to Bennett's room to revise for the French test, practise hairstyles and listen to Radio Luxembourg. Now all this. She took a deep breath. 'They're having a party,' she said. 'It's called Armageddon, or something. Because of Cuba.'

'Will there be art students?' Bennett sounded hopeful, excited. She adored the Lovelocks.

'Probably,' said Cissie, who thought art students were sneering, horrible people from another planet. 'And now Jude's going to be there, so I'll have to go back, in case she does something awful – you know what she's like. Will you come?'

They had paused outside the Methodist hall entrance. In the dark, a few people were still filing in. The organ could be heard, playing something mournful.

'Try and keep me away!' Bennett's eyes were shining in the light from the entrance porch. 'I'll tell the Germans there's a change of plan – homework at yours.'

They went inside.

The hall was stuffy after Cissie's chilly walk from Brigadoon, and steam rose from the array of damp overcoats draped near the wall heaters. Bennett sidled through the murmuring congregation still bunched in the centre aisle searching for friends or vacant seats. Cissie followed. In the front row an unruly collection of children, large and small, squabbled and fidgeted, watched over benignly by a small, sharp-featured woman with a perm. She looked up and beckoned enthusiastically at Cissie.

'Just wave back!' Bennett hissed. 'For God's sake, don't go and sit down there or we'll never escape at the end!'

Cissie smiled at the woman across the querulous heads of several small children. 'Evening, Mrs Jermyn!' she called, trying to sound cheery.

Mrs Jermyn shook her head and wagged a finger in mock reproach. 'You must call me Josie!' she corrected. 'I keep telling you, Cissie. We're a very informal family, very like your own, aren't we, Susan?' Susan was Bennett's real name.

The two girls sat down at the far end of the row, near the centre aisle. 'Too bleeding informal,' Bennett said under her breath. She paused for a moment to prod a small boy next to Cissie, who was wiping his nose on his sleeve. 'Pig!' she said, savage. The small boy continued with his activity, unperturbed. Bennett began drumming, impatient, on the Methodist hymnbook she had removed from her chair before sitting down. Bennett was always drumming. The congregation was beginning to settle now, and the murmuring had subsided to a low hum.

'Where's Mr Jermyn?' Cissie asked.

'Polishing his halo round the back,' said Bennett, glum, leafing through the hymnbook. 'He's taking the service today. Vicar's got the flu.'

The Jermyns were Bennett's foster parents. They lived in a large, unimaginative modern house in the middle of the village and filled it with children – their own as well as several supplied by the Welfare Department – and enthusiastic, unequivocal love. Bennett hated it.

Cissie eyed the fidgeting children. 'Which ones are actual Germans?' she whispered. Bennett surveyed the brood, unsure.

'Definitely those three with the bulbous noses,' she decided finally, 'and that oik next to you definitely isn't a German – he arrived after me. I think that ugly one with the plaits has got parents in Africa or somewhere. And those two with the spots and the wellington boots are brothers. They're on probation.'

Cissie studied them, impressed. 'What did they do?'

Bennett shrugged. 'Nicked bottles of Tizer from the Co-op. Nothing very thrilling.'

There was a stir, as Jim Jermyn suddenly made his entrance and stepped up to the plain pulpit, holding his bible. He caught sight of Cissie gazing up at him and beamed at her. His eyes focussed on Cissie's lipstick and the beatific gaze faltered. She smiled back, embarrassed.

'Excuse me while I puke,' Bennett murmured, head down. The service began.

An interminable hour and a half later, they sang the final chorus of 'Lead Me O Thou Great Redeemer' and Bennett's weekly ordeal was over. With indecent haste she knotted her headscarf under her chin and struggled into her mac, as the rest of the congregation stacked hymnbooks and engaged in subdued speculation about Cuba, which had been the subject of several prayers, the theme of three bible readings and the basis for all the hymns. Cissie sat slumped in her seat, leafing through the tattered Sankey's hymnbook. They hadn't sung her favourite, 'Dear Lord And Father Of Mankind'. She hummed it under her breath now, to compensate. It would have been a good one: '. . . *Speak through the earthquake, wind and fire, O still small voice of calm . . .*'

Bennett was pulling at her arm, concerned. 'Quick, before the Germans get us!' She hustled Cissie into the aisle, her coat only half on, taking advantage of Mrs Jermyn's brisk organization of her brood into their winter accessories. 'Trevor – where is your cap? Sandra – mittens!'

Cissie was still reluctant. 'Couldn't we do homework at yours first and then go back to mine? Jude won't be there yet –'

'Jude will have been there for hours,' Bennett said. Cissie knew she was right. Defeated, she buttoned up her coat.

Bennett waved at her foster mother, her face bright. 'Josie!' she called, 'I'm going to Cissie's to do my maths – back before bedtime!' Together they shoved through the departing congregation, squeezing past voluminous overcoats and tripping over the galoshes lined up near the exit, causing more than one disapproving frown.

'Cissie!' It was Jim Jermyn, bearing down on them from his place by the door, where he was performing the farewells usually carried out by the vicar. 'So nice to see you –' Cissie barely had time to murmur something incoherent before Bennett pulled at her arm and then suddenly they were outside.

'Quick!' And Bennett was away, running down the road in the darkness, fast in spite of her bulk, liberated at last. Cissie raced after her. Together they ran, screaming down the dark alley, until they rounded the corner, and collapsed outside the village shop, breathless and giggling. 'Once more the Germans are thwarted,' panted Cissie.

'Ve haf vays off making you pray!' Bennett did her imitation Nazi walk, kicking the Lyons Maid sign as she did so and setting it clanging rustily in the silence. Hurriedly, still giggling, they set off back down the road to Brigadoon.

'Thank goodness I'm wearing my straight skirt.' Bennett had paused for a moment and was applying lipstick with the aid of a small compact she had pulled from her coat pocket, grimacing in the dim light from a nearby bungalow. 'Did your dad say how many students were coming?'

'Mike's not my dad.' Cissie's voice was terse. Bennett glanced at her friend, but her face was not visible in the darkness.

'He's more of a dad than I've ever had,' Bennett said. They set off again.

'Yes, well. He's not my dad. He's my step-dad.'

'So how many?'

'What?'

'Students, cloth ears!'

'I don't know.'

But Bennett, excited by the prospect of the party, persisted. 'All right then – how many of your mum's friends?'

'Don't know.'

'That woman who writes poems and owns the wool shop?'

'Probably.'

'That funny little man with the moustache who writes about cowboys and Indians – what's his name?'

'Arthur. Look, Bennett,' – Cissie was irritable now – 'can we just get there and get it over with? You'll see who's there once we're there, won't you?'

Bennett, sulking a little, subsided. They walked along in silence for a while, listening to the companionably co-ordinated tramp of their feet. Every now and then one of them would skip, playful, and force the other to miss a beat. Then they would fall in together again, marching, harmony restored, their breath pluming white in the cold air.

Bennett spoke first. 'What's your favourite play?' she asked, innocent.

Cissie groaned. 'No . . .' This was Bennett's favourite game.

'*Pig*malion!' Bennett was triumphant. 'Favourite composer?'

'Bennett –'

'*Pig*anini! Your turn!'

Cissie racked her brains. She was hopeless at this. 'Favourite jockey?' she ventured.

It was Bennett's turn to groan. 'Don't be silly. Lester Piggot doesn't count.'

'Why not?'

Bennett sighed, explaining patiently as if she were talking to a very small, stupid child. 'Because he really *is* Piggot.'

'So?'

'So the rule is they mustn't really have pig in the name.'

Cissie's mouth was set. 'I don't get it. It's daft.'

'Favourite artist?'

Cissie racked her brains. 'Pigicelli?'

Bennett stopped, indignant. 'Who?'

'Pigicelli.'

'Never heard of him. You made it up.'

'I didn't!' They were walking again. 'Botticelli. Mike's got a postcard by him pinned up in the studio.'

'Botticelli!' Bennett's tone was scornful.

'Sort of nymphs. In flowery dresses.'

'It doesn't work.'

'So what's the answer, then?'

But Bennett had paused again. 'Listen!' she said. They stood, listening. Then Cissie heard it.

'Pat Boone,' she said. '"Speedy Gonzales".' She had heard little tinny voices floating across the fields: '*Hey Rosita, come quick, down at the cantina they're giving green stamps with tequila . . .*'

Bennett was hurrying on, excited. 'Come on!' she called, 'Come on!' Reluctantly, Cissie followed.

By the time they reached the front gate of Brigadoon, Pat Boone had subsided, and the shrill sound of 'Telstar' emanated from the front room. It was Cissie's record. Through the steamed-up windows, Cissie could see students gyrating, and the figure of Mill, exactly where she had been when Cissie left, in her armchair, surveying the guests with a Woodbine between her lips. Cissie groaned inwardly. Bennett had already gone inside. Toulouse appeared, over-excited and barking, and leapt into Cissie's arms. She carried him down the path at the side of the house and into the kitchen, where she was immediately half-blinded by smoke. Someone took the dog away from her, and there was Peggy, smiling, her hair more tousled than ever, her mascara slightly smudged.

'Ah,' she said, to no one in particular, 'it's a missionary!' She helped Cissie off with her coat and was about to throw it over a chair when Cissie rescued it and headed moodily to the cupboard to hang it up. She hated her mother at parties, all vivacity and sparkling eyes, as if she'd been let out of prison. Peggy had turned away again, distracted by a guest, and Cissie was left alone by the cupboard under the stairs. For a moment she was sorely tempted simply to duck inside, to sit curled up among the damp raincoats and the discarded overshoes until the party was over, but common sense prevailed. After all, she told herself, it would only mean a fuss. She hung up her coat and closed the door.

Mike had appeared at her side. He handed her a glass with something fizzy in it. She sniffed at it, suspicious. Mike raised an eyebrow. 'Lemonade,' he said, and went into the living room. Cissie stood for a moment, pressed against the cupboard door. The kitchen seemed to be full of people in navy and black – blue jeans, black dresses, black jumpers – with an occasional flash of brightness – someone's coral lipstick, a pair of bright green socks. The noise was deafening.

Bennett was standing by the sink, smoking inexpertly, her forehead glistening, listening intently to a boy in hornrimmed glasses.

13

Cissie edged over to hear the conversation. 'I saw it in L-L-London,' he was saying, tense. 'It's bound to come to Norwich soon. *Last Year in Marienbad*. Puts *A Bout de Souffle* in the shade, I think. I mean, I think Seberg's t-t-terrific . . .' Bennett seemed to be transfixed, whether by the boy's stutter or by his incomprehensible conversation Cissie couldn't tell. He had gone on to talk about something called Troofoe. She turned away, wondering if she could simply escape to her bedroom, but was impeded by Mike, who had come to find her.

'Jude's in there,' he said, indicating the living room. Cissie looked at him. He was grinning, his teeth clamped around his pipe. 'Don't look so worried,' he said. 'It's my students I fear for.'

Cissie pushed past him to the living room, clutching her lemonade glass. 'It's your fault she's here,' she said.

'But I didn't mean —' Mike began to say, but Cissie had shoved her way through the crowd round the doorway and out of earshot. She adjusted her ears to the deafening sound of Elvis Presley, and her eyes to the gloom of the 'dancing room', where only a glow from the fire (and an accompanying glint from Mill's sequinned bosom) supplied illumination. In the semi-darkness, Cissie could see couples dancing, bodies close, arms entwined, foreheads pressed together. She could see, in the middle of the throng, the skinny form of Jude swaying to the music, her arms looped round the neck of a boy in a leather jacket. Jude was laughing, her teeth gleaming in the dark. She took a cigarette from between the boy's lips, inhaled on it, blew the smoke carelessly over his shoulder and then kissed him on the mouth. Then she pushed the cigarette back between his lips, laughing.

'Surely she isn't fifteen.' It was Oliver, who had somehow materialized next to Cissie and who stood surveying Jude, his hands in his pockets, interested. Cissie gave him a cold look.

'She's seventeen,' she said. 'Not that it's any of your business.'

Oliver looked at Cissie for a moment, surprised. 'Seventeen? Is she still at school?' Cissie shook her head. 'What's she doing hanging about with you and Bennett, then?'

'Thanks a lot!'

'I just meant —' Oliver struggled to think of a polite way to express his surprise. 'How did you become friends?'

'We were in the school play. *Admirable Crichton*. She was the tweeny — don't you remember? You came to see it.'

'Did I?' Oliver was grinning in Jude's direction. 'She must have looked a bit different then.'

Jude had noticed that she had an audience. She nuzzled the boy's neck and murmured something to him, and then abandoned him abruptly, crossing over to where Oliver and Cissie stood.

'Watcha,' she said, taking the lemonade glass out of Cissie's hand and drinking from it. Her arms were glittering with cheap Indian bracelets. Her eyes never left Oliver's face. 'Who's this?' she asked, bold.

'You know who it is.' Cissie snatched her lemonade back. Why on earth did Jude have to come here? She was bound to do something dreadful.

'Oliver. I'm Cissie's step-brother. Apparently I saw you in the school play.'

'Was I any good?'

'Brilliant.'

'Was I?'

'Best thing in the play.' Oliver had seemingly forgotten that Cissie had also been in the play. She had been Lady Mary, and had got to wear all the best costumes; but Jude had stolen the show as the maid, a mob-cap pulled down over her ears, and an instinct for comic timing.

Oliver and Jude were flirting. Cissie felt rejected. Disgusted. Alone. Small. Young. Stupid. But Oliver was moving away, smiling. 'Got to go and see a man about a drink. See you.'

'Get me one!' Jude called after him, but if he heard he gave no indication, ducking away through the crowd without a backward glance. Jude watched him go.

'He didn't remember you really,' Cissie told her. 'He was just saying that to be kind.'

'See him over there? The one I was dancing with?' Jude didn't

15

appear to have heard what she said. 'He's from the North. Art school.'

'He's got sticky-out ears.'

'He's twenty-two.'

'He's still got sticky-out ears.'

Jude waved at the boy in the leather jacket. He beckoned to her. 'It's not his ears I'm worried about,' she said, heading back towards him, abandoning Cissie once again.

Cissie pretended to relax, leaning against the bookcase. Mill was watching from her armchair. She caught Cissie's eye, and pointed at Jude. She was mouthing something. Cissie looked at her questioningly. 'Virgin,' Mill mouthed, waving her Woodbine in Jude's direction. Cissie looked away, embarrassed. Probably not. Jude always said she had lost her virginity when she was fourteen. How should Cissie know? Jude never told the truth about anything anyway. She wondered if she could successfully escape to her bedroom now; after all, she had put in an appearance. And she had to revise Chapter nine verbs for the test tomorrow. Jude was draped over the art student in the leather jacket. His hand was resting on her bottom in a shockingly intimate way as they danced. Cissie felt cold, angry. How could Jude behave like that? She hardly knew him! She probably didn't even know his name! She watched her friend, disgust mingling with a strange, unwonted pride. Jude was so strong, so powerful, with her white skin and her dark eyes, those long limbs and that scrawny body. There was something seedily glamorous about Jude, something older than her years, knowing, clever. But kind. Sometimes. She had a big mouth and a big head, but she had a big heart, too. She would give Cissie her last sixpence if she had to; but then again she would probably steal a shilling back from her purse the next day.

A group near Cissie had begun to raise their voices, angrily arguing, inhaling on their cigarettes savagely and waving their arms about. It seemed to be a dispute about jazz, mainly conducted by a bearded man in a navy sweater, and someone Cissie recognized as a teacher from the art school. Various young men listened, absorbed, while their girlfriends shuffled, bored, raising soulful eyes to the ceiling in what they hoped were passable imitations of Juliette Greco. Cissie sidled past, Toulouse at her heels. In the kitchen, Peggy was perched on the edge of the table, surrounded by some of her odd friends: desperate unemployed and undiscovered poets from surrounding villages, bright-eyed spinsters from the Writers' Circle, the bad-tempered old woman who claimed she was descended from the Romanies, and who, according to Peggy, told fortunes at the funfair in Great Yarmouth; and Bennett, who was now gazing up at Peggy with a look of naked adoration. Cissie drew a sharp breath. The strap of Peggy's dress had slipped a little, and the black lace of her bra was visible. Cissie blushed on her mother's behalf, ashamed. She made her way to the stairs, meeting no one's eyes, for fear of being prevented from her exit (although a small corner of her wanted to be begged to stay). Toulouse followed. They negotiated a couple kissing on the bend of the stairs, and headed along the landing to Cissie's room.

Nervously she opened the door, wondering what horrors she would find. A sigh of relief: nothing. Her room was as she had left it, apart from a few coats and a bag thrown across the bed. She gathered them up in a bundle and deposited them on the carpet outside the door. She recognized the bag as Jude's. Sticking out of it was this week's copy of *Melody Maker*. Cissie pulled it out and then went back inside and shut the door. Toulouse jumped up on to the candlewick bedspread, snorting and digging in the soft pile, and finally curled up. The throb of someone playing boogie woogie on Peggy's piano reverberated through the floorboards, mingling with the high sound of someone's laughter. Deciding to save the *Melody Maker* until later, Cissie sorted through the pile of school textbooks stacked neatly under her dressing-table, and pulled out Whitman's *Cours Supérieur*. Page seventy-three, Chapter nine. Government of Verbs. She pulled the bedspread over her, hunched herself into a ball, curled round the dog, and concentrated, a small, solemn-faced figure, motionless beneath a large poster of Bobby Vee pinned to the wall. *Verbs governing the dative*. She wondered what Jude was doing with the boy with the ears and the leather jacket . . . *s'attendre, to expect*. She hoped Peggy wasn't doing the twist. There was something embarrassing about watching your mother dance . . . *se fier, to trust; s'intéresser, to be interested.* She wondered if anyone had noticed her absence . . . *plaire, to please; déplaire, to displease* . . . Probably not . . . *obéir, to obey; désobéir, to disobey.* Did she disobey? *Elle désobéit à sa mère.* Cissie was good at French. *Elle déplaît à sa mère.* She grinned a little to herself, enjoying the game. *Renoncer, to renounce. Elle renonce à sa mère. Résister, to resist. Elle résiste à sa mère* . . .

The door burst open and Bennett came in, pink-cheeked and hot in her home-knitted Sloppy Joe. 'Why didn't you tell me the time? The Germans'll kill me!' She studied Cissie. 'You've been asleep!' Her tone was accusing.

'What time is it?'

'Ten-thirty. Someone's reading *Under Milk* something downstairs.'

'Dylan Thomas?'

'I dunno. Sort of poems.' Cissie grimaced to herself. Of course. Then it would be folk songs. Mike would hand out the brandy, and someone would be sick over the hedge into the cabbage field, and then they would all sing 'Kumbaya' or some such dreary song. But then at least they would all go home.

'Mill's pissed as a newt. She nearly fell into the fire just now.' Bennett was combing her hair, peering into Cissie's mirror. She had a very round face, framed by an austere, mousey, bobbed haircut. 'Keeps saying if it's the end of the world then she might as well go out laughing.'

'Do you want me to walk back with you?' Cissie tried not to sound reluctant. It was cold out there, and walking home with Bennett meant running the gauntlet of the drunken students in the kitchen; and then the terror of walking back again alone, wondering as usual if one of the inmates of the mental hospital was on the loose. It never seemed to occur to Peggy or Mike that she might be frightened, she thought indignantly. But Bennett was shaking her head. 'Your brother's taking me – said he fancied a walk to clear his head.'

'Bennett! Oliver's not my brother, for the millionth time.'

'Jude's disappeared out the back. I bet she's having it off with that bloke in one of your dad's sheds,' said Bennett, trying a little Peachy Pink on her lips, stretching her mouth in a grimace.

He's not my dad, Cissie thought, but said nothing.

Bennett looked at her reflection, satisfied. 'Right,' she said, 'I'm off. See you on the bus, if the nuclear war doesn't start tonight. Good party!' She headed for the door, then remembered something and turned. 'Do you want me to deal with Jude?'

'I'd like to see you try,' said Cissie. The door closed, and she turned back to her French book. Sod Jude. Why did she always have to spoil things? Someone downstairs had started singing, one of those monotonous songs that had an endlessly repeating chorus. There was a low hum, as others joined in. Cissie leaned over to her dressing-table, cross, and pulled her transistor radio towards her. She turned the dial to 208, and as the sound of tinny music filled the room, drowning out the singing downstairs, she lay back against the pillow, eyes closed, wishing not for the first time that she lived in a normal house with a normal family. It would be a solid, semi-detached affair, called Deneholme or The Willows, not Brigadoon. It would be in a sunny, tree-lined suburban street, not next to a cabbage field just off the Yarmouth Road. The family, this normal family of her dreams, would all be in bed, early to bed on a Sunday, ready for the working week ahead, mum in a quilted dressing-gown, dad with a proper haircut, not like Mike's, and a dog called Fido or Rex, not named after some stupid French artist. And she wouldn't be called Cecilia, she'd be Susan, or Carole or Janet, like ordinary girls . . . She drifted away again, faintly aware of Jimmy Savile talking away nineteen to the dozen on the radio, and then the strident sound of a harmonica. Not a record she knew. As the singing started, she let the sound wash over her, drowning out the murmuring of voices downstairs. It was a strange song, plaintive, not like anything she had heard before. It was about the usual things – love me, I'll be true, plea-yee-yeese; but somewhere in the pit of her stomach, the voices and the words and the music resonated, touching her, making her sit up, blinking, excited. It faded away, that strange wailing harmonica sound again.

'That was the Beatles, on the edge of the charts with "Love Me

Do",' said Jimmy Savile. 'Four guys from Liverpool in case you gals out there are interested. And you gals usually are interested, I'm glad to say, on behalf of all the guys. And speaking of guys, here's one for you – it's the newie from Helen Shapiro and my guess is, it's another biggie . . .'

Cissie groped for the *Melody Maker*, discarded under the bed. Toulouse groaned in his sleep, disturbed by the movement. She sat propped up in bed, leafing through the paper, studying the pictures. Sure enough, there they were, under the heading 'New on the Scene'. The Beatles. She repeated it to herself. Beatles. She studied the picture, her finger moving slowly over the words beneath. John Lennon. Ringo Starr. That one. She looked at the face, long and hard. It was a nice face, enquiring, even-featured, gentle. George Harrison. She tried to remember the song, but she couldn't. She wondered if it had been George Harrison singing. George. It sounded reassuring, old-fashioned, the sort of name an uncle might have. Only this wasn't an uncle. She looked at the face again. Shy. He looked shy. Floating mysteriously into the bedroom in Polston Wood, vibrating along the airwaves from a strange little country somewhere near France, Helen Shapiro was telling someone to keep away from other girls in her deep voice. Cissie turned it off. She didn't want to hear Helen Shapiro. She wanted to think about this new thing, this new feeling. She turned to look up at Bobby Vee, who smiled cleanly down at her from the wall, his teeth perfectly white, his skin flawless, his hair neat, his gaze direct. She slumped back down again. Somehow Bobby Vee was not as exciting as he had been yesterday . . .

'I can see it!' Peggy was standing at the back door, hungover, the baby balanced on her hip, peering across the fields.

Cissie didn't reply. She was staring at the framed photograph on the wall, next to the cupboard under the stairs. It was a picture of her father, Cecil, who had died of a brain tumour. Peggy had been expecting Cissie when he died, that was why she had named her Cecilia, after her father – and also because, as Peggy never tired of telling her brightly, Saint Cecilia was the patron saint of music; and

Peggy just adored music, especially musicals. *Carousel, Oklahoma, Funny Face, Showboat* . . . The silly, romantic, yearning songs constantly echoed round the house as Peggy worked on her books. Cissie hated them – the songs, the books.

Cecil had been an engineer. In the photograph he was standing by a river, grinning, holding a fishing rod, and wearing wide trousers tucked into wellington boots. Cecil. It was hard to make out his face. He had a moustache, and his eyes crinkled in a smile. It was part of Cissie's morning ritual, to stand here and say hello to the father she had never known, the father who looked so reassuringly ordinary; but today something kept getting in the way of her secret moment. It was George Harrison. His face kept appearing before her, that smile, frozen.

'It's reached the crossroads,' Peggy was saying. 'Get your skates on, kid!'

Cissie looked away from the picture, returning to the world. 'My beret!'

Mill was presiding over a chaotic breakfast table. 'Never mind your beret, what about these cornflakes?'

Peggy frowned. 'Can't you forget it for one day?'

'I'll get detention.' Cissie found the missing beret in her duffle bag. She snatched up her school mac and kissed the baby, then her mother. ''Bye!' She ran down the path, struggling into her mac. The top of the bus had drawn level with the big barn down by Fox Corner. She would just make it . . .

She leapt aboard just as the young conductor rang the bell. 'You in training for the England team?' She grinned at him, panting on the swaying platform. 'Your mate's upstairs,' he said, shaking his head when Cissie struggled to find her season ticket in the mess at the bottom of her bag. 'It's all right – up you go.'

Bennett was in her usual place on the back seat. The top deck was filled with younger children, most of them in the maroon uniform of Crookfield Secondary Modern, like Bennett. The noise was deafening. Two small girls wearing the navy blue of Crookfield Grammar turned to smile nervously at Cissie as she struggled to join Bennett, hanging on as the bus veered round a corner and on to the main Norwich Road. She nodded at them. It didn't do to be too kind to first-years: they tended to take advantage.

'Beret,' commanded Bennett. Cissie handed it over, and Bennett got to work, kneeling up on the seat, efficient with hairspray, hairgrips and backcombing, fixing Cissie's beret like a pancake on the back of her head as they talked, watched by several fascinated younger girls. Cissie's hair was an embarrassment, an abundance of waves that frizzed into a halo when it rained.

'I've got something to show you,' Cissie said, excited, ducking away from the hairbrush for a moment. She fished in her bag and produced the *Melody Maker*. 'Look,' she prodded at the picture she had studied so intently several times already this morning. Bennett, her mouth full of hairgrips, peered at the paper.

'What am I looking at?' she asked.

'The Beatles. Just look, will you?'

Bennett looked. 'That one,' she said finally, pointing at a face that was, mercifully, not George Harrison's.

'Why?'

'Because he's the drummer, stupid. Look, he's holding drumsticks.' She went back to her backcombing. 'And he's got a good name. Ringo Starr. I like it. Ringo. Like a cowboy.'

'He's not as handsome as that one,' said Cissie shyly. She was looking at George Harrison. She couldn't tell Bennett how strange it made her feel, this discovery. It wasn't like Bobby Vee, or Doctor Kildare. She felt as if she were about to discover something incredible. It wasn't here yet, but it was coming, and it was all to do with George Harrison. She wondered if this was something psychic. Peggy was always telling her she 'had the gift', that it was something you inherited, and that it was in Cissie's blood. What did it mean? Cissie Lovelock and George Harrison – were they connected in some strange way she didn't understand?

'There. Not bad.' Bennett had finished fixing the beret and was surveying her handiwork, pleased with herself. Further up the bus, some of the Crookfield Secondary Modern boys had started a fight, laughing at first, but now grim-faced and in earnest, fists flying, hacking at ankles, causing a squeal from a group of second-year girls. Bennett gave a mock sigh, then strode up the bus to deal with the fracas, brutally smacking a small boy round the head with the flat of her hand. 'Oy, piglet! I told you – once more and you walk to school, got it?'

She returned, glowering. 'I hate kids,' she said. 'Just think – this time next year and I won't be here!' Cissie preferred not to think about it. Bennett was in her last year at school, and would be leaving in the spring. The prospect of sitting alone on the morning bus depressed Cissie. It wasn't just the years they had spent together trundling to school on the upstairs back seat, doing homework and hairstyles, fighting and being friends again: it would be the end of everything. First Jude had gone, leaving Cissie friendless at school, and now Bennett would go, leaving gaps in the day that had been filled by her large, confident presence: break times, when they met on the playing fields that divided their two schools; lunchtimes, when they sneaked off to the fish and chip shop together, or even, daringly, took the bus into Norwich to eat buns in a seedy cafe on Exchange Street. There would only be the prospect of A levels, and days spent in classrooms full of people she didn't like, people who thought she was weird, with her arty family and her shy white face hidden behind a curtain of hair.

The bus was pulling into Crookfield Circle, where it would disgorge its noisy passengers. Already the others were pushing down the bus, eager to get off.

'Why is it small boys always *smell*?' Bennett asked loudly, addressing no one.

'Leave them alone,' said Cissie, her voice lacking conviction. Here we go, she was thinking. Monday again.

'Cheer up,' said Bennett. 'We may all be dead by lunchtime. The Germans were saying it says in the paper that the Yanks won't back off.'

They got up. 'At least that means I won't have to do the French test.' Cissie followed Bennett to the stairs, where a last small boy was hovering.

Bennett kicked him half-heartedly in the rear, hastening his descent. 'Talking of pigs,' she said, swinging down the stairs, 'you never did get the answer.'

'To what?'

'Favourite artist.' The conductor was busy counting change, too engrossed to say goodbye as they stepped off the platform on to the pavement, engulfed in a sea of uniforms pressing in both directions: maroon to the left, navy blue to the right.

'It was Pigasso,' said Bennett, 'Picasso. Pigasso. Get it?'

Cissie grimaced, the expected response, then waved, turning away. 'See you at the tree,' she said, joining the throng of navy blue. The tree was where they met at lunchtimes to eat their sandwiches, rain or shine, behind the caretaker's hut.

Bennett was still shouting, 'Pigasso – tell Mike! He can pass it on to his students!' Cissie waved again and hurried along the school drive to the main entrance. She might just have time to study those sodding verbs again before assembly . . .

She was busy sitting with her head hidden by the upturned desk lid – a favourite position which meant she did not have to participate in the what-did-you-do-this-weekend kind of talk that her classmates enjoyed at this time. Cissie never seemed to have done the kinds of things they had done – coffee bars, the pictures, the youth club. How could she talk about the Armageddon party and going voluntarily to church?

Inside the desk, her book was open at page seventy-three. Verbs Governing the Sodding Dative. She had cut out the picture of the Beatles, and it lay on top of the page, creases carefully smoothed out. George Harrison. Something was going to happen. She chewed a strand of hair, thoughtful.

'Cecilia?' It was Miss Desmond, the form teacher, a no-nonsense middle-aged woman with hornrimmed glasses and an extensive wardrobe of tartan skirts. 'This is Heather Lewis, who is starting today. Heather's from Edinburgh.' Cissie looked up. She had an impression of startling blue eyes and perfect blonde hair in sculpted flick-ups.

'Hello,' said the vision, in a soft Scottish accent.

'I thought you could look after Heather,' Miss Desmond was

saying, 'since you don't have anyone to sit next to at registration. And Heather's doing almost all the same options as you – French, Art, Latin. Right, I'll leave you to it, then.' And she was gone.

The new girl stared at Cissie, unblinking. There was silence. 'You don't have to do this if you don't want to,' she said finally, her voice trembling a little. One of the other girls overheard and laughed. 'Och aye the noo!' she said loudly, and her companions laughed. Cissie sighed inwardly and snapped her desk lid shut.

'You'd better sit down,' she said grudgingly. Heather did so. She had a neat black canvas school bag, from which she removed a notebook, pencil-sharpener and pencil case. These she placed inside the empty desk alongside Cissie's.

'What did she say your name was?' she asked. Now she had produced a comb, compact and manicure set. These items she ranged along the top of the desk, next to the hole where an inkwell had once been.

'I'd get rid of those,' Cissie said, 'or they'll get confiscated. Cissie. Cissie Lovelock.'

Those bright blue eyes turned to gaze at her. 'Lovelock? Och, how lovely! Like something out of Sir Walter Scott.'

'Who?'

The eyes grew rounder. 'You've never heard of Sir Walter Scott? I thought Miss – whatsit over there – I thought she said you were good at English.' She emitted a small, tinkling laugh. 'Not heard of Sir Walter Scott!'

'Cecilia!' Miss Desmond was calling from the front, setting off a wave of sarcastic singing from the boys by the window.

'Cec-eel-yah!' they chorused in mock posh voices, 'Cec-eel-yah!'

Cissie looked up, blushing. 'Yes, Miss?'

'Make sure you take Heather to the dining room at lunchtime, will you? Show her the ropes?'

'But I was going to –' Miss Desmond had turned back to marking her register. Cissie flung some books into her bag, depressed. Bugger.

'I don't want to be any trouble,' the blonde vision said, huffy. 'If you don't want to show me the dining room –'

'I'll show you the sodding dining room,' said Cissie, thinking of Bennett, who would wait by the tree in vain all lunchtime. 'Don't you worry, I'll show you the whole sodding school, all right?'

Heather Lewis subsided, hurt, and pretended to be sorting out her already perfectly packed bag of books.

Cissie opened her desk lid again. George Harrison smiled at her. *Is this what you meant?* she asked him, silently. *Is this the wonderful thing that's going to happen?*

Cissie knew she was not going to like Heather Lewis.

At ten to four, the bell rang to indicate the end of another school day, and Cissie thankfully stuffed her French books into her bag. Her new, unwanted companion turned to her.

'Where do you live?' she asked, in that accent which was beginning to severely test Cissie's tolerance. 'Is it near here? Because we could walk home together if you like. Mammy said it would be all right if I brought a friend home. Do you like drop scones?'

'I live miles away,' Cissie said, relieved, 'Polston Wood — it's a village.'

'You could telephone from my house. Tell them you'll be late.'

Cissie stood, trying to be polite. Bennett would be waiting for her at the gate. 'I've got to meet someone,' she said, unable to come up with an imaginative reason for avoiding Heather's company.

'Is it a boyfriend?'

Cissie picked up her bag and hurried towards the cloakrooms, flustered. 'No, it isn't. Look — I'll see you tomorrow, all right?'

She grabbed her school mac from the peg and beat a hasty retreat, struggling through the throng to reach the exit. Once out into the already darkening afternoon, she could see Bennett's maroon bulk waiting, as usual, by the gate; and next to her, lounging on the low wall by the entrance, was Jude, smoking a cigarette and jeering at some passing fifth-form girls. Cissie hurried to join them.

'Sorry about lunch,' she said to Bennett, 'I got lumbered with a new girl. Ghastly Scottish little madam.'

Bennett was reproachful. 'I waited twenty minutes.'

'More fool you, then,' said Jude.

'I didn't want her to come, so I had to take her to the dining room,' Cissie said. 'She's a pain in the neck. Oh, *shit.*' She had seen Heather Lewis's perfectly coiffed blonde head bobbing through the crowd of departing pupils, heading purposefully in her direction.

'I shagged that bloke in your garden shed,' Jude was telling her, unaware of the impending arrival.

'Liar,' said Bennett.

'I have the scars to prove it,' Jude said airily. She pulled down the chiffon scarf at her neck, to reveal two purple love-bites.

'Yuk!' said Bennett. 'Anyway, that only proves he was a vampire. Why aren't you at work?'

'Told them I had period pains,' Jude said.

Heather had arrived. 'Hello!' She had halted in front of Cissie, clutching her school bag tightly, smiling and nervous. Cissie felt a pang of guilt. It was vile being a new girl. It was vile being on the edge of things, and feeling alone. Cissie knew.

'This is Heather,' she said, 'Heather Lewis. Started today.' Bennett mumbled a greeting. 'This is Bennett,' Cissie said, uncomfortable. 'And this is Jude, who used to go to our school but left last year.'

'Got slung out,' Jude said, looking directly at Heather for the first time. This was not true. 'Is that dyed, or natural, that hair?'

'Natural.'

They eyed the ash-blonde vision critically. There was no doubt about it, Heather Lewis was very pretty, in a doll-like kind of way. Jude turned away from her, assessment over. 'I only shagged him because he was from Liverpool,' she told Bennett, as if nothing had interrupted their earlier conversation.

'What's Liverpool got to do with it?'

'There's a bloke I fancy comes from there. A famous bloke. Well. Not famous yet. But he will be. Got a record.'

There was a small flip in Cissie's heart. She scrabbled in her bag until she found the picture. She handed it to Jude. 'Which one?' she asked.

Jude looked at the picture, then back at Cissie, grinning. Cissie remembered then why Jude was her friend. 'That one,' she said, pointing. They all looked. It was the one on the left, the one with the straight nose and the narrow eyes. John Lennon. 'He went to the art school in Liverpool,' Jude was saying.

Bennett understood. 'And so did that bloke with the ears at Brigadoon.'

Heather was lost. 'I'd better be going,' she said, disappointed.

'Right, then.' Cissie was unable to disguise her relief. She did not look up from the picture. 'See you, then.' She wanted Heather to go, so that they could get on with the important business of these Beatles.

'You like pop music, then.' Heather was busy pulling her beret on, at a most unfashionable angle. No one answered. 'Only I might be able to get you in to *Friday Beat*.' This had the desired effect. Three heads stopped poring over Cissie's crumpled photograph, and looked at her. *Friday Beat* was the weekly pop show transmitted on local television. Guest pop stars regularly appeared on it, and tickets to get inside the studio and be a part of it were like gold dust. Heather enjoyed the moment. 'I'd better be going, anyway,' she said. 'I can see you're busy.'

'How?' It was Jude who grabbed her arm.

'My father works at Anglia Television,' Heather said.

Jude, Bennett and Cissie exchanged a glance. This could be useful.

'Who do you like, then?' Jude asked, sarcastic. 'Frank Ifield? No – don't tell me – Kenneth McKellar.'

Heather pulled her arm away, dignified, temporarily powerful. 'Actually, no,' she said, in her soft Scottish accent, so that the word came out as *naw*. 'I like him.' She was prodding at Cissie's photograph. They looked at her, suspicious.

'Which one?' Cissie asked. This could be the end. If this awful Scottish intruder said George Harrison, then all was lost. Heather scanned the picture, her eyes moving quickly across the caption.

'That one!' She pointed, triumphant. They all looked. 'Paul McCartney!'

Cissie peered at the face in the picture, relieved. Paul McCartney.

'How much would you pay for his address?' Jude asked Heather, unexpectedly.

Heather was taken aback. 'Paul McCartney's address?'

'No, Kenneth McKellar's, stupid.'

Heather did not seem to notice the insult. 'Paul McCartney's address? A million pounds.'

Jude grinned, triumphant. 'Good. Because I can sell it to you.' She surveyed the three amazed faces before her, exultant. 'I've got them,' she said, 'I've got all their addresses.'

'I don't believe you,' said Bennett flatly.

'How?' Even Cissie, usually so quick to defend Jude's wildest claims, found it difficult to swallow.

Jude, in turn enjoying her moment, leaned against the wall, digging her hands deep into the pockets of her suedette jacket. 'The boy with the ears – at Brigadoon.'

'What's Brigadoon?' Everyone ignored Heather's question.

'You mean – he knows the Beatles?' Bennett was still not ready to be convinced.

Jude nodded. 'Well – not all of them. He knows John, because he went to the art school, and he knows their addresses. He said half of Liverpool does – they play in clubs a lot up North, they're dead popular up there already.'

Bennett frowned. 'And this bloke just handed over the addresses? Just like that?' Jude nodded. 'Ringo's address?'

'He didn't just hand them over,' Jude grinned at them. 'I had to perform a few favours –'

Bennett groaned. 'Spare us the details, for God's sake –'

A great shout went up from the school building. The girls turned, surprised, to see a stream of sixth-formers racing out of the main entrance, whooping and cheering, hugging each other. A couple of girls were crying.

'What is it?' Bennett yelled at a boy doing a little victory dance on the school wall.

'It's over!' He shouted back. 'The Cuban thing! Kruschev's backed down!'

'Whoopee!' said Bennett, dry. Cissie hardly absorbed what he said. The four girls began to walk away, engrossed in their own excitement.

'Five bob each,' Jude said.

'Bus!' Bennett suddenly shouted, pointing. 'Cissie, run!' Together they raced towards the bus-stop in Crookfield Circle.

'Five bob!' Jude shouted at their receding backs.

'Done!' shouted Cissie. Just ahead of Bennett she leapt on the moving bus, and together they bounded noisily up the stairs, laughing. They threw themselves on the back seat, and waved at Jude and Heather, who were still walking slowly along the road together, an incongruous couple, one in her neat uniform, blonde hair bobbing glossily, the other scruffy in a brown jacket and trews, dark hair uncombed.

Cissie watched their receding figures, panting, smiling. George Harrison's address. This is what she had sensed would happen, the something wonderful just around the corner, just like in *West Side Story*. This was the dream. And it was coming true.

CHAPTER TWO

You Really Got a Hold on Me – 1963

THE SCREAM REVERBERATED across the narrow back gardens of the Carrow Estate, causing a man in Spixworth Close to come out of his shed, looking up into the sky for the source of the sound, as if he thought it might be a low-flying Spitfire. A woman going into the house next door with a bag full of shopping caught his eye and jerked her head in the direction of a row of prefabricated bungalows further along the street. The scream still floated shrilly across the sagging conifers.

'Need you ask?' the woman said, cryptic, before disappearing inside. The man sighed and went back to cleaning his shears.

Inside the prefab, Jude groped behind her for a weapon. Blood was dripping from her nose. She could taste it in the corner of her mouth.

'You want something to scream about? You really want something to scream about? I'll give you something to scream about –' Her father was swaying, one hand on the back of the sofa, the last blow seeming to have momentarily slowed him down.

'Harry –' Jude's mother was in the doorway, too afraid to step into the room. Jude was panting, her heart banging loudly in her throat, the rasp of her breathing the only sound. Her hand groped blindly along the mantelpiece, until her fingers closed round something. She recognized it. It was the brass bird with the beak on a hinge that opened and closed; you were supposed to keep your letters in the beak, but no one ever did. Sometimes when her dad came back from the pub in a good mood he would insert a cigarette into the bird's beak and Jude and her sisters would laugh dutifully, relieved that his attentions were concentrated on a mere ornament, instead of on one of his children.

'Come here,' he was saying. 'Just come here.' Jude did not move.

'Better do as he says,' her mother said nervously from the door-way. Jude did not look at her. Traitor. Her father took a step towards her. At the same moment, Jude raised her hand aloft, the one holding the brass bird, and then with a yell she hurled the bird at the swaying figure in front of her, and as she heard the sound of the crash, she leapt forward and raced past him, past her gaping mother, knocking one of her sisters flying in the kitchen, and she was out, out into the back garden, past the dogs and the guinea pig cages and racing down the path, yelling a full-throated triumphant yell, as she pitched herself into the dark entrance of the outside toilet. Once inside, trembling, she fumbled at the rusting bolt. It slid into place, miraculously, at the first attempt.

Jude sank on to the wooden seat, and waited, panting. She would know soon if it was all over, or only just beginning. She counted to ten, very slowly, staring at the slats of light between the blistered, warping wood of the toilet door. Five . . . Six . . . She tore off one of the squares of torn-up newspaper on the nail by the door as she counted, and carefully folded it into an aeroplane. She could see a blurred picture of Christine Keeler on the piece she was folding, Christine Keeler in a perky hat, smiling. Nine . . . Ten. It was all over. She was safe. The bird must have missed.

She climbed up on to the seat and peered out of the hole in the top of the door. One of the dogs looked in her direction and then trailed over to the back door, to the very extremity of the rope attaching it to the fence, and dismally sank down on the step. There was no sound from the house. She launched the paper aero-plane through the hole in the door, and watched, squinting, as it nosedived into a bare patch of lawn. The dogs took no notice. She climbed down slowly. The toilet smelled of Elsan and years of excrement. She had better wait until he was asleep. She sat back on the seat and folded her legs beneath her, rocking slowly backwards and forwards, sniffing blood back into her nose, tearless.

32

She would just think about John, she would just think about John . . .

Peggy heard it as she hurried down the lane in her muddy boots, carrying a string bag full of sprouts and pushing the baby in a ramshackle pram: it came from Brigadoon, and it was a full-throated scream. Peggy hurried on, her head bowed against the wind.

Mike, chiselling at a large piece of stone in his shed, heard it. He looked up, his hands still for a moment, and wondered if it was the wind. But no – there it was again!

Bennett raced along the passage from the bathroom where she had been plucking her eyebrows with Peggy's tweezers, towards Cissie's room, the dog yapping at her heels, excited. Cissie was kneeling up on the bed, turning the volume knob of her transistor full on, her face alight.

'Beatles!' she said. 'The new one! Shut up, Toulouse!'

Bennett gasped a little, and came inside, creeping on tiptoe, as if any noise she made might prevent the Beatles from singing. She joined Cissie, kneeling clumsily next to her on the bed, her ear pressed to the transistor, intent. Cissie grasped her arm. Together they listened as the Beatles sang. *'Oh please, say to me, you'll let me be your man . . .'* Toulouse licked Cissie's face, concerned.

Then the house began to shake. Bennett turned, fleetingly wondering if you could have earthquakes in Norfolk, but even as the thought entered her head, she knew that the thundering was Mike racing up the stairs two at a time, and now he was here, in the doorway, out of breath, his face white.

'What is it?' he said. 'Cissie –'

'Sssh!' Cissie glowered at him, her ear still pressed to the radio, straining to hear every note. 'Beatles!'

Mike stood for a moment, seemingly dumbfounded, staring at the two girls, who had returned to their previous position, kneeling together on the bed in a parody of prayer, listening as the Beatles sang. The sound quivered tinnily in the room. Then Mike strode forward and snatched the radio away.

Cissie stared at him, taken aback. 'What are you –'

Not until that moment had Bennett or Cissie realized that Mike was angry. He could hardly speak. When he did, his voice was low, controlled. 'You screamed,' he said to Cissie evenly, his voice larger than the singing.

'Beatles' new record,' Cissie said.

'Beatles' new record,' he repeated. Bennett felt rather than heard the rumble of storm clouds.

'Mike!' Cissie's voice rose, 'Can you shut up until it's over, at least —'

He snapped the radio off. Cissie froze for a moment, shocked. Then she climbed off the bed, cheeks pink. 'Give me that back!' she said.

Bennett groaned inwardly. She heard the back door slam, as Peggy came into the house. Cissie was standing facing Mike now, her hand outstretched, her voice angry and urgent. 'They're playing it for the first time!' she said. 'Mike! It's the new record!'

'You're mad,' he said, finally.

'Mike, just give me my radio back — quick — it'll be over —' Cissie reached out but Mike pulled away. Peggy was hurrying up the stairs.

'The dustbin is the best place for this,' Mike said. The hand holding the radio was actually trembling, Bennett noticed with some surprise. Peggy appeared behind Mike, the baby dozing in her arms, hat askew.

'What on earth was that scream?' she asked. 'Are you all right, Cissie? Bennett?' Her face was bright with cold, and a few snow-flakes still quivered on the collar of her coat.

'He's got my radio,' Cissie said, 'and the Beatles are singing — the Beatles are singing and it'll be almost over by now.'

'Mike?' Peggy put out a gloved hand to take the radio, but he pulled away.

'He's a pig!' Cissie shouted, her face very red. 'I hate him!'

'And you're getting ridiculous,' Mike said, ignoring Peggy and glaring at Cissie. There was something faintly ludicrous about this large man in rough blue overalls filling up the doorway and holding the tiny transistor as if it were the most disgusting thing on earth, grimly, between dusty fingers.

34

'Mike –' Peggy began to unbutton her coat with her free hand, exasperated. 'They're teenagers, for heaven's sake.'

'Yes!' he said. 'Yes! I know!'

'They get excited –'

'Did you hear the scream?' he turned to his wife. 'I was in the shed – I thought she was hurt – I thought the house was on fire – I didn't know what to think –'

Cissie was crying now. 'It'll be finished now!' she sobbed. 'The most important moment of my life and you ruined it! I hate you! You ruin everything!'

Peggy sighed, tiredly. 'Cissie . . .' Bennett stared at the carpet, embarrassed. On the floor there were little trails of plaster dust where Mike had crossed the room to take the transistor from Cissie. Toulouse had taken refuge under the bed, just his black snout visible under the edge of the candlewick cover.

'It was the first time!' Cissie was saying, drawing great shuddering breaths. 'It was the new record.'

'It's got stupid,' Mike said. He threw the transistor on to the bed. 'This obsession – it's ridiculous. Can't you like these characters quietly? Stick a few pictures on the walls, by all means. Buy a few records, enjoy yourself. I remember what it's like. But for God's sake don't go so over the top.'

Peggy smiled brightly. 'He was a sucker for Cathryn Grayson when we first met,' she said. 'I couldn't get a sensible word out of him if she was singing –'

Cissie's face was blotched with tears. 'I don't give a bugger about his stupid musicals!' she shouted. 'It's not the same! Nothing's the same! Tell him, Bennett – tell him!' She fiddled frantically with the radio. It sprang suddenly to life. It was the Dave Clark Five singing 'Glad all Over'. Cissie switched it off again. Bennett sat, head bowed, wishing she was anywhere but here. The baby woke and began to grizzle quietly, eyes half-closed.

'Oh, forget it.' Mike turned, disgusted, and headed off downstairs. 'Bloody over-compensating,' he called over his shoulder to Peggy. 'You're too damn soft.'

They listened to the heavy sound of his feet descending the stairs.

Then the back door slammed. There was a moment's silence. Peggy untied the baby's bonnet, her face expressionless.

'You want me to take Susie?' Bennett was eager. 'I could play with her, if you've got things to do –'

Peggy shook her head, hardly hearing. 'No, it's all right, Bennett –' She was watching Cissie, who scrubbed angrily at her tear-blotched face.

'I wish my dad was alive,' Cissie said. Peggy said nothing, only watched her daughter, pressing her lips together, as if preventing herself from saying something she might later regret. 'I'll put the kettle on,' she said. And then she, too, headed downstairs, the baby's complaints fading away with her footfalls.

The two girls sat, silent. 'I wish I was dead,' Cissie said.

'Better go,' Bennett said. She made no movement, however. 'The Germans. Expecting me. Health Visitor's coming.' Bennett's home life was punctuated by visits from minor officials from Government departments. Cissie did not reply. 'They'll play it again,' Bennett said.

'It won't be the same.'

'No.' Bennett got up. 'See you, then.'

'See you.'

Bennett clumped away, depressed. Down in the kitchen, Susie was in a high chair banging a spoon. Peggy was peeling sprouts at the sink, staring out of the kitchen window. Outside, the sleet was falling in diagonal stripes, driven by the wind.

From the other room could be heard the sound of Paul Robeson singing a negro spiritual. Mill was very keen on Paul Robeson. 'Now there's a man with strong convictions,' she was fond of saying. 'You can't beat a man with sound politics. Find yourself a man with sound politics and you can't go far wrong.'

'Will you be all right, Bennett?' Peggy did not turn round, intent on her task. She was referring to the walk back to Polston Wood.

'Fine. I got my boots.' Bennett went over to the back door, where her wellingtons stood on an old copy of the *Observer*. She struggled into them, having the usual difficulty. Pudgy legs, she thought glumly.

Peggy was crashing plates in the sink. 'Why did the pig fail its driving test?' Bennett asked, and then, before Peggy could respond: ''Cos it was a road hog.' Peggy laughed, cheerful. Bennett was pleased. 'See you, then.'

'See you, Bennett.'

Pulling on her woolly hat, Bennett turned for a second and saw, illuminated in the reflection of the window, that Peggy was crying. She pulled open the back door hastily, letting in a blast of sleet, and hurried out, her face pained.

In her room, Cissie heard the slam of the back door as Bennett left. The house was suddenly very quiet. She got up and went to look out of the window. Snow was already covering the roof of the coalshed, and one remaining chicken, only just visible in the gathering gloom, pecked disconsolately at the white ground before disappearing inside the coop, feathers fluffed up against the cold. Beyond the stillness of the cabbage field surrounding the house, there was rustling and groaning in the great trees which marked the boundary between Polston Wood and the neighbouring village of Foxheath, as the snow and the wind shifted the branches. A train made its way slowly across the flat horizon, its lights flickering as it passed through the beginnings of Polston Wood itself, on its way to Yarmouth. Cissie watched its progress, and wondered who could be sitting in those carriages, those little squares of light passing in the darkness. Unexpectedly the longing to be on that train came upon her; she felt a surge of desperation, a sense of being trapped in this house with its odd occupants, like Pip in *Great Expectations*, wandering about in a Gothic mansion dreading encounters with the imperious Estella, or the mad Miss Havisham.

Downstairs, Mill would be asleep by the fire, her knitting slipping off her lap, negro spirituals filling her dreams, oblivious to the recent ructions. Mike would be back in his shed, fuming, hammering at some oddly-shaped monolith, his face streaked with dirt. Peggy would be feeding the baby, and singing a silly song, so that Susie's round face, so like Mike's, would be lit up with pleasure. There was only Cissie, standing at the window like a wraith, who did not have a place, a fixed point in this scenario. I could be invisible, she thought. I *am* invisible.

She turned and looked at her most recent Beatles picture, cut out of *Rave* magazine. It was pinned immediately above her bed. The four looked out, smiling. George was wearing a jacket with a velvet collar. Unlike the others, he was not looking directly at the camera but slightly to one side, a smile on his lips that said to Cissie: 'I've got my own private thoughts.' She went over and kissed the picture, placing her lips tenderly on George's cheek. He was everything. He made her real.

She stayed in her room, refusing supper, until she knew Mike had gone back out to the shed. She went slowly downstairs when she heard the shifting of furniture in the living room, signalling preparations for the evening. Susie was in her playpen in the kitchen. At the sight of Cissie, she raised her arms and made little urgent sounds, indicating she wanted to be held. Cissie picked her up and made snorting noises into the baby's soft neck, making her squeal with delight. Cissie had wanted to resent the baby when she arrived – after all, she was the result of that unnameable act performed by – unthinkable thought – her mother and Mike; but Susie was a charming, cheerful baby with a mop of sandy curls and an infectious giggle. It was impossible to connect her with anything other than joy. Even now, in Cissie's darkest hour, her dimpled arms were clasped firmly around her big sister, vulnerable and trusting.

Cissie settled the baby on one hip, as she had seen Peggy do, and went into the living room. The table from the front room had been carried in, as it was every third Saturday in the month, and Mill was already ensconced in her position, Woodbines and ashtray arranged in front of her. Peggy was carrying chairs in from the front room and arranging them round the table. Someone banged on the back door.

'Can you get that, Cissie?' Peggy's voice bore no hint of the fact that her daughter had been at war with everyone for the past two hours. Jiggling the baby in her arms, Cissie went to open the door. In a flurry of snow several damp, dark figures in hats hurried inside, umbrellas flapping, voices raised.

'Hello, Cecilia. A filthy night!'

'Good evening, wood nymph!'

'Is there somewhere I can put my galoshes?'

Dutifully Cissie took coats and organized a place for dripping umbrellas and boots. These were the members of the trio her mother privately called the Village Visionaries: a very small man called Peter with a goatee beard who lived in a brand new bungalow and believed in fairies, the formidable Mrs Michaels from the sweet shop, and a long thin woman with a tragic face and what Mill called 'a past', who seemed simply to be called Miss W.

Miss W, the last inside, had turned and was giggling girlishly at someone behind her, and Cissie saw that following the Village Visionaries came Mike, a layer of snowflakes on his shoulders. He had come in from his shed to fetch Susie, as was agreed on these occasions. Wordlessly, Cissie passed the baby to him. He tried to catch her eye, but she looked away. Silently, Mike left again.

By the time Cissie had struggled with snow-sodden outer garments in the cupboard under the stairs, the visitors were seated round the table in the living room, their faces expectant.

'Come along, my little nymph!' called the man with the beard. Cissie entered slowly. Mill caught her eye across the table-top and grimaced conspiratorially. Peter, the fairy man, had breath that smelt of Parma Violets and large, translucent ears; but worse, he had a twinkling, eager demeanour which he employed whatever the conversation, however inappropriate. He could discuss the afterlife (which this group did frequently) with a demented sparkle in his eye that hinted at dark shadows in his psyche. Mill felt sure he was a murderer, and often said so to her granddaughter. Cissie sidled nervously round the table to her seat in between her mother and the tragic Miss W, ignoring Peter's manic smile on the way.

'Lights?'

Mrs Michaels leaned across and switched off the standard lamp. Now, apart from a small light in the corner, there was only the glow from the fire illuminating the circle of faces. Although it was now dark outside, Peggy had left the curtains open, and a white blizzard was blowing silently on the other side of the windows. There was silence.

'Hands,' Peggy said quietly. Round the table, everyone joined hands. Cissie felt her mother's hand, warm, clutch hers on the table-top. On the other side, Miss W's bony fingers sat unhappily in her palm, limp and slightly damp. Miss W never made eye contact. She was sitting now with her eyes clamped tightly shut, her face screwed up as if in pain.

'The circle is joined,' Mrs Michaels said, grim. They sat, heads bowed. Cissie could hear the sound of Mill's breathing across the table. The waiting was interminable: this was always the most difficult bit, the waiting, the silence. A lump of coal shifted on the fire.

Behind her eyelids, Cissie concentrated. She would speak to him, she would tell him, he would understand. His thoughts could cross this great divide and touch hers, and they would be united, if only in spirit. Her heart pounded. If only their souls could touch for a moment, he would know then to come and find her, to take her away from Brigadoon and keep her safe and happy . . .

'There's a barrier.' It was Mrs Michaels. Cissie felt her mother's hand go limp in hers. 'Someone is preventing the circle from being joined.' Mrs Michaels' tone implied that this was a capital offence. Cissie opened her eyes. Her mother was looking at her.

'Cissie?'

Shamefaced, she opened her palm. It held a small square of dark blue cloth.

Peggy sighed. 'Cissie . . .' she said patiently. 'You know I can't do this if you hold something –'

Cissie screwed the piece of cloth in her hand, defensive. 'It's only tiny.'

Peggy shook her head. Miss W made a murmur of discontent, and Mrs Michaels tutted. Peter smiled his murderous smile. 'You'll have to get rid of it,' Peggy said. 'I'm sorry . . .'

'No.'

'It's distracting the flow –'

Cissie pushed back her chair. 'It's not distracting *my* flow!' she said, her voice uncharacteristically loud. 'It's helping me! It could help you –'

Peter the fairy man chose that moment to intervene. 'Come and sit next to me,' he said, twinkling at her in the gloom, 'You'll feel better over here.'

Mill glared at him over her bosom. 'And how will *you* feel?' she asked.

Peggy tensed. 'Mill,' she said, 'give it a rest, will you?'

Miss W drew herself up. 'Can we get on with the business in hand?' Her voice was plaintive.

Cissie stood up. 'I think you'll get on better without me,' she said, gulping back an angry sob. She headed for the door, ignoring the pleas and remonstrances of the Visionaries, the groan from Mill and the hurt expression in Peggy's eyes.

She slammed upstairs to her room. She found her precious copy of *With the Beatles*, pulled out the record and put it on to the turntable of the record player on the floor in the corner. Kneeling down, she lowered her head so that her eye was on a level with the grooves of the record. Third track, side two. There was the squeak that indicated the end of 'Hold Me Tight'. She turned the volume knob up a little and then threw herself on the bed as the piano began to play and the voices burst into the room, John's raw, George's plaintive, singing 'You Really Got A Hold On Me'. She rolled over on to her stomach, still clutching the record cover, still holding her little square of blue cloth. From the black glossy record sleeve only George's face stared out at her, impassive, half of it in shadow. She looked at the dark eye, right into it. She held the fabric to her cheek. He would not hear her across the windy miles between London and Norfolk, he would not sit up somewhere and feel the tingle of another spirit touching his . . .

'Cissie?' Mike was in the doorway, holding a sleeping Susie in his arms, his face full of concern. Cissie sat bolt upright, pink and flustered. 'Are you all right?'

She nodded. He took a step into the room. Cissie realized with surprise that he was hesitant about entering. 'Peggy said you were upset,' he said. Susie stirred and sighed against his shoulder, lost in a

41

baby's dream a million miles from them, relaxed in his arms. Cissie felt her defences melting away. In spite of herself, she knew she was going to forgive him for his earlier crime with the radio. She held out her hand, wordlessly, the one containing the piece of blue cloth. Mike stepped closer and examined it.

'It belonged to George,' she said shyly.

Mike looked at her, surprised. 'It did?'

'Mrs Harrison sent it to me,' she said. 'It was a bit of the jacket George wore when they played in Hamburg.'

Mike nodded, his face serious, examining the cloth, turning it over in his hand. 'Mohair,' he said.

She could have hugged him for not sounding cynical, for not suggesting, as Mill had done, that George Harrison's mother might have acquired roomfuls of jackets to cut up and appease eager fans.

'The Star Club,' Cissie said, 'that's where they played.'

He nodded again, thoughtfully. Then he looked at her. 'Were you trying to contact your father in the seance?' He asked. It was evident that this was not an easy topic for him. 'Is that why you were upset? You were trying to get in touch with your dad?' She did not reply for a moment. Then, unexpectedly, she grinned at him.

'Of course not!' she said. 'I was trying to get in touch with George! George Harrison! I thought I might get some vibrations from the jacket . . .'

There was a moment of stunned incomprehension. Then Mike said carefully, 'But George isn't dead.'

Silence. Then Cissie's face began to wobble. 'I never thought of that,' she said, and began to laugh. Mike joined in, relieved. 'I think I'm losing my marbles,' Cissie said, eventually, when the laughter had died away. She was only half-joking, and Mike knew it.

'You'll be all right,' he said. 'Believe me.' And he was gone, tiptoeing up the passage to put Susie to bed.

Cissie lay back on the bed for a moment, closing her eyes. She felt weak, on the verge of laughter or tears, it didn't seem to matter which. She leaned over and pulled her George Box from under the bed. It was a cigar box, painstakingly covered in cut-out pictures of

George, glued down and then varnished. She opened the lid and fingered the handful of letters inside. She caught glimpses of phrases, words, all written in the same careful looped handwriting. '. . .John in the kitchen . . .', '. . .don't like them going on tour . . .', '. . . the boys love it . . .'. There was a birthday card, too. And a glossy photograph of the Beatles, posed in a studio, with their signatures scrawled across it. Cissie held the photograph up to the light and examined it – yes, the signatures were genuine, you could see where John had pressed really hard to make the 'J'; you could see where Ringo had gone a bit wrong on the 'O' and had gone over it again. They had written on this photo. They had held it. George looked out at her, smiling, unconcerned. Gently, she returned the photograph, and laid the scrap of cloth on top of it, closing the lid.

The Beatles were singing '*Oh no, not a second time . . .*'. She lay on the bed like a small white corpse, her George Box placed carefully on her chest, where it rose and fell with her breathing. She stared at the ceiling. George looked down at her from a large poster, wearing a leather jacket, his face serious.

I will find you, she told him from her heart, *I will* . . . For a moment she was up there, on the ceiling, looking down at herself. *Yes, I will come, I will find you . . .*

Christmas Eve would never be the same again. In the back of Mike's mud-splattered Ford, Bennett and Cissie put the finishing touches to their appearance as they drove towards Crookfield Park, the neat Norwich suburb where Heather lived.

'You'll phone me when you get back,' Mike was saying, struggling to see the road in between the erratic motions of the windscreen wipers. It was pouring with rain.

Cissie nodded, too busy applying lipstick to speak.

'You think Jude'll turn up?' Bennett asked. She was peering into her compact mirror, carefully combing the fringe of hair that covered her forehead.

'Of course she'll turn up.'

Mike looked at them in his rear-view mirror. 'I thought you had gone off Jude,' he said. The two girls looked slightly uncomfortable.

'No . . . well . . .' Bennett tried to sound nonchalant. 'We were pissed off with her because of that tickets business –'

'Mike doesn't know about it,' Cissie cut in quickly. Bennett looked at her, surprised.

'You didn't tell him?'

Mike leaned forward in his seat, squinting through the rain at the murky road. 'Didn't you know?' he said. 'Cissie never tells us anything.'

Bennett had no such reservations. 'It was about the tickets,' she said, rubbing at a pencilled-in eyebrow with a chewed finger. 'When the Beatles were coming to the Grosvenor Rooms. Jude promised to get us tickets and then she just never did. Can you believe it? She tells us she's going to get the tickets, no sweat, and then she just doesn't. Meanwhile we don't bother to queue up with everyone else because Jude swears she's getting these special tickets, right up the front, through some bloke at the theatre. Just another one of her fairy stories, it turns out. So the Beatles come to Nor-wich, they come to *Norwich*! – her voice trembled with emotion – and we don't get to see them.'

Mike negotiated a bend carefully. 'Ah,' he said. 'That must have been in the spring, right?'

'How did you know that?' Cissie looked at the back of his head, surprised.

'You went into deep mourning around that time, as I recall,' he said.

Bennett snorted. 'He's having you on, Cissie! He knows bloody well when the Beatles came to Norwich, everyone bloody knew . . . Sorry, Mr Lovelock,' – this because she had remembered finally that Mike was a parent of sorts, and you weren't supposed to swear at parents. But Mike merely smiled. 'We went to the Grosvenor Rooms anyway,' Bennett continued, encouraged by the smile, 'and we stood about outside, but we couldn't see a bloody thing, could we, Cissie? There was hundreds of girls – hundreds. We never saw nothing,' she concluded ungrammatically, sighing.

'Well – you'll definitely see them tonight,' Mike said.

Cissie stared out of the window, not quite believing it. She was

44

going to see George. She was going to be in the same place as George. He would be there, breathing the same air, seeing the same things, hearing the same sounds. Cissie Lovelock. George Harrison. Together.

Mike pulled up in the driveway of Heather's house. 'Here we are, then,' he said. 'You want me to come in with you?'

'No!' Cissie's reply was too quick. She had not meant to be quite so rude, but the thought of scruffy Mike in his wellingtons and threadbare jumper standing on the pristine hall carpet in the primness of the Lewises' semi-detached was just too awful to contemplate. Bennett seemed to be having her own doubts about the impending trip.

'Can't you take us, Mr Lovelock?' she was imploring. 'Just drive us to London? You could go and see Oliver while we were at the concert –'

Mike laughed and shook his head. 'What – and miss Susie's first Christmas? Sorry, Bennett – out of the question. And my name's Mike, for the hundredth time.'

Bennett glowed. She was besotted by the Lovelocks' informality; it never failed to delight and amaze her, after the forced, impersonal jollity of the Jermyns.

Cissie was tying a plastic Rainmate carefully over her hair. She wished they could just shut their eyes and be in London, this endless journey done with. 'We'll be fine,' she said. 'We'll be home about one in the morning. Or two.' She pulled the hood of her duffle coat over the Rainmate, just to be on the safe side. She had just spent an hour hunched over the ironing board while Peggy ironed her hair strand by strand, spreading it out under brown paper, patiently smoothing it to perfection. Now her carefully manufactured sleekness would curl up in the rain. She despaired. She would see George and she would have frizzy hair.

'I'll be sitting by the phone,' Mike said, reassuring. 'It doesn't matter what time it is – the moment you get back here, you phone. All right?'

Cissie's hand was already on the door handle. Bennett put a hand on Mike's shoulder, wanting to hug him but not daring to. 'Thank

45

you, Mike,' she said tremulously. 'This is the best Christmas present in the whole universe.'

He turned and looked at them, their two faces blazing with excitement. 'I'm just the chauffeur for phase one,' he said. 'It's the Lewises you should thank, isn't it? They got you the tickets.' It was true. Somehow, miraculously, Heather's dad had acquired the tickets from someone at Anglia Television. Unbelievably, it was Heather – irritating, prissy Heather Lewis, Paul McCartney devotee – who had given them access to heaven. It was a sobering lesson to learn about human possibilities.

'Give them a scream from me,' Mike was saying.

Cissie paused, indignant. 'We're not going to scream,' she said. She opened the door and climbed out into the rain. Mike wound down the window. 'Thanks,' she said, her voice gruff. 'Tell Mum Happy Christmas from me when midnight strikes.' She wanted to say more, to say she knew she had mucked up Christmas with this trip, that she was sorry she would miss the Christmas Eve carol singers, and stuffing the presents into Susie's stocking, and the mince pies, and Mill pounding out 'It Came Upon The Midnight Clear' on the piano. She wanted to say she knew she was lucky. Instead, she turned away, pulling the Rainmate further over her eyes.

He began reversing down the drive. 'Go on!' he called. 'Get inside! You're getting soaked!'

They raced, squealing, to the haven of the porch, where an over-head light illuminated 'Hazlemere', the words cut into a piece of wood shaped to imply that it had recently been carved from a felled oak. By the time they were inside, the rear lights of the Ford were disappearing in the downpour. Bennett and Cissie looked at each other, savouring this moment. This was really happening, at last!

'Happy Christmas,' said Bennett, grinning.

'Are you seeing your mum this year?' Cissie asked carefully. She never knew what to say about Bennett's absent mother, but felt she should say something.

Bennett, who had been about to ring the doorbell, paused. 'I've been,' she said.

'Was she all right?'

Bennett would not meet her eyes. 'She's been having that electric shock treatment. She thought I was a cleaner.'

Cissie's laugh was nervous. 'A cleaner! Were you carrying a mop?'

In spite of her amused tone, there was a tell-tale tremor in Bennett's voice. ''Course I was! I always visit mental hospitals with my mop and bucket. Don't you?' Cissie laughed longer and louder than the sarcasm deserved. Neither girl could look at the other, and there was a moment of jagged silence. Then Bennett rang the doorbell.

Mrs Lewis opened the door. She was a small woman with a deceptively sweet smile and a look of Her Majesty the Queen about her. 'There you are,' she said, still standing in the doorway. 'No Jude? You can take your shoes and coats off and leave them out there. And umbrellas in the corner, please. You weren't going to bring that Rainmate in to drip all over my parquet, were you, Cecilia?'

'Aren't we leaving now?' Bennett loomed over Mrs Lewis, suddenly large and loud. 'Isn't Heather ready?'

'We're waiting for your friend,' Mrs Lewis said. 'Susan – I think you'd better leave those socks off as well. They're leaving marks on the tiles. Does your foster mother allow you to wear trousers? I'm surprised.'

The two girls padded, shoeless, into the gleaming hall, and stood politely under a large, dark reproduction of a stag at bay. 'Daddy's just sorting out the car,' Mrs Lewis said, ushering the girls into the kitchen. They were rarely allowed into the sanctum of the living room, with its gleaming coffee table and unrumpled three-piece suite. 'And Heather's got a surprise for you.'

Bennett and Cissie exchanged a glance, as Mrs Lewis busied herself, humming, with the completion of a stack of ham sandwiches she was constructing for the journey.

'Surprises I can do without,' murmured Bennett in her Humphrey Bogart voice.

'What, dear?'

'Nothing.' Mrs Lewis was able to reduce both girls to mumbling,

47

inarticulate lumps, with just the twitch of an eyebrow or a quiver of the lip. In Mrs Lewis's case, the twitch or the quiver could herald a lengthy outburst of cruel disapproval, delivered in that tiny little implacable Scots voice: a small rivulet of annoyance hiding what was clearly the torrent of fury beneath.

'Ta–dah!' Heather appeared in the doorway, a triumphant vision in orange and black, and twirled for their approval. 'What do you think?'

Cissie and Bennett stared, stunned. Heather was modelling a huge tangerine-coloured sweater with 'BEATLES' knitted across the chest in large black letters. Down each sleeve the words 'FAB FOUR' were emblazoned, and on the back they could see, as Heather turned, the names 'JOHN', 'PAUL', 'GEORGE' and 'RINGO' knitted diagonally into the yarn.

'Wow,' said Bennett, finally.

'Paton's Jaffa double knit,' Mrs Lewis said, pleased with herself, 'and Sirdar Black Extra Soft. With a little bit of mohair in it, I'd say.'

Cissie and Bennett were fingering the sweater, jealousy mingling with admiration. 'It's brilliant,' Cissie said.

'Yes, it is, isn't it?' said Heather. 'It's a surprise. Mum's been knitting it for weeks.'

Neither Bennett nor Cissie had experience of a mother who knitted for weeks, and for a second their envy was almost palpable.

'You'll get your picture in the paper in that,' Bennett said, her tone grudging.

Heather twirled again, aware that she cut a dash. 'I know,' she said. 'That's what I'm hoping. Then Paul will see it and he'll get in touch –'

This dream was interrupted by Mrs Lewis. 'Get your things together, Heather. We ought to be going. And' – sharply – 'don't think you'll be leaving in those earrings. I'm not blind.'

'What about Jude?' Cissie said.

Mrs Lewis looked at the kitchen clock, pointedly. 'We did say three o'clock, didn't we?' Her husband was coming through the back door, rolling down his shirt-sleeves.

'Oil checked,' he said. 'Ready for the off. All set, girls?' Mr Lewis was tall and spare with a neat grey moustache.

'Feet, Donald.' Mrs Lewis's tone was tetchy. Meekly, he struggled out of his shoes. Within the walls of Hazlemere, Mrs Lewis's word was law.

'No Jude yet,' said Heather, removing her earrings as instructed. Silently, unseen by her mother, she handed them to Cissie, who put them in the pocket of her slacks. Heather would put them back on later.

Mr Lewis looked at the clock in exaggerated alarm. 'But we're fifteen minutes late already!'

Mrs Lewis had finished with the sandwiches and was wrapping them in greaseproof-paper with rigid precision. 'We'll have to go,' she said.

Cissie, Heather and Bennett exchanged horrified glances. 'We can't go without Jude,' Cissie said. 'We just can't.'

Mrs Lewis had already gone to get her coat from the hall cupboard. 'You want to see the Beatles, don't you?' she asked from its recesses. 'If we're late to the theatre they may not let you in.' She re-emerged, and began to struggle into a smart cherry-red swagger coat. Her husband hurried to assist her, but was thwarted by a look. 'Shoes, Donald,' she said. He hurried away again. Mrs Lewis arranged a small red felt hat on top of her curls, staring critically at herself in the hall mirror. The three girls stood, watching. Finally she turned, satisfied with what she had seen. 'Right, then,' she said, firm. 'Daddy's put the car in the drive. Put your shoes and coats on in the hall and wait for the signal before you run out. And don't come back in the house with your outdoor shoes on!' There was a moment, as the three girls stood, uncertain what to do or say. They could not leave without Jude; but, equally, they were unable to challenge the small, steely-eyed woman even now heading for the porch.

'Come on!' she was saying, brightly. 'Cheer up! You're going to see the Beatles!'

The car had just swung out into the road when a figure hurled itself against the bonnet, and for a moment Jude's face appeared, grotesque, shouting into the windscreen through the rain. With a sharp intake of breath, Mr Lewis braked and the girls in the back were all thrown forward. The back door opened and a dishevelled Jude climbed in, dripping and angry.

'You bastards!' she panted. 'You were going without me!'

'Language!' Mrs Lewis said sharply from the front. 'We won't tolerate swearing, young lady. One more and you'll be out of this car.'

'Sorry, sorry . . .' Jude attempted to look contrite and failed. 'Shove up, you lot.' They did, complaining, as Mr Lewis set off again.

'You're late,' Mrs Lewis's voice was like ice.

'Police came round,' Jude said airily.

The girls were instantly agog. 'Why?'

Jude struggled out of her damp rain mac, elbowing Bennett, who was sitting next to her. 'My little sister – nicked six packets of Love Hearts from the tobacconist's.'

'Did they arrest her?' Heather's voice was almost a squeak from the combined shock of Jude's dramatic entrance and the knowledge that her mother was listening.

'Let her off with a warning.' Jude scrunched the wet mac into a bundle and placed it under her feet. 'She'll get it from my dad, though.'

'Wireless, Donald,' Mrs Lewis said firmly. She had had enough of Jude.

'*Parade of the Pops*'ll be on soon,' said Bennett, hopeful.

Mrs Lewis shook her head, as the car radio crackled into life. 'No, dear,' she said, smiling her sweet smile. '*Sing Something Simple*. Christmas Eve Concert.' Sure enough, the sound of the Mike Sammes Singers suddenly surged into the confines of the car. They were singing 'Mary's Boy Child'. Mrs Lewis hummed along. The girls exchanged glances. Pointedly, Heather held out her wrist and showed the other three her silver Timex. Half past three. They exchanged tremulous glances. Four hours to go!

The Lewises' Morris Minor made agonizingly slow progress in the torrential rain, edging its way out of the Norwich suburbs and only finally speeding up as it reached the A11 and headed towards Newmarket. Cissie stared out at the squally sky and the vast empty fields. They were leaving behind everything she knew, and they were going to London, where the world began. She was no longer sure whether this was a wonderful or a terrible prospect. The Beatles were in London, and they beckoned like a beacon; but at the same time, London was an ominous labyrinth where people like her step-brother Oliver lived mysteriously sophisticated lives, free from parental caretaking. The idea was alarming. A vision of her bedroom swam before her, with its Beatles pictures and Toulouse stretched across the candlewick bedspread. How safe, how warm! How dreadful to be alone in a huge, alien city! George had gone to Germany when he was only seventeen. But then George was full of courage . . .

She dozed and dreamed, drifting in and out of consciousness, lulled by the car's engine and the warmth of Heather's and Bennett's bodies, crammed either side of her on the back seat. George was in the kitchen of Brigadoon, leaning over Susie in her playpen. He looked at Cissie, his face thoughtful. 'You'll be all right,' he said. 'Believe me.'

'Cissie . . .' Bennett's face peered into hers. 'You asleep?'

Cissie sat up, sleepy. 'Where are we?'

'Baldock,' Mr Lewis said from the driver's seat. 'Won't be long now.'

Cissie looked. They were driving along a busy dual carriageway, lined on either side by large semi-detached houses. Bennett and Jude were having a muttered debate, not appearing to have noticed that the fields had become houses outside the car window.

'The thing about John,' Jude was saying seriously, 'is that he's – well, he doesn't say what you expect him to say, does he?'

Bennett agreed. 'Nasty,' she said; then, seeing Jude's darkening frown, added, almost apologetic, 'He can be a bit nasty, Jude. He was dead rude on *Thank Your Lucky Stars*.'

Jude grinned, pleased. 'I know.'

'You'd never catch Paul being rude,' Heather said.

Bennett glowered at her. She did not want to be seen as sharing the same opinion as Heather. She scrabbled about for a way out of this unwanted liaison. 'Mr Goody Two Shoes McCartney – he's just the handsome one, isn't he,' she said finally, in a crushing tone. 'He's the *obvious* one.'

Heather bristled. 'Well you certainly can't say that about Ringo.'

Bennett, surprisingly unperturbed by this provocation, leaned back comfortably in her seat. 'Yes, but you can't cuddle Paul, can you?' she said, dreamily. 'You can't just love him, can you.'

'Why not?' Heather's voice was high, indignant.

Bennett shot her a pitying look. 'Because he's too good-looking. Can't be trusted.' She caught Cissie's eye and grinned.

Cissie stared at her feet, remembering what Bennett had said once to her, in a moment of blurted confidence in the bedroom at Brigadoon. 'Too good-looking. That was the trouble.' Bennett had been talking about her mother. 'Couldn't be trusted. Always running off with unsuitable blokes.'

'Traffic's building up,' Mr Lewis said suddenly, his hands grimly clutching the wheel, 'Next left, did you say, Navigator?'

Mrs Lewis was peering tensely at a map on her knees. 'Traffic lights,' she said, uncertainly. 'Left at a big junction . . .' Behind them, a car's horn hooted.

'Someone should tell him about the tortoise and the hare,' Mr Lewis said, unperturbed, glancing in his rear mirror. Jude, kneeling up on the seat and staring out of the back window, nudged Bennett.

'Talent,' she said, under her breath. The other girls squirmed round to have a look. The driver of the car behind was a young man with a fair, floppy fringe. He grinned at them. Next to him, a dark-haired version gave them a little wave.

'He looks like that one who was on *About Anglia*,' said Heather, excited, 'the blond one. Wayne Fontana and the Mindbenders.'

'That dark one's nice,' said Bennett. 'Looks a bit like Ringo.'

'His nose is too small. He's too good-looking,' Jude said, flinching ready for the blow she knew would be delivered by an angry Bennett.

'At least he doesn't wear *glasses*,' Bennett said savagely. This riposte, often used in times of heated debate about individual Beatle merits, was a weak one, because they all knew that John Lennon was one of the few people in the universe who could wear spectacles and still look fab.

'What's wrong with glasses?' Mrs Lewis wanted to know; then, having turned and seen the backs of four heads, she hissed, 'Sit down at once!' with such venom that they all automatically did as they were told. The car behind suddenly speeded up and screeched past, the dark-haired youth rolling down the window and making a V-sign at the Morris Minor, yelling incoherently into the wind, his hair flapping. The girls smirked and subsided, elated by what they felt to be their first encounter with London. The omens were good.

An hour later, the car finally drew to a halt in the gloom of a car park in north London. Stiff and rumpled, they climbed out, blinking, into the damp air. Cissie's heart was pounding. They had just driven past the entrance to the Astoria cinema, and that glimpse of crowds and lights and a giant picture of the Beatles shining out of the darkness had been almost too much to bear. She felt sick.

'Can we go, then?' Heather was asking her mother, desperately impatient, jiggling from one foot to the other. 'Can we have the tickets now?'

'Just be patient,' said Mrs Lewis, slowly folding her travelling rug. 'Daddy needs to tell you exactly the plan. Do you want to go to the lavatory, dear?'

Cissie paced away across the puddles, unable to contain her excitement, unwilling to listen while Mr Lewis gave Heather and Bennett a list of instructions. 'The car is two rows from the fence, tenth from the left – got that? Have a look, now, so you don't forget! And we're to the west of the theatre – that means you come out of the front after the show and you take the first road on the left . . .'

Jude had followed Cissie, and was jumping carefully over a large puddle near by, backwards and forwards, with great concentration.

'I won't be coming back with you,' she said.

Cissie, her head full of turmoil at the prospect of imminently seeing George, hardly heard her. 'Yes?' she said.

'I'm running away,' Jude said, leaping the puddle again, her face hidden in shadows. 'I'm not going home.'

Cissie looked up. Jude had stopped jumping and was standing staring out across the parked cars, her expression inscrutable.

'Where will you go?' she asked.

Jude shrugged. 'Don't know. I thought I'd start by staying with Oliver.'

Cissie stared at her, aghast. 'What – *my* Oliver?' she asked.

Jude smiled. 'Yes, *your* Oliver,' she teased.

Cissie, feeling giddy, leaned against a nearby car bonnet. The metal felt wet and cold under her hand. 'Jude,' she said, 'you can't.'

'Why not?'

'He'll never let you stay.'

Jude grinned. 'Yes he will,' she said, 'if you come with me and persuade him.' She stepped closer to Cissie, her face suddenly vulnerable, unexpectedly soft. 'We could run away together. Start a new life. One night at Oliver's, then – well, anywhere.' Cissie was staring at her. 'We could go to Liverpool,' she said finally, 'find the Beatles.'

There was a moment's silence. 'They're here,' Cissie said.

'What?'

'The Beatles – they're here. In London. They're not in Liverpool.'

Jude made an impatient noise. 'Yes, but they go home, don't they? And I've still got their addresses. I know they never wrote back to any of us' – Cissie shifted uncomfortably, aware of her secret – 'but we could go and visit their families. John's Aunty Mimi. Menlove Avenue. George's mum. Where was it?'

'Macket's Lane,' said Cissie, automatically, 'a hundred and seventy-four.'

She wondered whether now would be a good time to confess to Jude that in fact she was in touch with a Beatle – well, sort of. Although George had never written back in answer to Cissie's impassioned letter, his mother had. And Cissie had written back to her. And she had written back again. And now Cissie had a box full of letters from Mrs Harrison – letters full of secrets about the Beatles, details of George's life, tales from Mrs Harrison's own childhood in Liverpool: magic letters, letters that lifted Cissie up to heaven. She looked at Jude's grimly determined face, the shadow of a bruise under her left eye. No. This was not the time.

'Cissie! Jude!' Bennett was bellowing across the car park, 'Come on! It's time!'

Jude grabbed the sleeve of Cissie's duffle coat. 'I looked it up,' she said. 'We need the A1. We find ourselves a lorry-driver to give us a lift. Cissie!'

But Cissie was hurrying away, running across the glittering puddles towards the car and the safety of the Lewises and their last-minute admonitions. After a moment, Jude followed, scuffing her shoes on the concrete, depressed.

Heather was enduring a kiss from her mother. 'Straight back here!' Mr Lewis's tone was menacing. 'And if there's an emergency, we're at the Odeon, Leicester Square, *From Russia with Love.*'

Jude called to the others. 'This way!' she yelled. 'Come on!' She was already hurrying towards the lights of the Seven Sisters Road. Heather wrenched herself away from her mother's grip, triumphantly clutching the tickets.

'You can't get in without me!' she called to Jude, and began a slow, dignified walk in her direction, only to be swept along by Bennett and Cissie. The four of them raced away, exultant, screaming into the windy night.

For Cissie, what followed was a nightmare, heavenly jumble of images and sensations, hideous and beautiful, scaring and wonderful: a vicious crush of bodies pushing through a doorway too narrow to take them all; the chaos of the brightly-lit foyer, losing Bennett in the crowd, finding her again, her face red and grinning in a sea of other faces, her arm waving as if drowning, clutching a programme; Cissie clutching the belt of Jude's PVC mac as if it were a lifeline as they shuffled hysterically up the red plush stairs to their seats in the balcony. Then there was an unbearable wait in the steamy fug of damp raincoats and buoyant teenage bodies, tremulous and tearful faces. Cissie would always remember this moment: Bennett, pink and silent, Heather worrying about her shiny nose, as usual, and nervously folding her blonde flick-ups round her comb, peering into her compact mirror; Jude white-faced, staring into the middle distance, only the tense hand clamped on the seat in front revealing what she might be feeling. At the moment when Cissie thought she might actually be sick if something didn't happen soon, the house lights suddenly dimmed, and a great shout went up from the audience. Everyone stood up. Cissie craned her neck to see over the heads in front of her to the stage below, where two spotlights played on the closed curtains.

A roar. Then the curtains opened to reveal a small flickering screen. Cissie, slightly short-sighted, squinted but could not identify the moving shapes. A disembodied voice boomed from the shadows: 'By land . . . By sea . . . By air . . .' A deafening scream from the audience. 'Yes, by land, sea and by air come the stars of Brian Epstein's fabulous Beatles Christmas show.' The curtains opened completely and a helicopter lowered itself gingerly on to the stage, wires gleaming, from on high. 'And here's your pilot for the evening,' boomed the voice, 'ROLF HARRIS!' The theatre rumbled with the sound of a thousand mingled boos and screams as the familiar bearded figure appeared, clutching a clipboard, ready to announce his 'passenger list'. In a blur, Cissie saw tiny figures appearing: people she had seen on television now made flesh, tiny and colourful: a slight figure with shocking red hair in a pale blue dress, waving, could only be Cilla Black. Various groups in suits appeared from the helicopter, grinning and waving. Cissie leaned forward, desperate. 'The Fourmost', Bennett told her, pointing to a group gathering to the left of the stage, then 'Billy J. Kramer!' she shouted, excited. Confused and giddy, Cissie cheered and shouted with everyone else. She was ready to weep. Rolf Harris was saying something, and the theatre erupted into a barrage of noise. 'What did he say?' Cissie yelled into Bennett's ear, but Bennett was too busy jumping up and down and shouting 'Beatles!' with all her lung power to hear her. Cissie looked, and there they were, tiny, neat flesh-coloured dolls in grey suits, running down the ramp, arms waving. There they were. Her eyes found George. He stood looking out into the darkness of the theatre, grinning, and then stepped back to say something into the ear of his companion, who turned out to be John Lennon. Jude and Cissie exchanged a blazing glance. Their two. Together.

Then the moment had gone, and the Beatles had gone, and the Barron Knights began to play; and Cissie watched, small and silent, as the evening unfurled like a dream before her: Tommy Quickly, the Beatles doing a sketch about doctors, all wearing white coats, their jokes inaudible in the maelstrom of screams; then the Four-most; then the Beatles in a sketch, inaudible again, only the sight of George, ridiculous in a dress and headscarf, tied to the railway line by John as a villain in a top hat, causing Cissie to catch her breath, as she watched, unsmiling. He must not do that: he must not look ludicrous, or the dream would crumble. Other people appeared and sang, snatches of melody floating across the echoing clamour of several hundred delirious girls. There was an interval, in which Bennett, fighting her way to the Ladies, lost a shoe. Jude got into an argument with a girl in the row behind who objected to Jude standing on her seat. Heather busied herself making a small mountain of other peoples' handbags on the floor, so that she would have something to stand on when the Beatles reappeared, something to help her see across the chaos of a hundred straining, screaming fans down into the auditorium. Cissie sat, silent, waiting for it to start up again. When it did she stood like an automaton, staring down through the waving arms and dancing figures to the stage, where people sang and bands played and bits of noise jangled through the ether, and where, finally, the Beatles reappeared. Cissie watched, her eyes never leaving George Harrison.

He came to the front first, and sang. She thought it was 'Roll Over Beethoven', but she couldn't be sure. He frowned a little as the song progressed, and looked self-consciously across the teeming crowd, as if he feared them. Then he stepped back and stood apart from the others, intent on his guitar, his eyes rarely raised, as the Beatles performed and the screams of the crowd rose and fell, roll-ing round the ornate cinema, causing the chandeliers high up to sway and glitter, as the sound reverberated across the plaster cherubs and the peeling gold swags draped across crumbling urns around the walls of the auditorium. Cissie felt distanced, separate, as she watched and listened. Heather had scrambled up on her handbag heap, calling for Paul. Jude was jigging on the back of her seat, balanced precariously on the wooden arms in her stockinged feet, oblivious to the violent objections of the girl behind her. Out of the corner of her eye, Cissie could see Bennett, immobile, hands clutching her face, an expression of pain etched there, as if witnessing a terrible road accident.

I'm here, George. With all her being, with every molecule of her self, Cissie spoke to George across the heads of the crowd. He continued to play, head bowed over his guitar, a tiny, unreal figure in a spotlight. Then suddenly the four of them were at the front of the stage, bowing. Ringo waved his drumsticks, and then the curtains plunged down in front of the Beatles, cutting them off suddenly. The house lights came up, revealing a scene of mayhem and exhausted emotion, as girls sobbed and screamed, wept and laughed, sang and shouted – a huge, deafening declaration of love, issued on a crest of joy.

Silently, Cissie followed the others to the exit, down the red staircase, Bennett hopping on one shoe, Jude so excited at having seen her hero that she actually had her arm round Heather's shoulder, the two of them laughing and talking, remembering little moments.

'Did you see when Paul told John something and they both laughed?'

'He looked right at me – honestly, he looked right at me . . .'

Bennett was using the gilded stair-rail as a drum, banging on it with her hands as she descended, humming 'Twist And Shout'. She turned to Cissie and grinned. 'Wasn't that just the best moment in your entire life?' she asked. 'Aren't they just the best thing in the entire world?'

'Universe,' a girl in front of her corrected.

'Cosmos,' someone else added helpfully. Cissie said nothing.

'Here,' Bennett was saying to the girls around her, 'I've got a joke. Paul says to John, are those thick lens glasses you're wearing? And John says no, they're my own. Get it? They're my own – thick lens.' Appreciative groans filled the air. Below them, as the crowd made its laborious way to the foyer, a group of girls were singing 'I Want To Hold Your Hand', a strange mixture of sobs and laughter combining with the song. Cissie felt tears welling up and bit her lip. I mustn't cry, she told herself. She struggled with her feelings, arguing silently with herself: she had seen the Beatles, after all. So why did she feel so cheated? She knew why: she had seen four tiny marionettes on a distant stage, she had heard the great wave of screams rolling round the auditorium. No songs, no voices, no communication. Mouthing puppets. She hadn't heard a thing. She was shivering. No one else had heard a thing. Why didn't they say so? She had wanted to get close to George, to feel him as a living, breathing human being. Instead, she had stared at a minute cardboard cut-out that moved occasionally, in an unreal, remote space a million miles from her and her living, breathing body. She hadn't seen a thing. Didn't these other girls feel the same? Why didn't they say it hadn't measured up to their dreams? Didn't they *care*?

Jude was struggling back up the stairs towards her. 'You all right?'

Cissie nodded. She had made up her mind. 'We get to Oliver's on the underground,' she said. 'I remember him saying. The Circle Line. Bayswater.' She and Jude exchanged a look. 'Palace Court, Moscow Road,' she said, 'that's the address.' It was difficult to read what was in Jude's eyes.

She merely said, 'I'll tell the others,' and pushed her way down towards Heather and Bennett, now ahead of them in the crowd.

They all met on the front step of the Astoria, under the giant picture of the Beatles. Cissie looked up at it. George's face was a million dots, indistinguishable.

'You *can't*!' Heather was saying, aghast. 'You *can't*! Mammy'll kill me! She'll call the police!'

Jude shrugged. 'Won't do any good. They won't know where we are, will they?'

Bennett turned to Cissie, her face pink with emotion. 'Don't do this, Cissie,' she said. 'It'll ruin Peggy's Christmas. Please. For me.' Cissie did not reply. Everything had fallen apart. This small betrayal of Bennett seemed only right, the final bad thing in a bad day.

'You could come too,' Cissie said lamely.

Bennett looked at the ground. 'No, I can't. The Germans would get the Welfare on to me. I'd be put in a home.'

There seemed to be nothing more to say. Heather's face was a frightened mask, terrified by this unexpected turn of events. 'I'll tell Mammy you met a friend at the concert,' she was saying, thinking aloud, frantic. 'I'll tell her you've got an auntie and uncle in London, Jude, and you went off to stay with them.'

'Tell her what you like,' Jude said, indifferently.

A couple of boys in leather jackets hung about at the foot of the steps, a little drunk and provocative. 'They're rubbish, the Beatles,' one of them said.

'Shut up,' Jude snarled.

'Really poncy suits,' the other observed, grinning up at them. 'And those haircuts!'

Bennett would not be distracted. 'Please, Cissie,' she said again, her eyes large and pleading.

'Manufactured by their manager,' one of the boys said loudly, lighting a cigarette with what he hoped resembled Billy Fury cool, the flame of his match protected by his coat collar.

'Have you heard their weedy R and B stuff?' his friend asked loudly, half an eye on Jude. 'Can't hold a candle to the Rolling Stones.'

But they were not to be distracted, too caught up in their own small drama to be baited.

''Bye, Bennett.' Cissie would not look in her friend's eyes. She turned away, following Jude down the steps past the disappointed boys and into the rain. Turning back for a brief moment she saw them together, standing under the giant Beatles picture: Heather crying, Bennett anguished, one slender and swaying in her big orange sweater, its slogans unreadable in the brightness, the other solid and unflinching, watching them go, barefoot, clutching her one remaining shoe.

The journey on the underground was for Cissie a confusion of noisy, wind-blown tunnels, the scream of train engines, the opening and closing of tube train doors, and the blank, tired, alien faces of Londoners. Jude had taken control, studying the map at Finsbury

Park tube station, choosing the route via King's Cross, leading Cissie like a lamb down the escalators to change on to the Circle Line. Finally they emerged into the dark dampness of Queensway. The pubs were closing, and people were spilling out on to the wet pavements, calling 'Happy Christmas!' to each other, warmed by alcohol and sentiment. Jude knew where to go; she had interrogated a man selling the *Evening Standard* inside the entrance to the tube station.

'Here we are,' she said, triumphant, propelling Cissie off the main street, 'Moscow Road!' Silently, Cissie accompanied her. They passed a Greek Orthodox church, and a greengrocer's, still open despite the lateness of the hour. In the darkness of the entrance to a large building opposite, a drunk vomited.

'Palace Court,' Jude was reading from a brass plaque fixed to a wall outside an imposing red-brick building with balconies. 'This can't be it, surely?' They stood staring up at the ornate façade. Cissie saw several smaller plaques below the name plate.

'Sudanese Embassy,' she read aloud, 'Belgian Consulate.' She had obviously made a terrible mistake. Oliver didn't live here at all.

Jude had set off to stop a tired-looking woman who was heading towards the entrance carrying shopping bags. Cissie saw the woman point upwards, and then go inside. Jude beckoned. 'She says there's lots of bedsits higher up,' Jude's confidence had returned. 'The embassies are on the ground floor. Come on!'

They went inside. The foyer was intimidatingly tasteful, with embossed green carpet and a chandelier. Jude crossed to the lift shaft and peered up.

'Music,' she said, 'I can hear it, up there. Someone's having a party. We'll ask them if they know Oliver.' And she began to climb the stairs to one side of the lift, disappearing unnervingly round the first curve, leaving Cissie alone.

'Come on!' Her voice echoed, disembodied, from above Cissie's head. She hesitated for a moment. 'Cissie!' Jude's voice was fading. Cissie had no choice. She began to climb the stairs.

After three exhausting flights, the splendour of the décor deteriorated, and was replaced by peeling paint and lino engrained with years of dirt. From behind a battered-looking door, a baby cried as Cissie passed. Above, the sound of laughter and a Ray Charles record grew closer. Jude's footsteps echoed confidently above Cissie's head as she climbed. There was a strong smell of disinfectant and cabbage hovering on the faded landing of the fifth floor, where Cissie paused to catch her breath. The music was loud now, and Jude's footsteps had stopped. She was talking to some people by the lift gates; if Cissie peered up, she could see an elegant pair of legs in stilettos, and the sound of someone laughing descended the shaft. Evidently the party had spilled out on to the landing.

Cissie paused as she rounded the final curve of the stairs. Oliver was standing in the doorway, running a hand distractedly through his hair, staring at Jude. He was holding a bottle of wine. Cissie felt a flood of relief seep through her, so powerful that her knees almost buckled. Oliver was here. Everything would be all right. He turned and saw her.

'You idiot,' he said, 'you bloody little idiot.' Cissie stopped. He had turned back to Jude. 'You want your heads tested,' he said. 'Of course you can't stay here, are you mad?'

The normally brave Jude was hanging her head, shamefaced, and mumbling at the floor. 'We don't want to go home,' she said. 'We haven't got anywhere else to go.'

Oliver sighed, exasperated. The lift shaft suddenly sprang into life, the cables creaking. The couple waiting by the lift doors had turned their backs on Jude and Oliver, embarrassed, and were now darting furtive looks at Cissie, who hung back at the top of the stairs. The woman in the stilettos gave her a sympathetic smile. Ray Charles ended, and Peggy Lee began to sing. Someone squealed as the interior hall light was turned off, casting a red glow over the entrance, like the mouth of hell. Oliver glanced back inside at the party, frustrated. 'You'll have to go back,' he said, addressing Cissie, his voice firm. 'I'll phone Mike and Peggy. Whatever were you thinking of? It's Christmas Eve, you stupid girl, they'll be worried sick!'

'We've been to see the Beatles,' she heard her voice, sullen, as if it belonged to someone else – a miserable, lustreless, sulking creature.

The lift completed its arduous journey up the shaft and cranked into position with a shudder on their floor. With some relief the waiting couple pulled open the folding doors and stepped inside.

"Night, Ollie!' the young woman called, her voice teasing, as the lift descended. Oliver took a swig from the bottle and did not reply.

I've embarrassed him, Cissie realized with horror. I've embarrassed him in front of his friends. To her, this was the worst crime you could ever commit; and she had done it to Oliver – quiet, unassuming Oliver who had never done anything (knowingly) to hurt her.

'Can I have a drink?' Jude had become brave again, her usual defiant self. 'Come on, I'm eighteen now.'

Oliver looked at her. 'Yes,' he said. 'Yes, I suppose you are.' He handed the bottle over, resigned. There was a moment's silence, punctuated only by Peggy Lee. Jude drank from the bottle, then handed it back. 'Is that pot I can smell?' she asked loudly. Oliver made a sound of annoyance and suddenly pulled Jude inside the flat, half-closing the door, leaving his step-sister alone. Cissie waited, wondering what to do, abandoned out on the landing. From inside the party, she could hear laughter and then cheers. She sat down on the top step of the flight she had just ascended. She was exhausted. Her head was spinning with dizzying images – George Harrison, a tiny thoughtful figure engrossed in his guitar; Mrs Lewis fussily patting the collar of her red duster coat; the boy in the car shouting and making a V-sign; the rainbow-coloured, petrol-filled puddles in the car park . . .

She was leaning with her head against the wall, dozing, when she was suddenly aware that Oliver was standing over her. He was wearing a donkey jacket and was pulling on a pair of gloves. Jude was behind him. 'Come on,' he said coldly. 'We're going to the station.'

After a freezing, silent wait, Oliver finally hailed a taxi on Queensway, only just beating a crowd of revellers, and instructed the driver to take them to Liverpool Street station. Cissie was too tired to argue. She stared out at the festive streets as they hurtled through the City, aware that Oliver was maintaining an angry silence and that Jude had fallen asleep. Whenever she looked up, she would see

Oliver, sitting on the seat opposite, his arms folded, his face grim and puzzled, as if confronted by an alien being. Which I am, she thought . . .

The station was cold and quiet. Oliver left them in a waiting room while he went off to find out about trains. Jude woke up, shivering. Cissie glared at her. 'So we're just going back, then,' she said abruptly. 'I thought you really wanted to go.'

Jude shrugged, her face grey with fatigue. 'I do,' she said. 'Only now isn't the time, all right?' Cissie said nothing. The air crackled with her anger. Now she would have to go home and face Mike and her mother, those hurt, puzzled faces, the explanations, questions. It was horrible. And it was Christmas. She had ruined Christmas.

Oliver returned. 'Come on,' he said, unsmiling. 'You're two very lucky girls. I'm putting you on the milk train.'

There was only one carriage. The rest of the train was made up of freight wagons. The only other passenger was an old man in a trilby, who was already asleep down the far end, snoring. Oliver did not come inside. He stood on the platform and spoke to them through the open window, his breath pluming white in the cold.

'Mike will meet you at the station,' he told Cissie. 'I've told him you decided to come and visit me after the concert to wish me a happy Christmas.' He gave a wry smile at the thought. 'He doesn't know anything about you planning to run away, all right?'

The train began to move. Jude pushed Cissie aside and stuck her head out of the window to kiss Oliver on the cheek. 'You're not bad for an old bloke,' she said, pulling back inside. Cissie could see Oliver touching his cheek with a gloved hand, laughing, bemused. 'I'm twenty-one!' he said. The train pulled away, jolting, throwing Jude back on the seat. Cissie could see Oliver receding on the platform, one hand still up to his face, until the train rounded a bend and he disappeared.

She sat down opposite Jude, who had pulled a packet of cigarettes out of her pocket and was lighting one. 'How did you do it?' Cissie asked. 'How did you get him not to tell Mike we'd run away?'

'Easy.' Jude inhaled deeply, and leaned back against the faded upholstery. 'I told him that if he said we were running away, I'd tell Peggy and Mike that he was having a pot-smoking party and that he offered it to us.'

Cissie was appalled. 'But Oliver would never – he's not like that.'

Jude grinned at her, her eyes creasing from the cigarette smoke. 'Did the trick, though, didn't it,' she said. 'Kept you off the hook.' Then: 'Why don't you go to sleep? This train takes hours. We won't be in Norwich till nearly four o'clock in the morning.'

Cissie finally managed to get to sleep, curled up along a seat with her duffle coat tucked in around her, rolling and jolting with the movement of the train, fitfully aware that Jude was sitting bolt up-right opposite her, lighting one cigarette from another, humming Beatles songs.

The train suddenly juddered to a halt. Cissie sat up, bleary-eyed. Peggy had been gazing down at her. Cissie had opened her eyes and spoken sharply. 'Why don't you ever contact Cecil at the seances?' she had asked her mother. 'If you can get Miss W's sister and the fairy man's friend from the war, why can't you get my dad?' But Peggy had not replied, fading away into the blur of waking up. Cissie had been dreaming that she was at home in bed at Briga-doon. 'Where are we?' she asked, confused. Jude was standing at the door, the collar of her rain mac pulled up high so that her face was not visible. 'Maryland,' she said. She was opening the door.

'Where's Maryland?' Cissie was puzzled. Wasn't that a place in America?

A blast of icy air entered the carriage. 'Just outside London.' Jude stepped down on to the dark platform. 'I'm just not ready to go home yet. I'll see you,' she said. 'Happy Christmas!' The door slammed, and somewhere far away, a whistle blew shrilly. The train began to pull away. Cissie leapt up, her head spinning. She struggled with the window catch. Her hands were numb. Finally she hauled the window down and stuck her head out. Jude was walking away in the darkness, her head down against the wind. The train moved on. 'Jude! Jude!' Cissie called, but it was too late. Jude had gone.

'Shut up, can't you?' The man in the trilby had woken for a

moment, and glared at Cissie, his eyes glazed from sleep and alcohol. 'Just shut up, all right?'

The train lumbered on through the icy London outskirts, starting its laborious journey to the flat lands of East Anglia. In the steamy reflection of the train window Cissie saw her face for a moment, white, tear-streaked. She was going home, alone.

CHAPTER THREE

Do You Want to Know a Secret? – 1964

*T*HEY WERE STANDING BY *the side of the road, all four of them.
She was wearing the dress she had seen in* Honey *magazine, the
one with the keyhole neckline and the big pink daisies, and black
patent shoes with chunky heels, and just for once she had ironed her hair to
perfection and it hung perfectly coiled on to her shoulders. Her face was pale,
interesting – beautiful. Her eyes were wide and black-rimmed, framed by the
softest, thickest lashes, and her mouth shimmered, a frosted pink. The air
was breathless, not a leaf stirred. Somehow, in the silence, a long black car
glided alongside and stopped. Inside were the Beatles. Ringo was driving.
Something about a flat tyre. Bennett went to help. John Lennon and Jude
sat hunched in the back of the car, intent, studying a copy of John's book* In
His Own Write, *laughing at one of the scribbled cartoons. She supposed
that Heather and Paul were somewhere, but she hardly noticed. She watched
instead a tall, thin figure wandering away up the road. He paused under a
tree, leaning against its trunk, staring into space. Above him, white may
blossom hung suspended, the occasional petal floating past his thoughtful
profile. She approached. He felt rather than saw her coming, and looked at
her suddenly. Where had her fear gone? 'Hello,' she said. 'I'm the girl from
Norfolk with the flying table.' A moment. Then he smiled at her, that shy,
knowing grin. 'Hello,' he said.*

' 'Ello, 'ello, 'ello.' It was Bennett, doing her Dixon of Dock
Green voice. 'What 'ave we 'ere?' She was poking Cissie with a
drumstick. 'I hereby harrest you on a charge of serious daydreaming.'

Cissie sat up, the bubble burst.

'You're all pink in the face,' Bennett remarked.

'You're early,' was all Cissie managed to muster. Her head was still with George, somewhere on a blossom-covered bank.

'Couldn't stand the Germans' prattle another minute,' Bennett said. 'You'll get a damp bum down there.' George disappeared. The drifting may blossom faded. Cissie looked up at her friend in despair. Bennett looked impassively down, a safe, solid figure in a loud tartan cape and heavy shoes, silhouetted against the April sky. The cape was dreadfully ugly, and did nothing to flatter Bennett's triangular shape; but Cissie could never say so. She scrambled to her feet. There was Brigadoon, suddenly, on the other side of the hedge, where it always was. She followed Bennett through the gap in the hawthorn, wincing at the thorns, followed by Toulouse.

'Peggy says cabbage fields are mystical,' Bennett said, heading past the chicken coop ahead of Cissie. 'She says that's why you go and moon about in there.' Cissie did not answer. It was a typically romantic Peggy kind of explanation. It sounded more satisfactory than the truth – that 'mooning about' in the cabbage field was an escape from the seductive enclosure of Brigadoon and was therefore a tiny rebellion, a small betrayal. Peggy's versions of things were always more colourful, more exciting. It had become impossible for Cissie to contradict them. Peggy wanted to create Cissie in her own image – another bright butterfly to bewitch the world. It was hardly Cissie's fault if all she really got was a dark, crusty, dead thing, curled up in a permanent state of hibernation, doomed never to burst into life.

Mike was standing in the yard, drinking a mug of coffee and staring at a block of stone. Bennett and Cissie skirted round him, both knowing he was best left alone when contemplating what Mill called 'his lumps'. In the kitchen, Peggy was smoking a cigarette and gazing out of the window. Cissie realized that her mother had been watching them as they made their way from the gap in the hawthorn hedge across the shambles of the sheds and chicken coops and into the kitchen.

She turned her head as they entered. 'Have you eaten anything, Cissie?' she asked.

'Cornflakes.'

Peggy's eyes met hers. They contained a question. Cissie looked away hurriedly. Why did Peggy always seem to know everything? Bennett was making daft noises at the baby in the highchair, oblivious. 'Tea in the pot,' Peggy said, finally.

Cissie fetched two enamel mugs from the cupboard and the bottle of milk from the breakfast table, and took them to where the teapot was warming on the stove, next to a sleeping cat.

'How's the job, Bennett?' Peggy was asking, leaning back against the draining board, contemplating the two girls rather too intently.

Bennett shrugged. 'All right. It's *Mary Poppins* this week.' Bennett worked as a cashier at the Regal Cinema on Prince of Wales Road in Norwich. To her it seemed as unexciting as school. She caught the same bus from Polston Wood in the morning that she had always caught; there were the same strict dress codes, a disapproving manager who was always confiscating her drumsticks, and the hours spent in her tiny cubby hole with her rolls of coloured tickets and her bags of coins seemed not so far removed from the claustrophobia of Crookfield Secondary Modern.

Peggy pulled a face. 'Mike won't go. Says they don't know how to make musicals any more.'

'I've seen it four times,' Bennett said, without a trace of pride. 'Tell him it's crap.' She spent all her tea-breaks at the back of the cinema, eating KitKats and studying the prostitutes who occasionally brought a customer in out of the rain. There was something vaguely satisfying about listening to Julie Andrews singing about a spoonful of sugar while watching a furtive blow job in the back row of the stalls.

Cissie sipped her tea and wandered over to the cupboard under the stairs, to look at the picture of Cecil. He smiled, as usual, still standing by the river bank, frozen in black and white. Her father. He would be watching her now. He knew what she was going to do. She felt Peggy watching her and turned, defiant. But Peggy was busy at the cold tap at the sink, holding the last of her cigarette under the stream of water to extinguish it. She tossed the wet dog-end into the bin.

'Bus in a minute,' was all she said.

Cissie pulled her school mac out from the cupboard under the stairs. Her duffle bag, stuffed full, sat on top of the pile of discarded wellington boots. She stared at it for a moment. No, not yet . . .

'You ought to move into that cupboard.' It was Mill, watching her from the living room doorway, Woodbine dangling from a disapproving mouth. 'Always got your backside in there.' Cissie emerged hastily. 'You'll be back for tea.' This was a command, not a question.

'Of course I'll be back for tea,' Cissie said testily. 'I'm always back for tea, aren't I? Where else would I be going?'

Bennett shot her a warning look.

Mill lowered herself into a chair by the stove. A tabby cat immediately leapt into her lap. 'Wrong side of bed, was it?'

Mike came in, distracted, and stood washing his hands at the kitchen sink. 'Oliver's coming this afternoon,' he said over his shoulder to Cissie. 'Will you be back for tea?'

Bennett, spooning Ready Brek into the baby's eager mouth with occasional U-turns into her own, spluttered with laughter. 'This family!' she exclaimed. 'You're all psychic!'

'What did I say?' With a look of puzzlement Mike wiped his hands on a grey-looking tea towel, kissed Peggy on the back of the neck as he passed, and headed to the table to pour himself a cup of tea.

Mill was still pondering on Cissie's short temper. 'She's like the Red Queen,' she remarked. 'What was it she used to say all the time?'

'Off with his head,' Bennett said, helpful.

'Bus is coming!' called Peggy from her lookout post by the back door.

Cissie returned to the cupboard under the stairs and pulled out her duffle bag, heart pounding. 'You want me here for tea and bloody crumpets with Oliver,' she said, straightening up, trying to make her face nonchalant. 'You all keep telling me. Oliver's coming. You want me to be here? I'll be here. You want me to marry Oliver? I'll bloody marry him.'

'No need for language,' said Mill.

'I learned it all off you,' Cissie retorted. Bennett gazed at her sideways, face taut with anxiety.

'From you. I learned it all *from* you,' Peggy said absently. 'It's reached the crossroads!'

Cissie pulled the loaded bag on to her shoulder, careful not to wince as the cord bit into her skin. She dropped a kiss on Susie's downy forehead. This was it.

Peggy was looking at her, eyes soft. 'Here –' she said, handing Cissie a paper bag, '– sandwiches.'

Cissie's eyes slid away, ashamed. 'See you later,' she said gruffly.

'Tea! Don't forget!' Mill was shouting, as they headed for the door and outside. 'Oliver will want to see you . . .' Her voice floated away as they ran down the path. The bus was already at Fox Corner. They screeched down the lane, hair flying, exultant, as the bus paused, engine idling. The driver had seen them, and was waiting.

They scrambled up the stairs, out of breath, and flung themselves on to the back seat, oblivious of the bedlam of early morning upper-deck school pandemonium exploding around them.

'Phase One carried out successful-like, Sah!' said Bennett, in her Bootsy and Snudge Army Game voice. 'Phase Two now operational!'

When Cissie got off the bus at Crookfield Circle, Bennett stayed on. She travelled all the way into the city centre, alighting at Castle Meadow, where she caught another bus out to the Spixworth Road. From there she made her way down the familiar alleyways of the Carrow Estate, past the garage where they did the respray jobs on stolen cars, ignoring the taunts of the overalled boys who lounged in the doorway, paint-splattered in the sun, drinking tea from flasks.

The prefabs of Spixworth Close squatted morosely, oblivious of spring, their scrubby lawns still pale and bald. Bennett stood undecided outside Jude's house. Should she march bravely up to the front door and knock? She decided against it; in Jude's world, she was sure, front doors were for the rent man or the police, as they had been in Bennett's unhappy childhood living with her mother.

She headed down the path at the side of the bungalow, her heart sinking as the dogs began to bark ferociously at the sound of her footsteps. Jude's mother appeared at the back door, wearing her coat. She didn't recognize Bennett.

'Yes?' her tone was not friendly.

'I've come to see Jude,' Bennett tried to smile. Jude's mother eyed her tartan cape, making Bennett feel suddenly suspiciously overdressed and expensive. 'Mrs Reynolds, isn't it?'

'She can't come out.' Jude's mother pulled the back door firmly shut behind her. 'Her dad says she's got to stay in.' Mrs Reynolds began to head down the path, past Bennett, pulling on her gloves.

'But she can't!' Bennett was aghast. 'I mean – she's got to – it's – we've arranged it! It's important!'

Mrs Reynolds' back was expressive. She shrugged. 'Not today . . .' she said, without turning.

Bennett stared after her. 'Perhaps I could just have a word with her dad,' she began to say. Jude's mother stopped abruptly at the gate and then hurried back towards her. 'No,' she said, her voice low, 'I wouldn't do that – I really wouldn't do that –' She was close to Bennett now, her gloved hand on Bennett's arm, her face tense. She must have been pretty once, Bennett thought fleetingly. Suddenly the pressure on her arm eased, and Jude's mother once more headed down the path. This time she went through the gate, closed it quietly and hurried away down the street without a backward glance.

Bennett stood, uncertain. By the back door a hutch containing a bundle of hay suddenly heaved with activity, and she caught the glimpse of a small pink snout. Inside the bungalow, all was quiet. Bennett stepped up to the back door and peered in through the glass door. All she could see was a greasy cooker and a sink full of washing-up. She tapped on the door, tentatively at first, and then, when there was no reply, with more determination. The sound of the dogs reached a new, savage crescendo. This was Phase Two. She had to carry this out. Someone shouted from inside, telling her to come in.

She pushed open the door and stepped inside. The door to the adjacent sitting room was open. Bennett walked in. Jude's dad was lying on the sofa reading the *Daily Mirror*, a cup of tea on the floor beside him. He sat up when he saw her, and swung his feet on to the floor. He wasn't wearing shoes, she noticed, and he had a large hole in the toe of one of his socks.

'Hello,' he said, grinning. 'Who are you?' He had met Bennett before, but he had been drunk. She had forgotten how small he was, and wiry, like a grizzled terrier, the quiff of his hair grey.

'Friend of Jude's,' Bennett mumbled, scared. '. . . Come to get her . . . Going out.'

Harry Reynolds surveyed his visitor, enjoying the moment of power. 'Yes?' he said, 'Going out where?'

'Just – out . . .' Bennett's eyes slid away, taking in the plastic sofa, the crucifix above the fireplace.

'Sorry,' he said, still smiling, his eyes never leaving her face, 'no can do.'

'We had an arrangement –' Bennett began bravely, but he held up his hand.

'I only say things once,' he said, smiling. 'And I've said it, all right?'

Bennett turned to leave. Harry Reynolds resumed his prone position on the sofa. 'Here,' he called, as she reached the kitchen, 'you want a baby guinea pig? I got some nice chinchillas, ready now. Five bob.'

'No thanks!' she tried to make her voice sound cheerful.

'Bye!'

Two minutes later she was crawling, commando-style, under the front-room window, heading round to the other side of the bunga-low. The back way was blocked by the dogs. This was her only chance. She rounded the corner, grimacing as she felt the knee of her tights give way. Steve McQueen hadn't had this kind of trouble in *The Great Escape*, she thought wryly, hauling herself up and gingerly examining her reddened knees. A gentle tapping above her head made her turn and look up. Jude's face was pressed against the glass, white, desperate. Silently, and slowly, the window opened. Jude put a finger to her lips. Bennett clambered to her feet. A bag

73

was lowered through the window. Bennett took it and propped it carefully next to the wall. The window opened a little more, squeaking on its hinges. The dogs started up again, baying, disturbed. Jude's eyes were terrified.

'Go back,' she mouthed at Bennett. 'Go back!'

Misunderstanding, Bennett shook her head. 'No!' she whispered, 'I'm not leaving without you!'

Jude rolled her eyes heavenwards, exasperated. 'The guinea pigs!' she hissed. 'Go back and let them out,' as Bennett stared at her. 'Go on!'

Trembling, Bennett made the return journey, past the front of the house and round to the side. There was no sound from the living room, only the sound of the dogs, increasingly agitated, straining on the end of their tethers. She had reached the hutch opposite the back door. There was no movement from inside the house. Carefully, she turned the wooden latch and opened the hutch door. The bundle of straw was immobile. She reached her hand in, and was instantly rewarded with a sharp nip in her thumb from a tiny set of incisors and an indignant squeak. The barking of the dogs was more insistent, more disturbed. Mr Reynolds would surely come. Determined, she plunged her hand into the straw again, and this time managed to get hold of a small, squirming body. Tiptoeing to the kitchen door, she pushed it open and set the creature scampering across the lino. Crouching, she watched its progress, hardly daring to breathe. It had sniffed the mat for a second, and then hurried busily away and disappeared under the sink unit. Desperate, Bennett turned back to the hutch. Another guinea pig was shortsightedly twitching its nostrils at her, and she snatched it up and sent it after its companion. This one panicked on the doormat and began to run distractedly about the kitchen, criss-crossing the lino in alarm, squeaking loudly. Bennett heard a bellow from the living room, and scrambled to her feet, racing round the house again as Jude's father headed for the kitchen.

Jude had already climbed out of the window and was waiting, panting, grinning, her bag under her arm. 'Run!' was all she said, and they did, leaping over the sagging front hedge and thundering down the road, their hearts in their mouths, not stopping until they rounded the corner on to the main road, where they subsided in a giggling, hysterical, panting heap in an alleyway at the side of a betting shop.

'Guinea Pig Rescue,' said Bennett in her American coming-to-a-cinema-near-you voice. 'They came, they saw, they squeaked.'

'He'll go nuts,' Jude said, her voice filled with satisfaction. 'He'll go stark, staring bonkers.' A shadow crossed her face. She remembered that someone else would pay for this – her mother, her sister. Someone.

Bennett looked at her, understanding. Then she turned her head, hearing something. 'Quick!' she said. 'Bus!'

And they raced away to the bus-stop, dancing on the pavement and flapping their arms, excited and silly, light-headed and fearful. Phase Two was complete.

Miss Desmond was glaring at Cissie. She could feel the icy pressure of that gaze penetrating the back of her neck, and she knew why. As a member of the sixth form, she was expected to set an example. That meant singing. But she just could not – would not. She didn't believe in God. It would be hypocritical.

The hall was filled with the wavering sound of reluctant youthful voices attempting to hit the high notes of an unsingable hymn, and Cissie stood, staring ahead, biting her lip.

'*Bread of heaven, bread of heaven, feed me till I want no more . . .*' She felt Heather nudge her. They exchanged a knowing look, a half-smirk. Heather raised soulful eyes to the heavens and mouthed along with the chorus, unwilling to incur the ire of Miss Desmond, and wanting to display her profile. Standing on the other side of Heather was Ray, a tall pale youth with over-large hands, who admired the proffered profile wordlessly. Cissie saw that dog-like gaze and drew in her breath. What on earth did Heather see in Ray Broadbent? He had spots and big hands. Cissie could see a nerve trembling in Heather's cheek. She realized that she was jiggling her foot against the bench in front, and stopped, not wanting to attract attention. But it was so hard to keep still! There was something oddly exciting about being here, in assembly at Crookfield Grammar, and knowing the rest of the day would be totally unpredictable.

There was a rumble as four hundred bodies sat. The headmaster stood at his lectern and began the final prayer. Around Cissie, heads were bowed. She lowered her head, eyes wide open, willing the time to pass. Heather's hand suddenly grasped her elbow, and the blonde head indicated the window with a little bobbing movement. Miss Desmond frowned, then looked away. Cissie peered carefully round the girl in front, following Heather's gaze, and was in time to see the rotund shape of Bennett heading for the caretaker's shed, her demeanour brisk and business-like, as if the presence of a large tartan-caped young woman crossing the playground during assembly was commonplace. Heather's grip on her arm tightened, and then relaxed, as Bennett disappeared from view. They looked at each other, a million questions on their lips. The headmaster had arrived at the 'amen', which was echoed in a hundred mumbles from around the hall. Heather's eyes were like saucers. 'Jude?' she mouthed the question. Cissie shrugged. She had only seen Bennett. What if it had all gone wrong?

A mass movement, as the assembled schoolchildren got to their feet and the headmaster left the stage. Mrs Baxter began to play something rousing on the piano, and the first-years at the front of the hall filed out in a meek line, too new to misbehave. Miss Desmond was frowning at Cissie. She pointed towards the front of the hall, lips pursed. Cissie scrambled out and headed to her position by the middle doors, where her duty was to oversee the departure from the hall of the third-years. Opposite her, on the other side of the hall, Heather took up a similar position, her blonde hair dazzling against the light, Ray Broadbent hovering, as usual, near by. For an endless five minutes as the hall emptied, Cissie went through the prefectorial motions with her usual lack of enthusiasm. 'You – be quiet. Oy – get in line. You – wait behind.'

Finally, miraculously, it was over. Mrs Baxter closed the lid of the piano, folded her sheet music and hurried away. The other prefects strolled off to the sixth form common room, self-important and relaxed.

76

Cissie tensed as a couple of upper-sixth boys paused in front of her, engrossed in a debate. 'All the real jazz is from New Orleans,' one was saying, indignant. 'British bands can't do it properly, apart from Ken Colyer.' It was all right: they were not going to while away their spare time taking the mickey out of Cissie Lovelock, for a change. 'It's all crap,' the other said angrily, as they moved on through the hall, '*real* jazz started with be-bop, didn't it. Everything before Charlie Parker is so predictable . . .' They drifted away. Miss Desmond and the other teachers on patrol headed for the staff room. Ray Broadbent was dispatched. Heather and Cissie met at the back of the hall. The moment had come. Cissie felt as if every molecule of her blood was poised, quivering in her veins.

'Look,' she said, holding her hand out to show Heather, 'I'm trembling.'

'Och, you're lucky,' said Heather. 'I've had the most terrible runs all morning. Mammy asked me if I'd been eating marshmallows again. I had to pretend I had.'

'Ready, then?'

They looked at each other.

'Ready.'

The trick was to behave as if what they were doing was perfectly natural. They turned and walked out of the hall into the corridor, and steadily progressed towards the side door beyond the cloak-rooms, heads up, aggressive, watchful. No one stopped them. Heather pushed open the door and silently they made their way across the bright playground, feeling exposed in the sunlight, in the direction they had watched Bennett go.

It was all going to be all right. They reached the caretaker's shed unchallenged, and pushed open the door. Miraculously, they were there – Jude, squatting on the damp ground smoking a cigarette and spitting on to her mascara brush, frowning; Bennett hauling a skinny-rib jumper down across her ample chest, her face flushed and tense.

'Hurry up!' Bennett panted. 'We ought to get out of here quick –'

Heather was already pulling off her school skirt and scrabbling in her bag, the tic in her cheek more pronounced than ever.

'Here —' Jude handed Cissie her duffle bag, which had been hidden in a bush outside, as pre-arranged, since before assembly, 'you'd better get your stuff on.' Cissie took the bag, aware, amid the excited giggles and whispers of Bennett and Heather, that Jude was quiet, watching her with unusual intensity. Something was wrong. Cissie waited, filled with dread, to hear what sharp-tongued accusations Jude would heap upon her bowed head, but Jude turned away, grinning to herself, and alighted instead on Bennett.

'You're not going in that cape,' she said, with an air of finality. Bennett paused in mid-preen and looked anxious.

'I haven't got anything else,' she said. 'The Germans bought it for me. Said it was the latest thing. From Richard Shops.'

Jude looked pained. 'It's just — not right,' she said, brutal.

'Why not?'

'It's not mod,' Jude said, with an air of finality. That was that. If it was not mod, it could not be worn. The others were not entirely sure what constituted mod, but Jude was; and she was always right about these things. 'Your shoes are good,' she was saying to Bennett, to soften the blow. 'Your shoes are dead mod.'

Bennett looked pleased. 'Church jumble sale,' she said. 'Some old bat in the village — they were her dance shoes before the war.'

'Here —' Heather peered in her bag, 'you could borrow my orange and black Beatles jumper if you like.'

Bennett hesitated; the jumper was old hat now, but no one had the heart to tell Heather that. 'I've got my big blue jumper,' Cissie said kindly. 'It's a bit sweaty and there's some chocolate down the sleeve —'

'I'll take it,' Bennett beamed, grateful.

Jude was watching Cissie, who stood, hesitant for a moment, her face reflecting her fears.

'What's up with you?' Jude demanded.

'Nothing.'

Heather looked up from her bag, from which she had been pulling various crumpled garments. 'Don't worry, Cissie,' she said kindly. 'I'm peeing myself as well. If Mammy ever finds out what I'm doing it'll be no television for a year.'

Bennett looked horrified at the thought. 'No *Ready Steady Go!* I'd die!'

'You're scared,' Jude said flatly.

'I'm not! It's only —' Cissie struggled miserably to explain, '— Oliver's coming, they made a big fuss about me being there for tea —'

'That hunky brother?'

'He's not my brother.'

'Peggy won't mind,' Bennett said, pulling Cissie's blue sweater over her head, in a fever of preparation.

'You don't know that,' Cissie said stubbornly. 'She's nuts about Oliver. Not wanting to see Oliver — biggest crime in the universe.'

'Hurry up!' Jude was peering nervously outside. 'We should get going . . .'

Cissie bit her lip. No one understood. Anyway, it was too late to back out now.

Divested of their uniforms, Cissie and Heather crouched on the ground and frantically applied ivory PanStick to their flushed cheeks, peering into tiny little compact mirrors, struggling with pots of eyeliner.

Jude twitched in the doorway. 'He said we had to be out of here by nine-fifteen . . .' She had bribed the assistant caretaker with a snog and ten Woodbines. 'I'm desperate for a bacon sarnie . . .'

'Didn't you have any breakfast?' Heather asked innocently, pulling her face into a taut grimace as she applied a beauty spot to her cheek.

'Eat my sandwiches,' Cissie offered.

Jude pulled a misshapen paper bag from under Cissie's discarded uniform. 'In here?' She took out a squashed sandwich and bit into it. 'Mmm,' she said. 'Jam . . .'

'Yuk,' said Heather.

Jude handed Cissie a slip of paper, grinning. 'Here,' she said, 'it was in with the sandwiches. You're full of secrets, Cissie Lovelock.'

Cissie took the slip of paper and turned it over in her hand. On it, someone had written 'LIFE IS SHORT' firmly, in biro.

Her eyes met Jude's. 'My mum,' she said, her tone apologetic.

Bennett peered at it over her shoulder. 'What does it *mean*?' she asked.

Heather looked, too. 'It's a sign,' she said, her voice full of awe. Cissie screwed the note up in her fist and hurled it into a dark corner, where a lawnmower stood propped against a row of rakes.

'Nothing,' she said, her voice fierce. 'It doesn't mean anything. It's a sign I've got a loony mother, that's all.'

There was a frozen moment, while three girls remembered someone's mother in a mental hospital on the outskirts of Norwich, and Bennett's cheeks were suddenly hot and red.

'Come *on*,' Jude said, scowling, rescuing them. 'We've got to go!'

Finally they were ready, and they tiptoed out of the shed, giggling and unsteady, clutching each other, until they reached the shadows of the main building. Ahead of them was a clear, manicured path to the front gate, under the windows of the chemistry labs and past the tennis courts. They paused for a moment, wide-eyed at their own daring. Then suddenly not caring that they might be seen, no longer afraid, they broke into a wild run, screaming, racing away towards the gate, white-faced, black-eyed, mini-skirted and bursting – a wild and wonderful moment when everything was going to be possible, when dreams were going to be realized and nothing and no one could stop them.

They had made it to the gate. Gasping, elated, Cissie turned to see the school secretary, rigid in a twin set, pause in the playground, staring after them. It didn't matter. She didn't care. Jude had reached the gates first and she swung over the top, in spite of the fact they were open. She was shinning down the other side, her face bright with laughter as the others scrambled breathlessly through the wrought-iron gates.

'Heather! Don't go!' It was Ray Broadbent, doe-eyed and desperate. He had been crouching in a row of small conifers by the gate, waiting for her.

Jude groaned. 'Go away, prat!'

The school secretary had paused, and was standing motionless in the front playground, watching them, shading her eyes with her hand, as if to see them better.

80

'Can't stop, Ray,' Heather panted, her wistful hand on his sleeve.

'Don't go!' he repeated.

'Antony and bleedin' Cleopatra!' Jude pulled Heather away, and they left him standing, large hands dangling, desperate, as the school secretary loomed.

'More like Pinky and Perky,' observed a panting Bennett, pleased to be able to make a pig reference at such a dramatic moment.

'I'll be back!' Heather called, blowing Ray a kiss, running after the others. The bus was revving up in Crookfield Circle. The conductor watched them, grinning.

The secretary had reached Ray. As they bundled aboard they could see him, head lowered, receiving the admonishment that was theirs by rights. The bus moved off. They threw themselves on to the seat, breathless. Heather knelt up, gazing at the receding figure of Ray, as they swerved round the Circle.

'Isn't he lovely!' she breathed.

'Not as lovely as Paul McCartney,' said Jude, nudging Bennett.

Heather turned, eyes bright. 'No,' she said, Ray forgotten. 'No . . .'

And the bus rumbled away towards Norwich, empty but for its giggling cargo of truants.

They were doing it. They were actually doing it – trundling down the A11, away from Norwich, heading towards London.

This was not what Cissie had imagined, but she was doing her best to turn even this cramped journey into a viable George fantasy.

The first one had been so perfect: the standing by the road, the silent car, Ringo at the wheel, George wandering away to stand under the blossom, just waiting for the moment when Cissie Lovelock entered his life . . .

They were crammed into the cab of an articulated lorry, hot and uncomfortable. The driver, a large, cheerful, sweating man in a plaid shirt, would take them to the other side of Thetford, he had said – but there would be a brief detour first.

And the detour, miraculously, is a pretty farmhouse in Thetford forest, set amid the tall pines, smoke curling from the chimney. It's a holiday retreat for his nephew, the lorry-driver explains. His nephew leads a busy life, and he and his friends need somewhere quiet to relax every now and then. Looks like they're in there . . . And they climb down from the hot, smelly cab and the others go inside. Cissie is the last to descend, and as her feet hit the grass, a hand reaches for her elbow, helping her to make the last step. She turns, and of course, it's George. Of course it is. Because the truck-driver is Paul's uncle, and the cottage is the Beatles' retreat. No one knows about it, no one. Only them. And the uncle. And now Cissie, Bennett, Jude, Heather. Cissie is trembling. He is even more soft and beautiful than she had believed. His face is serious. He knows, like she does, just how significant this moment is. It will change their lives forever.

'Hello,' she says, 'I'm the girl from Norfolk with the flying table.'

'I think I'm going to be sick.' Heather was whispering desperately in her ear. Bennett's thigh pressed against Cissie's like a dead weight, and her foot had gone to sleep, crushed under Jude's bag. The smell in the cab was overpowering. It was the ripe stench of panicking pig. Heather was gagging into her hankie. The driver looked over, grinning.

'Open the window,' he said. Cissie struggled with the handle, and eventually managed to lower the window a little. The sound of squealing from the back of the truck became instantly louder. Heather groaned.

Bennett and Jude were still euphoric, excited that the trip was under way, united by events at Jude's house.

'Pigadilly,' Bennett was saying, 'get it?'

Jude snorted. Then, after a moment: 'West Ham.' Silence. 'West Ham!' They both exploded again, Jude's face wet with tears of laughter.

'I can't bear it!' Heather was hissing loudly above the screaming pigs. 'That awful noise –'

The driver turned down the radio, sympathetic. 'Sorry, love,' he said, his eyes not leaving the road, 'they always get bad around here –'

Cissie looked at him, interested. 'Why?'

'Hammersmith,' Bennett was murmuring to herself, almost too weak to speak, '*Ham*mersmith . . .'

He shrugged. 'Only a couple of miles to the slaughterhouse. They know, see. Smell the blood, I expect.'

Jude, who had been screeching at Bennett's offering, paused and exchanged a horrified glance with Cissie.

'The slaughterhouse?'

He nodded. 'I told you we had to make a stop.'

Heather's retching became noticeably louder. The girls fell silent for a moment.

'Close the window,' Jude said wearily. 'I'd rather listen to Heather puking than listen to a hundred pigs waiting to die.'

Cissie rolled the window up again. They continued in silence, all trying not to hear the muted terror of the pigs behind them. Cissie closed her eyes. She would make no adjustments. After all, they hadn't turned off the main road yet. The cottage could still be there. It would just happen before they got to the slaughterhouse . . .

The others are inside. She can hear them laughing, talking. But George has taken her hand and he's leading her away from the cottage, into the shadow of the tall trees in Thetford Chase, where once King Henry the Eighth rode with his courtiers . . .

There was a slight detour while Cissie became momentarily a lady of the court in a green velvet gown, riding side-saddle in the dappled light, and the enigmatic profile at her side turned suddenly and gazed upon her with the dark brown eyes of George.

'Hold on,' the driver was warning, as they suddenly lurched to one side, Jude toppling into Cissie's lap, the contents of Bennett's handbag tumbling to the floor of the truck. They had turned off the main road.

'Not long now, girls,' he said, turning the radio up louder, as the pigs screamed. Cilla Black was singing 'Anyone Who Had A Heart'.

Cissie closed her eyes, determined.

He still has hold of her hand, and they walk slowly together, talking and yet not talking, their lips not moving but words and feelings and thoughts being exchanged, because they are as one, they are one being, they are meant

to be together. And he has stopped now, and he has pulled her towards him –
gently, always gently, and he tips her chin a little with his finger and she can
look right into those thoughtful, humorous eyes at last, and she can part her
lips slightly, and she can see those lips, and they are frozen at the moment
before they will descend on to her lips –

The truck rumbled over some humps in the road. They turned into a gateway.

'Stop!' Heather screamed. The driver pulled on the handbrake and Heather burst out of the cab, flying into a nearby hedge, where she disappeared.

'Hang on, girls,' he was saying. 'Let me get the damn thing in the yard –' They lurched forward a few more feet and then pulled up. With the cab door open, the terror of the pigs – the screaming, the smell, the desperate strugglings behind them – all became real and overpowering. Bennett, Jude and Cissie sat paralysed, staring ahead through the cab windscreen at what looked like a scene from the depths of hell. Streams of bellowing pigs were being poked and prodded into the darkness of an enormous hangar. The clamour had reached deafening proportions.

The driver was already swinging expertly out of the cab. 'Come on!' he said, grinning, enjoying their discomfort, 'I got to get these chaps on the chopping block.'

Hurriedly they scrambled down, and stood in the yard, self-conscious, their mod finery somehow ludicrous in the face of all this blood and suffering.

'We better look for Heather,' Jude was shivering, in spite of the sunshine.

'Spewing in the hedge,' Bennett pointed. Heather suddenly straightened up and was visible. She walked slowly towards them, her mascara streaked into ugly rivulets down her cheeks.

Cissie fought the sudden desire to sit down heavily on the tarmac and weep, amid the red puddles and the screaming and the laughing slaughterhouse boys in their blood-stained overalls sweeping the bloody water into the drains. 'We're not going to get to London, are we.' It was a statement, rather than a question.

Jude bristled. 'Of course we are. I got us a lift this far, didn't I?' –

for she had been the one who had persuaded the driver to take them.

'You got us a lift to the middle of nowhere,' Cissie said coldly. An electrical moment of anger flashed between them.

'Yes, but I did something,' Jude said loudly above the noise. 'I did something. What have you ever done?'

There was a small, icy moment of silence. Their world was crumbling. They both felt the panic, the pounding heart, the sick intuition that nothing would ever be the same again. Then Bennett appeared at their side, triumphant, a Boadicea in mod shoes.

'It's all right,' she said breathlessly, indicating a weasel-faced boy grinning behind her. 'He says he'll take us – in his van.'

Jude eyed him disbelievingly. 'You going to London?'

'West One.'

'Brilliant!' She grinned at Cissie, all rancour forgotten.

And the boy in the van suddenly said, 'I've got to make a detour, I've got this cottage in the woods where my uncle goes to stay at weekends. He leads a busy life and he needs somewhere where he can relax with his friends . . .'

Heather had turned suddenly and was vomiting loudly into a nearby water trough.

'Heather!' Bennett said, exasperated. 'Not now!'

Weasel-face was jingling his car keys. 'You girls coming, or what?'

'Hang on –' Cissie was leaning over Heather, a reluctant hand on her shoulder, feigning sympathy while trying to keep her eyes averted from what Heather was depositing in the trough.

The boy shrugged. 'Can't. Got to go now.' His eyes swivelled and found Bennett, with whom he was evidently taken. 'You want to come on ahead with me?'

Bennett hesitated. 'Bring one of your mates?' he suggested, waving the keys enticingly, as if they were the keys to heaven. Which, of course, they could be . . .

Heather's vomiting grew louder, more anguished. The boy observed her with interest. 'She a vegetarian?' he asked.

Bennett was biting her lip, looking at Cissie.

'We can't split up,' Cissie said, desperate. Bennett looked from her to Jude.

'You could follow later. When Heather's finished throwing up her haggis,' Jude said. Cissie's eyes went back to Bennett, mute, desperate. If Bennett left her, it would be the end of everything.

'If we see the Beatles, we see them together. That's what we always said.' Bennett's eyes met hers. A decision was made.

'We stick together,' Bennett said, finally. 'She's right. That's what we said. We stick together.'

The boy shrugged, disappointed, and climbed into the van. 'Your funeral,' he said. 'Anyway, they're not very original, are they – the Beatles. That George Harrison – he tries to copy Carl Perkins' playing all the time. Note for note.' They watched him drive out of the yard, the pigs screaming in their ears.

'He had spots, anyway,' Jude was saying. 'A big one, on his chin – full of pus.' Heather's shoulders had stopped heaving. She hung limply over the trough, exhausted. Bennett stared at the empty road where the van had gone, as if she could conjure it up again by sheer force of longing.

'He wore two rings on one hand and two on the other,' she said eventually, as if that explained everything.

Cissie patted her shoulder, understanding. 'But he wasn't as funny as Ringo,' she said. 'And his jeans were too short.'

Heather had got the old pump at one end of the trough working, and was sluicing her face with one hand, pumping with the other, grey-faced and depressed. They watched her, each struggling with an intense desire to push Heather Lewis's blonde head under the gushing water. The dream had already been tarnished, certainly, what with the endless wait on the road outside Norwich, the niggling quarrels as they lost their sense of excitement and became bored with hitch-hiking; then the pigs and the evil-smelling truck and this nightmarish place; but it had taken Heather Lewis with her weak stomach to really destroy the magic. Heather Lewis, intruder. Heather Lewis, Scottish person. Heather Lewis, with her perfect flick-ups and her perfect little nose.

'Heather bloody Lewis,' Bennett said finally, softly. Heather

86

looked up then, and saw the three resentful, cold, accusing faces of her friends. She began to cry.

The car, a gleaming red Ford Granada, was speeding along a dual carriageway. The flat Norfolk plains had given way to the clapboarded villages of Essex, and these in turn had spread into the outlying suburbs of London: Ongar, Epping, small towns separated by the occasional field, rows of houses startlingly alike, only the occasional odd front porch or wrought-iron gate indicating a rebellious occupant.

Heather was in the front, next to the driver, a florid man in a crumpled brown suit and argyll socks who drove with one hand on the steering wheel and only half an eye on the road. He was a sales rep for Gordon's Jam, he told them. In the back, Cissie, Bennett and Jude were crammed together, sharing the space with the driver's jacket, which swung noisily from a coat hanger and obscured the view out of the right-hand window.

Cissie was pretending to be asleep, trying in vain to recreate her George fantasy, and failing. The voice of the man driving kept interrupting her vision.

'All the way to London, girls,' he had said when the car had miraculously stopped for them. 'All the way. I'll take you all the way, heh-heh . . .'

Whenever she opened her eyes, they met his, watchful, in the rear-view mirror. Jude chewed bubble gum and blew the occasional large bubble, but was silent. Bennett had pulled her drumsticks out of her bag and was banging them quietly on her knees, intent on defining the rhythm of some song. This left Heather obliged to deal with the man at the wheel, who had given her a dog-eared copy of *The A–Z of London* and which Heather was supposed to be studying. Every now and then she would say desperately, 'Maybe we should have turned left there –' and the man would lean across, ostensibly to touch the pages of the book, his hand straying over Heather's frozen knee.

'Let me see . . .' He would say, grinning, watching Heather's face for a reaction. 'No, it's all right . . . We're all right . . . I said – we're all right, aren't we, Natasha?' Natasha was the name Heather had told him was hers when they had climbed into the car. It was Jude's idea. She had told the man her name was Ethelreda. The others had giggled.

'Mine's Jocasta,' Bennett had told him solemnly.

Before Cissie could speak, Jude had said, 'And she's called Cecilia, aren't you, Cissie?'

The man had grinned his wolfish grin, not believing any of them. 'Funny sort of a name,' he had said. 'Funny name, funny girl, is that it? Cecilia. Cecilia, I'd like to feelya. Heh-heh.' Cissie had glared at Jude and said nothing, making sure that Bennett sat between them. Sometimes she hated Jude so much she had real thoughts of murder in her heart.

Bennett began drumming on the back of the man's seat, slowly at first, then with more urgency, more insistence.

'Oy!' he said. 'Do you mind?'

Bennett subsided, pulling a face behind him. She began to sing 'Can't Buy Me Love', quietly at first, then with more gusto, as Jude and then Cissie joined in.

'So —' the man said, his eyes sliding over Heather, 'you're going to be in the Beatles' film, then?'

'We're going to be extras,' Heather said proudly. The man raised an eyebrow. 'You know — pretend to be fans.'

'Pretend . . .!' scoffed Jude.

The rep seemed to find the idea amusing. 'Going to meet the boys, then, are you?' he asked drily. 'Going to meet the Beatles? Heh-heh . . .'

Bennett clenched her drumsticks. 'What's so funny about that?'

'Come on darling,' he said, carelessly negotiating a bend. 'You and ten thousand others.'

'Jealous?' Jude asked tartly.

'What — four spotty oiks from the sticks?' He laughed again.

'George isn't spotty!' Cissie had suddenly found her voice.

'Ringo is,' Jude said, to provoke Bennett.

'No he isn't. Bitch.'

The rep was twisting the expanding bracelet of his gold watch thoughtfully with his free hand. The other rested on the driving wheel, fingers relaxed. Cissie was transfixed. Surely they would crash! What would happen if another car did something un-expected? A dream lurked hopefully. *The crash. George reads about it in the paper. He arrives at her bedside in the hospital, where she lies, pale and beautiful. She opens her eyes . . .*

'Wouldn't say no to some of their cash,' the man was saying. His hand returned to Heather's knees. 'You still on the right page there?'

Heather smiled at him, polite, scared. 'That's what my boyfriend says,' she shifted away in her seat, her body stiff. 'About the Beatles. He says he'd like their money . . .'

'You got a boyfriend?'

Jude was grinning in the back. 'We prefer to think of him as a hamster, actually,' she muttered audibly. Heather turned and glared.

'Got a name, has he, this boyfriend?'

'Ray,' Heather said. 'Ray. He looks like Paul McCartney.'

'Exactly,' Jude murmured, triumphant, 'a hamster.'

There was an explosion of mirth in the back of the car. The rep ignored the giggling trio, his attention focussed on Heather. The journey was coming to an end. Things were speeding up.

'And you and this Ray – you have a pretty steamy time, eh? In the cloakrooms after school?' He was rewarded by the sight of Heather's burning face. She stared ahead, silent. 'Do it round your mum's house, do you?' he persisted, grinning. 'Or in the car?'

Bennett was busy performing an elaborate mime of vomiting behind the driver. Cissie stared at her feet. Jude's eyes were closed, but she was listening.

'Ray hasn't got a car,' Heather was saying in a small voice.

'Not got a car? You want to be a bit more choosy.' The hand with the gold watch changed gear, patting Heather's thigh as it did so. 'Lot of freedom you get with a car. Take me for example –' he was evidently about to embark on a salesman's anecdote. 'Couple of weeks ago I was delivering out Essex way –'

'What did you say your name was?' Jude suddenly interrupted. 'Bob, was it?'

'Bill. Anyway. Picked up a couple of girl hitch-hikers on the A13, just outside Shoeburyness –'

'Bill what?' Jude persisted. Cissie looked at her.

The rep eyed her suspiciously in the mirror. 'Why?'

She shrugged. 'Just wondered.'

The man returned his gaze to the averted, pink profile of Heather. 'One of them looked a lot like you,' he said. 'Only not so attractive, of course.'

'Of course . . .' murmured Bennett unhelpfully from the back.

'Anyway, they were coming up to the smoke wanting to see a bit of excitement. So I say to them –'

Jude leaned forward again. 'Is it peculiar, or something, your surname? Is that it? Foreign, is it?'

The man bristled. 'No, it bleedin' well isn't. It's McKinnon, if you must know.'

'Like McCartney,' Bennett remarked.

Heather turned, angry tears in her eyes. 'Nothing like McCartney,' she said savagely.

'You navigating or what?' the rep said sharply. In despair, Heather turned back.

In the back seat, Jude was busy scribbling something in biro on her bubble-gum wrapper. The driver looked at her in his rear-view mirror, suspicious. Nonchalantly she returned his look, her hand sliding over the paper. 'Go there a lot, do you? London?'

'Well . . . the odd occasion,' he said, defensively. He had taken a dislike to the clever, dark one behind him. She was too knowing by half. 'Anyway,' he said, returning with enthusiasm to his story, 'I take these two schoolgirls to one of these Soho clubs, see . . . Know what I mean by a Soho club?'

Heather's voice was faint. 'A strip club?'

'We're sitting at the table, see. Heh-heh. And one of them, the dark-haired one, leans forward and puts her hand on my leg. Like this, kind of thing –' His hand reached out and pressed gently against Heather's upper thigh. He gave her a sidelong glance to see how she was responding. Heather, paralysed, unable to remove his hand, which was beginning to press more insistently against her, could only see that her three so-called friends in the back seemed intent on each other, their heads lowered together, leaving her abandoned. What she did not see was the note Jude had composed. It read: 'Dear Mrs McKinnon, I had sexual intercourse with your husband in this car, Signed: A well-wisher.'

Jude leaned across and placed the paper so that it protruded from the ashtray in the front passenger door next to Heather, who was too rigid with embarrassment at the thought of a Soho strip club to notice.

'You have to turn left here,' Jude suddenly said, her voice authoritative.

The rep glanced at her in his mirror. 'You sure?'

'Second set of lights, isn't it, Heather?'

The man frowned. 'I thought your name was Natasha.'

'It is!' Jude said brightly, 'Natasha Heather. Go on – you'll miss it – second set of lights –'

The car slowed, as the man changed gear, removing his hand from Heather's thigh for a moment. 'So I was telling you,' he said, determinedly, '– about the club with these girls – so there's this hand, right, under the table, doing God knows what, then the other one – the blonde –' He had pulled up at a set of traffic lights. 'You're not going to believe this –'

'No,' said Jude, opening the door nearest to the pavement, 'you're probably right.' She struggled out, grabbing Cissie's sleeve as she did so. Cissie and Bennett writhed across the plastic seat towards freedom.

'Come on,' said the driver. 'Stop pissing about!'

Heather turned in her seat and saw the three of them scrabbling their way out. 'Don't leave me!' she screamed. 'Don't leave me!'

'Jump!' yelled Bennett. 'Jump, you silly cow!'

Heather struggled wordlessly with the door handle, her cheeks a flash of scarlet, the sales rep mouthing angrily at her. Jude wrenched the door open and began to haul Heather out on to the tarmac. The lights turned green, and behind them, a queue of cars began to hoot their horns impatiently. The man leaned over as Heather finally landed in the road.

'Come on girls,' he said. 'I'll take you wherever you want to go –'

The honking of car horns became more insistent. 'Yeah,' said Bennett, 'all the way. We heard you.'

She slammed the door. 'You'll be late!' he shouted, his face creased in an expression of helpless rage. 'You're miles away from the West End!'

The car jerked away. Bennett whacked at the gleaming boot with her drumsticks in a triumphant flourish as it passed, and then joined the others shinning over the fence that divided the dual carriageway from the pavement. Their escapade had caused chaos in the road, and the air was filled with car horns and angry voices as they raced away together, breathless and relieved, roused by the sudden fresh air after the claustrophobic heat of the car. It had begun to rain gently, the pavement spattered with dark stains. It felt cool on their hot cheeks.

They paused, panting, on the corner. 'This way,' said Jude, pointing an imperious finger. Bennett and Cissie followed.

'Hang on.' They turned, irritated. Heather was triumphantly brandishing the salesman's *A–Z of London*. 'I'm on the right page,' she said. 'Leytonstone High Road – see? We just have to go back this way and we can get the underground –'

Jude kept walking. 'Bus is cheaper,' she said. 'Bus-stop's up here – come on . . .'

There was no one at the bus-stop. The rain began to fall steadily, large globules of dirty water clinging to the discarded rubbish in the gutter. The girls rooted about in their bags for headscarves, and groaned as the pace of the rain suddenly quickened and they were caught in the kind of savage downpour only possible in an English spring. Heather ran squealing to shelter under the awning of a nearby shop. She turned to adjust her scarf in the reflection of the window, only to pause, horrified, at the sight of a plastic pig's head smiling benignly at her from a bed of fake parsley. The others joined her.

'I'll never eat meat again,' she said, shuddering.

A bus appeared. Jude ran out into the torrent waving her arms and the bus careered to a halt, sending a spray of water on to the pavement and Jude's feet.

Cissie shivered, watching as the conductor and Jude exchanged shouted words above the noise of the bus's engine. Jude returned, disconsolate. The bus moved away.

'Two changes if we want to get to the West End,' she said. 'Or we can wait forty minutes for the number twenty-five, which goes to Oxford Street. But the journey takes an hour.'

Cissie stared at her, aghast. 'We can't wait that long!' she said, anguished. 'We were supposed to have been there hours ago!'

Heather returned to her study of *The A–Z of London*, unable to resist an I-told-you-so lift of one eyebrow. 'Leytonstone,' she announced, 'is on the Central Line. The Central Line takes us all the way to Tottenham Court Road.' she paused and looked up, enjoying her moment. 'The Scala theatre is just off the Tottenham Court Road,' she said, coolly triumphant. 'And it's only ten stops.'

Cissie and Bennett looked at Jude. She was gracious in defeat. 'Let's go,' she said, and headed out into the rain without a backward glance.

The rain had diminished to a persistent drizzle. For a while they plodded on, silent and intent on their destination; then, as they continued to walk, they began to take in their surroundings. Jude walked ahead, looking around her aggressively, as if any indication of fear might result in an unexpected attack. Heather and Bennett paused to stare in shop windows, dazzled by the array of glittering sari lengths, heaps of unnamed and unnameable foods in foreign-looking emporiums, odd rubrics – 'Halal Meat', 'Mirza Fashions', 'Baklava Freshly Made on Premises', signs written in strange hieroglyphics outside mundane barbers' shops and vegetable stalls. Cissie straggled along behind, trying not to stare at the passers-by, who went about their daily business without seeming to register the dazzlingly exotic apparitions with whom they shared the pavement. Old ladies in felt hats with shopping trolleys headed grumpily past Africans in beaded embroidered hats without appearing to notice. Two giggling dark-skinned girls in purple silk trousers and sequinned tunics fluttered by, like two brilliant butterflies, ignored by the housewives with their pushchairs and carrier bags. An Asian wearing a grubby apron blew Cissie a kiss as she passed. She only had time to fearfully register that he had the most beautiful eyes she had ever seen.

For a moment she wished desperately to be back in the field behind Brigadoon, with Toulouse's head in her lap, and her dreams of George taking her wherever she wanted to go – not here, not this real, grey, loud place full of aliens, but to the peak of any fantasy she cared to pursue. It was safe in that world – she had control, she made things happen. Here, all was random, dangerous, prone to failure. She forced herself to think about the reality, the world beyond the field behind Brigadoon – Mill grumbling by the stove, Oliver silently chain-smoking and staring out over the garden, her mother with that silly, permanently smiling expression she wore whenever Oliver came to visit . . . Funny, a little voice said in the dim recesses of this vision, funny how Mike is never there in these pictures. She pondered this for a moment guiltily. It was because Mike never *was* there, she told herself: he was always in his shed or in the back yard, hammering away at one of his lumps. She had a sudden picture of him standing in the doorway to her bedroom, uncomfortable, un-happy, holding the sleeping baby in his arms, Susie's face soft against his shoulder, and asking, 'Cissie? Are you all right?'

Only it wasn't Mike. It was the smiling face of the man with the wellington boots, standing in the river; it was her father. Stop it, she told herself, *stop it* . . . She realized suddenly that her face was wet, and for a ridiculous moment she wondered if she had been crying without realizing it. Then she remembered the rain.

The others had paused for shelter outside a betting shop. Heather was studying *The A–Z of London* again, without much hope. 'It says here the stations are marked with a black dot,' she was telling Jude. The blonde head and the dark one bent together over the pages. 'We should be there by now.' They both stared hopelessly out at the road, as if a tube station marked with a black dot might appear by magic.

'She's lost us, hasn't she,' Bennett said, drumming morosely on the window sill. 'We're not going to get there, are we.'

'Stop moaning!' Jude said abstractedly, studying the book. 'We must be near it –'

'Why don't we just go to a cafe and have egg and chips?' Bennett brightened considerably at the thought. 'Then we can just turn round and hitch home again –'

She was rewarded with a sharp *thwack* of the book on her head. 'Egg and bloody chips!' Jude had started walking again, oblivious to the rain. 'Egg and bloody chips at a time like this!' The others followed. 'Most important day of our lives and she wants to eat egg and bloody chips!'

They were getting cold now, clothes clinging damply, hair wilting. 'Maybe Bennett's right –' Cissie said hesitantly, ducking to avoid a dripping awning. 'Maybe we should turn round –'

Jude stopped dramatically, her face an exaggerated parody of pained betrayal. The others stood, half-hopeful, waiting to see what happened next. 'Turn around!' she repeated. 'Turn around!'

Cissie wilted. 'No,' she said slowly. 'We've come this far . . .'

Jude's eyes were fixed on her face. Rain trickled from the soaking folds of her headscarf, causing dark rivulets in the PanStick-covered paleness of her cheeks. 'Miss Flying Table wants to go home,' she said. 'Miss bloody secretive Flying Table wants to go home.'

'Shut up,' Cissie said quickly, her face suddenly burning, her eyes sliding to Bennett, who was watching, interested.

'What table?' Bennett asked, the rain forgotten, the egg and chips forgotten.

'Ask her,' Jude was saying, her eyes still resting coldly on Cissie. 'Ask her.'

Cissie was quivering. 'You've been in my bag,' she said to Jude. Her anger was like a white flash – bright, searing. 'You've been nosying in my bag –'

'I was looking for some rouge,' Jude said.

'You read my letters.'

Bennett was getting tired of this. 'What letters? Can we get on?' They had all stopped in a doorway, as if by tacit agreement. They were crammed between a newsagent's and a shop with travel posters plastered over the windows. Through the smeared glass,

Cissie could just see a bare room, scattered tables, and swarthy men hunched in groups, playing cards and drinking from tiny glasses.

'What letters? Just tell us, Cissie, eh?' Heather had reached into her bag and was applying a layer of 'Peppy Pink' to a damp mouth, making a *moue* with her lips.

'Go on, then,' Jude said, challenging. 'Miss secretive – tell them.'

Cissie turned her back on them and glared through the window. 'You tell them,' she said. Inside, a group of men looked up from their cards and grinned at her. They were old, with dark skin and yellowing teeth. She turned back hastily. Jude was producing Cissie's precious bundle of letters with a flourish from her shoulder bag. Ostentatiously, she began to read, holding one of the letters aloft, as if it were a proclamation. 'Dear Cecilia,' she read, 'Thank you for your letter. I'm afraid George is too busy to write. I hope you won't mind if I write instead –'

She had the full attention of Heather and Bennett now, who stood transfixed, listening, oblivious to the raindrops dripping from the doorway on to their necks. Bennett's mouth had dropped open, so that to Cissie, suddenly, she looked ludicrously like a fish, her face dripping, her lips parted, her eyes wide. Jude's voice droned on, revealing those secret words, those treasured paragraphs, her tone dry and accusatory.

She was reading another letter now. 'I liked the story about the seances,' she intoned in mock Liverpudlian, savouring each word, enjoying the dramatic effect. 'I told George about it when he phoned up –'

Heather turned to Cissie, her face brightly impressed. 'You wrote to George's mother?' she gasped, her accent suddenly strong, as it was when she became excited. 'You wrote to George's mam and she *answered*!'

Cissie looked at the pavement, aware of Bennett's face, hurt, betrayed. 'I meant to tell you,' she said gruffly, 'I was just waiting for the right moment –'

'You told George Harrison's mammy about the seances . . .?' Heather's voice was shrill with envy, disbelief, excitement. 'And she told George –'

Jude interrupted, continuing her inexorable recitation of the letter. 'I told George about it when he phoned up,' she repeated in her Mrs Harrison voice, 'and he was very interested . . .' Cissie was aware of Bennett's silence, as each word was absorbed. 'He liked the story about the table lifting off the ground when the spirits arrive. He always asks after you when he phones, and he calls you the girl from Norfolk with the flying table.' Jude looked at her audience, triumphant. 'The girl from Norfolk with the flying table,' she repeated. Cissie looked at her feet.

'The girl from Norfolk with the flying table.' It was Bennett's voice, reverently intoning the words. Cissie looked up. Bennett's face was ecstatic. She clutched Cissie's arm. 'He knows who you are,' she breathed. 'George knows!'

Jude folded the letter, nettled. 'She didn't tell us,' she reminded Bennett. 'She's been getting these letters for weeks and she never said a word.'

'Doesn't matter!' Bennett's eyes were like saucers. 'He knows, Cissie! He knows you exist!' For a tiny moment, there was just Bennett and Cissie, locked together in understanding, Cissie's heart flooded with relief. Bennett was not going to be angry. She understood.

Heather stood, wounded. 'I wrote to Paul,' she said, almost to herself. 'Twenty Forthlin Road. But I never heard anything.'

Jude handed the bundle of letters back to Cissie. 'Come on,' she said. 'We'll never get there if we don't keep going.' She ducked out into the rain again, clearly annoyed that her thunder had been stolen. Cissie stuffed the letters back into the recesses of her bag, happy again.

'Come on!' she called to the others, hurrying away after Jude, suddenly excited. 'Come on!'

It was Bennett who found the tube station – they had nearly missed the entrance completely in their haste along the increasingly busy High Road. They clattered down the stairs and fidgeted on the damp platform, calling to each other in high, hysterical voices, making too much noise, exhilarated at the thought of being so close to their destination, ignored by the other waiting passengers.

Finally, the train thundered into the station and they clambered on, giggling.

In the carriage, a weary man in a cloth cap dozed behind his *Daily Express*, swaying gently with the rhythm of the train. The four girls flung themselves down, exhausted. Jude pulled out a cigarette and lit it, blowing the smoke in a confident plume towards an advertisement for Polo mints above the window opposite. There was a moment's satisfied silence.

Bennett nudged Cissie. 'The girl from Norfolk with the flying table,' she said, her voice awed.

Cissie nodded, calm. Her heart was pounding, her head was spinning. This was it. The train rattled on towards the West End, leaving the outlying sprawl of London behind, heading for its heart. Everything was a portent. The escape from school. The note from Peggy. Mrs Harrison's letters. The moment was coming. She was going to meet George.

CHAPTER FOUR

Everybody's Trying to be My Baby

LIVERPOOL STREET. BANK. ST PAUL'S. The tube train was crowded now. The four girls were clutching on to leather ceiling straps near the doors, too excited to remain seated. Jaded-looking passengers shuffled on and disembarked at each station, indifferent to Cissie's furtive scrutiny, Heather's wide eyes, Bennett's murmured remarks. Jude pretended not to be interested, hanging by one arm with what she hoped was a certain *insouciance*, concentrating on not losing her balance and yet retaining an air of casual familiarity with the mysteries of strap-hanging on the underground.

Cissie tried desperately to drink it all in – the sights, the smells. These bright pictures would have to last her over the lean Norfolk months ahead when all she had to anticipate was her A-level revision. The two girls seated near by, with their perfect white faces, their glossy hair, their neat pastel-coloured A-line dresses – Cissie had thought these visions only existed in the pages of *Honey* magazine. The man in the pin-striped suit staring coldly ahead; the Italian family shouting at each other loudly over the heads of the standing commuters; the old woman in the hat with a veil, a tiny Pekinese trembling in a wicker shopping basket on her lap – these people were the stuff of London, where every eccentricity was tolerated – no, better than that – ignored! No slow Norfolk voice interrupted this orgy of individualism with a disparaging mutter of 'Don't see the use in that' or 'That's just plain daft' . . . No horde of cruel schoolmates pointed and sneered.

The doors slid open at Holborn, and more men in suits equipped with newspapers and briefcases struggled in. The carriage was becoming tightly packed, and Cissie was thrust against a tall African in a white robe. He smiled down at her kindly, revealing a row of white teeth. He smelled of sweat and Parma Violets. A wizened drunk in a trilby staggered on as the doors were closing, causing the packed carriage to shuffle reluctantly ever closer. Cissie felt enveloped in white cotton, straining desperately to avoid touching anything under the folds of fabric that might be a shiny black leg, or a knee – or worse. She wondered what was under the robe. Did Africans wear underpants? Through a gap under someone's arm she could just see Bennett, sandwiched between two nurses, hot in their navy capes. The drunk began to sing 'I Can't Stop Loving You' in an excruciating baritone, hovering over every syllable with a tremulous warble. Cissie tried to move away, but there was nowhere to go, as the train lurched through the blackness.

'Next stop!' It was Bennett, shouting above the crowd, waving an arm frantically, like a panicking swimmer. 'Tottenham Court Road!'

The train jerked to a halt, and Cissie fell against the African, who smiled still, seeming not to take offence at her frozen, horrified face. She had never touched a black man before. She felt as if she would faint. The crowd was shuffling off, carrying her with it. The smiling black face receded. Heather was calling somewhere behind her. A mass of heaving red and white shoved at them from another platform, alien Northern accents mingling with the reverberation of a hundred feet clattering across the concrete to the escalators. It was like a dream – Cissie was hustled along, dazed, while in her ears echoed a myriad voices all speaking in the tone of George Harrison.

'Watch it, you daft get!'

'Coom on, 'Arry! Shift yerself, lad!'

Somehow the girls found themselves together in the tiled passageway as a train thundered away from the platform opposite, its carriages a blur of red and white.

'Bloody Liverpool,' someone said.

They stared after the train.

'Playing Spurs, aren't they?'

'Kick-off's at three . . .'

Another portent, thought Cissie. Liverpudlians in London – not just the four on whom they focussed their every waking thought, but hundreds and hundreds of them, red and white rosettes and scarves proclaiming their provenance. They were propping up the walls of the station, hanging about in groups singing, an exuberant, noisy foreign army of invaders, from the same country as George. The girls headed towards the exit, weak with relief and excitement. They had done the journey. They had gone from Crookfield Grammar to Tottenham Court Road. It was only one o'clock. It was going to happen.

They were on the escalator, travelling upwards, trying not to cling too hard to the handrail, trying not to gawk at the cool sophistication of the *habitués* who ran up the moving staircase on the left-hand side, not holding on, just running upwards, defying gravity, heading higher and higher . . .

'I'm going to shag him if I get the chance.' Jude was standing backwards, looking down at the others, taking up too much space and irritating the upward-runners on her right.

'Who?'

'John.' Jude lit a cigarette, staring defiantly at the passing climbers, blowing smoke at them, daring them to react. No one did. 'If I can't get John I'll go for one of the others,' she added.

Cissie stiffened. 'You're not blonde,' she said. 'George likes blonde girls.'

Jude raised a scornful eyebrow. 'You don't believe that squit, do you?' she said. 'He'd shag anybody, I bet. They all would.'

'Jude . . .' Heather was squirming, wishing Jude would lower her voice.

'They all would,' Jude repeated, inexorable. 'Even James Paul.' This elicited the desired result from Heather, whose eyes filled with angry tears.

'Take no notice,' Bennett instructed, pink-faced. 'It's not going to happen, is it.'

'You don't know that.' Jude's face hardened.

The escalator jerked a little, rumbling upwards.

'I can see it now,' Bennett said, sarcastic. 'Jude and the Beatles all in a room together, and her saying "Which one first?" . . .'

Jude's look, intended to be both crushing and dismissive, was hindered by her sudden arrival at the top, where she almost toppled over backwards. Each struggled to maintain an attitude of casual mastery of the moving staircase as they stepped off it on to steadier ground, and gathered together, trying to get their bearings.

'Scala Street.' Bennett said. 'We want Scala Street.'

'Tottenham Court Road – which exit?'

Heather had been side-tracked by a passing blonde in a suedette coat. She nudged Bennett, excited. 'Look!' she whispered, 'isn't that Julie Christie?'

Bennett looked at her pityingly. 'You think she goes on the tube?' she asked. Heather subsided, mortified.

Jude was leading them up a crowded staircase, up to the light beyond. They emerged, blinking, on to a crowded pavement, bewildered by the roar of traffic, the shouts of a newspaper vendor, the hubbub of shoppers, all hurrying confidently towards unknown destinations. Jude led them down a side street, into the shadows.

'Down here, turn right, we should be there,' she said, snapping shut *The A–Z of London*. The others followed, anxious. They passed some Indian restaurants, inexplicably grouped together, their flaking façades of purple and green a bright dash of exotica among the faded grey office blocks. The sound of pop music suddenly blasted at them from an open doorway, and they turned hopefully – but it was only a small and scruffy record shop, the figures of serious-faced youths leafing through banks of singles, shadowy in the dark recesses.

'My shoes hurt,' complained Bennett. Her ankles were beginning to swell.

They were overtaken by a couple of girls in school blazers, stuffing their striped ties into their pockets, half-running along the kerb, faces anxious.

'What if we can't find it?' Cissie was asking.

'Don't be such a bloody pessimist!' Jude turned and frowned.

Three more girls hurried past, giggling together, their heels clacking on the pavement. Cissie turned, too, and saw behind them several small gaggles of girls all hurrying, as they were, towards the road junction ahead, where cars darted past in the sunshine. They speeded up, catching the air of excitement.

Ahead of them they heard what sounded like a muffled sighing beyond the adjacent buildings – and then Cissie knew. The sigh was not a sigh. It was a muted collective scream.

She caught up with Heather. 'It's them!' she breathed. They turned the corner into Charlotte Street. The pavements were crowded here, and amongst the shoppers and the office workers, small groups of fans were identifiable, milling together in fidgeting, excitable clusters, their numbers growing, one group detaching itself from a crowd and joining up with another, like a swarm of confused bees searching for their queen. The girls quickened their step to keep pace with Jude, who was beginning to push impatiently past some of the slower in the throng.

Once again Cissie felt as if her feet were not her own, as she was propelled along in a growing and ever more excited crowd. Bennett was next to her, and Heather was somewhere behind – and Jude, as usual, was just visible ahead, turning occasionally to make sure the others were still there, her face twisted with anxiety and anticipation. They had turned a corner. The crowd stopped suddenly. Cissie's face was crushed against the plastic mac of someone in front of her. She heard a groan, like the complaint of a large, multi-throated beast, rumbling ahead.

'What is it?'

'Why have we stopped?'

'My leg! Ow – my leg –!'

Jude was struggling back towards them, her face bleak, shaking her head. 'It's no good,' she panted, squirming under someone's arm to reach Cissie and Bennett, 'we're not going to get in – doors are closed.'

Around them, the crowd swelled and shoved. Cissie felt herself become heavy, as if her feet had suddenly touched the earth again. They reached the shadow of a doorway. The powerful aroma of coffee assailed them. In the shop window, Cissie could see neat displays of brown beans, and the gleam of a coffee grinder. She wondered briefly why on earth such a shop should exist. What was it for?

'We've got to get in,' Heather was wailing, her accent suddenly stronger, as it was when emotion got the better of her. 'I've got to see Paul! I canna bear it – I canna bear it –'

Jude stared at them, her face working through several emotions. 'Come on,' she said grimly. 'I'll get us in. I promise I'll get us in . . .'

Again they followed her, straining to keep together as they threaded their way through the packed mass of bodies. Finally, Cissie glimpsed gilt double doors, a cordon, the desperate faces of policemen wrestling with stray screaming girls who suddenly breached the defences in a wild dash, or burst through the doors at breakneck speed, only to be ejected with equal ferocity a few seconds later. Here the crowd was so tightly packed it was almost impossible to breathe. There would be a sudden swaying in one direction and Cissie would be lifted up and carried along, gasping for breath, wildly keeping her eyes fixed on the bobbing head of Jude in front of her, the dishevelled blonde tresses of Heather to one side, Bennett's pink, desperate face on the other.

'Let us in!' the crowd yelled, 'Let us in! We want the Beatles!'

Cissie felt as if her lungs would burst. She was crushed against a furious-looking Amazon in a mohair cardigan and giant pink button earrings. 'Bastards!' the girl panted. 'Bastards!' She turned to Cissie, fuming. 'They're in there!' she said indignantly, 'I saw them!' She had a thick layer of black eyeliner circling her eyes and smudging her cheeks, where the occasional tear had slid down her face.

'Did you see George?' Cissie gasped, but the girl had turned again, and was yelling along with the crowd, a full-throated bellow: 'Let us in!'

Somewhere behind them, something was happening to make the crowd twist back on itself, causing screams of terror as girls fell on top of other girls. Cissie managed to manoeuvre her body round and saw the gleaming bonnet of a long, low black limousine nosing its way through the crowd. It was immediately besieged, disappearing under a heaving, screaming mass of girls, who climbed on the roof, banged on the darkened windows and hammered at the windscreen, where Cissie caught a glimpse of a cowering, uniformed driver. For a moment she thought she really would die, suffocated under the hysterical scrum of bodies – and even in that moment, the fantasy took hold, even as she fought to keep breathing.

She faints and is taken into the theatre. She wakes and there he is, bending over her, shy grin, brown eyes. 'Watcha,' he says in that guttural voice she knows better than her own. And gently he brushes a lock of hair from her cheek, his fingers tender, like a butterfly's wings . . .

The blackness swirled for a heart-stopping second, and then there was the sky above her head, and the struggling mass, and the car passing, and the girls falling back, disappointed, angry.

'It wasn't them!'

'It was that fat bloke – you know –'

'It wasn't anyone!'

'It was Ringo, wasn't it?'

'Norman Rossington – it was Norman Rossington!'

'Who's Norman Rossington?'

'It was Brian Epstein!'

Jude had managed to fight her way through to Cissie. 'I'll get us in!' she yelled above the din. 'I promise!' But even as she bellowed her promise, another car appeared, and the chaos began again. This time Cissie was swept away with the relentless throng, still somehow attached to the girl with the mohair cardigan, but losing sight, in a terrible blank moment of panic, of Heather, of Bennett, of Jude. Again the car disappeared under a deluge of scrambling girls, like a tasty morsel consumed suddenly by an army of ants, and Cissie was shoved against the bodywork with a thud that knocked the breath out of her. In that brief, gasping second, with her face slammed against the tinted windows, she glimpsed a white, terrified face staring back at her. The face was very wrinkled and white, with blood-red lips, and for a second, the mouth fell open, revealing small yellow teeth. There was a blurred impression of fur swathing a sagging, chicken neck and then Cissie was thrown back on to the crowd as the car suddenly accelerated and roared savagely through, scattering girls like seagulls in its wake.

'Who was it?' Someone shook her, breathless.

'No one,' she said, gulping air, glad to be alive. 'No one. Just some old woman.'

'Probably a Beatle's mum,' said someone, helpfully.

This idea was immediately taken up.

'A Beatle's mum!'

'Ringo's mum was in there!'

'It was John's Aunty Mimi! She had red hair!'

Cissie scrambled through the thinning crowd, searching for the others. She reached the haven of a small mews to one side of the street, where, apart from a lone girl squatting limply in the gutter sobbing into her handbag, there was space. She looked around. The screaming continued, the fighting for position, the mad scramble of girls jockeying for position outside the theatre doors − it was still there, the madness, the noise, the lung-crushing hysteria. Cissie stared. She could see only strangers. Dumbly, she turned and walked away.

Jude watched him thoughtfully. He reminded her of Tom Jones, the singer − curly hair, sideburns, a strong, cruel mouth. He was wearing a half-hearted attempt at a uniform: a blue shirt with epaulettes, blue serge trousers, a narrow tie. He was leaning against the stage door, assessing the girls around him with a weary cynicism, aware of his power. They clustered around, pleading.

'Go on − five minutes!'

'I won't tell, honest!'

'You could pretend we knocked you unconscious and then you won't get into trouble.'

One girl, slightly older and braver than the others, was pushing through the crowd. She approached him, chin up. 'I'm Mr Epstein's niece,' she said. 'He said I should meet him inside.'

Tom Jones grinned, studying her, his head cocked on one side, like a bird. 'You're the fifth niece today,' he said.

'Mr Epstein will be very angry −'

He laughed, and pulled a cigarette from behind his ear. 'Mr Epstein will have to give me my cards, then, won't he?' he said. The girl subsided and melted back into the throng, to the groans of her friends.

Jude watched, waiting until the girls near by had drifted away. Then she approached, calm.

'Got a ciggy?' she asked. There was a moment, while he looked her up and down, taking in the black tights, the long legs, the knowing face. Then he reached in his pocket and pulled out a packet of Number Six. She took one, holding it between her teeth, as she had seen Honor Blackman do in *The Avengers*.

'Light?'

He lit a match, and she held his wrist steady while lighting her cigarette, looking at him from under her eyelashes, a gesture copied from a hundred 'B' films. For a second she felt his pulse quicken under her fingers, and she knew she would succeed.

'I don't expect you like the Beatles,' she said.

He shrugged, watching her. 'I'm a rock and roll man myself. I like to dance when I listen to music.'

Jude nodded. 'Me too.'

'You can't move to a band that hasn't got a saxophone,' he said, warming to his subject, 'a good screaming tenor sax solo.' Jude was listening, submissive. 'Listen to Bill Haley,' he instructed. 'He'd be rubbish without old Rudi Pompilli. Those honking solos . . .'

'Yeah. He's good,' Jude said, forcing herself to sound enthusiastic. She had never heard of Rudi Pompilli.

'What's your name?' he asked.

'Francesca,' she said. 'What's yours?'

Bennett and Heather, inexplicably still together, were standing in a street behind the theatre, studying possible means of entry. Bennett and an exhausted-looking girl in a leather coat were eyeing a small window high up in a huge blank wall towering above them.

'If we get on the roof,' Bennett was saying thoughtfully, 'one of us could stand on the other one's shoulders and get in there.' They turned to Heather, who was scuffing the ground with her patent shoes, bored. She wanted to go home. The day was a failure.

'It'll have to be her,' the girl in the leather coat said decisively, her accent suggesting she had not come far today, 'she's the only one small enough to get through the window.'

Heather shook her head. 'Not me,' she said, fearful. 'It's breaking in, isn't it. I'll get arrested.'

Bennett headed towards a row of dustbins lined up against the wall. 'Don't be stupid,' she said. 'Come on!'

And before Heather could object, Bennett had clambered on top of one of the bins, teetered precariously on its lid for a second, and then, with surprising agility, had hauled herself up on to the flat roof above. The leather-coated girl was following eagerly. Bennett peered over the edge at Heather's agonized face below.

'You can't leave me here!' Heather wailed.

Bennett shrugged. 'Up to you. I'm going in there. Meet Ringo.'

Heather scrambled up after them. As she struggled to her feet on the roof, she was in time to see the girl handing something brightly-coloured to Bennett. Heather went to have a look. Bennett was studying some pink-coloured lozenges in her palm.

'Pastilles?' Heather held out her hand. 'Can I have one?'

'Uppers,' said the girl in the leather coat. 'You take two.'

Heather stepped back, shocked. Bennett cheerfully swallowed the pills. 'It's illegal,' said Heather.

The girl looked at her pityingly. 'Where'd she spring from?' she asked Bennett.

'Scotland,' Bennett said.

'Oh,' said the girl, as if that explained everything. Then, turning her attention to the current problem, she eyed Heather thoughtfully. 'You'll have to put your bag down,' she said.

Heather clutched her bag defensively. 'It's got my sanitary whats-its in it,' she said in a hoarse whisper. 'I'm not leaving it anywhere.'

Bennett was peering over the edge of the roof. Other girls were hurrying down the alleyway, looking up, heading towards them. 'If you don't do it now, there won't be another chance,' she said desperately. 'Look! There's thirty-five Paul McCartney fans coming this way!'

Heather dropped her bag. 'I came first in gymnastics,' she told the girl in the leather jacket, brisk. 'Kneel down – hurry up! That's it – now – I get to kneel on your shoulders – then I get my balance –'

Bennett was groaning. 'Forget it . . .'

Heather had one knee pressed into the girl's neck. She was beginning to enjoy herself. She could do this. She was going to get them inside, and she would be the hero of the hour.

Bennett was tugging at her ankle. 'Get down,' she hissed, 'Quick!'

Heather turned, annoyed. Appearing over the edge of the precipice was a policeman's helmet. She staggered to her feet, as the policeman's head appeared, and then his shoulders. He was middle-aged, red in the face with exertion, cursing under his breath. The girl in the leather coat laughed. 'Fat git!' she said. And then she was away, scooting across the flat roof and shinning untidily downwards, out of reach of the policeman.

Bennett peered over the edge. The girl was running away down the street without a backward glance, swerving to avoid more policemen who clattered over the cobblestones catching stray girls and sending them back the way they had come.

The policeman had succeeded in climbing on to the roof. His forehead was beaded with sweat. Bennett and Heather moved closer together. He studied them wearily. He was holding Heather's handbag. 'You should be in school,' he said, 'shouldn't you?'

Jude ground her cigarette out with the heel of her shoe. She could feel his eyes on her, assessing his chances. His name was Malcolm.

'So,' he said, leaning back against the closed door, arms folded. 'You want to meet the Beatles.'

Jude shrugged. 'I'm not bothered,' she said. She made herself look straight at him. 'Pity you're busy,' she said. Behind her she could hear the sound of voices. Other girls were going to come and try their luck. She had to be quick. But not too quick.

'I'm not that busy,' he said. She didn't take her eyes from his face.
'No?'

'Which one do you like, then?'

'John. You look a bit like him.'

'I do?'

'I expect I'm not the first person to say it.'

'You reckon he's the best-looking, then?'

'Let's just say he's the one I'd – you know. He's the one I fancy.'

He looked past her, to where a group of girls were gathered, watching. Then he made a decision. He pushed the bar on the door and suddenly a dark corridor beckoned. 'Come on, then,' he said. 'I can shut this from the inside . . .'

She stepped in. It was suddenly cool. She closed her eyes, faint with relief. She had done it. Malcolm was pushing the door shut, reaching up and bolting it at the top, with a great scraping of rusty metal. Then he turned and grinned at her. He seemed very tall, very grown-up. 'I can't promise you John Lennon,' he said, 'but you'll certainly see some excitement.'

'It's your fault,' Heather said.

Bennett jiggled on her chair, not concentrating. She looked around the room. It was small and windowless, with folding chairs stacked against the walls, a peeling poster of a forgotten pantomime tacked to the door, and a coat stand in one corner. 'I wonder what happened to Cissie,' she said. Her mouth felt very dry. She wished someone would come in and offer them lemonade, but she supposed it was unlikely.

'Have we been arrested?' Heather asked. Two girls, weeping in one corner, began to sob loudly on hearing the question. One of them was quivering under a blanket, being tended to by an amused man in a St John's Ambulance Brigade uniform.

'Shut up,' said Bennett. The two girls were very young, she thought. 'Where are you from?' she asked them.

One of them looked up, her face blotched and made ugly with tears. 'White City,' she said.

'Oh,' said Bennett, wondering where White City was.

'Try not to talk,' said the St John's Ambulance man to the smaller of the girls, holding her shaking hands in his large, comforting ones.

The door opened and a policewoman came in with a tray of tea. She doled out the enamel mugs briskly. 'They've all got sugar in them,' she said.

'Haven't you got anything cold?' Bennett asked. 'Long, cold and wet?' Heather's hand was on her arm, warning her. She looked down, and realized she was twitching. She tried to stop, but found it impossible. She grinned to herself. Funny, really.

'Your mum and dad have been in touch,' the policewoman was saying to Heather. She was young and unsmiling, with a tight perm and a high colour flushing her face and neck. 'They reported you missing, you know.'

Heather was aghast. 'They'll kill me!'

Bennett forced herself to stop fixating on the policewoman's eyebrows. 'How did they know she was missing?' she asked. Her foot, jiggling under the seat, seemed to have a mind of its own.

The policewoman sipped at her own tea. 'Found your diary,' she told Heather.

'You mean – they read it?' Bennett couldn't believe it. 'They read her diary?'

The policewoman nodded. ' "Paul McCartney – today." That's what you wrote, I believe?'

Heather nodded, miserable.

'They read your sodding diary! The bastards!'

'That's enough of that language, young lady.' The policewoman straightened up, and turned her attention to the weeping pair from White City. 'Come on, you two – we're taking you home.'

The larger of the girls, a pale, mousey waif said, 'But will I meet John first?'

The policewoman shook her head. 'No can do. They're busy downstairs, love. Come on.'

The girl broke into fresh sobs, her face a pasty picture of tragic loss.

'I want to see John . . .!' she wailed.

Bennett was still staring at Heather. Funny how large Heather's face suddenly seemed, how sharp every contour, how vivid every mole, every freckle, every scar. 'If the Germans read my diary,' she said, 'I'd bloody kill them. I'd bloody kill them.'

'Language!' The policewoman said again, turning her head towards Bennett, frowning. Odd how every tiny curl of her hair was suddenly, emphatically a curl . . .

Heather began to cry quietly, hiding her face in the sleeve of her jacket, her knees hunched up on the chair, her hair falling across her face. Bennett patted her, sympathetic. And kept on patting.

It was beginning to rain. Cissie felt the coolness on her face with relief. Somehow it served to diminish the memory of the heated panic of the past few hours, to pull the world back into focus. They had failed. They were not going to be extras in the Beatles' film. They were not going to meet the Beatles. They were just part of the huge, howling, chaotic madness that the Beatles were about. They were not special, not important. Her love for George had no significance, other than what it was – the most powerful feeling she had ever had. But it was her feeling, not his. And this was her moment of misery, not his. Somewhere behind her, in the Scala theatre, he was. He just *was*.

She had crossed over the road from the theatre, and now she was in a silent street away from the chaos and the screaming. Here, some pigeons pecked in the gutter, their eyes bright, looking at her sideways. A solitary lorry passed slowly, its driver searching for somewhere to park. The rain began to fall more insistently, and the sky darkened. Suddenly there was a rumbling sound, and Cissie looked up, expecting a storm. Instead, some men began to back out of a nearby doorway, intent on carrying some huge object, manoeuvring it out into the street with cries of 'Steady there!', 'Down a bit!'. The rumbling had been the opening of a large sliding door in the wall next to her. She stood watching the men as they struggled with what appeared to be a large piece of scenery – she had a glimpse of a giant wall of canvas, a painted tree covered with improbably red apples. They struggled down the road with their burden towards the lorry, which had parked in the middle of the road, its engine throbbing, its back gaping open, the driver balanced on the sloping platform, ready to shout instructions.

The rain descended suddenly with a vengeance. Cissie ducked into the doorway, listening to the men's indignant yells as they battled with their cumbersome load in the downpour.

She turned. Ahead of her a darkened passage snaked downwards, out of sight. She thought suddenly of *Alice in Wonderland*. Almost before she could think about it, she had walked away from the teeming rain thundering in the doorway and into the gloom, down the passage ahead. *Down, down, down* . . . Her footsteps echoed in the silence. She half-expected to hear a shout, someone angrily calling her back, demanding to know her business, telling her she was trespassing. But nothing happened, and the only sound was the clip of her footsteps as she headed down the passage.

She reached a junction. Above her head, there was a notice stencilled in paint on the wall, illuminated by a light bulb dangling on a wire: 'SCALA THEATRE STOCKROOM, ACCESS ONLY, TOTTENHAM STREET SUBWAY'. There was an arrow, pointing to the right. Cissie peered into the gloom, and saw another passage, dark except for dim lights dotted along the ceiling. She looked back at the notice, then beyond to where she could still see daylight, and the rain. Then she turned back and hurried off in the direction of the arrow.

He had made a cosy hideaway for himself in here. It was little more than a cupboard, with a tatty armchair, a card table and a transistor radio, a kettle and mugs on a tray, an overflowing ashtray, a copy of the *Daily Mirror* with the Quick Crossword half-finished.

Jude stood in the doorway. 'Very nice,' she said eventually.

Malcolm was behind her. She felt his hands on her waist, pushing her gently into the room.

'Tea?'

'OK.' He had shut the door. Now he moved to the kettle, business-like. Perhaps it was going to be all right. Then he suddenly swerved towards her, holding the kettle, leaning down, his face close to hers.

'I won't be long,' he said. He had her pressed against the sharp edge of the card table, so that her knees were buckling, and he pressed his mouth against hers. She slid her arms round his shoulders and kissed him efficiently, her mouth wide open, her tongue exploring his. She wished he would hurry up. She could do with a cup of tea. His grip on her shoulder became more urgent, and he pressed against her, his mouth moving, until her face felt wet, violated, not her own. She pushed him away.

'Tea,' she said, laughing a little, pleased at her small display of power.

He watched her, his breathing uneven, smiling. 'In a minute,' he said. 'Come here.'

And then he deliberately put the kettle down again, on to the table, and she felt his strong hands pull her up a little, lifting her slightly, so that her feet nearly came off the ground. Resigned, she kissed him again, going through the motions of passion, grabbing his hair and clutching it, as she had seen countless sirens do in the 'X' films she had watched with Bennett, giggling in the stalls of the Regal cinema, having sneaked in through the exit by the ladies' toilets and thus avoiding the ticket kiosk. She would have to do this for a bit longer, and then she could creep away, while he made the tea . . .

He was groaning now, and his hand moved down to her sweater, pressing into her, hurting her. She pulled away. 'You said tea –' but he had forced her mouth back to his, and was holding her tightly, so that she could not move. She tried to kick at his shins with her foot, but she only encountered the leg of the table. Dimly, outside in the corridor, she heard someone sobbing, 'John! I want John! Please . . . I want John . . .'

The voice faded away, and there was only this moment, and Malcolm's hand pulling at her sweater. All right, she thought, all right . . . He had his hand on her breast now, and was pulling at her shirt.

'Just a moment . . .' she whispered. She could control this. She had done this before. She unbuttoned her blouse and tried to relax against him, as his hand reached in and pulled at her bra, forcing the fabric down until his rough fingers found her flesh. He was pushing her down into the armchair. It was difficult to stop him. Greedily his hand pulled at the fabric of her blouse.

'Off . . .' he murmured. 'Come on, take it off . . .'

She giggled a little nervously. He had succeeded in pressing her back into the armchair, so that she was half-sitting, half-lying, her face flushed, her blouse awry, her jumper pushed up under her chin. She thought how stupid this all was, wondered not for the first time why it was all supposed to be so important. To her, it was just rough hands, a struggle, hanging on so that you got what you wanted – a ride home in a car, a packet of fags, whatever . . .

'I don't do that . . .' she murmured, breathing into his neck, nibbling at his ear. This was supposed to turn men into willing slaves, according to her well-thumbed copy of *Forever Amber*. Sure enough he buried his face into her blouse, groaning. She smiled at the ceiling, exultant.

But he was pushing his other hand up her skirt now, pulling at her tights, his expression unseen, his breath on her flesh. She grabbed his hand, determined. 'No,' she said. 'No . . . Not that.'

'Yes,' he said, his voice muffled.

'No. I don't . . .' She was beginning to panic now. His hand was like a rock, gripping her thigh, working its way upwards. Her fingers tried to pull at his, but they were solid, immovable. She must not show fear. She knew that.

'Come on, Malcolm,' she murmured. 'Play the game . . .'

He looked at her suddenly. She recognized that look. Glazed, excited, anonymous. 'Here, then,' he said. And he took her hand and guided it downwards, pressing it against himself. She felt something moving, bulging there, and her heart quickened. 'Come on,' he was saying, 'Come on . . .'

She touched the swelling warmth pressing against her. All right. She would have to do this. It wasn't the first time. She was angry with herself for letting it go this far, but it was all right. She would do this, and then he would get the tea and then she would go. She moved her hand and reached for his zipper. He groaned and writhed a little, his body heavy above her, as her hand finally grasped his penis. All right, you toad, she thought. I'll give you what you want and then I'll bugger off and you'll feel like a prat . . .

But he was moving again, pulling her hand away. She extracted her face from his chest, relieved no longer to have to breathe that combination of sweat, bri-nylon and Old Spice. He moved above her, suddenly determined, stronger, his knees pressing her into the back of the armchair, his breath coming in gasps. She struggled to extricate herself, to pull herself upwards where she might breathe, but she was held there, helpless, unable even to fight, the terrible taste of vomit rising in her mouth.

'Come on,' he was saying, somewhere far above her, his voice muffled, excited. 'Come on, you do this, you know you do this. It won't be the first time . . .'

Incongruously, somewhere in the distance, she heard music.

And he was pushing at her, his groin was in her face, his hand was scrabbling down there, pushing at her, pulling her head down. She tried to gasp, but there was no air, there was no escape, there was only this moment of suffocating defeat, his flesh moving against her mouth, when she had to do what he wanted, when the world went spinning out of control and she had lost the game . . .

The man, stiff in a dark suit, was speaking brightly into the camera. 'While the Fab Four rehearse the next scene for their Running, Jumping and Standing Still film, directed by Dick Lester, backstage here life is imitating art . . .' he paused, frowning. 'No. Cut. Too intellectual. Go again, Brendan. Sorry.'

The weary-looking man squinting into the camera lens peered round for a moment. 'Still running,' he said.

The reporter sighed and began again. 'Pop Scene, Beatles item, take four.'

Bennett had found something in her pocket, and was rustling. The man frowned at her. 'While the Fab Four rehearse the next scene for their Dick Lester −' Bennett had triumphantly produced a crumpled paper bag and had dropped the contents on the floor.

116

'—Their film directed by Dick Lester — sorry —' Bennett was crouched down now, retrieving jelly babies from the floor. She looked up, grinning.

Heather stood to attention, ready for her moment, hair brushed to sleek perfection, lipstick freshly applied, eyes bright. The St John's Ambulance man was perched on a trolley in the corner of the room watching, interested, his arms folded across his chest.

The reporter tried again. 'Beatlemania looks set to make headlines again, as Beatle fans from all over the country converge on their idols. Heather Lewis is one such fan. Where are you from, Heather?'

'Norfolk.' Heather blinked nervously into the eye of the camera.

'Norfolk?' The reporter sounded chirpily interested, casting a conspiratorial eye at the lens. 'That's quite a journey you've made, Heather. And how did you get to London?'

'By train,' said Heather.

'We hitched,' said Bennett at the same time, her mouth full of jelly babies, hidden from the camera, jiggling her leg and chewing, grinning.

Heather froze. 'Train,' she said quickly. 'To Liverpool Street. Then the tube.'

The reporter recovered. 'And which Beatle is your favourite?'

He pushed the microphone under Heather's chin. 'Paul,' she said sheepishly.

'Paul McCartney,' he told the camera, in case there was anyone left in England who was not clear about this. 'And have you seen Mr McCartney today?'

Heather shook her head. 'No.'

The sound of music drifted upwards. The cameraman signalled to the man in the suit to carry on.

'Are you disappointed?'

Heather thought for a moment. This was an important question. 'No,' she said finally. 'Because I know I'll meet him one day.' The man was about to speak again. She carried on. 'I know he'll be really nice,' she said quickly, 'because he's the thoughtful one, always very kind to his fans.' Suddenly, from somewhere inside her, she found courage. She looked straight into the gleaming lens, her voice passionate. 'And if you're watching this, Paul, I'd just like to say on behalf of all Paul fans everywhere that we love you, and we think you're the best-looking boy in the whole universe . . .' The reporter smiled indulgently. Heather's hand gripped the microphone. He tried to tug it away, but she held on grimly. This was her big moment. She was not about to have it sabotaged. 'And if you're ever in Norfolk,' she told the camera earnestly, 'you can be sure of a great welcome from everyone, because everyone in Norfolk loves the Beatles, especially me. Thank you.'

She looked at the man in the suit expectantly. He stared back at her. Then he turned to Bennett, keeping his expression enthusiastic. 'And what about you? What's your name, young lady?'

'Bennett,' she said, her mouth dry and full of jelly babies, 'Susan Bennett.' Her body was fighting to go in ten directions at once and her brain was in overdrive.

'And which of the boys is your fab favourite?'

'Ringo,' she mumbled, looking at her mod shoes. She had a ladder in her tights.

'And why are you here today?' She didn't answer, transfixed by her toes. He tried again. 'Why have you come all the way from Norfolk today, Susan?'

'We didn't come by train,' she said, glowering at Heather. 'We hitched.'

'Right. And you've come to see Ringo.'

Bennett was examining a jelly baby, sticky in her palm, and did not reply.

'Why is he your favourite?' persisted the man, trying still to sound bright and interested. He had been at the theatre all day, his feet were killing him, and he was dying for a snifter.

Bennett thought for a moment, then looked at him. 'He just is,' she said. Heather stepped forward discreetly, and took the glutinous red mess from her hand.

'Oy!' Bennett said, indignant. 'Give that back!'

'OK,' said the man. 'Cut. We'll use the first one. Thanks, girls.'

Heather smiled at him graciously. Bennett had forgotten he was there. She had found another jelly baby.

It was George's voice. Cissie would know it anywhere. It was George, singing a song she did not recognize, something about dancing, his voice plaintive, echoing in the distance somewhere. The music stopped suddenly, then started again. She rounded a corner, stepping carefully past the stacked crates and coiled wires.

Someone was sitting only a few feet away from her. She saw who it was and instantly her whole body was buzzing. It was George Harrison. He was smoking a cigarette, one leg crossed over the other, studying a piece of paper, frowning.

Cissie stood, silent. Above that dark, glossy head resonated the song, eerily loud – George's voice, but not emanating from him, coming from somewhere beyond them both, reverberating across the space. A song about dancing. '*I'm happy just to dance with you . . .*' the voice sang. '*Just to dance with you . . .*' The figure in front of her – George (she repeated the name, astonished, inside her head, for it *was* George) – George mouthed the words, his hand tapping against the silver-grey smoothness of his trouser leg. She thought to herself what long, handsome fingers he had.

Her hand crept to the bag on her shoulder. She reached in and pulled out her bundle of letters. '*Hello George,*' the voice inside her head said, '*Hello, George, I'm the girl from Norfolk with the flying table.*' The voice inside her head was clear, ringing, confident. The girl inside her head took a step forward, then another, crossing the space between them. Yet she stood, paralysed. There he was: a young man, a stranger, absorbed in his work. She was poised, trembling, on the brink. '*Hello, George . . .*'

The music stopped. Cissie had not moved. In the silence, George looked across at her. Time stopped. She had not spoken, but somehow he had heard her and looked up. He was looking at her now. George Harrison was looking at her. This was the moment. It was here. Possibilities shimmered between them.

Then, in that humming, twanging deafening second of silence and communication, a man wearing headphones appeared and, seeing Cissie, said, 'Christ! They're like bleeding ants – get in everywhere.' Stepping into that magic space between Cissie and George, the man began to talk to him, explaining something, waving his hands about, telling him they had to go. George nodded, getting up, unsmiling, listening. The man led him away, still officiously issuing instructions, George engrossed, serious.

Cissie stood, paralysed, holding the bundle of letters, her mouth slightly slack, disbelieving. Then suddenly there was someone standing in front of her. At first she thought he was a policeman, but then she realized this was a different kind of uniform, like the ones the men outside the theatre had been wearing.

'Come on,' he said wearily, taking her arm. 'Out.' He began to march her back along the corridor. She twisted in his grip, hoping for a last glimpse of George, but he had gone. There were only the piles of stacked sets, the tawdry backstage lights, the bored technicians.

She began to cry, propelled down the dark tunnel, hurrying to keep up with the man, hardly able to believe what had just happened, a brilliant moment of magic that hung, suspended, dazzling, in her memory. Nothing would ever be the same again.

On the other side of the street adjacent to the theatre, the doors of a black police van were open, and inside, the drooping bodies of weeping girls were draped over the benches, a small hot cell of intense emotion, presided over by an amused policewoman with her notebook and pencil poised to take names. The man took Cissie across the road and delivered her up.

'This one actually got in,' he told the policewoman, grinning. 'Watch her – she's obviously a bit cleverer than the others . . .'

Cissie stood, dazed, telling the policewoman her name and address, watched by an admiring crowd of girls, voluble in their support of a fellow fan.

'Let her go!' they shouted indignantly. 'You can't arrest her!'

The policewoman said, 'They're not under arrest,' in a tone which hinted that she had already said this several dozen times. She smiled at Cissie in a breezy way. 'Hop in, love,' she said. 'We're taking you to the police station and then we'll phone your mum and dad.'

'No!' Cissie went cold with horror. 'No – it's all right – listen, I'm seventeen, I can get home on my own –'

The policewoman carried on writing in her book, calm. 'We'll check it all at the station, love. In you get.'

Cissie had one leg up inside the van when she heard someone call her name. She turned, hopeful. It was Jude, hanging back on the pavement, half an eye on the police near by, fearfully waving.

'You under arrest?' she called.

Cissie shook her head. 'But I've got to go to the police station –'

The policewoman helped her into the van with a brisk shove. 'Come on, love, tell your friend to come to the station if she wants to talk.' She turned to Jude. 'Vine Street,' she said brightly. 'You can walk it from here.'

Squashed on to a bench in the van, Cissie could see Jude clearly. She seemed to be quivering from head to foot, her mouth red and bruised-looking, her eyes defiant.

'Did you get in?' she asked.

Jude shook her head. 'Did you?'

Cissie hesitated a moment. 'No . . .'

'Anyway I've gone off John,' Jude was saying, her voice harsh. Several girls in the van booed on hearing this. Jude glared at them all, clutching at the grubby sleeves of her sweater with her fingers, agitated. 'They're all prats!' she suddenly shouted, 'poncy prats, that's what they are –'

'Jude . . .!' Cissie was shocked. 'No they're not!'

Jude was backing away, a wild expression on her face, as if she might either burst into laughter or tears. 'Time you grew up and met some real men,' she yelled. 'You don't know you're born!'

'Jude! Jude!' It was Bennett and Heather, accompanied by a policeman. They had heard. Heather's face was streaked with tears. Bennett looked very white, her eyes like dark globes, the pupils enormous, staring out of a pallid face damp with sweat. The policeman pushed them towards the van, and as they clambered on

121

board, they looked out and saw Jude, her face standing out from the crowd, raw with emotion.

'Jude!' Heather called. 'I'm going to be on *Pop Scene!*' Jude stared at her blankly. Cissie held out a hand, but Jude did not see it. She had turned suddenly and melted away into the crowd.

'Shove up, young ladies,' said one of the policemen, 'still room for a couple more!'

Two very small girls, bright-eyed with excitement, climbed on, unrepentant. The doors were slammed shut, and then the van moved off with its cargo of fraught and frustrated girls.

'How will Jude get home?' Heather asked, worried at the separation. To her, the streets of London were a terrifying maze, not to be negotiated alone. Oddly, Edinburgh had never had the same effect.

Bennett shrugged. 'Dunno. Don't care.'

Someone started to sing 'It's A Long Way To Tipperary' in a loud, defiant tone, and Bennett joined in, nudging Heather jubilantly in the ribs when they got to '*Good-bye Piccadilly*', changing it volubly and triumphantly to '*Good-bye* Pig*adilly* . . .' and looking around gleefully for a response from Cissie and not getting one.

Bennett was not to be deflated. 'Come on,' she said, threading her arm companionably through Cissie's as the van lurched noisily round a corner. 'Just think – we're making history! One day you'll be able to tell your grandchildren you went to London to see the Beatles and ended up in police custody!' Her brain buzzed at the thought.

'I'm not going to have grandchildren,' came the tragic reply. 'I'm not going to have children. I'm not going to get married. I'm going to live on my own and think about George.' Another girl in the van cheered at the thought.

'I hate Jude Reynolds,' Cissie said suddenly, savage. 'I hate her.'

Someone began to sing, quietly at first, and then louder as others joined in, more and more, until everyone in the van was swaying, two rows of sad, smiling girls, locked together in unrequited love. '*Imagine I'm in love with you, it's easy 'cos I know . . . I've imagined I'm in love with you, many many many times before . . .*' They sang on, each thinking of their own Beatle, each exuding a deathless longing, a terrible, romantic, unrequited, passionate, desperate desire for someone they would never know. '*It's not like me to pretend. . .*' The van drew up and they lurched forward, laughing now, exultant, shouting, '*I'll get you! I'll get you in the end!*'

The doors were opened. They piled out, defiant and giggling, spirits restored, and were ushered into the dark portals of the police station.

'I'm *ravished*,' said Heather.

'She means famished,' Cissie said.

It had been four hours now. Heather lay balanced along the narrow wooden bench, slowly raising and lowering her perfectly-shaped legs one after the other, like they did in the gym at school, aware she was being admired by a young sergeant behind the reception desk.

Cissie sat hunched forward, chewing on a strand of hair, an action she often performed when bored or nervous. At the moment she was both. It was like waiting for your execution, she thought. She remembered Virginia McKenna in *Carve Her Name with Pride*, preparing to be shot by the Gestapo. She studied the damp poker of sucked hair she had just removed from her mouth. Heroines didn't suck their hair. They offered a tragic profile, an accepting smile, their chins defiant, their necks like swans.

'You two doing exercises?' Bennett was watching Heather's leg-waving, Cissie's neck-stretching, drumming her drumsticks on the bench. 'I can see your knickers, Heath.'

'No you can't.'

'Peach with white spots.'

Heather sat up, pink. Cissie stopped being Virginia McKenna. The desk sergeant returned to his files.

They sat in a row, flattened by their day. Cissie had filed her unbelievable encounter away to be taken out and studied later in the quiet of her bedroom at Brigadoon. It was not a moment to focus on now, here, in this drab, real place. Instead, she talked as she had always talked, her voice sounding unreal, their mundane conversation like the script of a play called *Girls Talking*. She played her part well enough, but she longed to go home, to get this over with, to be alone with George.

'I wonder where Jude is,' Heather looked at the others.

'Probably shagging Brian Epstein,' Bennett said sarcastically.

'Do you think she does?' Cissie asked.

'What?'

It was Cissie's turn to go pink. The other two were looking at her. 'You know. It.'

'Of course she does.' Bennett's voice brooked no argument. 'She's been doing it for years.'

'She says she's been doing it for years,' Cissie corrected. 'I know what she says. But do you think she *does*?'

There was silence for the moment while the three of them pondered the question. Or questions. For each knew that this was not really what was being asked. In their hearts and in their heads they were breathlessly wondering if the others knew what they did. Cissie was convinced she was the only virgin left – except for Heather, of course, who couldn't possibly be doing it with clumsy Ray Broadbent. He wouldn't dare do it with anybody. And she certainly wouldn't be doing it with anyone else. But Bennett . . .? What about all those nights at the Church Youth Club? What about that time on the playing fields, when Bennett had emerged grinning from the gorse bushes, furtively followed by Jim Dones, the assistant from Polston Wood's butcher's?

Heather wondered tensely whether the others knew. Did it show, that she had allowed Ray to go 'fifty' with her in the front room while her parents sat in the living room listening to *Down Your Way*? Her body shrank inwards at the thought. It had been an unpleasant, muddling, shoddy experience. She imagined that Ray must have got some pleasure out of it, since she remembered his flushed face, suffused with a kind of desperate, groaning gratitude as he struggled to button up her blouse in case Mrs Lewis came in and told them off for mussing up the cushions.

'She was the first one to use Tampax,' Bennett volunteered helpfully. 'She was only thirteen. I remember.'

The use of Tampax as opposed to the bulky sanitary towels they had all been given by their mothers had at one time indicated a certain sexual sophistication to their teenage minds: something you had to insert into your body! The intrigue! The mystery! To know that intimate part of you so well that you could poke a tube into it with impunity! But now that Cissie had graduated to Tampax herself, persuaded by Peggy that the insertion of a cardboard tube 'up there' did not signal the end of precious innocence, she was dubious about such a distinction.

'I think it's all talk,' she said, not for the first time. The subject of Jude's sexual experience was a well-worn path down which the three of them frequently meandered. 'I think she's gone seventy-five, but no more.'

'Maybe eighty,' offered Bennett, jiggling her drumsticks.

Heather was silent. She knew what seventy-five was. But what on earth was eighty? It didn't bear thinking about. Opposite, a gaggle of men in blue and white scarves were singing a solemn version of 'Smoke Gets In Your Eyes', swaying together, with the occasional stray clatter of a football rattle earning them a frown from the front desk. Heather eyed them, disgusted. They were all drunk. Their wives would be wondering where they were. She would never let Ray go off like that with his friends for the day . . .

'Hamster alert,' said Bennett.

Ray Broadbent, the subject of Heather's musings, had appeared in the doorway, his face a grey expanse of anxiety.

'Ray!' Heather leapt up, delighted, and ran across the scuffed lino to be caught in his clumsy embrace.

Bennett watched, sardonic, from the bench. 'Rhett Butler eat your heart out,' she murmured. Heather and Ray were being applauded by the men in blue and white, some of whom were making slurping and squelching noises.

'You were on the six o'clock news,' Ray said, his voice quivering with emotion, 'And *About Anglia*. You were brilliant.'

Heather turned, still clutching Ray's arm in a fever of proprietorial pride. 'Bennett! We were on the telly!'

But Ray shook his head. 'No. Just you. It was brilliant. All that stuff about Paul coming to Norfolk. The *Eastern Daily Press* rang

125

your dad. They want to do a bit about you for the paper. They're parking the car.'

'Who – the *Eastern Daily Press*?'

'No – your mum and dad.'

'God,' said Bennett loudly, irritated, and still trying to arrange her brain around orderly thought. 'Old Uncle Tom Cobley and all. Three people to get you home.' She tittered to herself.

Heather glared. 'Where's your family then?' she demanded from the safe haven of Ray's enfolding arm. 'Are they coming to collect you? And where's your precious mother, Cissie Lovelock, when she's needed?'

'She's on her way,' Cissie said defensively. 'The policeman told me.' Cissie moved closer to Bennett. There were times when she wondered why she had any other friends.

'At least I won't be hung, drawn and quartered just for coming to London for the day,' Bennett said.

'No, of course you won't,' said Heather angrily, 'because no one cares. Because your mum isn't coming. Where is she, Bennett? Where is your mum?'

'She's on holiday,' Bennett mumbled, her head down. Cissie's heart sank.

'Holiday!' Heather's voice rose, mocking. 'Holiday! Since when do people get locked up in loony bins for their holiday?'

The dreaded explosion erupted. Bennett flew at Heather with a bellow and began to beat her about the head with her drumsticks, Cissie and Ray struggling to separate them. The sticks clattered to the floor. Bennett's face was grim and white. Her hands were closing round Heather's neck.

'Stop that!' It was the desk sergeant, opening up his desk flap and hurrying across to join in the fray. The Spurs supporters cheered. The girls were pulled forcibly apart, and sent to sit down, a glowering Bennett joining Cissie. Heather, triumphantly equipped with boyfriend, led Ray away to take up intensive embracing positions at the far end of the bench.

The doors swung open mid-kiss, and in a flurry of cries, embraces, and agitation, the Lewises appeared, Mrs Lewis immaculate

126

in a powder-blue suit and matching handbag, dabbing at her face with a small lace handkerchief.

'You naughty girl!' she murmured to the embarrassed blonde head she had pressed to her bosom. 'Mammy's been so worried . . .'

'Excuse me while I puke,' muttered Bennett. Cissie wasn't paying attention. Through the swing doors she could see the Lovelocks approaching. Now, she thought: I get it — the tolerant we-were-young-once acceptance, the silent reproach, the pained, liberal attempt to understand.

She braced herself. Bennett was already on her feet, eager to see Peggy and Mike and be rescued. Cissie looked up. Mike was standing over her, his arms folded. She registered only that he had a streak of grey plaster in his hair, giving him an oddly patrician look, that his face was unusually grim, his stance not one she had seen before.

'You selfish little madam,' he was saying. 'You selfish, self-centred little *bitch*.'

'Mike —' Peggy was behind him, pulling at him, as if she could physically stop the words. He shook her off.

'Do you have any idea,' he continued, implacable, ' — any idea at all about how worried your mother has been about you? She's been sick — she's been physically sick with worry!' He was shouting now. The football fans were watching with glassy-eyed interest. The sergeant was back behind the safety of his desk, evidently thankful that someone was doing his job for him. 'She thought you'd gone for good, you stupid little idiot! She thought you'd run away!'

Cissie looked at the floor, her head throbbing. The humiliation was too much. She had a brief, giddy image of the Lewises listening, agog, of Heather smirking, Ray gawping, Bennett red and silent. And Peggy. Peggy standing there, saying nothing. Nothing.

'I'd like to belt you from here to kingdom come,' Mike's tone was almost conversational now, the words coming fast, saved up through three hours of fuming on the train, articulated over and over again in his head until they emerged sounding like lines from a well-rehearsed play. 'I'd like to knock your block off, but since I'm a civilized man, I won't. I'll just ask you to look your mother in the face and tell her you will never – and I mean never – do anything like this again.'

There was silence. Cissie thought she would die. 'I'm sorry,' she murmured, her lips quivering dangerously. She must not cry. She must not. She must not look at Peggy either. She dare not.

'You think that's enough, do you?' He was demanding. 'You say sorry and then we all forget it and go home, is that it?'

'Mike – stop –'

Peggy had intervened, her face pained. Cissie saw for the first time that Peggy was wearing trousers, and she felt a flash of irritation. Honestly! There was Mrs Lewis looking like something out of Hollywood, and her own mother looked like she'd been gardening, with her dishevelled birds'-nest hair and gloveless, grubby hands.

Mike shook her off. 'No, Peggy. It's got to be said. She can't go on treating us as if we're some minor irritation she has to contend with. We're her parents, for God's sake –'

'You're not,' Cissie said, under her breath.

Mike's face loomed very close to hers. 'What did you say?'

Cissie's heart pounded. 'You heard,' she said. The sheer, sensational terror of being rude to Mike in front of an interested audience egged her on to further bravado. 'You're not my dad and it's none of your business what I do.'

Mike had a hand on her arm now, hurting her. 'You nasty little bitch,' he said, his voice shaking. 'You vicious little –'

'Mike . . .' Peggy's face appeared behind Mike, tense. 'Not now –'

He shook her off. 'After everything I've done,' he said, his eyes never leaving Cissie's, his face flushed a peculiarly livid colour she had never seen before. 'Years. Years of it. Helped you with your homework, gone to the parents' evenings, put up with your bloody music –'

'No one asked you to.' Cissie could hardly believe she was hearing her own voice; was that sulky mumble really her? She could not stop herself. She wanted this to end, this nightmare, public quarrel which no one could win; but she hated him so much it was almost tangible. He had spoilt everything. She had seen George today, it was a memory that would last all of her life, that precious, glittering

128

moment when he had looked at her and everything had been possible. She wanted to savour it, dream it, live it, over and over again. Only now it was ruined in a horrible, chaotic mishmash of argument and confrontation. It was Mike's fault. He had muddied it all, coming here with his angry speeches, trying to act like a dad.

The grip on her arm tightened. 'You're still under-age, my girl,' Mike was saying between clenched teeth, 'and don't you forget it —'

Peggy pulled at him. 'For God's sake!' Her voice was raised, now. 'Leave her alone! The girl went and had an adventure! She went and did something off her own bat for once in her life — I'm glad! I'm telling you I'm glad!'

'She can't speak to me like that,' he said. But he had let go of her arm. She rubbed at it, where his grip had left a burning sensation. 'After everything I've done . . .' His voice trailed away. Peggy would not look at him. No one would look at him. There was an embarrassed silence. He stared at Peggy, hurt. 'You cried on the train,' he said slowly.

Peggy pulled Cissie up from the bench. She put one arm round her daughter, the other round Bennett, her face flushed. 'Oh, shut up, can't you?' she said. She turned to the policeman, who watched them, interested, sucking a pencil. 'Can we go, officer?' she called.

He nodded. 'Be my guest.'

'This way,' Peggy said to the two girls, her eyes avoiding Mike's. 'We can get a taxi to the station . . .'

The train rattled evenly through the dark, flat fields, a bright snake on the silent landscape. In the second-class carriage Bennett lay flat out, spread across three seats, face up, mouth open, making small snoring noises, her eyes closed, her secret smile hinting at happy dreams.

Cissie stared out at the blackness flashing past. Behind her, reflected in the glass of the window pane, she could see Peggy and Mike, sitting stiffly opposite each other with heads averted. They had hardly spoken since Peggy's outburst at the police station.

Cissie looked down at the letter she was holding. '*Dear Cecilia*,' it read, '*Thanks for your letter. George is very busy learning his lines for the film. I expect you have read about it. We've had a lot of rain here, but I expect it's the same where you are. George sends his love. Love from Louise Harrison.*'

Cissie studied her own face, pale, dramatic, her eyes dark hollows in the shadowy glass. Cissie Lovelock. The girl from Norfolk. The boy from Liverpool. *George sends his love.* Eventually she fell asleep, a half-heard, half-remembered song about dancing vibrating in her brain. Finally she dreamed a dream, a fleeting picture of that glossy head bent in thought, those white fingers holding the paper, the slight frown across his forehead, the glossy sheen of his suit, and him looking up and saying, 'Hello. I always knew we'd meet one day.'

CHAPTER FIVE

If I Needed Someone – 1966

IT WAS ONLY five o'clock and already the sky was dark, with flakes of snow drifting down in little eddies, swirling away again as gusts of wind circled Brigadoon. Mike had just come in, rubbing his hands together and stamping his feet, his face tinged blue with the cold.

'That's that,' he announced. 'She's finally installed.'

'Is she all right?'

'Last seen smoking a Woodbine and telling her sister how the world could be put to rights if only Harold Wilson would consult her.'

Peggy was making tea and humming tunes from *West Side Story*. Mike settled himself in Mill's chair by the fire in the living room, and Toulouse jumped on his lap. He had just delivered his mother to her sister's in Brundall for the night, and now he could relax. He stroked Toulouse's ears and grinned to himself at the picture of Mill, formidable in a bucket-shaped green mohair hat, grumbling in the tiny modern bungalow where he had left her.

'Call this a house?' She demanded of her sister, who was, fortunately, deaf. 'Call this a house? With no stairs?' The sister had merely smiled hospitably and made another pot of tea. Mike could relax. Mill was going to be all right.

Peggy came in with a tea tray, a cigarette dangling from her lips. 'Stop worrying,' she said, shifting a reluctant tabby cat and depositing the tray on the rug in front of the hearth. 'It'll do her good to sleep somewhere else for a change.'

'All this for madam's birthday,' Mike observed wryly.

'You're only nineteen once.'

Mike recognized the defensive tone and changed the subject. 'Does Oliver know what time we're arriving?'

'Of course he does. I thought you'd be pleased.'

'About what?'

Peggy was sitting on the rug, her legs curled up under her, pouring the tea into odd, chipped cups. She was wearing one of Mike's old sweaters, a stained black skirt with an uneven hem, and ballet shoes. She looked at her husband reproachfully and handed him his tea. 'About Cissie. That she actually *wants* to have a birthday party.'

They had had this conversation before. 'I am pleased. Did I say I wasn't?'

Peggy had pulled a packet of cigarettes out of her skirt pocket and, tearing a strip of newspaper from the discarded *Daily Mirror* under Mike's seat, she leaned towards the fire and held the taper into the flames, waiting until the fire leapt on to the paper and consumed half of it in a great plume before lighting her cigarette.

'You'll set your hair on fire one of these days.' Mike was watching her, affectionate, exasperated.

She stayed where she was, hugging her knees, staring into the fire, her hair burnished by the light of the flames. 'She's invited all her friends from the Tech.'

'I know.'

'Do you think they'll come?'

Mike laughed. 'Of course they'll come. A bunch of red-blooded young blokes, a house with no parents in it – and she asks if they'll come!'

'Only, I'm worried for her. She'd be so upset if it was a flop.'

'I'd be upset if it was a flop,' Mike observed dryly. 'Being sent out of my own house so that a bunch of teenagers can have a private orgy –'

Peggy looked at him, pained. 'You think we shouldn't go?'

He groaned theatrically. 'God, woman!' An indulgent hand reached out and rearranged a tendril of red hair. 'Three weeks she nags me to get out of the house for the brat's birthday, and now she's having second thoughts!'

Peggy stared at him, not really listening. 'Do you think – you know – do you think Cissie's . . .' she let the question hang there in the smoky air, unspoken. It was the sex question. It always made Mike uncomfortable. He didn't like to think about Cissie and sex, it told him too many things about himself – about how middle-aged he was becoming, about how his youth had gone . . .

He shrugged with a nonchalance he did not feel. 'Who knows?' he said. 'Your guess is as good as mine. But we can't cancel the weekend just because you have the vaguest suspicion this might be the eve of your daughter's –' he looked suddenly furtive and lowered his voice, twirling an imaginary moustache like a music hall villain, ' – deflowering.'

Peggy stared at him, the very suggestion making her anxious.

'I was joking!' he exclaimed. Peggy did not smile, caught up in some worrisome fantasy about Cissie and the loss of her virginity. 'Where is she?' Mike asked, to restore the atmosphere. 'Our Little Miss Party Girl?'

'Maybe she's already slept with someone.' Peggy sipped her tea, thoughtful. 'She's always talking about this boy at college – Dave Someone-or-Other.'

'Well I hope she found out his surname before they did it,' Mike said.

Peggy seemed suddenly to hear his last question, and looked up at him. 'I don't know where she is,' she said. 'She was up in her room, and then she went outside.'

'In this weather?'

'She wasn't wearing her coat. I thought she was going to get some coal in, or feed the chickens, or something.' She stared at Mike, her face anxious.

He sighed and pulled himself out of the lumpy depths of Mill's armchair, pushing a grumbling Toulouse on to the floor. 'You want me to go and look?'

Peggy shook her head. 'No – you go up and finish packing your things. I've done mine. I'll give her a shout.'

Peggy carried the tea things back into the kitchen, Toulouse at her heels. She pulled on Mike's old mac hanging from a peg on the back door, and struggled outside, in the teeth of the wind. She stood in the square of light cast from the kitchen and called, her voice lost in the clamour of groaning trees, a bucket rolling around the yard, the wind screaming round the corners. Beyond the garden, the cabbage fields were cloaked in the deep blackness of a winter night, chill and invisible beyond the rustling hedge.

Peggy went back inside, worried.

'Mike!' She called him, standing at the foot of the stairs, hugging the mac round her. He came down.

'I can't see her out there,' she said.

'She's not in her room – I checked,' he said. 'She's left the radio on.' They looked at each other. 'I'll get my coat,' he said.

Outside, the cold had taken hold, gripping everything with icy fingers. Together they searched, staring into the beam of light from Mike's torch, blinking away wind-induced tears in the bitter blast.

They had disturbed the chickens, who complained from their perches, bodies fluffed out against the cold. They had searched Mike's shed, peering behind the large, dark shapes of his sculptures in the hope they might find Cissie crouching inexplicably there; but there was nothing, just the muted scurrying of mice making for the shadows, and the clatter of the wind outside, as it turned the stray bucket over and over in the yard.

They were beginning to get anxious now, each trying not to show it to the other, shouting to one another over the gale in what they hoped were studiedly calm voices.

'Perhaps she went to see Bennett . . .'

'Her bicycle's still in the shed.'

'What about the outside lav?'

'I looked there. The potting shed?'

'Did that . . .'

They paused finally, tense and breathless, under the light from Cissie's bedroom window. Helplessly they stared around them, as if inspiration might come out of the shadows on a gust of January wind.

'She wouldn't be in the cabbage field, would she?' Mike ventured. 'Surely not in this weather –'

They headed off down the muddy garden, Peggy's shoes squelching in the clay. Mike gallantly held back the prickly tentacles of the hedge so that Peggy could struggle through, and then followed her, wincing as a thorn embedded itself in his trouser leg. They stood, disorientated in the darkness for a moment, balanced on a muddy furrow, clutching each other. Then Mike shone his torch carefully to the left of him, and they peered after the light, squinting, hopeful.

'Look —' Peggy pointed, 'over there — by the hedge, further along.'

They both saw it, then — a small flame, flickering defiantly in the blackness, under the hedge, and a crouching figure, face invisible. They struggled towards it, the torch beam wavering as Mike negotiated the ditch on the edge of the field, occasionally plunging a wet foot into the mire.

Finally, panting, faces wet with sleet, they reached Cissie. She was kneeling in the mud, sobbing, her wet, shaking hands struggling to light matches from a giant kitchen-size box of Ship matches she had evidently taken from the kitchen.

'What the hell . . .?' Mike demanded, his voice disappearing into the fields with the wind. Peggy nudged him sharply and bent over Cissie, two wet red heads together. Blinking in the wavering torch light, she squinted over her daughter's shoulder, struggling to see what she was doing. On the ground were several scorched pictures, and Cissie was struggling, one hand cupped over the other, to keep alight a small flame as she burned another picture. Peggy pulled the torch away from Mike and peered more closely. The pictures were of George Harrison. For a moment Cissie was successful, and the picture she was holding began to curl and blacken at the edges, George's head surrounded by a halo of charred paper, and then the flame ate into his face, consuming his eyes, eating into his grin, before damply dying.

'Cissie . . .'

She turned her head then, and her face was stark white in the torch light, her eyes dazzled, her mouth drawn back in a strange half-gasp, half-sob. 'It's George.' Peggy heard her strangled voice above the wind, syllables swallowed up in the storm-tossed din.

'George?' She heard Mike turn away, voice full of muted fury. 'Dear God . . .!'

Cissie was still kneeling, her hair wetly plastered to her cheeks. She held out the crumpled pictures mutely, as if in explanation.

Peggy took them, upset, despairing. 'What is it, Cissie?' She reached out and touched Cissie's thin shoulder, feeling it shivering through the soaking wool of her jumper. As if in reply, the figure crumpled suddenly, creasing up in the middle as if someone had kicked her in the stomach.

'George . . . married!' Her daughter's voice wailed through the wind like a banshee. 'George . . . married!' For a moment Peggy almost laughed, so great was her surprise and relief. Was that all? Careful to keep her face composed, she looked down at the bundle of paper in her wet palm. The sleet was gradually reducing the images of George's smiling face to a grey soggy mass, features distorted and disappearing.

'Come on,' she said, kindly. Cissie did not hear, kneeling up in the mud, her face buried in her hands, looking for all the world, as Mike would tell an incredulous Oliver later that night, like an early Christian martyr awaiting execution.

It was Mike who took control then. Without a word he leaned across Peggy and pulled Cissie roughly to her feet. 'Inside!' He shouted above the wind. Dumbly she followed him, sliding across the sludge of the cabbage field in his wake, helpless with grief. Peggy followed, wet and depressed.

Finally they stood, dishevelled, in the warmth of the kitchen, an oddly quiet place after the racket of the storm. Still quivering, Cissie dislodged a warm, sleeping cat from its resting place on the stove, and, lifting the heavy black plate, she stuffed the rest of her pictures of George into the flames. Mike and Peggy watched, silent. Cissie remained with her back to them, head bowed over the stove, not speaking. After a moment, Peggy crossed to the kettle and began to fill it under the tap at the sink. Mike leaned over and took down his pipe from the window sill.

'Who did he marry?' He made the mistake of asking, as he attempted to light his pipe from the damp box of matches.

Peggy looked at him, pained. Cissie still had not moved. 'Patti Boyd,' Peggy told him. 'The girl he's been going out with. The model. The one in *A Hard Day's Night*.'

'So – it was on the cards then?' He was genuinely trying to make sense of Cissie's explosion of grief. 'They were engaged, were they?'

Peggy lit the gas under the kettle. 'We all need a nice cup of tea,' she said. She looked anxiously at her daughter's bowed head. 'Party in a few hours!' she said brightly. 'That should take your mind off –'

This was the wrong thing to say. With an anguished sob Cissie flew up the stairs, a clumsy cyclone of emotion, thundering upwards with such anger that the banister creaked and shook. Upstairs, the baby woke with a whimper. Footsteps could be heard pounding along the landing, and then there was the loud slam of Cissie's bedroom door. Susie began to cry from her cot with more determination, fully awake and indignant.

Peggy looked at Mike. 'Don't,' he said, 'don't say it.'

'Perhaps we shouldn't go.'

Mike sighed, a pained, weary sound. He slumped at the kitchen table, pipe still unlit. 'Peggy,' he said, finally. 'Don't do this. We've planned to see Oliver. He's expecting us. He's looking forward to it. I'm looking forward to it.'

Peggy was rather too busy with the teapot, her face not visible. 'She's very upset. Go and see to the baby, will you?'

Mike tried to keep his voice even, reasonable. 'Some ruddy pop star's got married, Peg. It's hardly Hiroshima, is it.'

'I think you and I both know that George Harrison is hardly "some ruddy pop star".' Her voice was cold.

He got up and crossed the room, standing behind her, rubbing her shoulders. For a moment she remained tense, and then he felt her yielding, leaning back slightly. He kissed the back of her neck. 'She's eighteen . . .' he said.

'Nineteen.' She had stopped fiddling with the tea caddy and stood, her head leaning back against his chest. All was quiet upstairs, Susie had gone back to sleep. 'And I thought this was all behind her . . .'

'So did I. She seemed to have grown up all of a sudden.'

'You don't think – could she be *ill*, do you think?'

They pondered the question silently, standing together, locked in thought, remembering the times over the past year when Cissie had seemed alive, vibrant. She had failed her A levels at school, and had gone reluctantly to the local college, where suddenly she had blossomed. George Harrison was mentioned less, the Beatles still dominated but seemed to have settled in a position somewhere in her life between clothes and French essays. They had both thought the future held more hopeful prospects for Cissie. And now this . . .

There was a sudden commotion at the back door, causing them to pull apart, surprised, and Bennett appeared, a dripping figure in a sou'wester, long PVC mac and wellingtons. She gesticulated through the glass. She was going to put her bike in the chicken shed. Peggy straightened up, smiled and waved.

'You're early,' Mike mouthed, pointing at his watch.

Bennett opened the door, and an icy blast swept in. 'I heard it on the radio,' she panted, rain from the brim of her hat dripping on to the lino, 'about George and Patti. Thought I'd better get over here.' And she was gone again, ducking into the darkness, clutching her bicycle. Peggy and Mike exchanged a relieved look.

'Susan Bennett, Angel of Mercy,' he said. 'I'm going up to pack.'

Dear Mrs Harrison, she wrote, *I know it's not my turn to write, but I've just heard about George and Patti on the News. I've never said anything to you about Patti before, because I know it isn't really any of my business. I'm sure she's a very nice girl. She must be, if George likes her. She's very pretty and I'm sure she made a beautiful bride. Please send George my very best wishes for the future. I hope he will be very happy. I'm afraid I won't be able to write to you any more because I have unexpectedly been offered a job in Australia. Thank you for writing to me for so long, I have really enjoyed your letters. Best wishes –*

She paused, and stared at her scrawled handwriting. This was not what she wanted to say. She wanted to tell Mrs Harrison that it was over, that there was no point in writing any more, because George was lost to them both. She frowned at herself, depressed by her own cowardice. She didn't even have the guts to tell Mrs Harrison how she really felt — not even dear Mrs Harrison, who had written her those cheery letters, scribbled on the backs of old Christmas cards, telling her tales of Liverpool, of tangoing with John in the kitchen at Macket's Lane, of her daughter in America, of George's latest phone call. She should have read the signs: the gradual appearance of Patti's name in the letters: 'went with George and Patti to a film première', 'saw Patti in London', 'went shopping with Patti' . . . Then there had been the letters from the bungalow George had bought his mother. 'Patti is here with me', she had written once; and another time: 'I'm sitting in the garden with Patti'. Patti had been there all the time. *All the time.* Cissie thought there was no one in the world she hated as much as Patti Boyd at that moment: Patti Boyd, with her perfect flick-ups and her goofy smile and her pale, slim body in its flawlessly fashionable clothes, and her infinite, impeccably shapely legs. Patti Boyd. Patti Harrison. *George Harrison s'est marié avec Patti Boyd.*

She realized that someone was standing in the doorway of her bedroom, observing her silently. She turned her head, not surprised to see Bennett standing there, resplendent in a tubular maroon sweater dress that did not flatter her. She was holding a bottle of vodka. Behind her, the sound of *Rubber Soul* floated up the stairs. John Lennon was singing 'Norwegian Wood'.

'You going to stay up here all night?' she asked.

Cissie did not reply, turning her head away. She was spread out across the bed, still wearing the jeans she had worn in the cabbage field, the mud now encrusted and flaking off on to the candlewick bedspread. Toulouse was lying with his head on Cissie's legs, his bright eyes on Bennett, watchful.

'Party's warming up,' Bennett said. 'That lot from the King's Head have just turned up. And Barney's here. And Carol.'

'Good,' said Cissie, folding up her letter, her face invisible behind a curtain of hair. 'They can all have a good time then, can't they.'

There was a creak as Bennett plonked herself on the end of the bed, causing it to shift and sag. Cissie heard her unscrewing the cap of the vodka bottle.

'Swig?'

'No thanks.'

Bennett ignored the torn wallpaper, where pictures of George had been ripped from the walls. Instead, she studied a purple dress hanging on the door of the wardrobe. 'That your party gear? Very nice. Did Peggy make it?'

'I'm not coming to the party, Bennett. Why don't you just piss off downstairs?'

She heard Bennett strike a match and turned, curious. 'I thought cigarettes made you sick.'

'They do. This isn't an ordinary cigarette.' She inhaled noisily, her eyes watering. Cissie watched her, interested in spite of herself.

'You mean it's cannabis?'

Bennett shook her head. 'Marijuana. M. J.' She took another noisy toke, self-satisfied, grinning. 'The old Mary Jane.'

'You'll end up on heroin.' Cissie was sitting up now, cross-legged and red-eyed, the lavender-coloured sheet of note paper still in her hand.

Bennett snorted. ''Course I won't! Spotty Herbert's been smoking it for a year. You think he's a heroin addict?'

Cissie absorbed this information with amazement. 'Herbert Pegram smokes that stuff?'

Bennett nodded. 'Gets it off some bloke in Acle. He gets it off someone up London.' Spotty Herbert was the pudding-faced boy from Pegrams Dairy who helped his dad with the milk round. He was famed for his unrestrained dancing style at the Friday night Methodist youth club, which Bennett was occasionally forced to attend by her bright-eyed foster parents. Cissie wondered fleetingly if it was marijuana that caused him to dance like a demented dragonfly.

Bennett offered her the ratty-looking cigarette. After a moment Cissie took it, stared at it, then put it to her lips. 'Will I pass out?' she asked.

Bennett grinned. 'Have I?'

'The difference,' said Cissie, inhaling and trying not to choke, 'is that I *want* to.' The smoke was sweet, rather sickly.

Bennett was swigging vodka. 'I've got some news,' she said. Cissie drew on the damp end of the thing again, waiting for the top of her head to blow off. Instead she felt light-headed, as if she could lie back and float away. It's because I'm unhappy, she told herself. My brain wants to escape.

'I'm pregnant,' Bennett said. She was looking at Cissie over the rim of the vodka bottle, watching for her reaction.

Her eyes full of smoke, Cissie blinked at her. 'Pregnant?' she repeated stupidly. 'As in having a baby?'

Bennett nodded. She handed Cissie the bottle and retrieved the joint for herself. 'Three months, nearly. Sick as a dog every morning.'

Cissie was still staring, nonplussed. She had no idea what she was supposed to say. There seemed to be no rules governing this conversation. Bennett was exhaling smoke in a white plume, trying to make smoke rings. Cissie took a swig of vodka. It tasted as if it ought to be petrol, she thought.

'Aren't you going to say anything?' Bennett leaned back on the bed. Toulouse wriggled across the counterpane to rest his head on her belly. Bennett stroked his head. 'See?' she said. 'The dog knows. They always know.'

'What do you want me to say?' Cissie could feel her face becoming warm and hated herself inwardly. Why did she always blush at the very moment when it was the last thing she ought to be doing?

Bennett shrugged, affecting indifference. 'I dunno. Congratulations?'

'Have you told the Germans?'

'You're joking!' Bennett snorted. 'They'd send me to a nunnery! Or a home for unmarried mothers.' She stared ahead of her for a moment, her face blank, causing Cissie to realize then that Bennett was suffering. 'Ve haf vays off making you abort . . .' she said slowly, unsmiling, in her mock-German accent. Under the veneer of unconcern, she was scared.

'What are you going to do?'

Bennett looked at her. 'I'm going to have the baby.'

'What – you mean – have it adopted?'

Bennett shook her head. 'I'm going to keep it.'

'The Germans will never let you.'

Bennett handed the joint again, calm. 'The Germans can go and stuff themselves, then, can't they.' She eyed Cissie, mischievous. 'Aren't you even going to ask me who the father is?'

Cissie's head was swimming, overloaded with stimulants and sensational information. 'I don't know. Is it Freddy?'

Bennett snorted again. ''Course it's Freddy! You think I'm knocking off some other bloke as well? A one-man woman, that's me.'

Freddy Lemon was the assistant manager at the cinema, a pasty-faced, stoop-shouldered man in his thirties with startled eyes and a stammer. He was married. Cissie had never understood what Bennett saw in him. He never seemed to say anything when they met, dwarfed by Bennett's loud guffaw and overwhelming stature, always standing back, glancing furtively over his shoulder as if he expected his wife to appear like an avenging angel out of the shadow of the one-and-nines.

'He's taken it very well, all things considered,' Bennett was saying. Cissie stared at her. Bennett was slipping away.

'What things?'

'Pardon?'

'Considering all what things?' She was overwhelmed by this sudden desire to hurt her friend in some way, to slap her, to wake her up, or if she couldn't do that (which of course she couldn't) then to injure her with words.

Bennett stroked Toulouse's ears vigorously. 'He says he'll pay me some money. Put me in a bedsit. You know. Pay for the baby.'

Cissie's head swam. Bennett was becoming more intangible by the minute. She took another swig of vodka.

'Of course he would only be able to see me at work. And then Tuesday nights, when Sandra was doing the late shift.' Sandra was Freddy Lemon's wife, who worked in a handbag factory. Bennett's voice droned on, resigned, as if she was reciting an extract from

Leviticus at one of the Jermyn's interminable Bible-reading sessions. 'He tries to phone me at home, but I have to be careful. The Führer answered the phone once and was dead suspicious. You'd have thought I'd got blimmin' Fidel Castro ringing me up. He said he'd try and come to the doctor's with me but it's difficult with sergeant-major Sandra behind him every five minutes . . .'

Her voice faded away. Her mouth was still moving. She was still speaking, waving the joint about as she explained something, a frown on her forehead, as if the situation puzzled her. Cissie was silent, getting drunk and dispirited. Bennett was slipping away, with all this talk of secret meetings, telephone trysts, broken promises. And Freddy Lemon looked nothing like Ringo Starr: he was boring and middle-aged. Cissie could not understand it. First Jude lost, now Bennett. First John married, then Ringo. Then George . . .

Her mind slid away from the present and lighted as it so often did on a face from the past: Jude. She had disappeared that night in London and had never been heard from since; no phone call, no letter, nothing. Just an ominous, tantalizing silence. And Heather – she might just as well have disappeared. She had left school with mediocre A levels and had gone on to attend a private secretarial college, where she was required to dress neatly in a pleated skirt and white blouse and learn something mysterious called Pitman's. From then on she had slipped out of Cissie's life almost completely, apart from occasional embarrassed, unlooked-for encounters in the bou-tiques of Norwich. They had met only a few weeks previously, in Saxone's, among the shoes in the Size Five Sale Rack, and Cissie, eager to escape and backing towards the door, had politely invited Heather to her birthday party, safe in the knowledge that this strange, distant, post-school Heather would not come.

Bennett had stopped talking. Cissie slid off the bed and stood up, surprised at how difficult this was. Pulling off her jeans and sweater, she lifted the purple dress from its hanger. Bennett watched, impass-ive. Cissie pulled it over her head, losing herself in its soft, dark folds for a moment and then emerging, struggling into the sleeves. She stood, swaying slightly, staring at her reflection in the dressing-table mirror. A startled face looked back, a skinny figure in the knee-length 'mod' dress, with its Peter Pan collar, its modest three buttons at the neck. 'Good.' Bennett nodded, approving, her voice distorted by the neck of the vodka bottle, from which she was drinking, so that she sounded as if she were speaking from the bottom of the sea. Unsteadily, Cissie sat down at the mirror and began to glue on her eyelashes.

'I wonder what happened to Jude,' she said.

Cissie did not reply. There was no need. The question had been asked a hundred times before, and they had no answer. These days, they did not ask it so often.

'Maybe she'll turn up tonight, out of the blue,' Bennett said, her tone unconvincing. 'You've left the corner unstuck. By your nose. The left one.'

Downstairs, they heard the sound of breaking glass. Bennett crossed to the window and opened it, tossing the dog-end out into the swirling sleet. She leaned out for a moment, squinting into the flurries of snow. 'Loads of cars out here,' she said, her voice floating back into the warmth of the room on a gust of freezing wind. 'Someone's parked on the verge and knocked over Mike's statue.' Cissie joined her at the window, eyelashes firmly in place. Sure enough, Mike's bulbous stone homage to Leonard Bernstein ('Looks like a large baked bean,' Mill had remarked at the unveiling) was leaning drunkenly at an angle in the settling snow, nestling up to the bonnet of a Ford Escort, with several scooters propped against it. A car was pulling in behind, and several people fell out, screaming with laughter, into the snow, disappearing into a drift by the front hedge.

'He'll kill me,' Cissie said dolefully. Bennett pulled her inside and shut the window.

'I doubt it,' she said. 'He never tells you off about anything. Not really.' She was thinking about the Jermyns. They never exactly appeared to be angry, but seemed to hover in a state of permanent disappointment over the conduct of their longest-serving foster child, like small birds who had found a cuckoo in the nest and couldn't think why they found it difficult to love. God alone knew what they would make of her latest misdemeanour. She grinned bleakly to herself. Maybe even God didn't know this time . . .

Cissie was staring blankly up at the ceiling, from where George looked down, his expression benign. She hadn't thought to remove the pictures from the ceiling.

The sound of Rufus Thomas blasted up the stairs suddenly, and someone below gave a whoop of approval. This seemed to galvanize Cissie. 'I hope they're dancing in the front room,' she said. 'That's what we planned. Dancing in the front room, drinking in the kitchen —'

'— Sex in the living room,' Bennett supplied helpfully. She held open the door. 'Shall we?' Together, they made a dignified if drunken descent towards the noise. 'Open your mouth,' said Bennett, as they reached the bottom.

'Why?'

Bennett grinned. 'Just do it!'

Cissie obeyed. Bennett was holding the vodka bottle to her mouth. 'Swallow!'

She did, feeling something go down her throat. 'What was it?' she asked.

'Dexy.'

'Oh.' She tried to sound as if this was not of consequence. Be cool at all times. Bennett was rather keen on drugs, she mused. 'Will I go mad now?'

Bennett led her into the living room, past throngs of strangers crammed into the kitchen. 'If you do I'll go madder. I've had three. Plus my mum's in the loony bin.' She squinted back at a crowd of leather-coated, stone-faced young men crowding in the back door. 'Blimey! The Spixworth Faces!'

Cissie turned to look. The Spixworth Faces were infamous. Dark stories of their dirty deeds were repeated with awe by lesser mods in Norwich cafes. Bennett was impressed. 'Fancy having them in your house!' she breathed.

Cissie was more realistic. 'We must be the only party tonight,' she said, anxious. 'That means we'll get *everyone* . . .'

Ahead, the living room was completely dark and impenetrable,

145

the hubbub of voices competing with the urgent throb of soul music from the adjacent room. Someone sidled past, feet crunching on broken glass, caressing Cissie's thigh as he went. Disconcerted, she turned to see a tall mod in a long pale blue leather coat disappearing in the direction of the dancing.

'Come on,' she said to Bennett, still half-crazy with despair over George. 'Watch me. I'm going to get off with that bloke. The Ace Face.'

'I wouldn't if I were –'

But Cissie had already threaded her way into the front room, where the sound of the Miracles boomed out above the bobbing heads of intense dancers. She squinted into the darkness. She hardly recognized anyone. Across the room she could see the pale blue coat. He was leaning against the wall, surrounded by his acolytes, chewing and staring out at the throng. It was now or never. She crossed over to him.

'Hello,' she said.

He seemed to look at her from a great height. He had cold, bright blue eyes, and a pale scar under his chin. 'Who are you?' he asked. She recognized the accent, it was so like Jude's, the flat vowels, the nasal Norfolk intonation.

'Cissie. It's my party.' She was aware suddenly of her own voice, sounding oddly posh.

He studied her, interested. 'Do I know you?' he asked.

She shrugged, her befuddled senses making her confident. 'Does it matter?'

He was half-smiling at her, making some kind of assessment, calculating. She noticed he had fine, pale, downy hairs on his cheeks, and pale, gingery lashes. There was something alien about him, something dangerous and exciting.

'Dance.' It was a command rather than a request. She followed him into the middle of the gyrating throng and began to move, relieved that she at least knew how to dance. She would not shame him by doing last month's steps; she prided herself on keeping up to date, studying how they danced on pop shows on TV, practising endlessly in front of her mirror.

Smokey Robinson was singing 'Going To A Go-Go', and the mod was doing his minimal footwork, eyes fixed, bored, on some invisible spot on the wall, as if he were dancing alone. It didn't matter. What mattered was that Cissie knew that just for a moment, a small, bright moment, she was with the Ace Face of Spixworth, and everyone was watching. They would talk about it in the Tech common room on Monday, and heads would swivel when she walked by.

'You like Motown?' she asked nervously, above the noise.

He shrugged. 'Smokey writes good pop songs, but the real soul's on labels like Sue.' She smiled, uncomprehending. 'Everything on the British Sue label's really ream,' he added.

'The British Sue label? Is there another one?'

He looked down at her pityingly. 'American Sue,' he said, as if only a moron would have to ask the question. 'Mostly dross. They put out some good stuff, I suppose. In fact some of it came out on Sue over here. But the good stuff's on the red and yellow UK label.' He had almost forgotten her presence. 'Funny,' he mused, 'that red and yellow colour scheme . . .'

'Is it?' She was determined to keep up, to keep a foothold on this obscure, one-sided conversation.

'The Pye R and B label's red and yellow as well,' he said. 'And that's another great label. Both yellow and red labels.'

Cissie smiled up at him, murmuring a suitable sound of interested surprise at this observation. How on earth did boys manage to make music so *boring*?

The song ended. He pulled her towards him for a moment and smiled down at her, showing very white teeth.

'Drink?'

She followed him through the dark mass of bodies into the kitchen, aware that Bennett was watching, agog. She smiled to herself. This was easy. She could have anyone she wanted.

They had arrived at the kitchen table, which was a jumble of spilt wine, dirty glasses, cigarette ends and half-empty bottles. He found two abandoned glasses and pulled a small bottle of Scotch from his pocket. 'You from London?' he asked, pouring some of the whisky into each glass. Before she could reply there was the sound of loud laughter, a hostile voice, someone speaking apologetically, another hoot of unsympathetic laughter.

She saw, then. Standing in the doorway, his chin up, was Peter the fairy man from the village. Her head spun. What on earth was a Village Visionary doing here, now, of all places, of all times? She had a sudden mad intuition that her mother had somehow conjured him up, but even as she thought it she realized it could not be true; for Peter the fairy man was in trouble. He was surrounded by a gang of boys that Cissie did not recognize. They looked like rugby players, all with the same beefy necks and broad shoulders, the same braying laughter and overbearing *bonhomie*. One of them was trying to pull Peter inside.

'Come on,' he was saying. 'One little drinkie-poo. Won't kill you.'

'I'm teetotal,' Peter the fairy man was saying, his voice high and desperate.

'You a poof?' Another suddenly moved in close, peering into Peter's eyes as though he might find the answer there. 'You a shirt-lifter?' He tweaked, grinning, at Peter's goatee beard.

Suddenly Peter saw Cissie and his face brightened. 'Cissie!' he called, his voice louder than usual. 'Cissie! It's me! I thought it was one of our seance nights –'

'No,' she said, embarrassed. 'Not tonight.'

The rugby players were leaning in towards Peter now, oppressively close, arms around his shoulders.

'Is your mother in?' he asked, his frightened eyes never leaving her face. Beads of sweat were beginning to mingle on his brow with the melting snow dripping from his cap.

Cissie watched as the men jostled him. Suddenly they had lifted him up, with a great shout of triumph. For a second she saw his terrified face heading for the ceiling, then he disappeared again, dropping out of sight amid the beefy arms and legs of his oppressors.

'No,' she said, turning desperately to look for the mod in the pale blue coat, who had drifted away, bored. 'No. My mother's gone to London.'

She heard a whoop, then another, then the slam of the back door as the activity in the kitchen doorway progressed outside and down the garden path. She guessed they were going to throw Peter the fairy man into the cabbage field, or into the pond on the corner, or into the path of oncoming traffic on the Yarmouth Road. She didn't much care. Blindly, she took a swig of whisky from the glass she found she was holding.

The argument at the back door seemed to be continuing. The rugby players had been replaced by the Spixworth mods, who jostled in the doorway, eyes bright with amphetamines. They were intimidating someone who was trying to get in. Bennett was pulling at Cissie's sleeve. 'It's Dave!' she mouthed. 'Your Dave!'

Cissie tried to sort this message out. Your Dave. Then she looked up, suddenly wide awake, suddenly aware, anxious. Dave! Dave, who sat smiling at her in English when she was trying to concentrate on *Othello*, Dave, who wore an anti-apartheid badge and played Pretty Things records in the common room. She suddenly saw the mod in the pale blue coat. He was leaning against the doorpost, deceptively casual. 'Fucking long-haired git,' he was saying to someone, unexpectedly sounding very Norfolk, very provincial. 'Fucking students. Fuck off.'

The leather coats pressed forward menacingly. Cissie struggled through the crowd. 'No!' she called, hearing her own voice with surprise. It was loud and commanding. 'Don't – he's a friend.' She had arrived, breathless, at the centre of the dispute. Dave Williams was standing in the snow, trying not to shiver in his PVC mac. His eyes fell on Cissie. 'Hello,' he said ruefully. 'Do you want me to go?'

'No!' Her voice sounded raucous, indignant. Roughly she pulled him over the threshold, elbowing the pale blue leather coat out of the way. She turned to the Ace Face. He was just a boy, after all. 'I invited him,' she said coldly. 'I say who gets to come in.' There was a tiny moment, when she thought he might club her over the head with a bottle, or stab her sharply in the ribs, or drag her by the hair, screaming, into the snow. Instead, he blinked, pale eyelashes fringing those cold blue eyes. He looked away, his eyes meeting those of his cohorts. 'Fucking crap party,' he said. 'No fucking decent sounds. Fucking college kids.' He headed out of the door, beckoning to his companions. Only one, a small, swarthy boy in a baseball jacket, hung back. The party-goers waited to see what he would do. Aware of his audience he contemplated the room, thoughtful. *He's going to hurt someone*, Cissie thought, *he's going to hurt Dave*. The cold eyes lighted on Peggy's dresser, with its piles of odd plates stacked on shelves, a row of chipped mugs dangling from hooks. He crossed the room, the crowd falling back, anxious not to get in his way. In a strange, slow moment, he swept his arm along the shelf, and Cissie watched as the plates sailed silently to the tiled floor, where they smashed into a hundred pieces, girls squealing and jumping out of the way. He left, satisfied. Someone began to cry.

Dave looked at Cissie. He had brown eyes and brown hair falling in a fringe, long at the back. 'Sorry,' he said. Bennett appeared with a dustpan and brush.

'Dance?' Cissie said. She pulled him away, towards the music. Her heart was pounding. Her heart was breaking. George was married. She had to move, or she would stand frozen forever. 'Come on!' He allowed her to lead him through into the darkness of the living room, but she stopped there, leaning into him, smiling still. 'You've still got your coat on,' she said. She peeled it away from him, and then leaned drunkenly back to throw it into the cupboard under the stairs. Her father smiled out at her from his picture. 'Go away,' she said crossly. Dave was wearing cord trousers and a brown crew-necked sweater. He looked nice – not hard and sharp and bright like the mod in the pale blue coat, but soft and brown and gentle. She had been hoping for this moment for months now, but she had never dreamed it would be this easy. Ace Face. Dave Williams, best-looking boy at the Tech. *I can get anyone . . .*

She leaned into him, feeling his arm go round her waist. She buried her head in his shoulder, which smelled of Pears soap and tobacco.

'Cissie!' Reluctantly she looked up. Incredulous, she saw a vision coming towards her, pale face as pretty as ever, hair solidly perfect, that bright, silly smile stamped on her face. 'Cissie! Hello! I told you

I'd come . . .' Cissie disentangled herself from Dave, and tried to focus her eyes on the new arrival.

'Heather,' she said dully.

'And Ray. You remember Ray.'

He was standing bashfully behind her, eyes on Cissie. Ray Broadbent!

'We're engaged now,' Heather trilled, waving her left hand triumphantly under Cissie's nose. 'Two sapphires and a ruby. I want you to be my bridesmaid. Promise me, will you? And who's this?' Her eyes had alighted on Dave, who was watching the reunion, bemused.

'Dave,' he said, smiling. 'Dave Williams.'

Heather lowered her mink eyelashes. Dave was very good-looking. She was glad she was wearing her new Ossie Clark dress. Hers was the only genuine Ossie Clark in the room, although she had spotted several imitations from Chelsea Girl and Bus Stop . . . Keeping Dave Williams in her sights, she turned to address Cissie again. 'I'm in the newsroom at Anglia TV now,' she said proudly. 'PA to the producer.'

'Great!' said Cissie brightly, not knowing what a PA was.

'And trainee journalist. They're grooming me to go on air. Remember *About Anglia*, me going on about Paul McCartney? They did nothing but talk about it at the interview. Said I was a natural.'

Bennett had joined them, scowling at Ray, swigging from a bottle of cider. 'Engaged! I thought you were going to marry Paul.'

Heather turned, annoyed to find Bennett still in the picture. She had rather hoped that Bennett would have disappeared by now. 'That was when I was young. I'm a bit more mature now.'

Dave was admiring her slender figure in the glamorous dress. 'You certainly are.'

Ray suddenly loomed. 'What do you mean by that?' he asked.

Dave shrugged, grinning. 'Nothing, mate.'

'She's my fiancée.'

Bennett hooted. 'Your what?'

'Oh shut up, Bennett,' Heather flashed. 'I see you don't have a boyfriend to speak of.'

Bennett merely took another swig of cider, refusing to take the bait. Cissie nudged her. 'Should you be doing that – drinking like that?'

Bennett gazed at her, stone-faced and enigmatic. 'Why not?'

Ray was prodding Dave in the chest. 'You find your own woman, all right?'

Dave assumed an expression of mock amazement. 'Sorry . . .? I don't think I heard you right.'

'No,' said Ray, irritated. 'Hardly surprising with that row on.'

'He means John Lee Hooker!' Bennett said, smirking. The sound of 'Dimples' was blasting through from the living room.

Cissie suddenly felt an overwhelming desire to be sick. 'Excuse me . . .' she said, and hurried towards the back door. Outside it had stopped snowing and the wind had dropped. The yard was filled with the booming strains of the Marvelettes. Cissie vomited behind the coalshed, quickly and violently, and then stood upright, shivering. She could not go back in there. Through the glass of the back door she could see the pack of people, all shouting and laughing, gesticulating, drinking. It was like Hieronymus Bosch. She walked away from the noise and the lights and found herself by the hen coop. Inside, there was a scurry and a flutter, as her arrival disturbed the birds. She ducked inside, comforted by the sweet barnyard smell of hay, the aroma of that other world she inhabited when she was not being grown up, the world of warm hens' eggs and straw bales in the shed and Mike's ferret, and Toulouse . . . She sank into the straw, causing a raucous flurry of indignant fowl, and then all was silent, apart from the faint throb of the music in the far, far distance, and the occasional flutter of a feathered wing on a nearby perch . . .

It was the sound of a police car. She sat upright suddenly, making her head spin. Her mouth was dry and tasted bitter and poisonous. For a moment she had no idea where she was. Then she saw the rounded, shuffling shapes above, and remembered. The hen house. She had fallen asleep in the hen house. Dazed, she stumbled outside. There were two policemen heading down the path towards the back door.

'Hello,' one of them said, stamping his feet in the snow. 'You know whose party this is?'

'Mine,' she said.

'Only we had a complaint.' He was rather overweight for a policeman, with a red face and a tired demeanour. Saturday night was not his favourite shift. 'Someone in the village. Said things were getting out of hand.'

'No,' said Cissie loudly, hoping to drown out the uproar that seemed to be emanating from the house. 'No, I don't think so —'

But the policemen were pushing their way in. She followed them, wincing at the sound of what appeared to be a fight somewhere ahead. Someone was screaming, and the throng in the kitchen swayed and shoved, then broke back in a panic as something or someone suddenly moved their way. She stared, bemused, as Ray and Dave suddenly burst into view, grappling, struggling, their faces puce, Dave's sweater pulled up to reveal the white skin of his back, Ray's shirt flapping. The two policemen pulled them apart, handling them with a deft efficiency, almost casually, as if they were small children.

'He was chatting up my fiancée!' Ray was gasping for air, panting and enraged, tears in his eyes. 'He was trying to get off with her, I saw —'

'Hey, I don't fight people,' Dave was saying desperately, caught in the clutches of a firm police armlock. 'I wasn't doing anything . . .'

Heather appeared, pink-faced but otherwise calm. She was holding Ray's coat. 'It's all right, officer,' she said, in her best posh Edinburgh accent, 'we're leaving. Aren't we, Ray.' This was a command, not a question. The policeman released his hold and Ray struggled into his coat, ashamed, head bowed, blinking back tears. 'You go near her again —' he said to Dave Williams, whose eye was beginning to swell.

Heather led Ray out, passing Cissie coldly without a backward glance. The music had stopped. The back door slammed shut after them. The two policemen, enjoying their moment, surveyed the debris of the kitchen with interest. 'Like Sodom and Gomorrah,' one of them said.

People began to sidle out, deflated after the drama of the fight, collecting their coats, crunching over the remains of the broken china, their voices muted. 'Yes,' said the chubby policeman, 'Good idea, that. Why don't you all go home, eh?' He turned to Cissie. 'Your mum and dad gone away? They know you're having a party?'

'They'll be back tomorrow,' Cissie said, her voice defiant. 'Why don't you come back and ask them?'

Someone nudged her, warningly. It was Bennett. 'Thanks, officer,' Bennett said, flashing the man a bright, insincere smile. 'We can manage now, thank you.'

He gazed around suspiciously. 'There have been complaints,' he said darkly. 'They can hear you up at the vicarage on the other side of Polston Wood.'

'Well it's all over now,' Bennett said sweetly. 'See? Everyone's leaving . . .'

Gradually the guests disappeared, fading away into the bright snowy night, the sound of car engines dissolving into the dark, scooters puttering away towards the Yarmouth Road, back to Norwich. The policemen departed, the blue light of their squad car flashing brightly against the snow-weighted hedges as they headed through the snow furrows towards their sub-station at Rackheath.

There was only Bennett, standing glumly in the living room, staring round at the mess, and Dave Williams, slumped on the sofa nursing his bruised face. Cissie wandered through from the forlorn chaos of the front room, where she had discovered the cover of her *Long Tall Sally* Beatles EP had been used as a beermat, and that someone had stolen all her Rolling Stones records.

Dave Williams got up, murmuring something about putting cold water on his wound, and headed towards the kitchen and the stairs.

'You want me to help you clear up?' Bennett asked.

Cissie shook her head. 'I'll do it tomorrow.'

Bennett eyed her, grinning. 'I see. I'd better leave you alone, then. Don't want to be a gooseberry.'

Cissie sank into Mill's armchair by the fire. 'Don't be stupid.'

Bennett frowned. 'Why is it so stupid? I thought you fancied

154

him. I thought he was the one you'd been going on about ever since you started at the Tech.'

Cissie stared into the empty grate. It was full of cigarette ends. 'I changed my mind.'

Bennett made a sudden, angry movement. 'No you didn't. You're just saying that 'cos you're scared.' Her eyes met Cissie's.

So she knows, Cissie thought. *She knows I'm still a virgin* . . . 'I'm not scared.' Her eyes slid away. She fingered the arm of the chair. 'I've just gone off him, that's all.' She looked furtively in the direction of the stairs, hoping Dave would not return and hear her lies. 'Anyway,' she added, 'I couldn't have got off with him tonight. Not tonight.'

She pretended to inspect the worn chintz on Mill's chair, picking at loose threads, head bowed.

'You mean,' Bennett's voice was cold, 'you mean because it's George's wedding night, don't you?'

Cissie did not reply. She could not. Tears were welling up, threatening to spill down her cheeks in a torrent she would not be able to stop. She heard Bennett stride out. She was pulling her PVC mac from the cupboard under the stairs. 'Grow up!' she called angrily from the kitchen. 'You can't let George Harrison rule your ruddy life!'

And she was gone, slamming out and down the path, her footsteps heavy as she stumped away in the snow, past the windows of Brigadoon.

Cissie let the tears come, then. She had never quarrelled with Bennett before. Everything had collapsed. Bennett was pregnant and needed her and now she was walking home to the Jermyn's soulless house alone in the snow.

She felt suddenly enfolded in someone's arms. It was Dave Williams, his face close to hers, his soft brown hair touching her cheek. 'Don't cry,' he said gently. 'Don't cry . . .'

They stayed without moving for what seemed like a long time, entwined together. Then they sank on to the floor, and amid the debris of the disastrous party Dave made love to Cissie in a drunken, fumbling travesty of the act she had always fantasized would take place with someone else. Someone famous. She had dreamed that it would be beautiful, intangible, the gossamer touch of magic, a million fantasies exploding into a moment of nameless ecstasy. Instead here she was, lying amid the crumbs of crisps, the crushed and empty Party Four cans, on the damp carpet, being fumbled at by a well-meaning and pretty boy she didn't know at all. He had fallen asleep on top of her, his hair still falling on her face, his mouth slack, the swelling above his eye now a livid purple. She stared upwards, dry-eyed, emotionless. *I can get anyone I want . . .*

Peggy was hanging out of the window of the baby's room, listening. There it was: the plaintive sound of Paul McCartney singing 'We Can Work It Out' floating back across the hawthorn hedge from the cabbage field. She glimpsed Cissie's red hair through the thicket of bare branches, and then saw the wire leading from the window at the back of the straw shed through the brambles and beyond. Cissie had set up her record player by the hedge.

'It's all right,' she called to Mike, 'I can see her – she's in the cabbage field.'

Mike came slowly up the stairs, carrying Susie, treading carefully over a broken glass on the landing, followed by a joyful, bouncing Toulouse. 'I can't bring Mill home,' he said, 'not to this . . .'

Peggy laughed, a little tense. 'You're just upset because Leonard Bernstein took a nasty knock. Someone just parked badly, that's all.' She closed the window. 'It's not so bad,' she said, her voice bright. 'If we all muck in –'

Mike snorted. He put Susie in her cot, removing her shoes. She immediately relaxed and lay on her side, sucking her thumb and watching her parents with contented eyes. 'I'm not cleaning up after her,' he said, 'and neither are you.'

Peggy glanced out of the window again. 'Listen, she's out there with her record player listening to her music and minding her own business. Remember what a state she was in when we left? At least she's calm –'

'Calm! She's probably catatonic! She's probably off her head on pep pills, or whatever it is they all seem to be taking –'

Peggy gave him a look full of reproach. 'And when you were her age, what were you doing? Getting drunk every night, I'll bet.'

'It wasn't the same —'

Peggy headed for the door, annoyed. 'Do you have any idea how old-fashioned you sound? If your students could hear you now!'

Mike looked back at Susie, whose eyelids were drooping. He followed Peggy out on to the landing and carefully closed the door.

'When are you going to stop making excuses for her?' he demanded in an angry whisper. 'She's wrecked the damn house and now she's lying about in the bloody snow like a madwoman, as if she hasn't got a care in the world!'

Peggy stalked across the landing to Cissie's door and paused, gripping the door handle. 'You're always so quick to criticize Cissie,' she flashed, 'but not a word against Oliver!' She regretted the words almost as she uttered them. Mike stared at her, hurt.

'Oliver's never given us cause for worry,' he said slowly.

She was not able to stop now. Something drove her on to inflict more pain, to defend Cissie, to stop Mike saying those hurtful things. 'Oliver's never given us cause to do *anything*,' she said. 'Oliver never does anything, does he? Stuck away in that tatty flat living a half-life —'

'He's got a job. He pays the rent. He's self-sufficient.'

Peggy wrenched open the door. The smell of stale wine wafted out. 'And you're happy with that, are you?' she demanded. 'You're happy watching him waste his life mending other people's television sets when he could have been doing Fine Art at the Slade?'

Mike was silent for a moment. Then he said, 'We don't choose what our children become.'

She looked at him, distressed and triumphant. 'You said it, not me.' She turned and entered Cissie's room, hearing him clump heavily downstairs. She sat on the bed. The curtains were closed, the bed unmade. On the floor, she caught sight of a piece of lavender-coloured paper, only partly visible under the hanging folds of the counterpane. She picked it up.

Dear Mrs Harrison . . . Slowly, she got up and went downstairs, reading the letter as she went, pausing to pick up a discarded wine bottle on the stairs. *Please send George my very best wishes for the future* . . . She collected some more bottles from the heap on the kitchen table. Mike was nowhere to be seen. *Thank you for writing to me for so long. I have really enjoyed your letters* . . .

She opened the back door and stepped outside with her armful of bottles, wincing at the sharp air. Cissie must be freezing . . . She headed for the dustbin, pausing a moment as she lifted the lid to listen. From across the garden, a taunting song insinuated itself into the stillness of the snow-bright morning, the cruel voice of John Lennon. Mike heard it too, listening in his shed, brooding about how to mend the cracks in his statue and the larger ones in his marriage. Peggy dropped the bottles into the bin with a loud clatter. She must go and clear up, Mill was due home in a couple of hours . . . She hesitated for a second, then she screwed up the lavender letter and dropped that in as well. *She's very pretty and I'm sure she made a beautiful bride* . . .

CHAPTER SIX

With a Little Help from My Friends – 1967

T HE HASH CAKES HAD taken effect rather earlier than Bennett had anticipated. They had still been in the car on the outskirts of Esher when things had begun to get a little strange. They had managed to cope with the driver's conversation by being monosyllabic and avoiding each other's eyes, which suited Cissie, who wanted to organize in her mind the events that had led to her being crammed, stoned, in the back of a stranger's car heading towards George Harrison's house on a hot day in August.

It had been Bennett's idea, of course: the final, careful mending of their damaged friendship. It had taken the birth of Bennett's son to re-unite them – a stiff, embarrassed encounter in the maternity ward of the Norfolk and Norwich Hospital, Bennett a grinning stranger hugging that small alien thing to her breast while Cissie watched, half-filled with envy and half with incomprehension. The baby was called Gandalf; Bennett had been reading *Lord of the Rings*. Gradually Cissie had begun to visit Bennett's tatty room in Norwich and slowly they had rediscovered the bonds of their friendship in the sad backstreet that Bennett shared with the bedsitter flotsam and jetsam of the city.

She looked across at her friend gazing serenely out at the blossoming Surrey suburbs, and smiled to herself. Life was good. They were together, they were friends, and they were going to see George. They were going to see George! It sounded so casual, the kind of thing you said about anyone: 'I'm going to see Bob', 'I'm going to see Bill'. *I'm going to see George.* The outing had been Bennett's idea: hitch to Esher to George's bungalow, then go to

London, to an exotic-sounding place they had read about called Middle Earth where, according to *International Times*, you could dance all night. Baby Gandalf was installed at Brigadoon in Susie's old cot, being spoilt by Mill and Peggy; they had hitched to their destination with no problems; they were nearly in Esher; the sun was shining. It was all too beautiful.

Dear Mrs Harrison, Today I went to Esher with my friend to see George at his bungalow. As luck would have it, he was at home, and he invited us in for tea . . .

Bennett had rolled the window down and a cool breeze danced on Cissie's cheek. Occasionally, her hand would stray across to rub Bennett's distended belly, and the eyes of the driver who had picked up these two hippy hitch-hikers would slide away in the rear-view mirror, disconcerted by this display of affection. 'Soon be there, baby,' Cissie would murmur, happy. 'Soon be there . . .' Bennett was seven months pregnant. Cissie could see the baby clearly through the tie-dye swirl of Bennett's huge smock. The baby was curled up and smiling, one hand under its chin, like Rodin's *The Thinker*. This baby, Cissie knew, was going to be a goddess. She wondered who the father was. Bennett had never said. Not that it mattered. After all, baby Gandy had a father – that silly little man from the cinema – but he didn't exist, not really. Sometimes he put in an embarrassed appearance at Bennett's bedsit carrying unsuit- ably violent toys for his son, and was given short shrift by Bennett, who had lost interest in extra-marital affairs with oppressed hus- bands, thank goodness. Bennett appeared to know what she was thinking; as the car crawled in the heat along a suburban high street, turning suddenly and solemnly, she said, 'I'm not going to tell Freddy Lemon where I'm moving to.' Bennett was about to move into a commune in the country.

Cissie was interested in this announcement. She tore her atten- tion away from the snaking intricacies of a passing row of trees, and stared at her friend.

'You're not going to tell him?' she repeated. 'Not ever?'

Bennett caressed her tie-dyed bulge serenely. 'Gandy doesn't even like him,' she said. 'And I certainly don't. Anyway,' she added, leaning back, relaxed, 'I think he'd be glad, really. He only visits out of duty. Duty!' She snorted, causing the driver to twitch slightly. 'What a concept! The guy is thirty-five going on a hundred and ten.' She flapped a hand. 'I mustn't think about it,' she said firmly. 'Bad karma.'

The car had slowed down and finally stopped. They staggered out, heads spinning, and murmured thanks to the driver, who drove away silently without acknowledgement, like a figure in a dream landscape. Indeed, this *was* a dream landscape. This was Esher – magic centre of Cissie's dreams. Somehow they made their way to the pavement, Cissie clutching at Bennett's skirt, dazed. They were here. They were going to see George. They were going to the famous psychedelic bungalow called Kinfauns. It was a terrible risk, of course – he might still be away with the Maharishi Mahesh Yogi – but it had been days now since the Beatles had headed off in a hysterical hubbub of media interest to pursue their spiritual quest in the Welsh mountains. Surely they would be back by now?

'What if he's in?' Cissie asked Bennett fearfully.

'That's what we want, isn't it?'

Cissie was not sure. What would they do – just march up the path and knock on the front door?

She nudged at Bennett, who was propelling her briskly along the pavement, apparently with a clear idea of where they were heading. 'What if Patti answers the door?'

Bennett looked at her pityingly. 'We ask her if George is in.'

Dear Mrs Harrison, Today I went with my friend to Esher to see George in his bungalow. Patti answered the door. She told us to get lost. I tried to tell her I was a friend of yours, but she wouldn't listen.

Cissie had slowed down. 'I'm not sure about this,' she said. Her voice sounded far away. 'It's not a very cool thing to do, is it?'

Bennett stopped and looked at her. 'You're not just anyone, are you,' she said, her tone confident. 'You're special. You've got all those letters in your bag. You're not just a fan. You're the girl from Norfolk with the flying table.'

Cissie realized suddenly that they had arrived. They were

standing in front of wrought-iron gates, and a high wall lined with poplars. No house was visible. Her heart sank.

'Oh shit,' said Bennett.

There were at least a dozen of them, sitting on the pavement, lounging against the gate, draped across the bonnets of parked cars, scratching their names into the gate posts with nail files, transistor radios pressed to their ears, shrieking and squabbling, a gaggle of sullen-faced, long-legged teenage girls, all hair and kohl-ringed eyes, pale, sulky mouths and bitten fingernails.

Bennett and Cissie stood, swaying, staring at these apparitions from hell.

'Piss off,' one of them said. 'You're not regulars.'

'You don't own the pavement,' Bennett said.

'We do, actually.' A small girl in a grubby pink kaftan and bare feet stepped forward, scrutinizing them with a critical stare. 'Anyway, George isn't in.'

Bennett stood her ground. 'We'll wait.'

The girl shrugged. Indifferent. 'Suit yourself. But I'm telling you – George is still in Wales with that Indian bloke.'

'So why are you all hanging about, then?'

Another girl spoke. 'We're waiting for Patti,' she said. 'She's just nipped out to the shops. In the Jag.'

'The red Jag,' someone else said, as if to confirm their special knowledge.

Cissie turned away, depressed. 'Come on, Bennett. Let's go.'

The girl in the pink kaftan nodded. 'Good idea,' she said. 'Piss off. This is our turf.'

Cissie began to walk away. 'Look!' someone shouted behind her. 'Look at them! They're *old*!'

'That one's so old she's going to have a baby!'

There was a united teenage snicker. Bennett joined Cissie and together they hastened away, the girls' cries echoing in their ears: 'We're going to scratch Patti's car when she comes back!' 'We're going to tear the number-plate off when she's waiting for the gates to open!' 'We're going to kill Patti and have George all to ourselves!'

They stumbled on to the main road, where Bennett crumpled into a heap on the dry, grassy verge. 'Sorry, Cissie,' she groaned. 'I wanted it to be wonderful . . .' She lay back, staring at the sun, one hand on the bulge that would be a baby soon. The hash cakes were beginning to take hold with a vengeance. Had they just encountered a coven full of witches? Cissie stepped out, hot and depressed, into the fug of oncoming traffic and stuck out her thumb.

Dear Mrs Harrison, I was going to go to Esher to visit George at his bungalow, but I changed my mind . . .

They had tumbled out on to the pavement outside a cinema, only Cissie had been confused by the sudden appearance of what seemed to be hundreds of magical people in brightly coloured, shimmering robes. She had been so busy staring at them that she had forgotten to thank the driver, who had driven away into the rumble of traffic with a friendly wave of the hand, never to be seen again, leaving Cissie in a swirl of brightness and unintelligible chatter. 'Indians,' Bennett had explained. Cissie struggled briefly with a vision of Sioux braves – feathers, horses, tepees, squaws – and then realized. Of course. Indians. Saris, colours, chatter. Indians. They were outside an Indian cinema. There was a poster on the wall, garish colours and the silhouettes of a couple embracing, he with impossibly perfect features, she desperate in a scarlet veil, an opal in her nose, camellias looped through dark hair. To Cissie it had been more beautiful than any work of art and she had stood transfixed by it until Bennett had coaxed her away.

Now they were on the underground, having coped with the change from the District Line to the Central Line successfully, in a kind of smirking daze, propping each other up on the seat and eyeing the other passengers as if they were creatures from Mars.

The train had stopped at Bank station. A herd of numb-faced commuters left the carriage, and others replaced them. Cissie watched with interest. How dead their faces, how dull their lives. She felt a brief moment of lilting happiness at the lucky chance that had led her to be Cissie Lovelock in this exciting time, and not that woman over there with the shopping bags, not that ramrod-backed bank manager with his briefcase, that gaggle of spotty youths in shirt-sleeves, yawning and sweating their way home. That man opposite with the moustache . . . She looked again. Surely he was not a stranger. She studied him closely. That moustache, drooping slightly, that hair.

Bennett nudged her. 'George moustache,' she said, evidently looking in the same direction. Cissie had seen him before, of course, once, many years ago, perched on a stool backstage in a theatre, mohair suit, long fingers, the divine one.

She leaned forward, solemn, a striking picture in diaphanous pink muslin and a drooping velvet skirt, painted boots and ropes of translucent blue beads, strung together by sister Susie at infant school and filched from her toy box. 'Excuse me,' she said, her voice clear and calm. 'Excuse me —' George Harrison looked up at her reluctantly, not wanting to be part of a spectacle. 'I am the girl from Norfolk with the flying table,' she told him. 'I didn't catch you at the bungalow.'

Bennett's hand was on her arm. 'No,' she said. 'No, Cissie — it isn't him.' The man was examining his hands carefully, as if every fold of flesh, every fingernail, contained some important secret. Cissie waited patiently for him to respond, but he did not raise his eyes again. She understood. It must be hell, she pondered, to have your life invaded all the time by fans, like those evil little girls outside Kinfauns. Only of course she wasn't just a fan. She was Cissie Lovelock, she was his friend. She didn't want to violate the very private being that was him; she just wanted to be there, to be part of what he was. I should be wearing a scarlet veil, she thought sadly. I should have a jewel in my nose and camellias laced through my hair . . . Or I should look like Patti. She closed her eyes, pushing the thought of Patti away, trying to organize her brain so that she would not get upset. Had that little coven of monsters descended on Patti and destroyed her? They had looked as if they wanted to tear her to pieces. Cissie didn't know whether to be pleased or disgusted.

The man with the moustache was wearing wellington boots now, and a fisherman's sweater — navy blue, with a darn in the sleeve.

That's a strange outfit for a pilot, Cissie thought. But then she remembered – of course, he had been fishing in the picture, holding a fishing rod and smiling at her, with his eyes crinkling at the corners. She nudged Bennett. 'Look!' she hissed. 'It's my dad!' Bennett peered, but did not see. Cissie smiled at him. She had always imagined that Cecil was a pilot, although no one had ever said he was. It just seemed the right kind of careless, romantic occupation for her missing father. He examined his hands as George had done, oddly self-conscious, disconcerted by this Pre-Raphaelite vision seated opposite him who smiled and seemed to know him.

'He should be wearing a helmet,' Cissie said to Bennett. 'Don't they wear leather helmets? And goggles?'

'Who?'

'Pilots. Fathers.'

'Which?'

They both began to giggle, amused by this inconsequential exchange. The train stopped again, at Chancery Lane, and Cecil got up and left the train without a backward glance. Cissie pressed her forehead against the grimy glass and watched him disappear along the platform as the doors closed and they moved off. How very disappointing!

'It's not every day you meet your father on the Central Line,' she told Bennett, upset. Bennett struggled to her feet, swaying above Cissie. 'Holborn,' she said mysteriously.

Cissie followed her off the train, clutching hold of the fabric of Bennett's smock as they threaded their way carefully along the platform, up the escalator, past a ringletted, stripey-trousered busker who blew them a kiss and then began to sing *Are You Going To San Francisco?* in a high-pitched voice, long grubby fingers picking at guitar strings, an ugly gnome's face under curls.

Up on the street the summer light was fading. The last few shoppers straggled towards the tube entrance, harassed in their cotton frocks and their hot suits. Going in the opposite direction were the other people, the ones Cissie and Bennett recognized, swarming in their imaginations, the ones who were like them: pirates, gypsies, witch-doctors, Hell's Angels, flower children, all shimmering and alive and going somewhere, wandering, grinning into the shadows of tall buildings, sitting cross-legged on pavements in patches of late, lingering sunshine, loafing outside alternative bookshops in Covent Garden, brown-skinned, freckled, adorned with rags from Asia, Grenadier Guards jackets, jingling silver, bare feet, unruly hair and laughter. They were all going to Middle Earth.

The market had long ago closed for the day, only heaps of rotting vegetables and a few broken pallets to be clambered over. A girl in a patchwork skirt was sorting through a pile of discarded cabbages as they passed. She smiled at them, holding up a handful of leaves. 'Nice with pinto beans,' she said in an upper-class accent. Cissie was taken aback. Here was someone who sounded like a member of the Royal family, rooting about amongst the vegetables as if she had spent her life on her knees in Covent Garden.

Cissie smiled in a wobbly fashion at this vision and followed Bennett. Best to keep silent. It was advisable to keep cool at all times, and never to admit ignorance or surprise. In a way, the posh girl in the patchwork skirt was a consolation to her, it made her feel less uncomfortably better off than everyone around her. What did she have to rebel against in the Lovelocks? Peggy, with her *laissez-faire* attitude, Mike and his lumps, Mill and her Woodbines? Everyone at the Tech had always loved her family, they all envied her. She felt like a fraud, even this visit to London had been casually sanctioned. Bennett had had to find a baby-sitter for Gandy, had gone through endless negotiations to get someone to feed her disreputable horde of stray cats, had struggled to find spare money from her Social Security payments to bring with her – in short, Bennett had battled her way to London; Cissie had merely announced that she was going, to calm acceptance from Peggy, had scrounged ten pounds from Mill and had not even bothered to say good-bye to Mike, who had been busy in his shed at the time of her departure. No ripples on a pond caused by my leaving, she thought sadly, as they descended the steps into Middle Earth.

That was the last realistic thought she encountered for several hours. Time passed – or rather, did not pass – in a blur of sound and light, throbbing bass notes from Country Joe and the Fish songs she vaguely recognized, globules of colour cast on a wall that flickered and floated without meaning, faces appearing out of the darkness, some threatening and ugly, others kind and beautiful. She and Bennett sat on the floor in a dark corner and watched what happened, absorbing the shifting bodies, the music, the sudden, unexplained 'happenings', when a desperate figure would leap up suddenly from the gloom and begin to read incoherently from smudged pages of scribbled, intense poetry, or a girl with plaits like an Indian squaw would begin slowly and solemnly to dance around the reclining figures on the floor, weaving in and out of the dazed bodies as if hypnotized. As usual, Cissie felt shabby, uninteresting, unfashionable, faced with this array of what she thought of as London sophistication. All the girls seemed to be wearing amazing clothes, all the boys were exciting and exotic. It was all a far cry from Norwich Tech common room, where you could cause a major sensation just by wearing purple tights. Here, everyone wore everything, there were no rules. To her provincial eyes what unfolded before her in the half-light was a seductive tapestry of dancing, poetry, energy, politics, drugs, argument and music, woven by a magical troupe of beautiful freaks. Norwich, by comparison, seemed drearily out-of-date, trailing along several months behind what really mattered. You had to come here to be where it was at, and if you stayed behind and hung about in the half-hearted East Anglian alternative bookshops and humble happening venues, then you might as well be dead. Here, Swedes conversed with Italians, Parisians compared notes with New Yorkers, ten languages struggled to be heard over the noise. Denim sat alongside silk, velvet with plastic, leather with diamanté. California tans jostled with pale anaemic flesh. Woolly halos of frizzed hair met smooth helmets fashioned by Vidal Sassoon. And here they sat, a part of it!

She pulled a letter out of her bag, and sat, smiling in the half-light, reading it again. *Dear Cecilia, I was so pleased to get your letter. How is your little dog? George phoned last night, he sounded very happy. He and Patti are planning a holiday . . .* Patti again! Cissie felt suddenly, overwhelmingly ill. She managed to get to her feet, swaying and confused by the exertion. Bennett looked up at her.

'Loo,' Cissie said. Bennett nodded and lay down again, uncomfortably settling her head on her over-stuffed shoulder bag, clutching her belly, eyelids sagging.

Cissie made her way towards the exit, unsure of anything except her desire to vomit. She passed the stage, where a crowd was gathering to hear the main attraction, due to appear at any moment. She was moving across the great dark concrete space, struggling against the sound of the Doors, Jim Morrison's voice rasping across the ceiling from speakers wired to the walls. Then she saw the mouth of a tunnel, gaping red, ahead of her, flanked by snaking and crawling concrete, alive with scribbles. She paused there for a moment, her nausea forgotten, intently reading the scrawled graffiti, following it with her finger, anxious not to lose the thread. *Sonja, Amsterdam June 1967 . . . Haight is love . . . Benny, I'm going crazy, see you at the Arts Lab, bad karma getting to me, 23/6/67 . . . Soft Machine were here* . . . It all made perfect sense. Then she saw it. *Jude sucks dick*. She held her finger carefully under the words, anxious not to lose them. She turned her head hopefully in the direction of the crowds, anticipating being able to contact Bennett by telepathy, to tell her to *come here quickly, Jude is here*. But all she saw and felt was the tiny frozen moment just before John Lennon was going to sing 'Lucy In The Sky With Diamonds', a sharp intake of breath, a communal sigh from the people on the floor of Middle Earth as they recognized those magical tones from the most wonderful combination of noises they had ever encountered: *Sergeant Pepper* . . . She must concentrate. She studied the scrawled words again, telling John Lennon he must go and sing somewhere else, she had to find Jude, who was evidently here, and may even now, at this very moment, be in a boat on a river with plasticine trees and marmalade skies . . .

Somehow she struggled down into the red mouth of the tunnel and found the word 'CHICKS' chiselled into the concrete and then picked out in blood red. She went inside. Sure enough, there was Jude, the same scarlet smeared across her face, as if she had been eating strawberry jam.

'Is it blood?' Cissie asked sympathetically. There was a strange roaring in her ears, as if she were underwater.

Jude merely stared through her, glassy-eyed, intent on some business on the floor. There were several of them, all huddled together with the same haunted eyes (she thought immediately of Mike's Edvard Munch postcard pinned up above the door of the shed). They were shivering and holding each other, making little murmuring noises, like so many tiny gerbils clustered together. Jude with the blotched mouth was tightening a flowered scarf around the arm of another white-skinned girl, who leaned forward, her face intent, her mouth an 'O' of anticipation. There was a needle, and there was more blood, dripping on to the tatty lace of one girl's dyed silk night-dress, the drops melting into blackened, ugly splotches on the pale fabric. The Jude-girl had sunk the needle into white-face's alabaster flesh, and now she pushed the plunger, while the others swooned a little, breathing in tiny gasps, their murmuring and mutterings now like a hundred bats' wings. It was going to be a Hammer horror film, if Cissie wasn't very careful. Jude looked up at her, with nothing to say. Cissie gazed sadly back. *I loved you. You were my friend*, she said in her head. But the words did not emerge. She watched for a moment, unutterably depressed by the puddles of urine on the floor, the trailing, soggy strands of toilet paper in the filthy sink, the smell. Then she turned and headed giddily back the way she had come, down the tunnel towards the smoke-filled, heaving throb of the concrete chaos that was Middle Earth.

She found Bennett where she had left her, and pulled at her arm. Wordlessly, Bennett got up and followed her into the swaying throng. It was all right again, all falling into place. They belonged here after all. Together they swayed slowly to the music, arms twirling above their heads, eyes locked, lost to the sound of the flute and the mandolin, while the Incredible String Band dancers weaved sorcery on stage, silver head-dresses shimmering under the spotlights like fountains, their faces invisible, their bodies bewitching.

Later, Bennett and Cissie fell asleep in a jumble of discarded jackets in a corner, their finery crumpled, their eye make-up dissolving, only the throb of the music intruding into their dreamless sleep.

★

'Cissie!' Someone was pulling at her, wrenching her out of the dark pit where she had fallen. For a moment she had no idea where she was, and then she remembered. It was cold now, and she began to shiver. Around her, Middle Earth carried on, loud and colourful. Bennett's face loomed, round and anxious. 'Back pains – every five minutes.'

Cissie was instantly wide awake, horrified. 'You mean labour pains? But it's too early!'

Bennett grimaced, clutching her back. 'Try telling him that. Or her.'

Cissie scrambled to her feet. 'I'll find a phone – get an ambulance –'

'No!' Bennett's hand was on her arm again. 'You want the fuzz on our backs? We've been consuming illegal substances –'

'They won't know that –'

Bennett gave her a withering look. 'Urine samples, blood tests – you're joking! Of course they'll know. And I don't need to get busted while I'm giving birth, thanks all the same. We'll go to your brother's.' Bennett had decided.

Cissie stared at her stupidly. She felt ill and chilly and tired. 'Oliver?'

'It's not far. I checked it out on someone's *A–Z* while you were asleep. We can get the tube.' She winced a little. 'Only we'd better make it quick.'

Together they forged a path through the sleeping bodies, the occasional stoned dancer, the babble of Frank Zappa over the loud-speakers, until they reached the exit and climbed up to fresh air and a shockingly bright morning sky. They paused for a moment, con-fused by the change of atmosphere. It was clear and cold, with a watery sun lurking behind the grey buildings.

'Are you sure about this?' Cissie was staring at Bennett, terrified. What if Bennett suddenly gave birth here – on the street?

Bennett leaned against some railings, blinking at the light. 'Maybe I'm not in labour. Maybe if I just lie down for a couple of hours at Oliver's . . .'

They had caught the eye of some men perched on the back of a truck, busy unloading boxes of tomatoes. They paused in their work and stood, grinning.

'I can see one of 'em's a girl,' a man in a sweaty vest remarked loudly to his mates, 'unless blokes can get pregnant now as well . . .'

'Probably got a pill for that,' another said, mocking. 'They've got a pill for everything else.'

The man in the vest fixed his gaze on Cissie. 'You a boy?' he asked, his tone unfriendly. 'Only it's difficult to tell these days.'

Cissie looked beseechingly at Bennett from under her hair. 'Can't we at least get a taxi?'

'You on drugs?' Another man had materialized from the cab of the lorry. 'You on that LSD?'

Bennett was not to be persuaded from her plan. 'Tube station's only round the corner. It's not far,' she repeated, ignoring the taunts of the market men, her hand stealing to the small of her back. She caught sight of Cissie's white, tense face and grinned. 'Come on!' she said brightly. 'Oliver won't mind!'

The tube station was further away than it had looked on the map. Away from the market, the streets were almost deserted, with the bleak, clean, bereft look of a Sunday morning. The only activity was the hiss and rumble of a street-cleaning van hosing the dusty kerbs and the distant rumble of traffic on the Tottenham Court Road. They arrived at the station, only to find its gates pulled across, the interior bare, the ticket machines silent.

'Damn,' said Bennett. She rattled the gates hopelessly. A man dropping a pile of newspapers by the entrance shook his head. 'No chance, darlin'. You think they run all night?'

Bennett leaned against the wall, weary. 'What time is it?'

The man eyed her condition, concerned. 'Five o'clock. Here, you're not going to give birth on the pavement, are you?'

Bennett eyed him thoughtfully. 'Probably,' she said. Cissie glanced at her, surprised, but said nothing. 'We were going to go to the hospital,' Bennett was saying, her tone conversational, 'but we haven't got enough money for a taxi.'

The man had paused by the open doors of his van. Inside Cissie could see piles of Sunday newspapers, all tied in bundles. 'I could give you a lift,' he said, his brow furrowed. 'Gaffer'll do his nut – but I got three kids of my own. You hop in the front –'

'No!' Bennett's voice was desperately bright. 'We couldn't – it's miles away – Bayswater – the other side of London . . .'

He looked at her, suspicious. Cissie saw that his two front teeth were missing. 'Why Bayswater? What's wrong with the Middlesex? It's just off Tottenham Court Road – won't take five minutes –'

Bennett had straightened up with difficulty. 'No – really –' she said, ' – I'm registered at the one in Bayswater – and my mum lives there, and she'd be upset if I had the baby somewhere else –'

Cissie listened, impressed by Bennett's ability to tell tall tales to complete strangers with such ease. The man was looking sympathetic. 'No husband, eh?' He sighed, disapprovingly. 'You girls . . . I dunno. Haven't you heard of the Family Planning Clinic?'

A taxi was passing, and the man suddenly put his fingers to his lips and let out a piercing wolf whistle. The cab rumbled across and pulled up. The driver rolled down the window.

'Take these two to Bayswater,' the man said. Bennett was already climbing inside. Cissie followed. The newspaper man was handing the driver a rumpled five pound note. He leaned into the window of the cab, grinning, the gap in his teeth a black hollow. 'I got a daughter gone to Nepal,' he said, as if that explained everything. 'Shacked up with a Paki.' They smiled, polite. 'The name's George,' he said, as the taxi pulled away, calling after them, ' – just in case you want to name it after me . . .' He gradually diminished in size on the receding pavement, a small figure waving, until the taxi turned a corner and he disappeared from view.

Bennett and Cissie leaned back in the seat, grinning at each other, elated by their small adventure and the kindness of an unlikely-looking stranger. 'George!' Bennett repeated, rubbing her back. 'It's an omen!'

Cissie had not been to Bayswater since that Christmas with Jude. As they sped down a deserted Queensway and rattled round the corner into Moscow Road, she felt the same heart-stopping dread she had felt before on coming here, the same anxiety.

Oliver would be furious. At home, when Oliver appeared for his odd weekend visits, they maintained a polite distance, their conversation limited to exchanges about what was on television, or who would use the bathroom first. She had no connection to him: he was a stranger who visited Brigadoon, sat up drinking whisky with his father, and then left again. Coming here, she realized, was a terrible cheek; but what else could they do?

Palace Court had not changed. There were bright boxes of geraniums in the forecourt, and the gleam of brass name plates by the main entrance, causing Bennett to hesitate, unsure of her plan now that she had seen the imposing frontage of Oliver's residence.

'It's OK,' Cissie said, helping her up the marble steps to the foyer. 'Wait till you get to the fifth floor . . .'

'It's so early –' Bennett was not so sure of her plan now they had arrived.

The lift clattered upwards and shuddered to a standstill on the tatty landing.

They stepped out and stood, fearful and shivering outside the tatty door. Cissie pressed the bell, and waited. After a long wait, they heard footsteps approaching, and the door was opened.

'Hello?' A grizzled, T-shirted man with a Campbell's soup can emblazoned on his chest peered out into the darkness of the hall.

'Is Oliver in?' Cissie asked.

He shrugged. 'Might be. You'd better come in and find out.' The man had white stringy legs protruding from the T-shirt, and bare feet. The smell of French cigarettes followed him down the dark, threadbare passage. He paused outside a door halfway down, and indicated it with a jerk of his head.

'That one,' he said, and, as they still stood paralysed in the open doorway: 'Come on! I want to get back to bed!'

He disappeared into a room opposite, slamming the door. Bennett and Cissie tiptoed in, exchanging a troubled glance outside Oliver's door.

'You knock . . .' said Cissie.

'No, you . . .'

Cissie knocked. From across the hall came the sound of a radio. The Campbell's soup man had evidently decided that sleep was impossible now. Bennett, who was clutching her back, her face taut with pain, knocked again, harder. They heard a sound from within, then, after a pause, the door opened. A girl with long, straggly blonde hair peered out, still dazed with sleep.

'Is Oliver there?' Cissie asked. 'I'm his step-sister.'

The girl's eyes focussed a little more. 'You are?' She was American. 'He never said he had a sister.' She was awake now, studying them both, suspicious, clutching a pale silk kimono across her tanned breasts, a tousled, glamorous vision.

'Could you just call him?' Cissie was determined. She had come this far. She was not going to be deterred by some Yank with long legs and perfect cheekbones.

'Hey, Ollie!' The girl had turned, and was shouting into the room beyond. 'There's a chick here says she's your sister.' She turned back, eyeing Bennett with some concern. 'Hey – you all right? You better come inside.'

Gratefully they entered. It was a high-ceilinged room with tall windows looking out on to Moscow Road and the courtyard below. Bennett sank into a frail-looking, worn sofa with a groan of relief. The American girl disappeared through a bright red door into an adjacent room, leaving Cissie to stand, staring about her, intrigued. So this was where Oliver lived. She had never bothered to imagine what life for Oliver was like, so to come suddenly upon his life like this felt like an intrusion, as if she had suddenly found his diaries, or could read his mind: Oliver, who ever since she could remember had been a silent, inconstant presence in her life – shadowy, without interest. So this was where – and how – he lived. The walls were covered with posters and notes and sketches and paintings, jostling for attention, overlapping in a haphazard kaleidoscope of colour. A psychedelic poster of Jimi Hendrix hung next to a landscape in oils; an unidentifiable poem, carefully written out in beautiful copperplate, jostled for attention next to a sketch of a nude. Cissie approached it. It was the girl in the kimono, stretched out on a bed, gazing straight at the artist, her face challenging. Below it, to Cissie's surprise, she saw a polaroid picture of Brigadoon, enveloped in snow, with footsteps trodden in the path and a glimpse of Toulouse sniffing under a bush. It seemed incongruous somehow, to come across this piece of her own life in the foreignness of Oliver's flat, in London.

He had appeared behind her, bare-footed and in jeans, pulling on a T-shirt. 'Do you realize it's six o'clock in the morning?' he said. He was not pleased to see them at all. 'What have you done this time?'

'Ollie, that's not very kind.' The American girl was lighting a cigarette, perched on a large mountain of bulky objects covered by an Indian bedspread in a corner of the room. 'The girl's obviously in labour – we'd better get an ambulance.'

'No!' Bennett had collapsed against the grubby brocade of the sofa, clutching her back, anguished. 'We've been eating hash cakes, Oliver – I don't want to get busted – they'll take my other kid into care –'

Oliver turned to look at Bennett, annoyed, taking in her condition. 'Silly bitch. What on earth are you doing in London when you're about to give birth?'

'It's not due for two months yet,' Cissie told him, indignant.

'We went to see George Harrison.' Bennett explained, her mouth taut.

Cissie saw Oliver's expression. 'Then we were at Middle Earth,' she said quickly. 'And don't call her a silly bitch.'

Bennett struggled upright. 'If I could just lie down for a couple of hours . . .'

Oliver looked at the girl in the kimono. 'Do you know anything about babies?' he asked her. 'Is she in labour, do you think?'

The girl shrugged. 'I'm not a midwife, honey.' Cissie wondered fleetingly what she was: a model? an artist? She was certainly a vision. What on earth was she doing with Oliver?

'Please,' Bennett persisted, 'just a couple of hours' kip, Oliver. I don't think this is labour – just a bit of backache. I've been lying on the floor all night –' Only the whiteness of her knuckles as she gripped the threadbare arm of the settee revealed to Cissie that this might not be an accurate summing-up of Bennett's condition.

'Maybe we should call a doctor —' she said slowly.

Bennett turned to her, furious. 'No!' she snapped. 'I'm all right! I just need to lie down.'

The American girl made a decision. She slid off her perch and crossed the room to help Bennett to her feet. 'Come on,' she said, her voice kind. 'The bed's still warm.' She ushered Bennett away through the red door, leaving Cissie to face Oliver, who glowered at her from where he had flung himself into a sagging armchair draped in a tartan blanket.

'Sorry,' she said abruptly. 'I wouldn't have come if there had been anywhere else —'

'No?' He watched her, his hand tapping on a plaster skull perched on the table, the only sign of his anger.

Cissie looked around her. The sun was beginning to filter through the nicotine-coloured net curtains at the windows, dappling the room with light. 'Nice place,' she said, looking round. And it was, in a tatty, impoverished kind of student way. 'Are those your drawings on the wall?'

'Most of them.' He reached over and took a cigarette from a packet of Embassy on the table, and lit it from a book of matches, not offering Cissie one. 'You'd better sit down,' he said finally, inhaling, contemplating her coldly. 'Unless you're intending to dump your mate on me and bugger off home.'

'Of course not!' Cissie felt an angry blush rise up. 'Of course not!' She felt like weeping, she was so tired. Instead she wandered to the window and looked out. In the street below, someone was walking his dog, and a milk float lumbered past. Faintly, she could hear the sound of the radio from across the passage, playing classical music.

Oliver must have heard it too, because he said, 'Who let you in? Was it an oldish guy, grey hair?' She nodded. Oliver groaned. 'You woke Geoff up! I'll never hear the last of it — I'll have to keep him in Scotch for the next fortnight.' He seemed to relax suddenly, resigned to her presence and this interruption. She turned away from the window to find him watching her, curious. He needed a shave, she noticed. 'Sit down,' he repeated, his tone more friendly this time. 'When Cindy comes out I'll get her to make some tea, all right?'

She sat down in an armchair opposite him, facing a gas fire, unhappy at being scrutinized.

'So,' he said, after what seemed like a long silence, punctuated only by the movement and sound of his smoking. 'So what are you up to?'

She studied the toe of her painted boot. She did not want to communicate with Oliver. She wanted Bennett to get up and say she was all right, so they could hitch home together down the A11, like they always did, and everything would be focussed again, familiar, safe. She looked at the red door, willing Bennett to come through it, but she did not. There was just Oliver, his brown eyes watching her, observant.

'I told you,' she said finally. 'We've been to Middle Earth.'

'I didn't mean today. I meant generally.'

'Nothing much.' She twisted a ring round her finger. It was silver, with the sign of Yin and Yang on it. She had bought it at Barsham Fair a couple of months ago. A sudden vision of the fair sprang before her, with its fortune-telling tents and its 'medieval' dancing, the sound of flutes drifting over the camp-fires, the smell of marijuana clinging to skirts and sheepskins. Tears stung her eyes at the memory of it. There had been a rumour that George Harrison was coming, and she had wandered the muddy paths between the tents and the sideshows and the music stages, hoping to glimpse that face somewhere in the bedraggled crowd: but to no avail. Later she had heard that the Beatles had been recording in London all summer. The visit to Barsham by one of them had been a fantasy, a rumour, cooked up to entice visitors. Because, of course, they lived separate, magical lives. They did not descend to earth and mix with mortals.

Oliver sighed and shifted in the armchair. She gazed at him sideways through the screen of her hair. She could see his arm, brown against the fabric covering the chair. She could see the sinews in his wrist, and the long fingers holding the cigarette. 'God,' he said. 'It's like getting blood out of a stone.'

'I'm going to university,' she said finally, reluctant to give him any information. What business was it of his? 'In the autumn,' she added.

'You are?' He seemed surprised, almost pleased. 'Which one? What subject?'

'University of East Anglia. English Literature.'

There was a silence. 'Why there?' he demanded, stubbing out his cigarette. 'Why go to that concrete monstrosity? All those beautiful old universities you could have gone to –'

'I wanted to go there,' she said, stubborn. 'Anyway, I like modern architecture.'

'Liar!' he flashed. 'You've never liked anything modern in your life, apart from the fucking Beatles.' He snapped the word angrily.

She was completely taken aback. 'Don't you like them?' she asked, amazed. 'Don't you like the Beatles?'

'I like them,' Oliver said, 'but I'm not in love with them.'

'Neither am I!' she flashed back. Then, considering, trying to be honest, 'Not all of them.'

'I know,' was all he said.

Cissie was defensive, angry. 'I'm supposed to like music. It's in my blood, so my mother tells me. That's how I got my stupid name, didn't you know? Cecilia, patron saint of music. So I like music. The Beatles. It fits.'

'I looked it up,' he said. 'It also means blind.'

She stopped, her anger interrupted by surprise. 'What?'

'Your name. It means blind.'

There was a second of shocked silence. Then Cissie pushed it away. 'You don't know,' she said, stubborn, her mouth set in an angry line. 'You don't know anything about me. Why don't you mind your own business?'

'I know why you're going there,' he said, as if he had not heard her, '– to that university. Because you're too scared to get out.'

She flung her hair back, her face pink and angry, her eyes meeting his. 'Shut up!' she said. 'Shut up! You have no idea –'

'Oh, but I do,' he said. 'I do. You're scared to leave Norfolk, scared to leave Peg and that house and Polston Wood. Scared to

178

have a proper adventure. All you're going to do is stay in Norfolk and do what people expect bright girls like you to do.'

She got up, suddenly, in a furious, jerky movement. 'Fuck off!' she said, furious, her mouth trembling, fighting back tears. 'Fuck off!'

She went over to the mysterious mountain under the Indian bedspread in the corner, her back to Oliver, quivering with exhaustion and rage. How dare he! She fingered the paisley cloth, willing herself not to cry.

'Why are you so angry, Cissie?' Oliver asked her, his own voice taut. 'Is it because I've hit a nerve?'

She had never heard him say her name before. It sounded odd, this intimacy, from someone who had always been there in her life but who was a stranger. She felt irrationally insulted, as if he had said or done something obscene. She lifted the cloth a little to see what was underneath. She saw a corner of smooth veneer, a heap of tangled wires.

'Televisions,' Oliver said, by way of explanation. 'They're televisions. I mend them, remember?'

She turned again, triumphant. 'Exactly,' she said, her voice loud and hard, even to her own ears. 'A tin-pot electrician. A tin-pot electrician with a painting hobby who's never moved out of London. And he wants to lecture me on having adventures!'

There was a silence, only the fizz of their first real connection sparking between them in the sunlit room. Finally Oliver spoke. 'It's because of who I am,' he said, his voice quiet. 'You're right. I didn't do it.'

'So you want me to have adventures on your behalf.'

A muscle in his cheek was moving. She had never really seen Oliver upset before. 'I want you to stop posing as a hippy and go out there and *be* one. Go away. Have some fun. Do something unpredictable. I mean really unpredictable. Not following George Harrison about. I mean . . .' he hesitated, thinking, 'I mean something magical. Something special. Something just for you and no one else.'

She stared at him, surprised. His head was lowered so that she could not see his expression. He had never really spoken to her before, she realized. And she had never really spoken to him. He raised his eyes and looked at her, waiting to see what she would say, but the moment was interrupted by the opening of the red door, and the emergence of the American girl, now resplendent in velvet jeans and a lace vest, which she buttoned up as she crossed the room.

'I'm calling an ambulance,' she said over her shoulder. 'That kid's about to deliver.'

Cissie leapt up and hurried towards the other room, following Oliver. Bennett was sitting up, propped against an array of satin pillows, an oddly pink and fleshy creature in the opulence of the mock-leopardskin coverlet, the purple mosquito net draped from the ceiling, the gold-painted walls. She grinned at Cissie, sweating, her hands gripping a beaded cushion.

'What about this, then!' she exclaimed. 'It's like being in a bleedin' harem!'

'She's gone for an ambulance,' Oliver said, hovering by the bed. 'Shall I make you a cup of tea?'

Bennett's face suddenly creased with pain. 'No,' she gasped, reaching out and clutching his bare arm. 'No – I don't think there's time.'

Cissie stood helplessly by the door. 'Don't push, Bennett!' she said desperately, remembering an episode of *Emergency Ward Ten*. 'You mustn't push!'

'Can't help it!' yelped Bennett, suddenly kicking off the satin coverlet, her face a bluish purple as she strained and grimaced. 'It's coming!' she whooped. 'It's coming!' She sat forward, her shoulders hunched, grimacing, still holding on to Oliver, her nails making livid marks on his flesh. 'Sorry, Oliver,' she panted, 'making a mess on your sheets.'

'What do we do?' Oliver appealed to Cissie hopelessly. She was transfixed, staring at Bennett, paralysed.

'Don't worry –' Bennett gasped. 'I'm doing it –'

'Oh God,' murmured Oliver, leaning over the bed and grasping Bennett's other hand in his, 'Oh God . . .'

'Won't help me now –' cracked Bennett, grinning and frowning all at once, perspiration clamping her hair to her forehead, 'Not God, not Shiva, not Mohammed –' she suddenly let out a full-lunged cry, and Cissie leapt forward, galvanized by fear.

'I can see the head,' she said to Bennett, excited and revolted all at the same time, 'I can see the head! Push!'

'I am!' grunted Bennett.

'The shoulders – they're through –'

Oliver was hugging Bennett, who clutched at him as if she were drowning, terrible grunts emanating from deep inside her, her eyes bright with exhaustion. 'Come on!' he said. 'Come on, Bennett! You can do this – you've had practice –'

She laughed shakily at him, pausing suddenly from her labours. 'It doesn't get easier,' she panted.

'One more,' Cissie called, her voice unexpectedly strong from the foot of the bed. 'Come on Bennett – shut up and *push*!' She did, and suddenly in a great slimy rush there was a baby, blue-faced, wrinkled, writhing, silent, and a puddle of bloody mucus, and Bennett reaching forward and pulling the baby to her, its cord still attached, and sticking her fingers into its throat and a tiny mewling sound and then smiling at Cissie and saying, 'It's a girl.'

Bennett lay back among the bright pillows, exhausted, the baby on her breast, still bloody.

Oliver got up unsteadily and said something about fetching Geoff. He left the room. There was a moment of silence, just the hum of cars on the Bayswater Road in the distance, and the small snuffling sounds from the newly emerged creature, a little, bloody, newt-like thing resting on its mother, eyes closed.

'You choose the name,' Bennett said weakly. 'That man – the one called George. Outside Covent Garden. It was an omen. You choose the name.'

Cissie searched her exhausted brain for something suitable. It would be no good calling it something normal – Bennett would never forgive her. She ran through a list of pop stars' children: Tiffany? Rainbow? Saffron? She sat back on her heels on the faded carpet, trying to think. Her hand brushed her shoulder bag, still somehow on her shoulder, and she felt the bulk of the book inside, a book she had been trying to read and make sense of for weeks, to no avail. It had been a book that someone said George Harrison read. It was called the *Bhagavad Gita*. 'Doma,' she said. 'It's Tibetan for peace.'

Bennett closed her eyes, pleased. 'Doma,' she repeated. 'Doma Bennett.'

Oliver reappeared with the man in the Campbell's soup tin T-shirt. 'Geoff's going to cut the cord,' he announced. Geoff was carrying a bottle of Dettol and some nail scissors. Cissie was alarmed.

'Hadn't we better wait till the ambulance . . .?'

But it was too late. She turned her head, wincing, as Geoff leaned over the bed, scissors flashing in the light. She caught Oliver's eye. He was grinning at her. She looked away.

'Now,' Geoff was saying, 'if you would just push a little and allow me – we need to sort out the placenta –'

Cissie got to her feet, trembling. Her knees felt weak. She wondered when she could ever sleep. Outside, she could hear a siren approaching. She went over to the window and looked out. An ambulance was pulling into the entrance of Palace Court, and below her, like a tiny figure in a cartoon, she could see Cindy, Oliver's glamorous American, running down the steps to greet it.

Within ten minutes Bennett was on a stretcher, her sleeping baby wrapped in a blanket beside her, being manoeuvred into the antique lift. She blew Cissie a kiss and disappeared, too tired to speak. On the landing Cissie, Geoff, Oliver and Cindy watched her go.

They stood, an odd little group, staring down the lift shaft. Even when they heard the clang of the doors on the ground floor, the muffled shouts and instructions gradually disappearing into the foyer and outside, they still stood, dazed and speechless. Finally Cindy turned to Oliver, and kissed him lightly on the cheek. 'I'm going to work,' she said. She hugged Cissie, emotional. 'You did great, honey. Nice to meet you. Maybe one day I'll come to the famous Brigadoon . . .' And she was gone, down the stairs, disappearing into the darkness of the fourth floor.

Cissie stood, worrying about Bennett, too tired to clarify exactly what her worry was. 'You can see her later,' Oliver said, reading Cissie's thoughts. She had wanted to go in the ambulance, but the ambulanceman had said no, there was no point – Bennett would sleep most of the day; better to turn up at the hospital later – no point in sitting around for hours. 'Anyway,' he had added, eyeing Cissie's crumpled finery with cynicism, 'You look like you need a few hours' kip yourself.'

Geoff turned back to the front door. 'Do what you like, I'm going to get some shut-eye,' he said.

'I owe you a bottle of Bell's,' Oliver said.

Geoff looked at Cissie. 'By the way,' he said, his voice dry, 'I'm a doctor, in case you were wondering.'

He, too, disappeared. They heard the slam of his door. 'Is he?' Cissie asked. She followed Oliver back inside the hallway and then along the corridor into his flat.

'He was,' Oliver said. 'An abortionist with an alcohol problem.' He saw Cissie's expression. 'Don't worry,' he said, 'his hand was pretty steady this morning.'

Cissie smiled, a shaky smile. Oliver disappeared into the kitchen, returning a few minutes later with two mugs of instant coffee. Cissie had sunk into the armchair. 'Sorry,' Oliver said, handing her a mug, 'we've only got evaporated milk.'

He perched on the edge of the sofa, watching her. She looked away, suddenly shy. 'It's all right,' he said. 'I don't bite.'

He was smiling. There was something slightly shocking about seeing Oliver smile. Cissie could not remember him smiling before. Oddly, it made him seem even more vulnerable than usual, even more solitary; which was peculiar, because Oliver was rarely alone. He usually had a girlfriend in tow, or spent hours on the phone at Brigadoon, or was ensconced in front of the fire with Mill, or chatting to Peggy in the kitchen, or closeted away with Mike and his lumps in the shed.

'Do you ever see your mum?' she asked him suddenly, shocking herself with the intimacy of the question.

He shook his head. It was his turn now to avoid meeting her eyes.

'She left when I was three,' he said. 'Mill was my mum, to all intents and purposes.'

She had a sudden vision of a small, anxious boy suffering the indignities of being brought up by a large, opinionated grandmother; but he was smiling again. 'How do you think I know all the words to "Old Man River"?' He grinned. 'Paul Robeson sang me to sleep every night.'

'It must have been hard,' she said timidly.

He shrugged, his face suddenly closing up again. 'You know she's ill, don't you,' he said.

'Who?' She knew, but she did not want to acknowledge what was coming, she did not want to hear what he would say next.

'Mill. She's got cancer. She's dying.'

Cissie stood up, suddenly, splashing coffee on to the rug, distressed. 'Yes,' she said. 'Yes, of course I know.' Oliver stood up too, and gently took the mug away from her. The small moment of intimacy was over.

'What are you going to do now?' Oliver asked her. 'Do you want me to ring Peggy?'

'No!' She was vehement. 'No.' She tugged at her hair, weariness making her blunter than usual. 'I just want to sleep. I can't stay upright much longer. Can I borrow your bed? The nurse cleaned it up.'

'Sure,' he said. 'As long as you don't mind sharing it.' She looked at him. 'Just to sleep,' he said hastily, suddenly embarrassed. 'Only I didn't get to bed till four myself. And the sofa's only got three legs.'

Pink, she hurried past him towards the bedroom, where she sat down and pulled off her boots, her face once more shielded by a curtain of hair. He stood in the doorway.

'I won't come anywhere near you,' he said, offended. 'What do you think I am?'

She did not answer, merely lay down on one half of the bed, clutching a pillow, burying her face in it. There were no covers now, only the striped ticking of the mattress and a heap of exotic cushions smelling of someone's perfume. She supposed it was Cindy's. After a moment she felt the bed creak as Oliver sat down on the other side. She closed her eyes, tense; but he merely lay down and turned the other way so that his back was to her, his body stiff and pulling away, careful not to allow any contact.

She opened her eyes again. This was awful. What was she doing? She was in Oliver's bed! The thought made her heart pound. This was a dreadful, forbidden thing, she told herself. Why? asked her other half – why, what are you doing? You are going to sleep with your step-brother. To sleep. And you're not even related anyway. She pushed the thought away. Behind her, she could hear Oliver's breathing. She wondered if he, too, was awake, lying tensely on the mattress, muddled by the drama of the morning, too tired to relax. She closed her eyes, and a strange jumble of images began to gallop past her eyelids – the sullen girl in the pink kaftan at Kinfauns, Middle Earth, the Jude-girl with the smeared mouth and the hypo-dermic, the crumpled five pound note being given to the taxi driver, the Indian cinema, Oliver's brown hand holding a cigarette, Oliver's voice, angry, telling her to be a real hippy, Oliver standing in the doorway, his eyes hurt, saying, 'What do you think I am?'

She rolled over, drowsy, her bones sagging, until her body was close to his, her face against his back, her knees curled in behind his. Oliver was all right. She felt bad that she had made such a crude assumption about him. It was crass and unhip. She was a silly, pro-vincial, uptight little twerp. Slowly she reached her hand over his body, around his waist. She felt his hand, warm and steady, find hers, holding it, keeping it in his. Then she fell asleep.

The train swayed and rolled on its track heading through the flat, sunlit fields towards Norwich, on the last leg of its journey. Cissie stared out of the window, avoiding the silent, disapproving stare of the middle-aged couple opposite. Judging from their expressions, she represented everything they loathed about living in these un-predictable times. She wanted to lean across and hiss, 'Yes! I'm on the pill. Yes! I stayed up all night. Yes! My bloodstream's full of illegal things you can only imagine. Yes! My brain is befuddled – and yes! I'm happy!' Because for some indefinable reason, she was.

The sun was warm on her hair. The fields streaked past, yellow, green, orange, brown, a sudden flash of church spire or rooftop hinting at passing villages, gone in the blink of an eye. She thought about the trains passing Brigadoon, beyond the cabbage field at the back of the house, and the passengers glimpsing the rooftop of her home as they passed, their thoughts elsewhere. How unimportant we all are, she thought sadly.

She thought about Bennett, sitting up in the maternity ward, cup of tea in hand, already embroiled in ward gossip and maternal intrigue. 'See her at the end? She's an exotic dancer in Berlin. That's her third baby. Black father. And the one by the door — her baby looks like Malcolm Muggeridge. The sister's a gorgon, but staff nurse is a sweetie . . .' She had been glad to see Cissie, issuing her with a hundred instructions. 'If you take Gandy round to Fiona's, she'll look after him till I get back — she was going to have him when I had the baby anyway — and can you visit my mum? Tell her she's a granny again? And send me a parcel of baby nighties, will you? They're in the top drawer in the bedroom, left-hand side . . .' Cissie had acquiesced to everything, too dazed by events to put up a fight. She had not stayed long at the hospital. She wanted to keep moving, as if movement would somehow prevent thought. She wanted to keep her thoughts away from the strange, unsettling night she had spent in Moscow Road. Oliver, saying those words — 'Mill's dying'. Oliver's face, watching her. These things were all gathering, like a menacing cloud above her head, threatening change, chipping away at the little monument of stability she had constructed for herself. The thought of university was terrifying enough; she could not countenance any more upheaval to the fragile edifice of self-protection she had laboured so long to build. She did not want to think about the strange rush of emotion she had felt when — no, it did not matter. Now she was going home. Brigadoon. The university. Must get the books on that list. Must mug up for the 'rise of the novel' seminar.

She dozed, her head against the window, dreaming about George Harrison with his unfathomable dark eyes and his kind face. She saw him as she had seen him last, on television a few days ago (was it really only a few days ago?), boarding a train to Wales with the

Maharishi and the other Beatles and Mick Jagger and Marianne Faithfull, George in a brocade jacket, beads around his neck. And once again she asked herself why she had not spoken to him when she had the chance. She saw again the thin figure in the grey suit, the long white fingers, the frown. The moment seemed to glitter like a tiny spark in a huge firmament full of stars – a moment in time only visible through a telescope and already a million years past, just its glow beaming to earth from a magical second lost forever. Oliver is right, a voice in her head told her, I'm scared of everything. Life. The universe. Even George Harrison.

The train suddenly jolted to a halt. She sat up, dazed. The middle-aged couple were already reaching up to the luggage rack for their bags, the man placing his holdall on Cissie's copy of *Oz* on the table between them with a small gloating look of triumph. She waited until they had left before slowly standing and gathering up her belongings. This was Norwich, where she existed only as a pale, uninteresting thing. It was as if she had left that other, bright creature somewhere behind, in Bayswater, or Covent Garden.

She walked slowly down the platform, trance-like, trying to wake up. She had to get to St Andrew's Mental Hospital, to carry out her promise to Bennett. There must be a bus, surely . . .

'We can spend the whole day in Harrods, Mammy – we can even have lunch in there.'

The familiar voice made her look up. Coming down the platform towards her was Heather, neat in a pink shift dress and matching shoes, her hair bobbing perfectly as she walked. Accompanying her, grim in a floral two-piece and white peep-toes, was Mrs Lewis.

Cissie paused, swaying slightly and grinning. Heather Lewis. She hadn't seen her since that disastrous party. She stood, watching as they made their way down the platform towards her, waiting for the moment when Heather would look up and recognize her. She pushed her hair out of her eyes, noticing suddenly how grubby her fingers were, how sweaty her blouse. At that moment Heather saw her. Cissie opened her mouth to speak, but in a swift second Heather had absorbed the sight of her, reacted, and with pursed lips and hot cheeks had ushered her mother away, round a porter with a luggage trolley, talking brightly and quickly, hurrying her mother on to the train, without a backward glance. Cissie turned and watched as they climbed aboard and the door slammed.

'Heather . . .' she said reproachfully, half to herself. Then she turned and headed for the exit.

This was a day for unexpected encounters. She had walked to St Andrew's in the sunshine, realizing it was not far from the station. Inside the huge Victorian mausoleum of a building she had trekked the long blank corridors in search of Bennett's mother, finally tracking her down to a bright day room, the sun streaming through a glass dome in the ceiling, where a group of men silently wove raffia wastepaper baskets, and Bennett's mother sat staring out of the window, the sun in her hair. Cissie told her about the baby, about the birth amid the satin pillows in Bayswater, about the man cutting the cord, the late arrival of the ambulance, the naming of the baby. But Bennett's mother had not even moved her head to look at her, turning a white handkerchief over and over in her hand, her face averted, blinking away from the jiggling dust particles dancing in the light before her.

'It's too soon,' a man in a white jacket had whispered to Cissie, before she gave up and walked away. 'She only came out of ECT a few hours ago . . .'

She had stood in the main entrance to the hospital, staring out at the long driveway leading to the main road, unwilling to step out into the heat of the day to make the weary journey back to Polston Wood.

'Cissie!'

She turned, surprised to hear her name called in this alien place. A thin, long-haired youth in jeans and a bright, woven Mexican top was standing in the foyer by the reception desk, grinning at her.

'Dave Williams!'

'Hi. You visiting someone?' She had not seen him since the Tech, when they had sat in the sports hall with the other students struggling with their A level English examination paper. 'Come with me.'

He ushered her into a small room just off the main corridor. It was some kind of staff room, with a couple of easy chairs, a work roster pinned to the wall, stained mugs on a tatty coffee table heaped with copies of *Mental Health Weekly* and the *Nursing Times*. On a filing cabinet in the corner perched a black and white TV, with a *Tom and Jerry* cartoon burbling quietly.

'Sit down! Coffee?' She shook her head, but sat down in one of the chairs, surprised at his pleasure in seeing her. She always assumed that people forgot her the instant she left their presence, and was always gratified by enthusiastic greetings. Dave had pulled a small, thin joint out of his jeans pocket and was lighting it. 'You look great,' he said, leaning against the filing cabinet, ignoring the TV, which flickered and muttered behind him. 'You got a job yet?'

'I'm going to university.'

'Brilliant! You lucky sod!' He handed her the joint. She was finding this difficult. She could not equate this smiling, relaxed individual with the grubby memory of losing her virginity on the floor of the living room at Brigadoon. Meeting his eyes was difficult. She puffed at the joint, watching him through the shield of her hair. He was fiddling with a stray cotton thread on his tunic. His fingernails were bitten to the quick and he had yellow paint on his knuckles. She remembered with a pang that those hands had touched her, and she could hardly raise her head to look at him; but she knew she must.

'And you?' she asked breathlessly. 'What about you? Are you still going to art school?'

He nodded. 'Sure. In September.' She returned the joint and he took a long toke at it, inhaling deeply.

'Which one?'

'Eh?' He had turned and seemed suddenly to be engrossed in the cartoon.

'Which art school?'

He sat down in the other chair, his eyes not leaving the TV screen. 'Wolverhampton. Maybe. Or maybe Edinburgh. I'm not sure.'

'Surely you have to register by now?'

He did not reply, merely leaning forward in his chair and studying the television as if it might contain the answer. Cissie decided he was probably very stoned. It was probably the only way you could cope with doing a job like this – looking after a thousand Mrs Bennetts.

The cartoon ended with a loud fanfare and the *Six O'clock News* began. She stood up. 'I should go,' she said. 'My bus –'

Dave was looking at her, surprised, as if he had just realized she was there. She was about to say good-bye when she heard something on the news that made her gasp and look up. Dave heard it too and turned his head. On the TV screen, the Beatles were standing in a doorway, their faces frozen. Paul McCartney was answering a question, shaking his head. Cissie's eyes found George. He stared into the camera, his eyes very dark and tired, his mouth slightly open, as if he were about to speak; but he did not. Instead John Lennon leaned forward and said something. Then George said, 'There's no such thing as death, only in the physical sense. We know he's OK now.'

The newsreader reappeared and began to talk about Cambodia. Dave looked at Cissie, stunned. 'Brian Epstein dead!' he said. 'Do you think he killed himself?'

'I've got to go,' Cissie repeated. She wanted to be alone, to absorb this new horror. Why did everything have to change, why did it all have to become ugly? 'Good luck at art school,' she said; but he was already sitting with his back to her, engrossed once again in the news, the joint unsmoked in his hand.

Out in the corridor a woman leaned across the reception desk and smiled at Cissie. 'You a friend of Dave's?' she asked.

'Sort of.' Cissie wished she could just leave. Why on earth was Brian Epstein dead?

'He's doing well,' the woman behind the desk was saying. 'We're reducing his intake of sodium amytal all the time. He should be out by Christmas.'

Cissie was almost at the exit before she registered what the woman had said. By the time she had stepped out into the blistering heat of the sultry afternoon, she had understood. And by the time she was walking up the gravelled drive, under the bleached conifers, she was laughing, exhausted, in a world gone mad.

CHAPTER SEVEN

Piggies – 1969

THE BATTERED MINI pulled up in the car park of the Camelot Hotel, next to a row of executive saloons and a white Rolls Royce bedecked with ribbons and white carnations.

'Oh, God,' said Cissie, in the passenger seat.

'It'll be all right,' said the driver, pulling on the hand-brake, cheerful. He had long hair, a beard, and was wearing red trousers and a purple jacket, with a drooping yellow orchid in his buttonhole.

'You don't know these people,' Cissie said gloomily.

Steve sighed and leaned back in his seat, surveying his girlfriend with his customary air of puzzled resignation. 'Why are we here, then?' he asked. 'I thought you wanted to come. I thought this woman was a friend of yours.'

'*Was* is the operative word,' she said. She leaned forward and pulled at her hair in the rear-view mirror. She had tied it back and fastened it with velvet ribbons. 'Do I look all right?'

'You know the answer to that,' Steve said, climbing out of the car, shivering as the January wind caught at his clothes. Cissie climbed out too, and Steve leaned for a moment across the bonnet of the car, admiring her, as she stood rearranging her skirts. She was wearing a Moroccan dress Peggy had brought her back from a holiday in Tangiers, made up of heavy patchwork pieces of velvet and wool, brightly coloured, all stitched together in a riot of red and blue, with an embroidered bodice gleaming with tiny inlaid mirrors. On her feet she wore blue boots, and her hands gleamed with fistfuls of silver rings.

'You look like you should be pitching a tent with the Bedouins,' he said.

She turned, anxious. 'Do you think it's too much?'

He had locked the car, and now came round and hugged her. 'Don't be daft. Of course not. It's a bloody wedding, isn't it? I thought we agreed that weddings were a bourgeois ritual enabling the middle classes to dress up. So here we are, dressed up.'

Cissie pulled away from him, smiling her self-contained little smile. 'Have you got the invitation?'

Steve pulled it from his pocket and handed it to her. 'I still don't see why —'

'It's none of your business,' she said sharply, turning towards the hotel entrance, holding up her skirts to avoid the puddles.

'Weddings are supposed to be happy occasions,' he shouted behind her, raising his voice against the wind. 'You're not supposed to go in there wanting to kill the bride —'

'She invaded my privacy!' Cissie yelled back over her shoulder, stalking up the marble steps. 'She had no right.'

They had reached the hotel foyer, and they paused, taking in their surroundings.

'Jesus,' said Steve under his breath.

'Can I help you?' A woman in a suit was addressing them from behind the reception desk, a look of polite disdain on her face, her tone implying a certainty that she could *not* help them, since they were obviously not meant to be there.

Cissie pulled the invitation out of its envelope to show her, but Steve had moved over to the display board by the lounge entrance and was calling, 'This way! Wedding reception in the Round Table Room, first floor, it says here.'

Cissie followed him up the plush staircase, aware that the woman at the desk was watching their progress suspiciously. Steve paused at the top of the stairs, and then spotted a sign directing them along a thickly carpeted corridor. Already they could hear the sound of a thin musical attempt at a Hollies medley issuing from behind the double doors beyond. Two middle-aged women emerged from a door marked 'Guinevere's Boudoir' and headed in the direction of the music, not noticing Cissie and Steve. They talked loudly and excitably, plumply balanced on spindly high heels and weighed down by complex hairstyles involving towering hairpieces.

'Jesus,' said Steve again.

'You're not chickening out on me, are you?' asked Cissie, half-smiling. In an odd way, she relished the prospect of introducing Steve to what she felt was the 'real' Norwich — not the trendy, scruffy, left-wing status quo of the university, but the small-town, uptight, repressed paranoia of provincial city dwellers. She was sure there would be examples found here in plentiful supply.

Steve hooked her arm in his. 'I look on this as an interesting sociological exercise,' he said. Together they hurried along the corridor, as if fearful that hesitation might actually persuade them not to bother with any of this, and then together they pushed open the double doors and went inside.

They stood for a moment, uncertain, in the doorway, then the doors swung shut behind them, propelling them forward. They were suddenly in the midst of wedding guests murmuring quietly and self-consciously in small groups. It was evident that the reception was not yet in full swing. A few people turned and stared at Cissie and Steve, eyebrows raised. Cissie searched the rigid perms and the terylene two-pieces for a glimpse of the bride's mother, but recognized no one. A waiter appeared in front of them, dubious, proffering a tray. Steve took two glasses of champagne and began thankfully to drink.

'It's for the entry of the bride and groom,' the waiter told him, reproachful. 'There's only one glass per guest.' Cissie smirked. Steve stopped drinking.

'God!' he said. 'The complex rituals of the lower middle classes!'

The air was heavy with anticipation. Over in the corner an admiring gaggle of women discussed the wedding cake in stage whispers, studying its icing rococo intricacies with awe. The trio on the stage, three depressed-looking men in red jackets, struggled manfully with 'Jennifer Eccles', and occasionally a small bridesmaid skated across the empty dance floor. Suddenly the doors opened and a pimply youth in doublet and hose sidled in. 'Ladies and

Gentlemen!' he called in a wavering voice. 'Please welcome the bride and gar-ooom!' When all eyes turned to him, he seemed suddenly shocked by his central role in the proceedings, staring round at the assembled company with frightened eyes, and then, as the trio on stage fell silent, he held up a cornet and began to blow. The guests shuffled forward, eager. The cornet had a red fringed pennant hanging from it, with 'CAMELOT' embroidered in gold in what Cissie supposed was meant to be medieval text. There was a squeal from an excited little girl in frills as the youth finished his cornet solo, swept off his hat in a low, embarrassed bow, and opened the doors.

'Probably does the washing-up when he's not being Alan A-Dale,' whispered Steve.

'Isn't that Robin Hood . . .?' Cissie hissed back.

Their debate was curtailed by the band striking up a wavering version of the Wedding March, and the triumphal entry of the bride and groom, who paraded down the empty dance floor, pink-faced and self-conscious, amid much aahing and back-slapping from guests.

'I don't believe it,' murmured Cissie, peering round at the as-sembled company and counting the number of pink taffeta dresses dotted about. 'Eight bridesmaids. *Eight!* Trust Heather . . .'

Mr Lewis had climbed up on to the stage, and was holding the microphone he had picked up from the top of the organ, still in its stand. He held it nervously, as if it might explode, and when he spoke, his voice twanged from inaudible to deafening. 'Thank you . . . wedding . . . wonderful day . . . beautiful daughter,' he hemmed and coughed, stroking his grey moustache with a terrified finger, his face contorted into a frozen smile. '. . . Glad you could come . . . Far-flung corners . . . Drink a toast . . . AND GROOM!' Every-one raised their glasses, murmuring, and drank. Cissie could not see Heather over the heads of the guests gathered in front of her. She clinked Steve's glass, exchanged an ironic grin, and drank. There was muted applause. Mr Lewis breathed loudly into the micro-phone again. 'Long evening ahead . . . Dancing . . . Buffet meal . . . So *bon appétit* and . . . er . . .' His voice died away. He stared down at the crowd below the stage, blinking. 'Thank you,' he said lamely, and stepped down, to scattered, half-hearted applause.

The trio launched into 'Be Bop A Lula' and a few brave souls ventured on to the floor, defiant grannies with cardigans on over their dresses, giggling children, and a serious-looking couple who had evidently been practising the more intricate aspects of the jive for several years and were eager to give a demonstration.

'Right,' said Steve, who had been to fetch two glasses of wine, and was now leaning against the flock wallpaper, surveying the assembled guests. 'Tell me who's who.'

'Can't,' said Cissie. 'Don't know anyone.' She saw Heather, suddenly, surrounded by bridesmaids, only a few feet away, and at the same moment Heather saw her. Her face arranged itself into a pleased smile and she crossed over at once to greet her old friend, kissing her theatrically on the cheek, careful not to smudge her lipstick. 'You came!' she breathed, stepping back to absorb Cissie's colourful costume, admirably retaining her expression of pleasure and hiding any other emotions she might feel. 'Lovely frock. I looked for you in the church,' she said.

Heather, the only girl of her age in the universe to use the word 'frock', was prettier than ever, Cissie decided; only now that prettiness had the sheen of manufactured glamour about it: the perfect make-up, the manicured nails, the discreet false eyelashes, the glossy hair under the short white veil thrown back to show the bland, bright little heart-shaped face to perfection. 'I wasn't in the church,' she said bluntly. 'I'm not a Christian.'

For a second Heather wore that insecure expression Cissie remembered from their early teens, when someone (usually Jude) had told Heather her shoes were wrong, or it was no longer acceptable to like Cliff Richard. 'Are you not . . .?' she said politely, suddenly very Scottish. Her eyes lighted on Steve, who was studying this exchange with interest. 'Is this your boyfriend?' Steve stepped forward, polite. Heather's eyes widened. 'Och, Cissie! I can see why you picked him!'

Steve grinned, surprised by this outburst. Heather was studying his face closely, the embroidered edge of her veil grazing the shoulder of his purple jacket. 'The likeness is uncanny,' she said. Steve wilted. He knew what was coming. 'George Harrison to a T.' Heather smiled at him, dazzling. 'Only better looking, of course.'

'And nicer,' he said. 'Hi. I'm Steve.'

'No one is nicer,' Cissie murmured, indignant.

'I'm Heather,' she said.

'I know,' Steve was clearly a little impressed. 'I've seen you on the telly.'

Someone had materialized behind the bride, large and grinning.

''Lo, Cissie,' Ray Broadbent said, his face beaming with pleasure. 'Fancy seeing you here!' Remembering him in his Crookfield Grammar School blazer, it was difficult for Cissie to deal with this grown-up figure in a dark suit, hair slicked back neatly, the adolescent fuzz on his face gone. Only the large, embarrassed hands dangling from white shirt cuffs hinted at the gawky boy she had known.

Politely, she kissed him on the cheek. 'This is Steve,' she said. They shook hands. The encounter reminded Cissie of a gorilla meeting a spaniel, so little did they have in common, and she had to choke back a giggle.

'Shall I introduce you to my bridesmaids?' Heather was asking Cissie.

'No, really –'

'I'll just tell you who they all are, then. Julie – that's the tall blonde one – she's in make-up. Then Val – she's the dark one next to her – she's a PA to the producer. And Janet – she's the one with the perm – she's a secretary in the newsroom.'

'Fascinating,' murmured Cissie, politely looking in the direction of the pink taffeta figures scattered around the room. The dance floor was filling up now, as people mellowed a little after their first drink or two.

'See that little one by the stage? That's Pauline, my cousin on my dad's side. And the one with the red hair is Caroline, she's the links girl. You know. After the news.'

Cissie had stopped paying attention. 'The what?'

'She does the links,' Ray said helpfully. 'You know. Tells you what programme's coming on next.'

Steve had spotted a local celebrity at the bar. 'Isn't that thingy – the bloke who does the weather?'

Cissie frowned at him, irritated by his descent into star-struck fan. They were supposed to be above all this. She had imagined they would regard it all with a wry smile, from a safe, ironic distance and make their excuses rather early on. Now here was Steve goggling at a few nonentities from the television, and getting stuck into his third glass of wine.

She turned to Heather, her annoyance making her more out-spoken than usual. 'I'm very angry with you,' she said.

Heather looked fearful. 'Why? What have I done?'

'You can't be angry,' Ray intervened. 'It's her wedding day.'

Cissie was waving the wedding invitation. 'You sent it to Brigadoon.'

'I didn't know your address at the university –'

'You sent it to Brigadoon,' she said implacably, 'and my mother got it.'

Ray had taken the invitation, still in its envelope, out of Cissie's hand. 'So what?' he demanded.

Cissie prodded at the envelope, still glaring at the bride. 'It's addressed to the girl from Norfolk with the flying table,' she said.

Heather stared at her. 'I thought you liked the fact that George called you that.' Her cheeks were acquiring an ominous pink blush. Tears were imminent.

'Cissie –' Steve murmured.

'My mum saw it and so did my little sister. She gave me stick for weeks.' Even as she spoke she heard it echoing in her head, as she did every time she visited Brigadoon, and she saw Susie, her small face round and grinning with glee, chanting 'Flying table! Flying table! Flying table!' – then the freckled face crumpling into tears as her adored big sister shoved her in the chest and told her to shut up – then Peggy's face, pained, hurt – 'Oh do grow up, Cissie – she's only eight, for heaven's sake!' - and then Toulouse growling, and

Mike muttering, and the whole cycle of family alienation starting all over again.

Heather had recovered her poise. 'Oh, is that all?' she said. 'Sorry!' She sipped at a glass of champagne, her eyes wide and guileless. Cissie gave up. Heather had never quite understood anything.

Ray and Steve had lost interest in the argument and were returning to a debate they had apparently already started. 'I suppose you think drugs are going to change the world,' Ray was saying disparagingly, taking a defiant gulp of beer. 'One big happy family, all that old tosh.'

Steve considered this for a moment. 'Not exactly,' he said, finally. 'There are always going to be plenty of bread heads messing things up.'

'Steve –' Heather was trying to attract his attention, to introduce him to someone, but he would not be deflected from his lecture. 'We've got to overthrow the politicians,' he continued earnestly. 'And we've got to stop people like you –'

'Steve –' Cissie pulled at his arm, not wanting a fight.

'Wage slaves!' he exclaimed, animated, spilling his beer on to the carpet, 'nine-to-fivers, propping up a corrupt system.'

'Bullshit,' Ray said stoutly.

Steve sighed. 'You should listen to the Mothers, man.'

Mr Lewis had joined them, his moustache damp with beer foam. He pumped Steve's hand enthusiastically, determined to distribute *bonhomie* evenly in all directions, even to this grubby hippy. 'Don Lewis,' he said, 'father of the bride. Come far?' He moved Steve away from the group slightly, a proprietorial arm around his shoulder. Cissie grinned. So Steve wanted to mix with ordinary mortals. They didn't come much more ordinary than Mr Lewis, who was even at this moment asking, with genuine curiosity, 'So what exactly *is* sociology, then?'

Ray was nuzzling Heather's neck. Cissie surveyed them, slightly disgusted. 'So,' she said to Ray, when he finally came up for air, 'you won out over Paulie in the end, then?'

Ray grinned, pleased. 'Linda Eastman beat her to it, didn't she.'

Heather was not amused. 'Yes, thank you, Ray.'

'She still won't talk about Linda,' Ray said.

Cissie sipped at her wine. 'We all have our little hangups,' she said, smiling sourly.

'Yes, and we all know what yours is,' Heather snapped back. 'That's why your boyfriend even looks like him.'

Ray studied Steve's back with interest. 'Who?'

Cissie finished her drink and slammed it down on a nearby table, picking up another one. 'He doesn't,' she said flatly. 'Nobody does.'

'He's even got clothes like George,' Heather said.

'So has half the world, in case you hadn't noticed,' Cissie was savage. 'Outside this little backwater there's a revolution taking place, you know. It probably won't get here for another twenty years –'

Heather rearranged the delicate folds of her veil, unruffled. 'She's just niggled,' she said to Ray, 'because he got married. Patti Boyd got there first.'

'Marriage is a bourgeois institution,' Cissie said. 'Didn't you know?'

'Is that why George did it?' Heather flashed back tartly. 'Because it's a bourgeois institution?'

Ray was looking at the entrance, his eyes alight. 'Talk of the devil!' he exclaimed. They turned, one expecting to see Paul McCartney, the other George Harrison. Instead Cissie was aghast when the bright head of her mother appeared round the doorway, followed by Mike holding Susie's hand. Susie was wearing her best party dress.

'What the hell are they doing here?'

'I invited them,' Heather said. 'I always liked your mum.'

They were making their way to the buffet table at the far end of the hall, Peggy in an elegant kaftan, Mike in his usual rumpled cords.

'She looks like a ruddy fashion model,' Ray said, awed, watching Peggy's progress through the wedding guests. The crowds parted and heads turned as she passed, a flash of colour in a sea of muted shades, like a parrot suddenly fluttering into a forest, with her birds' nest hair, her jangly earrings and the shockingly vivid blue-green of her robe, set against the muted pastel shades of the other women's

200

wedding outfits. Only Cissie knew that Peggy had run the outfit up on her old Singer and that the fabric was actually curtain material.

'Who's that?' Cissie heard an interested guest ask.

'Local author,' someone said. 'Must be something to do with all these television chappies –'

Susie had spotted Cissie, and came skipping towards her, grinning. She paused, clinging on to her sister's hand, staring up at the vision that was Heather with the kind of bald effrontery that only children have.

'Hello,' said Heather graciously. She had never been very keen on Susie, even as a baby. Babies were grubby and unpredictable, given to ejecting portions of their food from one orifice or another, usually over your best skirt.

'I'm not keen on your dress,' Susie said. 'Why didn't you have a mini?'

Steve materialized next to them, with a hunted look on his face. Mr Lewis had drifted away, his duty done.

'Thank God for some sanity,' said Steve, who had also seen the arrival of the Lovelocks. 'Come on!' He ushered Cissie away across the dance floor, leaving Heather and Ray to the intense scrutiny of the smallest Lovelock, Susie circling them critically, saying to Ray, 'Why doesn't your tie match the bride's bouquet?' Susie was very interested in colour and style.

'Hello, you,' said Peggy, when they arrived at the buffet table. 'This is a turn-up, isn't it? Us hob-nobbing with the local stars.'

'You caused a bit of a sensation yourself,' Steve said. He was very keen on Peggy and Mike, silently comparing them with his own parents, who were dull teachers from Cornwall. Peggy and Mike had been on holiday to the Soviet Union. His mum and dad always went to the Scilly Isles.

'An interesting mix,' Mike was saying, biting into a vol-au-vent and surveying the guests. 'Norfolk snobbery and tweeness meets Anglia TV vulgarity and money.'

'The Lewises are from Edinburgh,' Peggy said. 'They can hardly be accused of Norfolk snobbery.'

'Well, all right then,' he conceded. 'But all the same . . .' He was studying a good example near by, where two bland-faced men in good suits and expensive shoes had been trapped by a large and enthusiastic matron in a tent-like creation. She was chatting brightly and spilling crumbs of cake down her ample front, while they sipped from whisky glasses and nodded and smiled, silent and supercilious.

'Ray Broadbent's mum,' Cissie said, following his gaze.

'And I bet that's a couple of Anglia TV types,' Mike said. 'Worse than almost any other kind of human,' he addressed Steve with a conspiratorial air. 'At least with a bank manager or an insurance salesman you know where you are. Or a Tory politician. But this lot' — he waved a dismissive hand — 'all long hair and pretending to be arty, but all after a fat wage packet and most of them producing unutterably bad television programmes for the masses.'

'They speak well of you, too,' Cissie said. She hated Mike when he went into one of his rants. It was so embarrassing. Why did he and Peggy have to analyse everything, why couldn't they just shut up, drink their glass of wine, do a few foxtrots round the dance floor and then totter home, like everyone else's parents?

'Oliver's popping in later,' Peggy was telling Cissie. Cissie stared at her, shocked. 'I cleared it with Heather's mum this morning,' she said airily. 'He's coming down for the rest of the weekend. Seemed a shame to leave him hanging about at Brigadoon with only the dog for company.'

'What your mother is not telling you,' said Mike, 'is that she's busting with curiosity because Oliver is bringing someone with him. His new lodger.'

'A girl,' Peggy said, breathless. Cissie still had not spoken.

Peggy misunderstood her silence and said, 'I know he's not your favourite person in the world, but you could at least be polite.'

Steve was watching her, anxious. He could smell a fight in the air. 'Is that all?' Cissie asked, her voice abrupt. 'Just Oliver and some girl? Aren't there any more stray relatives you could have rounded up and brought here? After all, it's only my best friend's wedding. Why stop at Oliver? Why didn't you bring Toulouse? The cats? Mrs Michaels from the sweet shop?'

Peggy, who had been about to bite into a piece of cherry flan, was staring at her, mouth open, hand paralysed halfway to her mouth, still holding the flan. Finally she managed to say, 'Since when has Heather Lewis been your best friend? You haven't seen her for years.'

Cissie turned away, annoyed, and concentrated on studying the dancers circling past, to the tune of 'I Am The Walrus'. It had been a mistake to come. Heather's family were sad, not funny. Weddings were not amusing, only depressing. And her sodding family always got in the way of everything and upstaged her. She watched two young girls jiggling together self-consciously on the edge of the dance floor. They were surreptitiously studying her outfit as they danced. She experienced a sudden sorrow for them, knowing how they felt in their cheap Chelsea Girl mini-skirts, confronted by this vision of everything that was trendy. They would have spent hours of giggling anticipation in a flurry of Carmen rollers and Miners lipsticks and choosing whether to wear the Tropical Tan tights or the Burnished Bronze, debating whether to stick with the skinny-rib or go for the polka-dotted shift. That would have been the best part, the breathless excitement over what might happen, how they might be the stars of the day, how the boy of their dreams might just be there, and today might just be the start of something wonderful. Instead they had come here and been nobody, and – worse – had been crushed by the sight of someone more exciting than they were. She had probably ruined their day, just like her mother had ruined hers.

There was some kind of small disturbance taking place by the entrance. It was Bennett, who had arrived pushing a dilapidated pushchair containing a sleeping, jam-smeared child. Another clung to her skirts, round-eyed and silent. Around her, guests began to edge away. Cissie waved, relieved, and Bennett, seeing her, wheeled the pushchair across the dance floor, scattering jitterbuggers and twisters as she went, and arrived beaming at the buffet table, cherubic in cheesecloth.

'Watcha,' she said to Cissie, then, seeing the others, 'Steve – Peggy – Mike – thank Christ you're here. It's like *Return of the*

Zombies, isn't it . . .' She thrust the boy clutching her skirt towards the food. 'Go on, Gandy – eat. Stuff your face. It's free.' He obeyed, grabbing a fistful of sausage rolls. Cissie was leaning over the push-chair, stroking the baby's forehead. 'Little Doma . . .' she murmured.

'Out for the count,' Bennett informed her. 'Stayed up till mid-night last night.'

Across the room Heather broke away from Ray and headed to-wards them, hobbling in her empire line dress, her veil bouncing.

'You came!' She was breathless with excitement. 'You came! I never thought you would!'

'You did it then,' Bennett said. 'You and the hamster.'

Heather's smile faltered a little. 'Don't call him that,' she said. 'He's a deputy department manager at Norwich Union.'

Bennett was looking around, bemused. 'I can't believe this shit!' she said. 'You really went and did it.'

A small man blinking behind large spectacles appeared. 'Trouble?' he enquired of the bride.

She shook her head, embarrassed. 'A friend from school . . . Susan.'

Bennett grinned at him. 'Bennett. No one calls me Susan. And this is Doma. And Gandy.'

'This is Ray's dad,' Heather explained, tense. 'Bob.'

'Ah,' said Bennett. 'Hamster parent.'

Mike turned away with a smothered noise and began a close study of the food.

Heather was desperate to change the subject. She stared at the sleeping Doma. 'Are they yours?' she asked, her tone implying that they were an unfortunate acquisition.

'Gandy, did you say?' asked Ray's dad, assuming an interested expression. 'After Mahatma, presumably. Marvelous man, if a little misguided. Can I get you a drink – er, Bennett?'

'Tequila?' she asked hopefully. 'And it's Gandalf. You know, *Lord of the Rings*.'

Ray's dad looked blank. Heather's tone was terse. 'Get her a vodka and lime, Bob. I'm sure that'll be fine.'

Bob obeyed, setting off across the dance floor to the bar. Bennett was hugging Peggy. 'My favourite woman,' she murmured. Cissie looked away, annoyed. 'You pregnant?' Bennett suddenly asked Heather. Then, seeing her expression, said, 'Sorry, sorry . . .' She turned towards a plate of sausages on sticks and helped herself to several.

'How's the commune?' Peggy asked.

Bennett shrugged, her mouth full of sausage. 'You know. Good and bad. Jez is still not pulling his weight in the kitchen department. Bren and Martin aren't together any more.' She brightened. 'But we've finished the hall and the garden's amazing.' She drummed happily on a salt cellar with a couple of serving spoons. 'And my band's got a gig on Saturday. At the Hare and Hounds. I can put you on the guest list if you like.'

Heather took the spoons away and returned them to a bowl of salad wilting under the lights. 'You're playing in a group?' she asked, unable to keep the incredulity out of her voice.

Bennett nodded, burping quietly on her sausage. 'All-girl. The Damsels.'

Heather looked concerned. 'Who baby-sits while you're playing in this group?'

Bennett sighed and gave her a pitying look. 'It's not like that,' she said. 'It's not organized, or anything. Sometimes the kids come with me, sometimes they hang out at the house, if someone's there.' She patted Heather on the shoulder, condescending. 'Baby-sitting is a bit of an outdated concept.'

The trio on stage had launched into the opening bars of 'Ob-La-Di, Ob-La-Da' and Ray appeared, searching for his new wife.

'Dance?' he asked. Heather smiled up at him, radiant.

'Ray,' said Bennett, grinning. 'Long time no see.'

He smiled at her nervously, pulling Heather on to the dance floor. 'Nice to see you,' he called. 'Glad you could come . . .' They hastened to the centre of the floor and disappeared in a huddle of dancers, all singing along to the song, lubricated by lager and wine.

Bennett lit a cigarette and watched him, thoughtful. 'He isn't quite as hamster-like as I remember him,' she said. 'In fact, he's quite sweet in a Tony Blackburn kind of way.'

Gandy had wandered off amongst the guests, still eating sausage rolls, crumbs all over his child-size patchwork jeans. A couple passed, intent on dancing.

'I like a nice Beatles number,' the man said.

'Only the early years,' the woman said, her hair bobbing. It was a fantastic creation of false ringlets. 'I'm not very keen on them these days. They seem to have lost their way.'

Bennett and Cissie grinned at each other, hearing this. It was always a relief to hear the Beatles being slagged off. Mike was taking Peggy on to the dance floor. Steve looked at Cissie. 'You must be joking,' she said.

'Got any dope?' Bennett asked. Steve nodded. By tacit agreement, the three of them threaded their way back through the guests towards the exit.

The reception had not been so awful really, Cissie mused. She was leaning over a fire escape, looking down into the hotel car park, slightly drunk, slightly stoned, smoking a cigarette. There had been crass speeches from relatives, smooth-talking charm from Heather's boss at Anglia TV, 'the usual rituals', as Steve called them. Now everyone was feeling too drunk and sentimental to behave with decorum, and the event had become more real, more human. Mrs Lewis's hairpiece had slipped to reveal a forest of kirby grips beneath. Ray's mum had developed severe hiccups and had been unable to communicate coherently for the best part of an hour. One of the bridesmaids had had to be taken to the Ladies' in floods of tears because Doma, who had woken up and escaped from her pushchair, had ladled trifle down the front of her pink bridesmaid's dress, destroying its pristine sheen forever. The Anglia Television contingent had become very drunk and were guffawing irritatingly by the bar, exchanging stories about What Happened The Last Time I Went On Location. Throughout, the red-jacketed musical combo had manfully plodded their way through almost every song in the Beatles' repertoire, giving rise to some tears from the bride, particularly during a spirited rendition of 'When I'm Sixty-Four'.

Now Steve was busy flirting with Peggy, Mike was dealing with the children, and Bennett had disappeared. Or at least Cissie thought she had, but now she could see, in the shadows of the car park below, a figure very like Bennett's, sitting incongruously in the back of the beribboned Rolls Royce. Someone was in there with her. Cissie smiled to herself. Trust Bennett. Any opportunity to screw some poor hapless bloke who happened to be passing. Not for the first time, she thanked God – or Shiva, or whatever – for the advent of the pill. Although in Bennett's case it had been employed a little too late.

Sighing, she went back inside. It was too cold to linger having philosophical thoughts in the open air. Besides, she wanted another drink. Inside the Round Table Room, the last vestiges of decorum were fading. Wives were smooching with other peoples' husbands, in a drunken and excited attempt to enliven their marriages. Men accepted 'just one more' brandy, knowing they would probably pass out. Boys from the Norwich Union careened drunkenly about doing impersonations of Mick Jagger. The dance floor was strewn with streamers and discarded paper plates and bits of cake. Under the buffet table, Cissie could see Doma eating, her cheeks bulging. Gandy had fallen asleep across two gilt-backed chairs by the stage. Cissie felt someone watching her, and looked across to the bar. Oliver was there. As she caught his eye, he turned away, thanking the barman and taking a glass of wine, which he handed to the girl standing by his side. He leaned over her and said something which made her laugh, tossing her long dark hair back, revealing brown shoulders. As Cissie watched, the warm feeling draining out of her, Mike crossed the floor and spoke to his son. They both looked across at Cissie, and Mike beckoned. Cissie's eyes met Oliver's. She crossed to the bar, slowly.

'I got you a gin and tonic,' Mike said.

'I'm drinking wine,' Cissie said.

'Fine.' Mike turned back to the bar and called the barman.

'This is Jackie,' Oliver was holding the girl's arm. She smiled at

Cissie, showing very white teeth. She looked foreign, exotic, but spoke with a Welsh accent.

'And you're Cissie,' she said. 'They were right. You *do* look like Lizzie Siddal.'

'Jackie's at St Martin's,' Oliver said.

'You and your mother have wonderful colouring.' She studied Cissie unselfconsciously. All Cissie could see was Oliver's hand on Jackie's arm, comfortable, belonging. She was aware of a shocking surge of jealousy rising up in her throat, making her want to strike out. She felt utterly confused, alone.

'Pure Celtic blood,' she told Jackie. 'Then my mother goes and mixes it with the Lovelock variety and we get sandy hair and freckles. Have you met my little sister? More Minnie the Minx than Lizzie Siddal, I think you'll find. Excuse me.' She took the glass of wine from Mike without thanking him, and walked away, trembling. She hated Oliver. Why had he come?

In the back of the Rolls Royce Bennett was expertly rolling a large joint. Ray watched her, drunk, holding a glass of whisky and leaning back against the soft leather. Bennett was crumbling softened cannabis between her fingers on to the prepared bed of tobacco.

'All I'm saying is I don't know why you bothered with all this palaver,' Bennett was saying. 'Why not just shack up together?'

'You're joking! You met Mrs Lewis?'

Bennett ignored the question, licking a stray end of cigarette paper. 'It just strikes me as a bit sad in this day and age,' she said. 'Anyway, where do you do it, then? On Mousehold Heath? Yarmouth beach? Back of the car?'

He drank some more whisky, offended. 'Mind your own business. Snouty.'

She paused for a moment, open-mouthed, staring at him. 'You don't,' she said, realizing. 'You don't do it, do you. You and Heather – you've never done it.'

He was looking out of the window, red-faced and angry. 'Fuck off, Bennett. You don't bloody know anything.'

She busied herself with the joint, rolling it carefully between her fingers, forming a perfect tube, carefully plucking out a stray strand of tobacco and stuffing it back in one end. 'You should try it,' she said, looking at him thoughtfully. 'Back of the car – it's good fun.'

'You'll end up an addict,' he said, uncomfortable. 'All that marijuana.'

Bennett laughed, putting the finishing touches to her creation and holding it up for scrutiny. 'Yeah. Only this isn't marijuana.'

'Whatever it is, it's against the law.'

She put the joint to her lips.

'Rots the brain,' Ray said.

'Light?'

He reached into his waistcoat pocket and pulled out a lighter, holding it tentatively at arm's length, watching Bennett's face in the flame. She waited until there was a flare on the end of the joint and held it for a moment, staring at it.

'Mind the upholstery!'

Bennett inhaled and then held the smoke in her throat for a moment before expelling it in a satisfied wheeze. Ray watched her in the darkness.

She laughed softly at his anxious expression. 'I'm fading . . .' she whispered. 'My brain's going . . . Help . . .'

He took a swig of whisky, annoyed. 'Ha ha.'

'Want some?'

He stared at her over the whisky glass. 'Don't be daft.'

A car wheeled into the car park, its lights exploding into their faces so that they were suddenly visible to each other, expressions naked, eyes surprised. With a muffled gasp, Ray pulled Bennett on to the floor of the car, where they crouched together, giggling, until the car pulled in somewhere near the entrance. Ray had spilled most of his whisky and he could feel it growing in a cold circle against his leg. They sat hunched, motionless, until they heard the engine cut out. Then they were suddenly in darkness again. Ray could see the gleam of Bennett's eyes in the darkness, and the red glow of the joint.

'What are we doing down here?' she whispered.

He had never noticed before what soft white arms she had. 'I don't know,' he whispered back.

She reached out and touched him gently. 'Here,' she said. 'Go on. Just a puff. It won't kill you, I promise.' He took the joint carefully from between her fingers and put it to his lips. She was still touching him. He closed his eyes and inhaled.

Neither of them saw the lurching figure who staggered out of the shadows of the car park and headed for the fire escape.

He climbed the stairs very quietly, making sure his boots did not clang against the metal, panting slightly from the exertion. A film of sweat gleamed on his forehead. When he reached the landing where Cissie had stood earlier, he paused for a moment. Inside, a woman in a red hat adorned with a bobbing red feather was passing.

'Excuse me,' he said, 'is this where the wedding is?'

The woman looked at him, taking in his donkey jacket, unkempt hair and blazing eyes. She hurried away down the corridor without replying.

'Thanks!' he called after her drily. 'Thanks for nothing . . .' He stepped inside. At least it was warm in here. And maybe he would find a drink, even if he didn't find what he had come looking for.

He followed the woman in the red hat into the Round Table Room, and stood pressed against the wall, watching the wedding guests, sizing up the place, locating the bar and the buffet, registering some bottles of champagne standing unopened under a table at the far end of the room, near the stage. Not yet, though. He looked around. Near by, the bride was sitting at a table with a girl with long red hair and some straight-looking jerks in suits. The bride appeared to be crying. They were rather too close to him for comfort; he did not want to attract attention. He edged away a little, his eyes roving round the room, searching for someone. She wasn't here. His eyes returned to the champagne. Not yet.

Cissie pushed another glass of wine at Heather, biting her lip. 'Don't cry, you silly bitch,' she said. 'He's probably puking up in the bog.'

'I'm not crying,' Heather said, wiping a tear from her eye. 'I just think Ray shouldn't have gone wandering off with his mates, not today.'

Cissie looked at her, glum. *Probably how the rest of your life is going to be,* she thought.

The trio on stage were asking for requests. 'Jeff Beck!' a boy at their table shouted, drunk. 'Anything off the *Truth* album!' They launched into a shaky version of 'Hi-Ho Silver Lining', and the boy groaned in despair and buried his head in his hands. Another of the besuited young men leaned across and put his hand over Cissie's. 'You probably don't remember me –' he began, slurring his words, his eyes unfocused, smiling a little desperately at her.

'I do,' she said coldly, removing her hand. 'Graham Beasley. fourth set French.'

He grinned round at the collected gathering. 'She remembers!' He leaned forward again. 'I always fancied you,' he said, blobbily sincere. 'You were so . . .' he searched for the word, 'so *weird.*'

Cissie was only half-listening. Across the room she could see Oliver and Jackie slowly dancing together, her arms locked around his neck, her face close to his.

Graham Beasley shoved a half-pint of beer across the table. 'Get some of that down your neck,' he said generously.

She pushed it back. 'The trouble with weird,' she said, 'is that it was completely unacceptable in 1964 and now suddenly everybody wants to be weird. Weird is cool. Weird is OK. You'll be telling me next you've taken acid.'

He stared at her. 'Of course I have.'

She stood up suddenly, jolting the table, and the beer mug toppled over, slurping its contents over the surface, so that Heather leapt back with a panic-stricken cry, and the youths round the table fell backwards, scattering chairs and whooping. The other guests turned for a moment, hearing the noise, and then turned back, shrugging, tipsily tolerant. 'Youthful high spirits,' they said.

'My dress!' Heather shrieked. Graham Beasley dabbed at the puddle on the table with his handkerchief, shooting Cissie a look full of reproach. 'You always have to spoil everything,' he said. 'Think you're so clever.'

Cissie stamped away, looking for Steve. It was time to go home. Her head was full of confused and painful thoughts, not helped by too much wine. Oliver caught up with her by the door.

'Where are you going?' he asked.

'Home. Back to the university.'

He sighed. 'Cissie . . .' He did not seem to know what to say.

She looked into his face, defiant. 'Yes?'

'You hurt Mike's feelings.'

She stared at him, trying to remember. Did she? When? 'His feelings are easily hurt,' she said glibly, instantly regretting her words.

Oliver frowned. 'You can be a selfish little bitch when you feel like it, you know,' he said finally.

Cissie shrugged. 'Listen. Mike's not my dad, all right? I can't help it if I don't treat him like a father. That's because he isn't my father. He's your father, Oliver. My father's dead.'

Oliver looked as if he was about to say something, but then seemed to change his mind. 'Yes. And he's been dead since 1949. That's twenty years.'

Cissie giggled softly to herself and leaned miserably against the wall. 'It was twenty years ago today . . .' she sang in a low voice.

'Funny,' Oliver said. 'Funny how you can still be so upset over someone who's been dead for years and who you didn't even know. But you couldn't even drag yourself to Mill's funeral.'

She looked away. Why did he have to spoil things? 'Study weekend,' she said. 'We were visiting Jane Austen's house.'

'Right,' he said drily. She began to sing 'Sergeant Pepper' again, her voice defiant. She did not want to talk to Oliver about Mill, and the funeral she had missed.

Further along the wall, she caught the eye of an unkempt, good-looking boy. On hearing her singing, he had turned, curious, to look at her. Oliver was shaking her shoulder. The boy looked away.

'Stop it,' Oliver said. 'Just stop it, will you?'

She shook his hand away, fighting the desire to weep. 'Why don't you just leave me alone? Why don't you and your dad just piss off back to wherever you came from?' Oliver's face had hardened. He stood there, listening to the angry torrent of words she produced from nowhere. 'Mike is just my mother's second husband, can't you get that into your head? No one will ever replace my dad – no one! And Mill was Mike's mother. She was your grandmother, not mine! And you –'

'Yes?'

She bit her lip. She had no idea what her runaway tongue might say next. 'Go back to your girlfriend,' she said sulkily. 'Just piss off and leave me alone.'

Just for a second their eyes locked, and she knew he was sharing this confusion, this lunatic intensity. With absolute and exciting certainty she knew for a heart-stopping millisecond, and then it was gone, and there was just her awful, petulant speech hanging there between them in the silence.

Oliver turned away without a word. Cissie stood, unsure, for a moment, and then hurried away down the corridor. She pushed open the door marked 'Guinevere's Boudoir'.

In the pinkly lit, perfume-smelling room Doma was curled up asleep under the towel dispenser and Heather sat perched against one of the sinks. Bennett was kneeling below her, sponging her wedding dress with a soggy paper towel and a great deal of stoned concentration. Their faces lit up as Cissie entered.

'Here she is!' Bennett exclaimed.

Cissie wished the boudoir had been empty. She didn't want to talk to anyone. She wanted to hug her thoughts to herself, examine them, dissect them in the safety of her own head.

'Here – come and convince this dingbat that the stain is about the size of a quarter of a farthing.'

Cissie peered. 'A quarter of a quarter of a farthing,' she told Heather solemnly.

'That's a sixteenth,' Heather said, smiling through tears.

'I never was any good at algebra.'

Bennett frowned. 'Isn't it geometry?' She gave a mock sigh. 'That's why I went to the secondary mod,' she said.

Cissie hoisted herself up on to the sink next to Heather, hitching her skirts up around her thighs. Heather delved into a large vanity case balanced in front of the mirrors and found a packet of Embassy.

She handed them round, and they were all quiet for a moment, busy with the business of matches, enjoying the familiarity of each others' company. Faintly, they could hear the strains of someone attempting to sing 'I Say A Little Prayer'. They exchanged a wry look.

'Aretha Franklin eat your heart out,' Bennett said. She had reached inside Heather's capacious beauty case and found a couple of Tampaxes. She had settled on the floor, and now she drummed in a desultory manner on the pink floor tiles, using the white tubes as sticks, the cigarette dangling from her mouth.

'I was really glad Peggy came,' Heather said.

'She's brilliant, Peggy,' Bennett said, doing a drum-roll on a piece of piping to prove her point.

Cissie was silent.

Bennett looked up at her. 'She only wanted to chuck a bit of confetti.' The improvised drumsticks had moved on to the grubby toes of Heather's white satin wedding shoes. 'More than Jude did.'

They stared into space, each thinking about Jude.

'She's not going to come, is she,' Cissie said. She realized now that Jude was what she had been waiting for. Jude was why she had come.

'I sent the invitation to her mum and dad's,' Heather said.

'I rang her mum once. She said Jude hadn't been home for years.'

Bennett did a drum-roll on Doma's inert bottom. 'Bet she has.'

'Bennett . . .!' Heather retrieved the Tampax and returned them to the recesses of her vanity case, irritated. 'So why didn't she come and see us, then?'

'Probably didn't want to.'

Heather had turned, and was staring at her reflection in the mirror. 'I wonder what she looks like now?'

Cissie was thoughtful. 'Maybe something awful's happened to her. That's why we can't find her.'

'Maybe she changed her identity.' Heather brightened, excited by the thought. 'Plastic surgery. Or changed her name.'

Bennett began to sing softly. '*Her name was Magill, and she called herself Lil, but everyone knew her as Nancy . . .*'

Someone pushed at the door, trying to get in. Bennett leaned firmly against the door. 'Sorry!' she called, 'someone being sick in here!' The intruder retreated.

Heather had tears in her eyes. 'I thought you'd all come. One last time. The four of us.'

Bennett and Cissie exchanged a look. This was Heather's wedding day, after all.

'Come on,' Bennett said softly. 'Beatles forever, remember?'

Heather began to sing, sadly and quietly. '*When I get older, losing my hair, many years from now . . .*'

In gentle tones, Cissie and Bennett supplied the chorus, '*oobe doobe dooh . . .*'

'*Will you still be sending me a Valentine, Birthday greetings, bottle of wine . . .*'

Heather's voice faded away. They sat, silent, lost in their own Beatle thoughts.

Finally Bennett said, 'Favourite novel by Charles Dickens.'

Cissie did not even look up. 'Pigwick Papers.'

Someone hammered on the door and shouted and Doma stirred in her sleep, moaning a little.

'Go away!' Bennett shouted, her back firmly pressed against the door. 'Boudoir's full! Guinevere's got all her mates in.'

'I know!' exclaimed Heather, suddenly bright. 'Let's go up on stage and sing "I Saw Her Standing There" – just for old times' sake, like we used to in the playground.'

They groaned loudly. The banging on the door resumed.

'We're not singing without Jude,' Bennett said firmly. She got slowly to her feet, stubbed her cigarette out in a sink, and leaned over to retrieve the sleeping Doma.

Cissie slid down from her perch on the sink. It was time to go back into the Round Table Room and face the Lovelocks and rescue Steve. She opened the door and was surprised to find the wild-eyed boy from the wedding reception standing immediately outside. She had a glimpse of stark cheekbones, a shock of black hair, a thin frame huddled into an oversized donkey jacket, and then he was bundled away, shouting incoherently, locked in the angry clutches of Bob Broadbent and Donald Lewis, fathers of the bride and bridegroom, their faces red and indignant. Cissie watched them dragging the boy down the corridor. He was shouting, incoherent.

'Caught him trying to steal the champagne!' Mr Lewis called over his shoulder.

'No!' the boy shouted hoarsely, 'I was just holding it, man . . . Don't call the fuzz, please . . .'

Ignoring his pleas, they were manhandling him away towards the stairs.

'Hey,' he called, eyeing Cissie, desperate. 'Let's talk about this . . .'

The trio disappeared round the corner.

Cissie led the way back into the Round Table Room. She found Steve where she had left him what seemed like hours ago, hunched in a corner with Peggy, lecturing her.

'The thing about Durkheim,' he was saying earnestly, in between gulps of lager, 'is that he didn't think marriage was that important.' Peggy listened, polite, her thoughts evidently elsewhere. 'Although he did say that a family without children isn't a sufficiently strong integrating milieu –' Cissie pulled at his sleeve, and he looked up.

'Time to go,' she said.

Steve looked pained. 'We can't!' he said. 'We'll miss the final ritual.'

'Bride and bridegroom's departure,' Peggy explained.

Cissie sighed. 'What time is it?'

'It's supposed to be happening now, but no one could find the bride.'

Cissie could see Heather being corralled by her mother and ushered back in the direction of Guinevere's Boudoir. Ray seemed to be paralysed by the sight of Bennett in the doorway and stood fiddling with his cufflinks, a glazed expression on his face. Then he was suddenly caught up by a gang of besuited young men, and tossed drunkenly in the air before being manhandled out of the room.

Bennett joined them, the sleeping Doma draped across her

shoulder. 'Where's Oliver?' she asked. 'I wanted to meet the new woman.'

'He's gone,' Peggy said. 'She's very nice. Doing Fine Art at St Martin's.'

'He's a bit old to be shacking up with art students, isn't he?' Cissie said abruptly. 'She looked about eighteen.'

Too late, she realized they were staring at her, as if she had said something odd. 'She's the same age as you,' Peggy said. 'And Oliver's twenty-seven. He won't be collecting his pension for a while yet.'

There was an awkward silence, broken by Bennett asking brightly, 'Do we know where the new Mrs Broadbent is spending her honeymoon?'

'Do we care?' Cissie muttered.

'They're having a night in a hotel in Great Yarmouth,' Steve told them.

It was his turn to be the object of surprised scrutiny.

'How do you know?'

'What on earth are they going to Yarmouth for?'

'Why just one night?'

He was proud to be the bearer of information. 'Apparently he proposed to her in Yarmouth. And she's reading the news again the day after tomorrow, so they can only have one night away. And I know because I asked the bridegroom.'

'He proposed in Yarmouth?'

'On the roller-coaster. Pleasure Beach. End of the prom.'

'Yuk,' said Bennett, succinctly.

The boy in the doublet and hose had reappeared with his cornet. He blew it a few times and then shouted something hoarsely above the noise of the music.

'Must be time,' said Steve, getting to his feet.

Peggy eyed him, smiling. 'Last ritual under the microscope, eh?'

He shuffled a little, embarrassed. 'I thought you'd be interested, being a writer.'

Peggy stood. 'Oh I am,' she said. 'I am.'

She scooped up the sleeping Gandy and called to Mike, who had been dozing near by, Susie asleep on his lap. They all made their way across the dance floor, following the other guests in a dazed and weary troupe along the corridor and down the staircase.

In the foyer Mrs Lewis was ushering everyone outside. 'If you would just wait on the steps,' she commanded, 'they'll be passing through in a wee moment.'

'Will they be on a donkey and should we be waving palms?' Bennett enquired. Mrs Lewis rewarded her with a tight little smile. They stepped outside into the cold January night, and joined the other guests shivering on the steps, pulling their coats around them over their rumpled outfits. The children began to wake up and complain. Mrs Lewis passed among them, distributing boxes of confetti. Below them on the pavement, passing drunks, fresh from the closing pubs, joined the wedding guests, eager for a spectacle.

Gandy, Doma and Susie were awake now, bleary-eyed and complaining, hanging round Peggy's skirts. Bennett put her arm round Cissie's shoulder. 'One down,' she said.

'I'm never getting married.'

'Neither am I. Unless Ringo proposes.'

There was a bustle of activity and a murmur of excitement as Ray and Heather suddenly appeared, arm-in-arm, in the doorway. There was a scream from various young girls as they raced down to the bottom of the steps, calling to Heather for the wedding bouquet. Bennett and Cissie scowled and drew back against the wall. The bouquet flew past them through the air and was caught by one of the skinny girls Cissie had watched earlier. Blushing, she buried her face in the white flowers, giggling and proud.

'She'll be sorry,' Bennett pronounced gloomily.

'Interesting bit of symbolism,' Steve was heard to remark.

'Oh, shut up,' said Cissie.

In a flurry of confetti and catcalls, the bride and groom struggled down the steps to the waiting Rolls Royce, surrounded by a press of people, all eager to kiss them and say their farewells. Cissie watched them from her perch on the top step, feeling oddly distanced from the proceedings. There was Heather, being spirited away, and she felt nothing but a kind of despair: for her, for everyone.

Across the road, she suddenly caught a glimpse of a frenzied, staring face. It was the boy she had seen being bundled out, the boy who had stolen the champagne. He was staring across the road at the crowd around the car, his face desperate. Cissie followed his gaze, and for a shocked moment saw what he saw: the white and frantic face of Jude. In a strange flash, Cissie saw it all: Jude's look of sadness as she watched Heather, her eyes suddenly moving up to meet Cissie's, the sudden slide of her eyes and Cissie's shocked realization that Jude did not want to be seen. At the same time she intercepted the sudden turn of Ray's head, spattered with confetti, as he ducked into the car and looked up for a split second, meeting Bennett's imperturbable gaze. Then the car door slammed, Cissie looked back across the road in time to see the unkempt boy begin to move, heading towards the spot where Jude had miraculously been standing.

'Bennett!' she said. 'Bennett!' But Bennett had already seen, and was moving clumsily down the steps, pushing through the crowd. Cissie followed her, craning her head above the wedding hats and the Brylcreemed heads to keep track of Jude.

'Jude!' they called. 'Wait!' But already it was too late. As Cissie watched, she saw Jude's eyes light on the stranger crossing the road. He was calling, incoherent, his words lost in the shouts of the wedding guests, as the car began to pull away almost in his path.

'Jude!' But they could both see that it was too late. Jude was no longer there. The crowds had folded in on her and she had disappeared, at the same moment as the boy stood rigidly in the middle of the road, his face contorted with desperation, and Heather's gloved white hand, waving out of the back window of the wedding car, fluttered out of sight, disappearing into the blackness of the icy Norwich night.

CHAPTER EIGHT

Long Long Long

IT HAD NOT BEEN Steve's fault that the car refused to start and had sat squatly and defiantly silent in the car park of the Camelot Hotel long after all the other wedding guests had departed; but somehow the sight of him struggling with his head inside the bonnet, smearing grease on the cuffs of his jacket, muttering knowledgeably to Mike about crankshafts and brake pads – all this had increased Cissie's mounting frustration and anger over the ridiculous day.

Now they were bumping along the Earlham Road towards the university in Mike's van, having abandoned the Mini in the hotel car park. Susie was asleep in the back on an old mattress, with Steve perched next to her, his knees up under his chin, his head lowered to prevent it colliding with the van roof, his red trousers collecting plaster dust from the rug Mike had given him to sit on. Cissie, squashed in the front with Mike and her mother, pressed her forehead against the side window, watching the darkened terraced houses flicker past them behind them and in front. She was thinking about Jude.

'Yoko Ono was on television last night,' Peggy said. She seemed always to be able to penetrate her daughter's thoughts, however obliquely.

'What was she doing?'

'Talking about conceptual art. It was only a minute or two.'

'Was she all in white?'

'Black.'

There was silence, as they pondered a vision of Yoko Ono in

black. Cissie wondered what Jude made of Yoko. She wished suddenly with a great longing to talk to Jude again – bright, fierce Jude, who had a definite opinion on everything. Black and white. Why had she run away?

She drifted into musing about the Beatles' women. It was very difficult to be in love with a Beatle and to feel anything other than loathing for their wives and lovers, but you had to try. Only Ringo's Maureen, an ordinary Liverpudlian, seemed to have somehow sidestepped the generally unspoken but passionate communal female hatred of most fans. The largest ladle of venom was reserved for Yoko Ono, enigmatically oriental and beyond understanding, and for Linda Eastman, Paul's new girlfriend, who had the effrontery to be American and to have ousted Jane Asher. Cissie supposed that for most people Patti seemed pleasant and harmless enough. She and George had been married for three years now. (Useless at remembering important dates in literature, this was one date etched into Cissie's brain: George and Patti's wedding day. For of course it had also been Cissie's birthday . . .) The Harrisons, the newspapers called them. Mr and Mrs George Harrison. George Harrison and his wife Patti. Photographs of them in the press arriving at functions together, leaving together, had become commonplace. Only not for Cissie. Every picture of Patti on the arm of George was a dagger in her heart. She tried not to mind, to be cool about it, to keep her silent passion inside her where it belonged, but sometimes it would leak out hysterically and she would weep for her lost love and her wasted life, longing for a man she would never meet, more tragic than one of her mother's Mills and Boon heroines – at least they usually got a kiss from the hero on the last page and the promise of a future. But of course she could not hate Patti. How could you hate the one thing He so evidently loved, especially when she was skinny and radiantly beautiful and wore all the clothes you would wear if you were married to a millionaire? So, not permitted to love and unable to hate, Cissie was left totally cut off, a crazed, dumb hermit meandering in a teeming world with only the thoughts in her head to offer her comfort through the busy days and the lonely Georgeless nights.

Dear Mrs Harrison, I wrote to you a few months ago and you never answered my letter. I wonder if it ever arrived, the post being what it is. So I wrote to you again, in December, and I sent you a Christmas card as usual, and a small present. It seems strange that I haven't heard from you.

They had reached Earlham Fiveways, and the van swung round the roundabout on to Bluebell Road. Now they could see the lights of the university ahead, bright rows of neat yellow squares set out in geometric patterns across the darkness of the fields. Everything about the university was aggressively grid-like and mathematic in its newness: the straight paths, the square windows, the angular lines of the windy walkways, the vertical heights of the concrete ventilator shafts poking out above the residences of Waveney Terrace, the futuristic outline of the ziggurats further back, 'like a pile of cardboard boxes dumped outside Tesco's', as Mill had dismissively described them on a visit to the campus. Cissie, made uncomfortable by this lucid observation, had not invited her again.

So that's three times I've written, and no reply. Have you got tired of answering my letters? I suppose you're so rich now you don't have to bother with people like me. I'm trying to understand, but I feel rather hurt. After all, it's people like me who made you rich, who made George rich. This is the last letter I intend to write.

'You'll come in for a coffee, won't you?' Steve was saying.

Peggy glanced at Cissie. 'Would you rather go straight to bed?'

Cissie shrugged. 'I'm not bothered.' She wanted to go to her room and dream about George, puzzle over Mrs Harrison's sudden silence. She felt Steve's hand, reproachful, press against her shoulder.

'We'd be sitting up anyway,' Steve said. 'Go on – Susie's out for the count. You might as well.'

They had turned into the main entrance and were passing the first long, solid block of student residences. Most of the rooms were still illuminated, although the curtains were drawn. The curtains were a constant source of irritation to Cissie. Whoever had charge of such things when the residences were first designed had had the idea of installing differently-coloured curtains in a graded colour system, so that at one end of the terrace the curtains were red, then gradually they changed to orange, then to burnt amber, through various shades of brown to beige. In the next block they were forest green at one end fading to pale almond at the other; in the next, royal purple progressing through dark blue to eggshell. Cissie had at first found this satisfying, soothing. Passing along the footpaths she would look up and see the slow change from one shade to another and be calm.

Life was ordered here. She knew the routine, she worked hard, she joined in the social life, she handed her essays in on time and still went to parties and got stoned on Saturday nights. She was the perfect student, hard-working, fun-loving – she knew how to be those things when required. She had ordered her life carefully, and the strategy she had chosen was successful.

But occasionally she would look up and see that the pattern of colours at the residence windows had been destroyed, and suddenly in the middle of a row of reds a rogue set of green curtains would appear, or a set of orange amongst the blues, where a rebellious student had swapped curtains with another, to destroy the harmony. Although she hated to admit it, this small act of anarchy unsettled Cissie. It was as if someone had leaned out of the offending window, wagged a finger at her knowingly and shouted 'Imposter!' for all the other students to hear. She could never tell anyone how she felt about the curtains. It would seem uptight, uncool.

They had driven round the campus on the perimeter road, under the underpass into the cavernous spaces beneath the residences, where rows of bicycles stood in the shadows. While Mike and Steve searched for a parking place for the van, Cissie and Peggy headed for Norfolk Terrace and Cissie's room, with Susie still fast asleep, draped over her mother's shoulder. Carefully they descended the giddily steep steps down to Corridor E, down into the depths of the concrete pyramid. Cissie ushered her mother inside, hoping the other students would be asleep or out. The last thing she wanted was one of those evenings with Peggy holding court in the communal kitchen surrounded by a flock of admiring girls who had never met a published author before, even if all she wrote were the romantic novels they never admitted to reading. She pointed to the door of her room and handed Peggy the keys. Peggy nodded and unlocked the door, carefully manoeuvring Susie inside. She lay her down on Cissie's rumpled bed and stood surveying her, thinking the thoughts about daughters that mothers think at times like this, when they are angelically sleeping with unwrinkled faces, their future ahead of them.

A few moments later she joined Cissie in the chaos of the kitchen, with its unwashed dishes, congealed food solidifying on plates on the window sill, and the crunch of spilt cornflakes underfoot. Someone had written a notice and fixed it to a cupboard. 'HANDS OFF MY BEANS', it read in angry, spiky lettering, 'OR ELSE'. Peggy read this, eyebrows raised, as Cissie silently filled four mugs with instant coffee.

'Are you the guilty baked bean thief?' Peggy asked. 'No – don't tell me. I know the answer to that.'

'What – you mean I'm too boring to do anything so wildly exciting as nick someone's tin of beans?'

Peggy sighed. She took one of the mugs of coffee and helped herself to powdered milk from a tin of Marvel. 'I didn't say that.'

'You didn't have to.'

'Look, do we have to fight?' There was silence. It appeared from Cissie's unyielding and angry back that indeed they did. Peggy tried again. 'Could we at least fight about something meaningful, then?'

Cissie was stirring the remaining cups of coffee with rather more vigour than necessary. 'Go ahead. Pick a topic. Any topic.'

'Cissie –'.

She turned then, annoyed. 'Go on, Mum. You've been busting to say something ever since the end of the wedding reception. Go on – now's your chance. Before the others come back.'

Peggy was watching her, searching for the right words to say. 'Cissie. I don't want to fight.'

'But? Come on. There must be a "but". There always is.'

Peggy sipped at her coffee, cupping her hands round the mug for warmth. Cissie was watching her now, wishing she had not spoken so harshly. She wanted to say, *I'm sorry, Mum, I'm sorry I get angry with the world and lash out at you. It's not your fault I'm not happy . . .*

'You gave Mike a hard time this evening,' was all Peggy managed to say.

Cissie stopped stirring. 'You've been talking to Oliver.'

'Of course I've been talking to Oliver. I haven't seen him for months.'

'You've been talking to Oliver about me.'

Peggy was staring at her, surprised. 'Why should I do that?' She carried her coffee over to the breakfast bar by the window and perched up on a tall stool, relaxed amid the debris of eight student lives. Picking up a sagging bag of sugar she licked her finger and dipped it inside in a sudden, childish gesture, pulling it out white with sugar grains. She sucked at it thoughtfully for a moment, then said, 'I loved your dad, you know.' Before Cissie could speak she continued, hurrying over the words, seeming to find them difficult to utter in the banality of Norfolk Terrace. 'I mean I really loved him. It was the war. It changed everything. Made everything more dramatic. More . . .' she searched for the right word, 'more romantic.' Cissie had stopped fiddling with the coffee mugs and teaspoons and was focussing, embarrassed, on a poster for Big Brother and the Holding Company tacked to a cupboard. Her mother never talked about Cecil. Now she was staring at the bright plastic surface of the breakfast bar, pressing her finger down on to stray grains of sugar, frowning a little. 'I felt about him the way you feel about George Harrison. No, I mean it.' This, as Cissie tried to interrupt. Peggy looked up suddenly, her face strained and desperate. 'But he's gone,' she said. 'Unattainable. Like George.'

Cissie felt complete surprise. It was as if her mother had suddenly stepped out of her exotic kaftan and paraded naked and weeping along the windy terraces. 'Mum,' she said, 'Mum . . .'

But Peggy seemed determined to finish what she had to say. Above their heads could be heard the sound of ringing voices and footsteps descending. Mike and Steve were making their way down the narrow descent to Corridor E. 'Your father's dead,' Peggy said harshly. 'George might as well be, as far as you're concerned.' She gazed across at her daughter, oddly upset. 'We can still dream about them,' she said, 'but we have to get on with life.'

Steve and Mike had reached the entrance to the corridor. Cissie heard Mike's deep, quiet laugh on the other side of the door. 'I see,' Cissie said coldly. 'I get the lecture because of what I said to Mike at the wedding, is that it?'

Peggy looked blank. 'What?'

'Oh, never mind.'

Mike and Steve had come in, rubbing their hands together to warm them up. Cissie handed them the mugs of coffee.

'Wind's getting up out there,' Mike said. 'We mustn't stop, Peg. Chickens need shutting up.' He perched on a stool next to his wife. 'Have you talked to Cissie about the dog?'

Cissie looked up. 'Toulouse? What about him?'

Peggy stared into her mug. 'Nothing really,' she said slowly.

Cissie waited, anxious. Not Toulouse. Nothing must happen to Toulouse, symbol of her childhood, representative of everything that was safe, loving, immovable and unchanging.

Peggy was looking at her now. 'We took him to the vet,' she said. 'He says we should have a think about his future.' Cissie stared at her, silent. 'He had another fit, Cissie. I think it was a kind of stroke. He's all right – but the next one could finish him off. Or could leave him so paralysed he'd have to be put down.'

Cissie stared at her. Toulouse. No. 'I'd better come home,' she said.

Peggy shook her head. 'No.' Her eyes met Cissie's. 'Come home when he's ill,' she said. Cissie understood. *Come home when he's ill and he needs you, not just because I've told you he's been ill and you're feeling guilty.* This was not a conversation about the dog; it was an unspoken, bitter dialogue about Mill.

'OK,' Cissie said gruffly.

There was a sad and uncomfortable silence, eventually broken by Steve, who had been scrubbing his grease-covered hands at the kitchen sink, embarrassed by the intensity of the Lovelocks' conversation. 'Do you know anything about Max Weber?' he asked Mike in a conversational tone. 'Only I've been reading his stuff on historical causality and I wondered if you thought it could be applied to art. You know – history of art . . . the progression through various artistic movements.'

Cissie smiled wanly to herself. What was it Mill had said? 'Find yourself a man with some politics.'

Mike pondered the question for a moment and then pulled his pipe out of the pocket of his cord trousers. 'Interesting you should ask,' he said, producing his tobacco tin. 'Some of my students were talking about value judgements the other day – you know, subjectivity and all that – and his name came up.'

Steve nodded sagely. 'It would,' he said.

Peggy looked across at Cissie, eyebrows raised. 'Walk?' she mouthed. Cissie shook her head. She did not want to be alone with her mother. It inevitably resulted in painful and unwanted emotions. Peggy stood up, hurt. 'I'll go and check on Susie,' she said, and left the room. Mike and Steve, engrossed in their conversation, did not notice.

Cissie stared out of the kitchen window into the darkness outside. Below her somewhere beyond the sloping grass was the university lake, scene of summer dope-smoking sessions and midnight swims. Over to one side she could see the lights of Suffolk Terrace still glimmering; hundreds of students were still not asleep. She closed her eyes and wondered, not for the first time, if there were other rooms on the campus where girls like her dreamed of unattainable men and wove the fantasy of loving and being loved in return into the fabric of their student lives: learning to look alert in seminars while daydreaming about Him suddenly walking in . . . Trying to concentrate in the echoing labyrinth of the campus library when outside the green slopes and leafy copses of the landscaped vistas were inviting you to imagine Him walking through the long grass, hand in hand with you . . . Lying on your narrow bed in the breeze-block cell of your room, staring at the pile of nineteenth-century novels waiting to be read (or chemistry textbooks, or economics, or French grammar) and instead dreaming of being here in this tiny haven on this uninviting bunk but with *Him* and all the untold and wonderful possibilities of the conversations you could have, the feelings you could share, the powerful and passionate things you could say to only Him, because only He would understand . . .

Would there be sex? That was always difficult. Only if it could be perfect, sublime – no sweating, no fumbling, no pain, no disappointment, no grunting, no flesh sticking glutinously to flesh, no waking up with furry teeth and embarrassment. Just a cosmic explosion of perfection. So probably no sex, then . . .

Peggy had returned, and was pulling on her coat, indicating to Mike that it was time to retrieve Susie and go home. Mike was stretching and getting to his feet, finishing some thought out loud. '*Entscheidung*,' he was saying mysteriously to Steve, 'commitment.' No, Cissie thought. There is no one else here like me. There is only me. The girl from Norfolk . . .

Cissie's study bedroom, third along from the kitchen, was bathed in a pink light emanating from a chiffon scarf thrown over the anglepoise lamp on the built-in desk under the window. The grey breeze blocks were covered with posters, shawls, scarves, masks, necklaces, but it was difficult to disguise the bland single armchair with the polished plastic arms, the sink in the corner, the melamine bookshelves, no matter how many cushions and rugs and decorations were draped about the room. The resulting effect was of a battle between two décors – the original grim and featureless study room, product of a designer's budget, and an exotic Eastern harem, brainchild of a poor but imaginative student.

Cissie was sitting with her back to Steve. He lay on the bed, smoking a joint and staring at the ceiling. Pictures of George Harrison were pinned haphazardly to the smoke-yellowed surface.

'Shall I put some sounds on?' he asked. She nodded absently, not turning round. 'Don't tell me,' he said, sitting up and hunching over her pile of records stacked by the bed. He pulled out the Beatles' *White Album.*

' "It's Been A Long Long Long Time",' Cissie said. 'It's the last track on side three. After "Helter Skelter".'

Steve pulled out the record. 'It's not called that,' he said, studying the label. 'It's called "Long Long Long".'

'Who bloody cares?' she said. 'Who bloody cares what it's bloody well called?'

228

He put the record on the turntable, and carefully placed the stylus arm above the grooves, lowering it gently into place. George Harrison's voice began quietly to fill the room. Steve lay back on the bed again. 'That geezer – Heather's dad, did you say? – kept going on about Harold Wilson. He thought sociology was social-ism. Asked me if I'd been to Paris recently.' He shook his head, amused. 'You know, like every sociology student in England crossed the Channel to man the barricades. Kept going on about it. Paris. Like he was saying Armageddon, or the Fall of the House of Usher or something.'

'Mmm . . .'

Steve looked up. 'What are you doing?'

Cissie did not reply. She fought a growing irritation with every-thing about Steve: the way he *talked* when she had specifically asked him to put George's song on; the way he said words like 'geezer' in a vain attempt to lose his middle-classness; the way he went on and on in that smug fashion about sociology when he probably hadn't even heard of it before he did his A levels.

She was re-reading an old letter from Mrs Harrison, from her precious George Box. The letter was dated January 1965. BP. Before Patti. *I'm sending you a note George left on the mantelpiece.* She fingered the crumpled brown envelope stapled to the letter. *Dear Mum*, it read, scrawled in biro in that familiar loopy handwriting, *get me up at 3, love George.* She had shown it to Steve once, in the first flush of romance and shared secrets. He had been very impressed. 'You should hang on to that,' he had said. 'It'll probably be worth a fortune one day.' She should have realized then it was never going to work.

'Oy!' A cushion flew across the room and hit her on the back of the head. 'I asked you a question!' Steve was sitting up, cross-legged, annoyed. 'God!' he exclaimed. 'It's like going out with Greta Garbo!'

Cissie leaned down and picked up the cushion. She put it on the desk in front of her and rested her head on it for a moment. She wished Steve would go back to his own room. Paul McCartney was singing about Rocky Raccoon. Something about the bright, inconsequential song made her snap.

'I'm sorry I don't measure up to your expectations,' she said coldly.

'It was a joke.'

'Very funny.'

'Come here.' She remained where she was, her head still resting on the cushion, her eyes focussing on a pair of bright pink plastic earrings clipped to one of Mrs Harrison's letters. Spring, 1964. She had worn them when she saw George.

'Cissie!' His voice was pleading. Sighing, she got up and approached him on the bed. He drew her down next to him, his arm round her shoulder. He handed her the joint.

'I finished with Sarah Holden to go out with you,' he said. She avoided looking at him, fiddling instead with the erratic fringe on the edge of the bedspread. She knew he was looking at her. 'You came up to me at that party, bold as brass,' he said. 'Remember?' She did not reply. 'You were bloody dead set on me. Everyone said so. So what's the problem?'

She turned to look at him. Small flakes of ash from the joint had settled in his beard. Still, he did have the same warm, brown eyes as George. And his nose was startlingly similar. She looked up, comparing him silently with a picture above her of George sitting at the feet of the Maharishi. 'The problem,' she said, touching his beard gently with her beringed fingers, 'the problem,' smiling in the melancholy way she had that so touched the heart of her lecturers (So bright! So waif-like! So like Lizzie Siddal!), 'the problem is that I got you . . .'

Making love. It was an odd expression, as if something was being manufactured in this hot and fleshy exchange. She wondered, as she often did in such moments, whether it was her fault that this sex business had never really been very exciting. Steve was always on top of her, as he was now, moving and murmuring, his face hidden, his beard scratching her face. She imagined all the couples she saw touching each other in the campus bar, knowingly smiling, hands playing in hair, fingers touching other fingers – they probably did it in all kinds of exotic ways, ways she could not even imagine. After all, everyone talked about the Kama Sutra, about opening your mind to new experiences, freeing up your consciousness. Maybe Steve did those things with other girls. She had a sudden vision of Steve writhing erotically in a sea of nakedness, like the women on the cover of *Electric Ladyland*, and she had to suppress a giggle. She had already learned that giggling during sex was considered by some to be offensive, unless you could claim to be stoned, in which case it was groovy. She was not stoned enough to get away with it tonight. She concentrated on making the right noises, arching her back when it seemed appropriate, sighing into Steve's hair when she felt him relax. Above her, George looked down impassively. She shut her eyes, embarrassed. She had forgotten to turn the light off.

Behind her eyelids, across the sweaty connection her body made with his, she heard a small, spattering explosion.

'Steve . . .?' she murmured.

Collapsed with his face in her hair, he was silent. She wondered if he was asleep. Then she heard it again. This time she opened her eyes. 'Steve.'

He grunted and shifted a little, freeing her shoulder. She pulled her tangled hair away from where it had been trapped between them, and sat up. 'There's something happening at the window.'

'Someone forgotten their key,' he mumbled into the pillow. She pushed back the sheet and climbed out, shivering, naked. Again, she heard the sound of something hitting the window – small, explosive sounds, then the same sound further along the terrace, and the sudden explosion of splintering glass. Steve groaned and pulled a pillow over his head. She found her Moroccan dress heaped on the floor where she had thrown it, and pulled it on over her head, padding to the window and pulling up the blind, blinking out into the darkness. She heard the girl in the room next door throw up her window, and her sharp-voiced exclamation. Someone was shouting below, standing in the blackness and the long grass.

Cissie leaned over the desk and pushed the window up, letting a great gust of wind into the room, which rustled the papers and sent an essay on Satire and Irony in the Work of Swift flying across the room. Steve made another complaining sound and burrowed further down the bed. Cissie looked out.

Down in the dark, a white, scared face looked up. 'Thank fuck,' Jude said. 'Can you let me in?'

She sat perched at the breakfast bar in the kitchen, in danger of falling off at any moment. She was wearing a grubby blue sweater and jeans. Her feet were grey and bare, with congealed blood blackening the toes. She had pulled a bottle of whisky from a bulging canvas bag and was drinking it, the hand holding the bottle trembling violently.

'Sorry,' she was saying to Cissie, her teeth clashing against the glass neck of the bottle, 'only there's a fucking loony out there following me. I had to take evasive action.'

A girl in rollers and a tartan dressing-gown was standing in the doorway, arms folded. 'Someone will have to pay for it,' she said.

'I will, Debs,' Cissie said.

'Only I can't sleep there now. There's glass all over the bed.'

'I'll get the porters over in the morning.'

'I could have been killed.'

Jude looked beseechingly at her old friend. 'Can't you shut her up? I can't handle all this heavy shit, not tonight.'

The girl glared at her. 'You smash my window and then you tell me to shut up.'

Steve had appeared in the doorway, pulling on a T-shirt. 'So,' he said. 'Jude the Obscure.' He and Jude studied each other for a moment, interested.

Finally Jude said 'Christ, Cissie.'

'I know,' Cissie said, proud.

'Yes,' Steve said. 'Only I'm not him. I'm Steve.'

'Where am I supposed to sleep?' the girl in the tartan dressing-gown was demanding. Steve handed her a key. 'My room. Suffolk Terrace, E7.'

'But that's a bloke's corridor.'

'I know,' Steve said patiently. 'They won't rape you, I promise.'

There was a snort from Jude, quickly repressed. The girl looked at the key in her hand for a moment, then at Steve, then at Cissie.

'First thing in the morning,' she said to Cissie in a threatening voice.

'I promise.'

The girl swept out.

Cissie touched Steve's arm. 'My hero,' she said.

Jude was drinking from the bottle, her eyelids sagging. She seemed hardly to have noticed the girl's anger. 'He's out there, hanging about. I can't go back out there.'

Steve put the kettle on and searched for a jar of coffee in someone else's cupboard. 'Coffee?'

Jude did not reply. She was staring at Cissie, her face white and ill, her eyelids reddened. 'His name's Robbie. He follows me about. I'm talking about seriously bad vibes, Cissie.'

'You mean he's out there?' Steve pressed his nose against the window, squinting out into the night. The wind had risen, and the mournful sound of it gusting round the concrete towers could be heard above the intermittent thumping of a Led Zeppelin song being played somewhere below them.

'Go and deal with it, will you, Steve?' Cissie shot him a meaningful look. She wanted to be alone with Jude. She wanted to know why the wonderful, powerful bad creature from her youth had been transformed into this grubby girl with a cold sore on her mouth and eyes that did not focus.

Steve left. Cissie stood leaning against the wall.

'Got a glass?' Jude asked. Surprised, Cissie rooted about in a cupboard and found her one. She settled on a stool next to Jude, who had placed a lump of dope on the plastic surface of the breakfast bar and was busy setting it alight, her fingers trembling as she struggled to hold the matches steady. Jude placed the glass over the dope and watched as the glass filled with smoke, her face set, concentrating. Then she leaned over and lifted the rim of the glass, contorting her neck so that her face was closer, and inhaling the smoke deeply. Gasping and inhaling, she turned to Cissie with tear-filled eyes and indicated that it was her turn. Cissie shook her head slowly.

'We all talk about you all the time,' Cissie said. 'Well – me and Bennett.'

Jude blew smoke into the room. 'Yeah?'

'We were worried. You disappeared.'

Jude's eyes slid away from hers. She took another slug of whisky. 'Stayed in London,' she said. 'Hung out. Met up with some people.' She looked suddenly at Cissie with her old directness. 'I can't believe you!' she said suddenly, in an outburst. 'English fucking Literature!'

'Why have you come back, Jude?'

She shrugged, fingering the glass. 'My sister's still living at home. God knows why. She sent me Heather's wedding invitation. I knew you'd be there. Old faithful.'

'So why did you run away – outside the hotel? Me and Bennett – we saw you. We wanted to talk to you.'

Jude made a sudden, twitching movement, almost upturning the whisky bottle. 'I told you!' she flashed. 'That madman out there – he followed me.' She took another gulp from the bottle. 'I knew he'd follow me here as well. We were in a pub by the bus station, scoring some dope. Someone mentioned the Beatles, we got talking. Turned out the guys we were scoring from were mates of your boyfriend. Went on about this mad, red-haired chick who was obsessed with George Harrison. I knew it was you. They gave me your room number. Mad, red-haired chick, they said. Obsessed.' She grinned at Cissie, the old adversary, stoned, demonic.

Cissie heard suddenly the voice of her mother, speaking very clearly in the kitchen. 'She's got a blue aura,' she was saying in a disapproving voice. Cissie turned, half-expecting to see her mother materializing in the doorway; but of course she was not there, only the powerful wave of her anxiety somehow reaching out as she bumped along somewhere on the Yarmouth Road in Mike's van, heading for Brigadoon.

There was silence, Cissie remembering suddenly how Jude could flatten her so easily, with just a few words, or a withering glance. And there did indeed seem to be a smoky blueness around Jude's head. 'It's really good to see you,' Cissie tried again, unconvincingly.

'Yeah,' Jude said drily. The blue faded. It had been the pall of cigarette smoke. Cissie saw then how very unhappy Jude was, how very scared.

'I mean it,' she said, her tone more genuine this time. Jude looked at her, and was about to say something, when the door crashed open and four students fell in the doorway, very drunk. One of them rushed to the sink and began to retch over the greasy dishes.

The others grinned in the doorway, propping each other up.

'What's happening?' one of them asked hopefully. The sound of vomiting increased.

Jude slid off her stool. 'I can't handle this,' she said decisively. 'I've got to split.'

Cissie smiled apologetically at the students, who were too drunk to notice, and, picking up the heavy canvas bag and rescuing the whisky bottle before Jude dropped it, she ushered her friend down the corridor, past a couple kissing in a doorway, past the bass thump of someone playing the Grateful Dead, to her own room.

The needle was clicking loudly on the end of the record still spinning on the turntable. Cissie stooped down and began to pick up the papers that had been scattered on the carpet by the wind. Jude went over and closed the window. 'Jesus,' she said, 'it's like Siberia in here.' Then she settled herself cross-legged on the unmade bed and helped herself to a cigarette from a packet she had spotted by the record player. She lay back against the pillows, relaxed now, more sure of herself, watching Cissie scooping up her essay and trying to sort it into a pile.

'English fucking literature,' she said finally. 'What good is that to the universe?'

Cissie paused for a moment and stared at her, her heart irrationally filled with love. 'Good question,' she said.

'You know why I'm here,' Jude said.

'No.' Cissie shoved the essay away under a copy of *Middlemarch*.

'I've come to take you away.'

Cissie laughed uneasily. 'I wish you could.'

'I can. I'm going to. Wait till you hear . . .' Jude had paused, irritatingly, and was hanging down over the bed, peering at the record player. With an unsteady hand she put the arm back on the record. After a scraping start, the insistent drums of 'Birthday' began to blast out. Cissie felt the beginnings of a headache.

Jude was leaning back again, enjoying her moment. Cissie waited.

'They're all in London,' Jude said. 'They're making a new album.'

'I know.' Cissie was disappointed. Since the Beatles' every move was catalogued, observed, reported on, analysed, discussed and dissected, this was old news.

Jude was unperturbed by this lukewarm response. She inhaled on her cigarette, eyeing Cissie with triumph. 'They're making a film of it. Somewhere in Twickenham. And probably in Apple as well.' She paused effectively. 'I can get us in,' she said. 'To Apple.' Cissie stared at her, disbelieving. 'I can get us in there,' Jude said. 'You want?' She had grabbed the bottle of whisky Cissie had deposited on the bed-side table and was waving it at her. Cissie shook her head. Jude drank. 'All of us,' she went on, wiping her mouth with her wrist. 'We'll all go.'

Cissie's heart was beating fast. She was coming alive again, hope growing in her dead heart. She reached and took the bottle from Jude, swallowing a mouthful of whisky, trying not to grimace at the taste of it.

'Bennett'll come,' Jude was saying. She unfolded herself from the bed and wove her way unsteadily to the desk. She picked up Mrs Harrison's letter, the one with the pink earrings clipped to it, and studied it for a moment.

'1964,' Cissie said.

'I know.' Jude smiled at her, conspiratorial. 'March the twenty-sixth it was.' She had unclipped one of the earrings and was studying it. 'Heather'll come or I'll break her legs.'

Cissie shook her head, slowly. 'I can phone her,' she said. 'At Anglia Television. She'll be back tomorrow.'

Jude had turned and moved closer to Cissie, her face moving in until it was only a few inches from her own. For a surprising second Cissie thought Jude was going to kiss her. Instead, she clipped the earring on to Cissie's earlobe. She studied it critically for a moment, her head on one side. Then she reached for the second earring, and, fumbling a little, she attached it to Cissie's other ear. 'Yes,' she said. 'You'll come.' She smiled at her friend then, a sudden, heartbreaking smile, like the sun bursting through the clouds, and Cissie was instantly ecstatic, quivering with life. She reached across for the whisky bottle. Yes. She would go . . .

They had finished the whisky. Outside, light was breaking over the oily calm of the university lake, and the dawn chorus had begun, raggedly cutting through the fading sounds of a hundred students collapsing into sleep and unconsciousness on a Sunday morning. Jude was on the verge of sleep, a copy of *International Times* across her chest. Cissie sat hunched up, cross-legged on the floor, wide awake.

Jude was blinking bleary-eyed up at a picture of George on the ceiling. In it, he was standing next to Ravi Shankar, unsmiling.

'You ever get out of this place?' Jude asked.

'Holidays.'

'Where do you go?'

'Home.'

Jude sat up a little, staring at her. 'But that's only down the road!' Cissie was silent. The song ended. 'I went to the States last year,' Jude said carelessly, lying back again. Then, when Cissie did not respond: 'Honestly. I was there when Nixon got in.'

The raucous sound of 'Yer Blues' started up. 'Great!' said Jude. 'This is my favourite.' She rolled over and reached out for a cigarette. 'Yeah . . . What a mess. I mean the liberals were devastated. The man is bad news. I went to Berkeley as well. We were demonstrating against the Tet thing. It was really cool. You know Berkeley?'

'Of course I know Berkeley. I do read the occasional newspaper, you know.' Cissie looked at Jude and wondered how much of what she was saying was true. 'How did you get the money to go to America?'

Jude lay back, having lit her cigarette, and blew a thin stream of smoke at George and Ravi Shankar. 'I was – you know – a kind of correspondent,' she said dreamily, poking the paper on her chest with a bitten finger. 'For them. They do that sometimes.'

'*International Times* sent you to Berkeley?'

'Well, no . . .' Jude frowned a little. 'They don't have the bread for that kind of thing. They helped. Contacts. You know. I help them, they help me.'

'They pay you?' Cissie was finding it hard to keep the incredulity out of her voice.

'No one pays anyone, Cissie,' Jude said irritably. 'It's not that kind of scene.'

Cissie began to wonder what had happened to Steve. Should she go outside and search for him? The whisky had had a paralysing effect on her body, leaving it inert and unwilling to move. Only her head was buzzing with a swarm of possibilities, busily darting from one fantasy to another, unable to alight anywhere for long. Above the Beatles, she could hear the sound of rowdiness from the kitchen, great whooping shouts and the crash of crockery. Then there would be an angry thud on some adjoining wall, as someone trying to sleep would shout something incoherent and angry through the breeze-blocked concrete walls.

Jude was drumming her fingers on the cigarette packet. 'So,' she said finally, 'Miss Prim got married then. To the hamster man.'

'She really wanted you to be there,' Cissie said. 'Why didn't you come?'

There was an awkward silence. For once Jude did not seem to have a ready reply. The moment was broken by a knock on the door. Slowly Cissie got up and went to open it, her head reeling from the sudden movement.

'No,' said Jude, seeing who was there.

'I found him down by the dustbins. I took him to the kitchen but he began to freak out –'

In the doorway was Steve, and, holding on to Steve's purple jacket as if for support was the unkempt boy Cissie had glimpsed at the wedding. He was swaying slightly, his mouth slack, his brow furrowed in a frown as if the act of staying upright was costing him dear. The sound of mayhem from the kitchen was louder now.

'Jesus Christ!' Jude exploded, and threw the *International Times* across the room, causing it to collapse in a chaotic flutter of news-print across the rug. 'Get him out of here!'

'Jude,' he said unsteadily. She turned her face to the wall, furious, trembling. 'Don't be angry. I only want to talk to you.' His voice was low and anxious. Cissie was surprised by its slurred gentleness, which seemed at odds with this ravaged, violent face and the stick-like, abused body.

'Let's go,' Jude said to Cissie, unexpectedly rising from the bed. 'Let's get out of here.'

Steve and Cissie exchanged a desperate look. 'They're having a food fight in the kitchen,' Steve said, hovering uncertainly in the doorway. Jude sank down again, defeated.

Steve made a decision and ushered the shaking visitor into the room, settling him in a rag-doll heap by the records. 'Hey, look man,' he said, pushing an album sleeve into his hand. 'You into Van Morrison?' He settled down next to his new companion, concerned, and pulled out his dope tin. Jude, seeing Steve arranging his paraphernalia on the cover of *A Saucerful of Secrets*, sank back on to the bed, seduced by the prospect of another joint.

'Is he all right?' Cissie stared at the newcomer, whose head was lolling on to his chest.

'He's fine,' Jude said abruptly. 'He's just out of his head.'

'Robbie . . .?' Steve shook him a little by the shoulder and he opened his eyes and smiled, his mouth a little slack.

'He won't die,' Jude snapped. 'More's the pity.'

Steve began a murmured conversation, a kind of monologue about the musical influences of Jimi Hendrix, and Robbie nodded, mutely hypnotized, watching Steve's fingers as he tore up Rizla papers.

'So –' Jude seemed eager to pretend that the apparition quivering on the floor did not exist, and had turned the intensity of her gaze back to Cissie. 'So – where does Bennett hang out these days, then?'

Cissie came and sat on the bed with her, curling her knees up under the heavy folds of the Moroccan dress. 'In a commune.

Brundall. It's an old rectory. Why didn't you come to the wedding, Jude? Heather was really hurt.'

'Brundall?' Jude's eyes were avoiding Robbie. 'That's not very far.'

'It's good there. The other people are nice.'

'Nice?' Jude looked at her, disgusted. Below her on the floor, Steve's voice, engaged in a monologue about Hendrix's musical career, had finally faded away in the face of the collapse of his audience. Robbie was now fast asleep, his breathing deep and regular. Cissie could see now that he was probably very beautiful. In sleep he looked like a small boy, pale and vulnerable, blue veins quivering in his eyelids, his mouth pale and full, like one of the Botticelli angels in Mike's art books at Brigadoon.

Jude climbed off the bed, yawned theatrically, her arms above her head, stretching like a cat, aware she was being admired. There was still something beautifully balletic about Jude, something lithe and feline, a glamour Cissie longed for but would never attain, because it came from not caring – or not seeming to care – about anything. Cissie's problem, she thought sadly to herself, was that she cared too bloody much.

Jude had subsided again, her arms folded behind her head. 'Let's go,' she said quietly.

'Where?' Steve had paused in the middle of his joint construction, surprised. 'It's seven o'clock in the morning.'

Jude gave him a withering look, as if the mere mention of time relegated him finally to the bleak anteroom of unhipness. Cissie knew all about this room. It was where the unknowing misunderstood eternally and forever what was happening in the main hall of the groovy and the well-informed. Cissie spent a lot of time in it.

'Can he drive? Has he got a car?' Jude asked her.

Cissie nodded. 'But it's –'

'Let's go to Brundall, then,' Jude said abruptly. She had crossed over to the doors of the built-in cupboard and was peering in at Cissie's wardrobe. 'You got a jacket I can borrow?' She selected Cissie's Afghan coat, another gift from the souks of Marrakesh brought back by Peggy.

240

Shivering in the grey morning they had reached the car park before Steve spotted a shambling silhouette erratically weaving behind them, lurking in the cold shadows of the English and American Studies building.

'It's Robbie,' he said. 'He must have woken up.'

'Hurry!' Jude pulled them along, stumbling on the dew-dampened grass. 'Which car is it?'

They had had to wake up Steve's friend on Waveney Terrace to borrow his car keys, and the transaction had exhausted and irritated him. After all, this demanding woman was nothing to do with him – some wraith wandering out of Cissie's past and taking over. In fact, he was rapidly becoming tired of Cissie's past. Because of it he had wasted a valuable Saturday night at some *petit bourgeois* wedding reception, his own car was now sitting immobile in a hotel car park in Norwich, he had had no sleep, Jude had interrupted a good lay – added to which she treated him as if he were some kind of mentally retarded nobody. He looked at Cissie out of the corner of his eye, her long hair drooping, her face haggard in the dawn. He wasn't entirely sure she was worth all this hassle. Divested of her glamorous coat, wearing instead an old cape which had been fashionable three years earlier, she didn't look so hot. Chicks were a total downer, all things considered.

They found the car eventually, parked under a dripping laburnum bush in the far corner of the car park.

'Hurry up!'

Steve fumbled with the lock as Jude clutched on to the door handle, peering into the mist, watchful.

'Why can't he come?' Cissie wanted to know. 'He seems harmless enough.'

'Just get going, will you?' They were installed in the car, Cissie and Jude in the back seat together, Steve's cold hands struggling with the ignition. The car, a sedate Vauxhall, sputtered reluctantly into life and sat chugging, emitting white exhaust fumes into the thickening light.

'Hurry!'

Slowly the car moved forward at the same moment that Robbie's face appeared, panicked, peering in the side window at Jude, his mouth opening and closing but no sound emerging. Steve struggled with the gears, coaxing the engine, angrily stamping his foot on the accelerator. For a hideous second the engine died, and then coughed resentfully again and they moved forward. Robbie was alongside them now, his face pressed against the dripping window, his eyes on Jude. She leaned forward. 'Quick!' Her voice was urgent, terrified, laughing. 'Quick, before he tries to climb in!' Sure enough he was struggling with the handle, jiggling at it frantically, his mouth working like a goldfish, shouting something they could not hear above the noise of the engine. Unexpectedly they lurched forward into another gear and began to move away, Robbie running now, still shouting noiselessly into the icy air, until finally they were going too fast and he had to let go, and fell behind, a crouching, despairing figure becoming smaller in the rear window as they hurtled towards the exit.

It was one of those sharp winter mornings when everything is focussed, shimmering and delicate as a spider's web. They were on the outskirts of Brundall, Jude and Cissie singing Beatles songs loudly, their arms looped around each others' necks, for all the world like the fifteen-year-olds who had shared this passion in the dimness of years ago. Steve struggled with the unfamiliar car, negotiating the bends with a grim jaw, his eyes occasionally flickering to the back, where they sang on, oblivious, all the way through all the LPs, singing automatically in chronological order, breathlessly raucous, right through *Please Please Me*, on through *With the Beatles*, moving on, exhausted and elated, to the first side of *A Hard Day's Night*. They had arrived at 'I'm Happy Just To Dance With You' when Steve shouted, 'Is it left at the crossroads?'

Cissie nodded, panting for breath. She and Jude collapsed back, grinning at each other. The George Box sat in Cissie's lap. Jude seemed suddenly to notice it. She reached over and pulled out one of Mrs Harrison's letters, fingering it, her face suddenly very serious.

'I was always so jealous,' she said finally.

Cissie stared at her, surprised. 'Of me?'

Jude shrugged. 'Your connection to George. I couldn't believe his mum wrote back. I wrote to John's Aunty Mimi, you know.'

'I know.'

'Nothing. I wrote four letters. Four!' She stared ahead, the hurt of the teenager repeating itself on her grown-up, tired face. Cissie was silent, hugging to herself the discovery that once – just once – she had been the object of envy among her friends. Just for a moment she forgave Mrs Harrison her mysterious silence. *I love you, Mrs Harrison. Thank you.*

'It made you special,' Jude went on. This was music to Cissie's ears. 'It made you closer to *Them*. It drove me on. For years.'

The car was slowing now, turning into the overgrown driveway that led to the rectory, dense with overhanging dead branches.

'That's good, isn't it?' Cissie said uncertainly, taken aback by the savagery of Jude's tone. 'To have something to drive you on. Give you a purpose.'

The grey pile of the rectory appeared through the front windscreen, its windows bright with odd curtains. A totem pole leaned drunkenly by the front door and a child's tricycle rusted near by.

'I always thought I had to better that connection,' Jude said. The car slid to a halt, its tyres crunching loudly on the gravel. Cissie looked up anxiously at the house, hardly listening. She hoped they hadn't woken the children; this would not put Bennett in a positive frame of mind for the news they were bringing her. Steve turned off the ignition. Jude already had her fingers on the handle and was opening the door nearest her. 'I had to get closer to the Beatles than you did,' she said.

'And did you?' Steve asked, since Cissie was evidently not listening.

'Oh yes,' Jude said, stepping out of the car. 'I slept with one of them.' She walked round the car towards the door.

For a moment Cissie stared at her through the window, frozen. Then she rolled the window down. 'Which one?' she asked. '*Which one?*'

But Jude merely laughed and ran the rest of the way to the front door, pushing at the heavy wood with her shoulder, unsurprised when it opened, disappearing inside.

Cissie made a small, choking sound. Steve turned. She was sitting hunched forward, her head against the plastic cover of the front seat, her face invisible. 'She hasn't changed a bit,' she said.

Jude had been met by a pretty-looking boy with tousled fair ringlets and a sweet, sleepy smile. 'Hiya,' he said, his Norfolk accent diminishing his attempt to sound transatlantic. 'You come to see Bren?'

Jude shook her head. 'Bennett.'

He looked regretful. 'She went off in the truck with the kids. It's her turn to do the market run. And I think she said something about bringing her mum back here for a day visit.'

Jude looked around her. The hall had a scratched parquet floor and the walls were covered with children's drawings – bright blotches of colour against the dour brown paintwork. 'Nice place,' she said.

'You want to wait?' He ushered her into a room near by. The sun was streaming in through high windows. Outside, through a tangle of laurel leaves, Jude could see the Vauxhall, with Steve still sitting at the wheel, but there was no sign of Cissie. She sank down gratefully into one of two large and sagging sofas covered in blankets. From this position she assessed the slight figure standing above her, his hair a halo against the sunlight. He really was very pretty. 'What's your name?'

'Jez.' He seemed suddenly shy. 'I'll make some tea. Bennett shouldn't be long . . .'

'That's fine,' she leaned back, smiling up at him, appraising. 'I'm not in a hurry.'

He left the room. Jude got up and began to wander about, examining the odd ornament, picking an apple out of a bowl and crunching into it, leafing through the pile of records on the floor. On the mantelpiece was a jar with some money in it. Jude tipped it into her palm. There were several silver coins and three five pound notes. She pocketed two of the notes and returned the rest of the money to the jar. Then she sat down again, reaching in Cissie's coat pocket for Steve's dope tin, which she had offered to carry for him. She relaxed back against the cushions, studying its contents, anticipating the pleasure that was to come.

Somewhere higher up in the house, someone was playing a flute or a recorder, the high, reedy notes floating down the stairwell into the hall. It reminded Jude of school, of passing the music room and hearing that sound. It was the sound of good girls, girls who joined the orchestra or the choir, girls who could read music and who did Latin instead of cookery. As she manufactured her joint with the ease of much practice, she thought about how Cissie was one of those girls. She hadn't wanted to be, but she was. So was Heather. Only Bennett was like Jude, Bennett with her loony mum and her foster parents and her messy life. Jude remembered the first time she had gone to Cissie's house, to Brigadoon. It was like a dream, a fairy tale, the kind of house girls lived in in books by Pamela Brown or Pat Smythe, a house with a proper garden and a dog and chickens, with a mad old granny and a lovely mum and an invisible dad. And there was that good-looking bloke who turned up there sometimes – Cissie's brother. Oliver. She racked her brains to remember something about him other than how he looked. Was he something arty? She was sure someone had said something about him painting pictures, but she had this memory of him leaning in the doorway of the kitchen at Brigadoon, smoking a roll-up and telling her in a dry voice that he mended televisions for a living. And she remembered his flat in London. Bayswater. Moscow Road. Palace Court. She must remember that. Palace Court. She might need somewhere to crash when she got back to London. And there was the added bonus that he was a bit of all right. It would make a change to sleep with someone a bit fanciable.

The boy came back carrying two chipped mugs of tea. In the sunshine his cheeks seemed covered in down, his mouth pink and baby-like. He sat down on the sofa next to her, and handed her one of the mugs. In exchange she handed him the joint, watching him speculatively. He really was very pretty.

'So, Jez,' she said, 'tell me about yourself.' London was a long way away. The guy with the televisions could wait. Meanwhile there was now . . .

In the car, Cissie wiped her face with her skirt, snuffling into the heavy folds. It smelled of cigarettes and whisky.

Steve tapped his fingers impatiently on the steering wheel. 'She's a crazy junkie,' he said. 'What do you expect?'

'She's my friend.' Cissie's voice was muffled, hurt.

'You mean she *was* your friend.'

'Do you think she has?'

'What?'

'You know – slept with . . .' she could not bring herself to say it. The thought was unthinkable.

Steve sighed. 'Look, why don't we go back? We could go to the refectory and have a proper breakfast, then we could go back to bed and forget all this.'

She shook her head, distraught. He tried again. 'You should drop it – this past thing,' he said. 'You've seen what she's like now, your so-called bosom buddy. She's a raving lunatic.'

'Shut up!' she shouted. 'Don't you understand?' He stared at her, shocked by the outburst. 'This is it!' she exclaimed. 'This is the biggest moment in our lives!' He looked blank. She opened the door and swung her legs out. Somewhere inside the house some-one was playing the Velvet Underground. 'It's the – the culmination of everything,' she said, almost unable to speak. 'It's our dream of the Beatles –'

'No,' he said. 'No it isn't, Cissie. It's the fantasy of a mad chick who's smoked too much Red Leb.'

She was standing on the gravel, staring in at him, her face still blotched with tears. 'Stay here,' she said abruptly. 'Don't come inside. I'm going to talk to Bennett.'

He sat, resigned, watching her as she stamped to the front door, pushed it open and went in.

Cissie automatically made her way to the kitchen. She knew the house well, but she disliked visiting it. Bennett's fellow commune-dwellers were a mysterious, silent bunch, prone to staring a lot and saying nothing. They were all local, and had the same strong Norfolk accents as Bennett. It was clear they regarded Cissie as an outsider. She had even heard one of them – Jez, the pretty one – referring to her to Bennett as 'your posh friend'.

A girl was sitting at the big wooden table in the kitchen savagely topping and tailing a pan of green beans.

'Hello, Bren,' Cissie said, her nervousness making her voice louder, brighter than usual. 'Is Bennett around?'

Bren pushed back a lank strand of brown hair and glared at her. 'Gone into Norwich to get her mum from the mental hospital.' She returned her concentration to the beans, her back eloquently hunched over the table.

Cissie hovered by a dilapidated sideboard, fingering a child's windmill she had found there. 'How's Martin?' she asked.

The girl bent lower over the beans. 'We're not together any more,' she said. 'I'm with Jez now.'

'Oh. Right.' Cissie wasn't sure how she should respond to this piece of news. Did this mean Bennett was now with Martin? Because surely Bennett had been with Jez? She didn't like to ask. She always had the sinking feeling that she could never keep up with events at the rectory. They all seemed to swap drugs, bodily fluids, friends, clothes, children, in a way that Cissie envied and feared all at once.

'Or at least I was.'

'Sorry?'

'I was with Jez,' Bren looked up. Cissie saw to her surprise that she was crying. 'Until your slag of a mate arrived.' She threw the knife down then, and burst into a flurry of embarrassed tears. The knife skewed across the table and clattered to the floor. Cissie went to pick it up, discomfited. She heard the sound of the commune van drawing up outside the house, the asthmatic wheeze of its engine clearly identifiable.

She brightened. 'Bennett's back!' The girl did not reply, red-faced and blowing her nose on the corner of a discoloured-looking tea towel that had been covering a bowl on the table. Cissie hurried out to the hall as Bennett and her cargo arrived, making a chaotic and noisy entrance. Gandy and Doma were eating toffee apples, red-cheeked and pleased with themselves, trailing their coats and leaving the muddy imprints of their wellingtons on the floor. Bennett staggered in under several wooden trays of carrots and an armful of cabbages, followed by a small, plump woman in a bouclé coat, clutching her handbag to her breast.

'Hello, Mrs Bennett,' Cissie said, hovering by the kitchen door, nervous. She had met Bennett's mother before, and still constantly battled with the ignoble fear that she might run amok at any moment.

Mrs Bennett smiled at her. 'Hello, dear.'

'It's Cissie, Mum,' Bennett yelled over her shoulder, going into the kitchen to unload her produce on to the table. 'You remember – from school. Gandy, take those boots off. What's the matter?' She had stopped in her tracks, staring at the tear-sodden Bren. But Cissie was more concerned by the arrival of Bennett's last passenger, who had made his way tentatively inside.

'Oh no,' she said. She turned to the kitchen. 'How the hell did he –'

Bennett was putting the kettle on, gazing at Bren, concerned. 'I found him hitching on the Yarmouth Road. Said he was a friend of Jude's. Amazing coincidence, eh? What's he call it? Arthur whatsit?'

'Synchronicity. Arthur Koestler.' Cissie stood weakly in the hall. Robbie had sunk on to the bottom stair, his legs finally giving out on him. He ran a chewed hand through his hair, making it stand up on end, staring at Cissie with bloodshot eyes. 'Don't I know you?' he asked.

Mrs Bennett was wandering away down the hall, still holding her handbag. Doma had begun to cry, repeating 'Juice! Juice!' over and over again.

Bennett shot a desperate look in the direction of her mother. 'Go and make sure she's all right, will you?' she said to Cissie. 'I'm a bit tied up here.'

Steve had appeared in the doorway. 'Cissie –'

'I told you to wait in the car!' she snapped at him, her voice uncharacteristically savage. He shrugged and left again.

'You're horrible to him,' Bennett called.

Robbie had shrunk into a foetal crouching position. 'Where's Jude?' he asked.

Cissie went away down the hall. She wished she had never come. Never gone to Heather's wedding. Never decided to go out with Steve just because he looked a bit like George Harrison. Never been born. It was all too complicated.

Mrs Bennett had disappeared. In the living room with the tall windows, the Beatles' *White Album* played to a sleeping cat curled up on one of the sofas. Cissie struggled with an overwhelming desire to lie down, to sink into the cushions and drift off to sleep, while George sang something gentle and understanding.

A row was developing in the kitchen. Cissie could hear Jude's voice, raised above the others'. Sighing, she turned and went back out into the hall. She could not leave Bennett to deal with all of this.

The pretty boy with the blond curls was standing sheepishly by the stairs, studiously making himself a roll-up, balancing his tobacco tin on the banister. He looked up at Cissie. 'Honest,' he said, 'we was just getting friendly. It wasn't sex or anything –'

Bren was still hunched over the beans, her face not visible. Bennett was leaning over her. 'You wanker,' she said to Jez, the boy in the hall.

'Christ!' Jude was pouring hot water from the kettle into a row of mugs, her hand shaking, her eyes glittering. 'I refuse to be the Wicked fucking Queen of the fucking West!'

'Shut up, Jude.'

'I didn't know he was anyone's *property*.' She spat the word out, as if the very pronouncement of it caused her pain.

Doma had retreated under the table and was sobbing heart-brokenly, murmuring 'juice' to herself. Gandy watched her, his eyes large and unsympathetic over the top of his toffee apple.

'Christ!' Jude said again into the tear-filled kitchen. She slapped a mug of coffee in front of Bren. 'Listen, I'm sorry, all right? A bit of a mistake.'

'Bren –' Jez fluttered in the doorway still. With a sudden

movement Bren stood up, scattering beans, pushed her chair back and stalked out.

'Excuse me,' she said, pushing past her boyfriend. 'Some of us have got yoga to do.'

They heard her footsteps ascend the stairs. Jez followed, more slowly. Bennett took Bren's mug of coffee and poured it down the sink.

'Thanks, Jude,' she said. Then, at full throttle: 'DOMA! Bloody shut up about the bloody juice!'

Doma's sobs went into a higher gear and Gandy strolled away with the pleased look children acquire when grief resides with someone else.

'Gandy, take those sodding boots off.' Bennett was crashing around angrily at the sink. 'Look,' she said. 'Was there something important? Only I'm on the rota to do the casserole and I haven't even started.'

Jude began to tell her, her voice growing louder over the cater-wauling of Doma under the table, about the Beatles, about Apple, about going to London. Cissie stood in the doorway still, listening, too tired to enthuse. 'And I can get us into Apple!' Jude was saying, 'This is once in a lifetime stuff, Bennett! You and Ringo. You and Ringo. You and Ringo fucking Starr.'

From further down the hall, the eerie tones of *Revolution 9* had started up. '*Number nine . . . Number nine . . . Number nine . . .*' Bennett struggled to fix the teat on to a bottle filled with orange juice. She thrust it under the table at Doma, who took it, studied it, her sobs shuddering for a moment. Then she made a decision and threw it resoundingly across the tiles, renewing her outcry with a louder wail.

'*Number nine . . .*'

'Richard Starkey MBE. You and him. Together.'

The music was rising to its unorthodox crescendo. Bennett leaned over the sink, clutching a burnt grill pan, distractedly squeez-ing a Brillo pad so that the pink foam squished through her clenched fist and dribbled to her wrist.

'Please, Bennett,' Cissie ventured. 'I'll go if you'll go.'

There was a screech from an interrupted John Lennon, and then silence from the living room, the great gulping sobs of Doma the only sound remaining. Bennett gave a little yelp and raced away into the hall. Cissie followed.

In the room with the sofas Mrs Bennett was standing by the record player, a confused look on her face. Between her gloved fingers she held the pickup arm at a drunken angle.

'I don't like that song,' she said.

Biting back tears of anger and frustration, Bennett crossed the room and put an arm about her shoulders. 'Come on, Mum,' she said kindly. 'Let's get that coat off and get a nice cup of tea, shall we? Settle you in . . .'

They left the room. Cissie turned the record player off. Jude was in the doorway. 'God!' she said. 'Parents!'

Cissie could not bring herself to say anything. She left Jude wandering about the room, humming to herself, picking up objects and putting them down again, pulling books from a bookshelf and flicking through them.

Cissie followed the sound of a television to a small room on the other side of the hall. She opened the door and peeked in. Mrs Bennett was ensconced in an armchair in front of a black and white television set with bad reception, lines zigzagging randomly across the screen. Bennett stood behind the armchair, clutching her mother's coat, watching with her.

'Look,' she said to Cissie without turning round. 'What would old Arthur Whatsit say about that?'

On the screen, Heather was reading the news, her face bright and bland. 'Severe weather warnings have caused local farmers to take extra precautions,' she was saying. She was replaced by a flock of sheep looking dazed in a paddock while someone hurled bales of hay in their direction.

'You've got to come to London,' Cissie said urgently. 'I can't cope with Jude on my own.'

Bennett looked at her. 'You won't be on your own,' she said, looking back at the television. Heather had returned, smiling sleekly, reading from her autocue.

'It won't be the same,' Cissie said, her voice rising in desperation. 'I need you.'

Bennett's shoulders had sagged. She stared down at the bouclé coat over her arm and stroked it a little, sad. 'I can't,' she said, her voice final.

They left shortly afterwards, Steve stiff and angry at the wheel, Robbie unconscious next to him, Jude staring out of the window, humming still and pretending not to mind about anything, Cissie tearless and tired.

Bennett watched them go from the window of the living room, waiting until the car had disappeared round the corner on to the main road before turning back into the room. Doma had subsided somewhere in the kitchen. Gandy was chattering brightly to Martin, who had just got up. Upstairs she could hear the muted murmurings of Bren and Jez dealing with this morning's setback in their relationship. The sound of the television burbling away across the hall told her that her mother was probably calm now. Picking up her scratched Beatles record, she allowed the luxury of a tear to slide down her face, as she examined its lacerated surface. It was too late for Ringo. This was real, this was now.

She heard her name called from outside and looked up, surprised. Someone was cycling down the weed-sprouting driveway, bouncing over the ruts, waving an arm, breath frosty in the winter morning, cherry-red coat like an explosion in the greyness. It was Peggy.

They sat together at the kitchen table, drinking rosehip tea, Peggy's fingers curled round the mug for warmth, her face uncharacteristically tense.

'The thing is,' she said finally, 'I want to tell you something, Bennett.'

'Me?' Bennett's modest heart filled with pride. This was real mum stuff. This was what she had always imagined. You sit with your mum in the kitchen drinking tea and telling each other secrets.

Peggy's eyes did not meet hers. 'It's something I should have told

Cissie years ago. Only I couldn't. I still can't.' At last she looked up, her face desperate. 'I want you to do it, Bennett. When the time is right.'

CHAPTER NINE

Come Together

THE STATION CLOCK TOLD Cissie that it was ten past eight; the train would be leaving in five minutes. She jiggled her foot against the metal barrier, listening to the throb of the train's engine rising up to the roof, spreading out across the red bricks, vying with the screech of brakes as a train from Yarmouth pulled in to platform three. As the last few stragglers headed past her to the London-bound train, the occupants descending from the Yarmouth Flyer suddenly filled the damp concourse: shoppers in headscarves, boys in uniform late for school, men in tweed jackets with sacks of vegetables, an old woman wandering, confused, with a shopping trolley. The ticket-collector at the barrier to platform one eyed Cissie. She stared back at him, defiant. She knew what he was thinking: another hippy who would try and get on the train without paying. Oddly, this lifted her spirits. He was on the outside, one of the world. She was one of the chosen few, cocooned in the knowledge that she was special. She listened to the tapping of her foot for a moment. Yes. It was the beat of 'Back In The USSR' . . .

Mrs Bennett was sitting calmly on the glass-covered veranda of St Andrew's Hospital. In spite of the smothering heat from the ancient radiators, Mrs Bennett was wearing her bouclé coat, with a serviceable but unattractive woollen scarf crossed across her chest beneath it and appearing at the neck. A small felt hat sat unhappily on her grey curls. A capacious handbag rested on her knees, and occasionally her gloved fingers would touch the brown plastic strap, stroking it gently.

Mrs Bennett was waiting. She knew she was going to go somewhere, and that it was a fairly momentous thing, but just for the moment she could not quite remember where or what it was. She looked out across the brown, bare land in front of the hospital. Beyond the wall at the end of the gravelled drive a bus was passing. She could hear the murmur of distant traffic, reminding her fleetingly of another, confused existence somewhere outside this building – but perhaps that was another person. Two men in the white jackets of the nursing staff were coming slowly up the drive, talking intently, their breath emerging in little white frosty gusts as they spoke, one leaning towards the other, as if he were saying something of the utmost importance. Mrs Bennett sat forward a little, frowning. Perhaps they were coming to fetch her. Something by her feet caught her eye and she looked down. Next to her chair was a small red suitcase. She recognized it. It was the one she had been carrying when she had first entered the hospital. Had it been during the Blitz? She remembered the sound of banging, the groaning, the terrible weight of fear and unhappiness. It must have been the Blitz. She looked out of the window again, suddenly anxious; but the men had disappeared. The driveway stretched to the road, the traffic hummed, another bus passed. She remembered then. Susan was coming to take her home for a few days. Was it Susan? She tried to remember. Perhaps Diana. Or Caroline. It didn't matter. She relaxed back against the creaking wicker of her chair, unconcerned. She was going to be taken home for a little while, whatever home was.

It was still Cissie's bedroom, even though she had not occupied it for any length of time for several years. Peggy stood in the doorway, contemplating the peeling pictures of George Harrison, the dust-covered dressing-table, the empty bed. Toulouse was curled up against the folded bedspread, snuffling in some ancient, dazed dog dream, his hair thinner now, not so soft, his whiskers grey.

Peggy looked down at the piece of fabric in her hand. It was blue, a small neat square, slightly fraying at the edges. George. Hamburg. Mike had told her. She pressed the fabric to her lips and closed her eyes, leaning against the door frame, a slight, intense figure with her burst of piled red hair, her odd clothes. *Go on, Cissie*, she breathed to herself. *Go on!*

'Cissie!' She turned, to see Steve hurrying towards her, threading his way through the small throng of people from the Yarmouth train. Her heart turned cold.

'Go away,' she said. 'I'm not going to change my mind.'

He stood in front of her, panting slightly. Suddenly his beard looked ridiculous, his ears too pointed, his eyes not warm enough, not soft enough to be George's. 'They haven't come, have they.' It was a triumphant statement rather than a question. 'You're the only one who turned up.'

'Sod off,' she said. 'It's finished. You and me. Go away.'

He stood, smiling slightly, not quite believing her. 'This is stupid,' he said. 'Let's go to Mac's Cafe and have bacon and eggs. My shout.'

'Finished. Kaput.' She felt, oddly, like grinning. Irreverent thoughts kept flashing into her head, not at all matched to the seriousness of the occasion. She was, after all, in the process of chucking her boyfriend of six months. It was hardly *Anna Karenina*, but it did merit a bit of solemnity. Instead she felt rather breathless, a little excited, inclined to giggle.

His smile faded. 'What do you think's going to happen?' He demanded. The driver was heading past them, carrying a metal lunch box, a folded newspaper under his arm. Steve's cheeks were flushed a dark pink. 'Do you think for one moment you're going to meet George Harrison?' She did not reply. The engine driver swung up on to the footplate and disappeared from view.

'And if you did – what then? He's going to gaze into your eyes and then you're both going to live happily ever after?'

The big minute hand on the clock above the station entrance had jerked forward again. Cissie felt in her pocket for her ticket. Her fingers closed round it. 'Good-bye,' she said to Steve.

His voice was steady, determined. 'I'll see you in the refectory Monday morning.'

She suddenly raised her voice, furious at his smugness, his

certainty that her precious dream could not be realized. 'You won't!' Then her heart lifted. Hurrying through the arched entrance was Heather, immaculate in a navy suit, blonde hair swinging, causing people to turn and nudge each other as they recognized her. 'Good-bye, Steve.' She waved her arm at Heather, shouting, 'Hurry up! It's going!'

Heather joined them, clutching a leopardskin holdall. 'Sorry,' she said, 'I had to do the farming report.' She registered Steve, failing to keep the disappointment out of her voice. 'Are you coming?' She turned to give Cissie an accusing frown. 'I thought this was just us. Otherwise I'd have told Ray –'

Two small girls appeared from nowhere, shyly clutching copies of *Bunty* and a biro. 'God forbid,' said Steve sourly. 'This is your pathetic little pilgrimage. Far be it from me –'

'Piss off, Steve. You're spoiling my day,' Cissie said.

Heather was signing autographs, scrawling something confident across the front of *Bunty*. Steve left. Heather beamed down at the girls. 'Name?' She enquired.

They were almost unable to speak. 'Heather,' one of them said, finally.

'No,' Heather's voice was patient, the smile unfaltering, 'I meant *your* name.'

The small face below shrivelled and became puce with embarrassment. 'Janet,' the girl said.

Cissie watched Steve disappear through the arch. She felt no emotion. The little girls melted away with their autographs, ecstatic, into the crowd.

'Where are the others?' Heather asked.

Cissie was staring at her, grinning. 'Does that happen a lot?'

'What?'

'Those girls?'

Heather shrugged, affecting a kind of weary nonchalance. 'It's my job, Cissie.' Cissie repressed a smirk.

The man at the barrier was about to close the gate. They hurried through, Cissie waving her ticket at him triumphantly.

'We've still got another minute,' Heather said, although around them doors were slamming, people were kissing through train windows, a porter was piling mail sacks into the guard's van.

'They're not coming,' Cissie said.

'I thought you said Bennett had to take her mum out. I thought she said she couldn't come.'

'I know, but . . .' Cissie's voice trailed away. She had been so sure that Bennett would find a way, Bennett, of all people. And Jude! Jude, who had instigated the whole plan, who had returned to Norfolk after all those years of wandering simply to make this happen! She knew what train they were getting, she knew they were going to meet at the barrier. Cissie sighed. Of course Jude was never going to make it; Jude, who probably never woke up till lunchtime – how on earth could she have thought for a moment that Jude would be here in the grey early morning, ready to board a train? They paused for a last hopeful second, looking back, Cissie's hand on the door, both of them craning round in spite of themselves for a glimpse of Bennett's voluminous skirts, Jude's spiky hair.

'You'll have to get on, ladies.' The guard was standing with his whistle to his lips. 'All doors closing now.'

They climbed in, slamming the door shut behind them as the train lurched forward and then began hesitantly to leave the station. Heather struggled with the window catch and succeeded in pushing down the window. She peered out. 'No sign –' she said, her voice disappearing into the creaking and groaning of the carriage as it jolted into action. 'We've gone round a curve now – can't see the barrier –'

She drew her head back in, trying not to look disappointed. 'Just you and me, then.'

Cissie smiled, unhappy. 'Yes.' They avoided each other's eyes, did not ask the hundred questions they had to ask: *How do we get to Apple? What do we say when we get there?*

'We'd better find seats,' Heather said eventually, picking up her holdall from the corner where she had thrown it on boarding. Glumly, Cissie followed her, struggling through a carriage full of shouting foreign students with huge amounts of luggage. They searched in vain for two seats.

'Next one,' Cissie said. They were heading up the train towards the front. Ahead of her, Heather had reached the end of the carriage and was struggling with the adjoining door and then suddenly they were away from student jabberings and cramped chaos and were on the threshold of a darker, silent carriage where the space diminished, and before them stretched a mock mahogany bar, a few seats, a couple of tired businessmen in suits already sipping coffee and staring out of the window at the slowly passing suburbs of Norwich.

An indifferent-looking girl mopped the counter. 'Help yew?' She asked, barely looking up from her task.

Heather was about to speak when she registered the other drinker at the bar.

'There you are.' Bennett turned towards them, glass in hand, smile as bright as sunshine. 'I thought it was just going to be me. I've been on this sodding train for hours.'

A bright stripe of sunlight was lowering across the brown earth. Mrs Bennett had watched its progress as slowly it passed across the small hillock by the entrance, catching a few leaves of the evergreen shrubs dangling tattily on the path's edge, leaves bruised by the careless heels of a hundred visitors. Now the light had edged up the concrete steps and filled the doorway, so that the people who came and went were temporarily gilded, their heads flashing bright, like a flock of angels, briefly glimpsed, hurrying about their business. Mrs Bennett stared at this radiant streak, transfixed. Standing in it was one particular angel in a red coat, her hair flaming, her face invisible. On each side of her were two small, solemn faces, like cherubim.

'Hello,' said the angel. 'Hello, Mrs Bennett. Remember me? I'm Cissie's mum.' She pushed forward the cherubim, who stared, unsmiling. 'And these are your grandchildren. We've come to take you to the seaside for the day.'

The train had picked up speed, and was clacking across the wintry fields in a gloomy chorus of wheels over points, wheels over rails. They had found an empty collection of seats near the front of the train, and had settled themselves in. Cissie sat by the window with her back to the engine, opposite Bennett and Heather, with a table separating them. Heather's leopardskin bag was opened in front of them, and Bennett was examining its contents.

'Christ, Heather!' She held up a pair of tights, vertically striped brown and turquoise. Heather snatched them away.

'Don't!' She stuffed them back into the bag, red-faced. 'Why do you always have to humiliate me?'

Bennett sank back, bored with the game. 'You'll look like a stick of rock in those.'

'Does Ray know you're here?' Cissie asked idly.

Heather bit her lip. 'I couldn't tell him – not so soon after the wedding. I told him I had to go to London to interview someone.'

They stared at her, impressed. 'Who? Who did you say you were going to interview?'

'Barbara Castle.'

Bennett snorted. 'And he believed you?'

Heather looked down ruefully at her neat suit. 'Why do you think I'm wearing this outfit? She's the Employment Minister, Bennett. He'd have been suspicious if I'd worn my jeans.' She gathered up the contents of the bag and stood up. 'I'm off to the Ladies',' she said. 'I'd better get changed before Ipswich.'

Bennett eyed her, cynical. 'Same old thing, then.'

'Sorry?' Heather was standing in the aisle, ignoring the nudges and murmurs of recognition from a family opposite.

Bennett leaned back, affecting an air of indifference. 'You. It's all just the same as it used to be. Having to tell fibs to get to do what you want. Changing your identity in the toilet.'

A slow flush rose up Heather's neck. 'Some of us don't like hurting people if we don't have to,' she said. Then she turned and headed down the train, hair bobbing, upset.

Cissie pulled her eyes away from the blur of muddy fields speeding past and rested them on Bennett, who was moodily lighting a cigarette. 'That was unkind,' she said mildly.

Bennett looked at her. 'Unkind?' she repeated. 'Didn't you tell me the last time you saw Heather before the wedding she snubbed you totally? On the platform at Norwich station?'

Cissie shuffled a little. 'She was with her mother,' she said, uncomfortable.

Bennett inhaled on her cigarette and shrugged. 'I thought friends were friends,' she said. 'Say anything to each other. Do anything to each other. What's that poem?'

'I don't know,' Cissie said, weary of being the repository for all Bennett's half-remembered theories.

'You know. Penguin Modern Poets.'

'Corso. You mean Gregory Corso.'

'That's the one!' Bennett was triumphant. She slid the packet of Embassy across the table, and Cissie took a cigarette for herself. 'How did it go? . . . *"Friends be kept, friends be gained"* . . .'

Cissie thought for a moment, running the poem over in her head. She remembered the line that followed, but instead picked another line from later on in the poem. '*"I have many friends yet sometimes I am nobody's friend"*.' she said, perverse.

Bennett frowned. 'That's not the bit I meant.'

They smoked in silence for a while, each avoiding the other's eyes, Cissie tracing a scratch on the table-top with a chewed fingernail, Bennett tapping her foot against the table leg and humming 'Bad Moon Rising'. Cissie found herself thinking about Oliver. She saw him in her mind's eye as she had seen him last, home for a weekend visit, sitting on the window sill in the living room at Brigadoon. She had been sprawled on the floor with Susie playing a desultory game of Happy Families, and she had looked up suddenly and found him watching her. To her surprise, this had made her feel nervous.

'Why don't you come and play?' she had asked.

He shook his head slowly. 'I don't know how to,' he said.

'It's only Happy Families.' She had sat up, cross-legged, clutching her cards, smiling at him.

'Exactly,' he had said, his face serious.

For a second she had seen how hurt he was, how excluded, how like her. And then the moment had passed and he had just been

261

Oliver again, an occasional mysterious presence descending on Brigadoon like a wraith. At least he hadn't brought the beautiful art student with him, she thought. Jackie, with the easy smile and the Welsh accent and the brown hands. Funny, she could see her so clearly, and yet she had only met her once. Oliver had never brought her again to Brigadoon, and had never spoken of her. Not that it mattered. What Oliver did with his life was his business. But she could not help the feeling that somehow his sadness was tied up with her own, that she was in some way the author of his melancholy. She swatted the thought away, irritated with herself. She tried to think about Steve, to feel some kind of regret that their relationship was over, but she could not feel anything. She tried to remember his face, but it had faded away.

'I shouldn't have come,' Bennett said suddenly, breaking the silence. Cissie looked at her, waiting to hear what she would say next. 'I should be with my kids. And my mum was expecting me . . .'

There was silence again, broken only by the repeated whine of a child further up the carriage: 'I want crisps, Mum, give me some crisps, I want crisps . . .'

'It's only one day . . .' Cissie said lamely, unable to think of anything more suitably comforting. 'And we'll get to see them, Bennett. Ringo. Remember? You're going to see Ringo.'

'How?' Bennett's face was openly disbelieving, pinkly desperate. 'Jude's not here. I don't even know how to get to the bloody Apple offices. Do you?'

Cissie's spine was rigid. 'Savile Row. It's in Savile Row.'

'Yes. And where the bloody hell is that?'

Once again London seemed to stretch out ahead of them, vast and unfathomable, as it had always been. Here they were, older, brighter, knowing so much *more*, and still they were ignorant.

'And even if we find it,' Bennett was implacable in her gloom, puffing on her cigarette, intense, swaying with the movement of the train, 'what then? How do we get in? Jude isn't here.'

Jude. The key to their excitement, unlocking their desires, sparking their imaginations, then disappearing just when they needed her.

Norfolk sped past, wet streaks of winter cabbage fields, heaps of rotting sugar beets, a herd of Friesians standing disconsolately under a bare elm. Heather returned to her seat, her face pinched and offended. She was wearing a very short red dress under a floor-length tweed coat. She sat down, pulling a copy of *Petticoat* magazine from her bag, and began to read, ostentatiously turning the pages.

'Good coat,' Cissie said.

'We were just wondering,' Bennett said conversationally, 'where Savile Row is. Do you know?'

The family opposite stared at the transformed Heather, mother with lips pursed in disapproval, father's eyes fixed slyly on the expanse of black, wool-covered leg Heather was revealing. She looked up from her magazine, caught his eye and smiled automatically at him before pulling her legs in under the table. 'Of course I know where Savile Row is,' she said coldly. 'I'm a journalist, Bennett. I have to know.'

'So – where is it, then?'

'The West End.'

'I could have told you that.'

'So why did you ask . . .?'

Cissie's thoughts drifted away, as they bickered. George was getting closer, she could feel it. Steve had disappeared, and a hundred possibilities suddenly burst into life in her head.

Perhaps they wouldn't even have to bother finding the mysterious Apple. Perhaps George, picking up her vibrations, would be waiting at the barrier at Liverpool Street station. She knew their heads were connected, their hearts interlocking, their souls just one beautiful soul, the two halves of the Apple that signified everything that mattered in her life. *The girl from Norfolk, the girl from Norfolk, the girl from Norfolk.* The girl from Norfolk is coming, she thought. Wait for me, George. *Go on, Cissie. Go on!*

Bennett had produced some photographs and was showing them to Heather. 'That's Jez in the hammock,' she was saying, 'and that's Doma up the top – on the branch – see?'

Heather peered. 'That looks awfully dangerous.'

'They have to find things out, Heather. Take risks.'

'Even if they break their legs in the process?'

'Free expression,' Bennett said patiently. 'Being spontaneous. It's a sort of educational theory. What's that woman called, Cissie?'

'Montessori. Maria Montessori.'

Heather was disbelieving. 'Isn't that a town in Italy?'

Bennett snorted. 'Honestly, Heather! I thought you were supposed to be Miss Sophisticated.' Bennett studied the photographs of her children, face glowing. 'I'm sending them to Summerhill when they're a bit older.'

Heather was aghast. 'Summerhill! That mad old man in the big house?'

'I thought you'd like him – he's Scottish, isn't he?'

Heather shuddered. 'I saw a documentary. Children running about like little wild animals. They don't have to go to lessons at all if they don't want to, did you know? They don't even have to *get up* in the morning if they don't want to!' She leaned forward confidentially. 'Someone told me the children eat their own – you know –'

'What?'

She put her hand over her mouth to mask the words, turning away from the interested family opposite, embarrassed. 'You know.'

'She means shit,' Cissie said bluntly. 'I've heard that story. You shouldn't believe that kind of rubbish, Heather. It's a myth perpetrated by the bourgeoisie.' She was pleased with that sentence, even if she had stolen it from Steve.

Bennett nodded sagely. 'Straights. They're always scared of new things. Anyway, what's wrong with eating your own shit?'

There was an explosion of incredulous giggles from the children opposite. Their mother stood up, rigid, and began to pull bags down from the luggage rack.

Cissie nudged Bennett, grinning. 'See what you've done?' she mouthed. But the train was slowing down, clacking through the run-down industrial muddle always to be found near railway stations in English towns. Heather peered out, blinking at a cluster of cranes pointing their metal elbows into the cold white sky. 'Ipswich!' she announced.

The family began to make their way down the aisle, struggling with bags and packages, the children still eyeing Heather, impressed by the sight of a celebrity. As the train rounded its final bend into the station, one of the small boys in the party came back towards them, swaying, excited. 'You're Heather Lewis, aren't you?' he said to Heather.

The train jerked and shuddered to a halt. 'Timothy! Come here!' the boy's mother called sharply.

Heather smiled a gracious smile. 'Actually I'm Heather Broadbent now,' she told the boy. 'I got married.'

'You read the news. On the telly.'

'That's right.' She was scrabbling in her bag, searching for a pen for the inevitable bestowal of an autograph.

'Me and my sister —' the boy hopped from one foot to another, agitated by his own effrontery, 'me and my sister — we think you're rubbish!' And he raced away down the carriage, whooping. For a frozen moment, Bennett and Cissie waited, staring at Heather, trying to gauge her reaction. Then all three of them burst out laughing.

'It's not easy being famous,' Heather said wryly. Cissie saw suddenly how much Heather was enjoying this adventure, so far removed from the rigidity of her work, her relationship with Ray.

'Look! Look!' Bennett was hammering on the window excitedly, causing a man in the seat behind to turn round and snap, 'Do you mind?'

'Look — it's her — it's Jude!' Sure enough, there she was, peaked face under Peruvian hat, hammering on the other side of the streaming glass, grinning and pulling faces. Cissie sank back in her seat, almost weeping. It was going to happen. It was going to happen this time: the magic was working. Jude was here after all. They were all here.

Bennett suddenly made a small explosive sound and sank back into her seat. 'Look,' she said, her voice despairing, 'she's brought Dracula along!'

Cissie squinted through the glass, craning her neck to catch a sight of Jude, who was already racing along the platform to the door at the end of the carriage. Behind her, hobbling shambolically, his hair a wild bird's nest, clothed in the same frayed sweater and grease-encrusted jeans, the same aura of panic and anxiety and incipient mayhem, was Robbie.

The four of them were singing 'Lady Madonna' in happy, raucous voices, all slightly stoned after smoking a joint in the Ladies' toilets. They had all crammed in together, hysterical, Heather doubting and disapproving, but caught up in the mood of excitement. Now Heather laughed giddily, smiling even more than the others, fuelled by drugs and adventure and their mutual sense of *something about to happen*.

In the seat behind, Robbie dozed, murmuring occasionally and opening a confused, bloodshot eye. When he heard the singing, he lapsed back into semi-consciousness, his head on the table in front of him, his mouth slack, dribbling slightly on to his sleeve.

They were going through the songs in chronological order, as they had always done, each of them remembering in turn which song followed which, priding themselves on recalling every harmony, every quirk, every murmured Beatles aside. This was their common language, this was the blood that bound them together.

Finally, they rested, breathless and satiated. They had reached the end of *Revolver*, screeching along to 'Tomorrow Never Knows', and the rest would be sung later.

Cissie and Jude smiled at each other. George and John. They were the special, strange ones, weren't they?

'I'll do it,' Jude was saying huskily. 'I'll get us into Apple. I promised, didn't I?' Her eyes locked with Cissie's.

'I thought you weren't coming,' Cissie said, breathless. 'When you weren't at the barrier —'

Jude rubbed at her face. 'Went to a party in Thetford,' she said. 'Seemed stupid to go back to Norwich when we could pick the train up here. Spent half the night hitching . . .'

'It'll be one of those days.' Bennett murmured.

'What days?'

'The ones you tell your grandchildren about,' Bennett said dreamily. 'The day I met the Beatles.'

Cissie remembered, then: Peg's bright head bent over hers, tucking her into bed, saying, 'Did I ever tell you I met Howard Keel once?' And Cissie saying, 'Howard Keel?' – her voice filled with scorn – 'Howard Keel? Isn't he dead? Anyway, who cares?' And the hurt on Peg's face as she withdrew, keeping her dreams to herself, sorry she had revealed her heart to her stony-faced child just for a second.

'Our grandchildren won't care,' Cissie said. 'They probably won't even know who the Beatles are.'

The others turned on her, angry and surprised. 'Of course they will!' Bennett's face frowned at her, round and red like a Bramley apple.

'They'll go down in history,' Heather said. 'Like Mozart.' She smoothed her dress down over her thighs, admiring her long white fingers.

Jude snorted. 'Not John,' she said. 'He'd hate to be like Mozart. Hitler, more like. Someone who pissed everyone off.'

The others ignored this provocation.

'Anyway,' Cissie said, 'I'm not getting married. So I won't have grandchildren.'

'Doesn't necessarily follow,' Bennett said.

Heather was twisting her wedding ring round on her finger, tense. 'Look, we're not going to have all that stuff about bourgeois institutions again, are we? Can't we just agree to differ?'

They lapsed into silence. Cissie wondered for a moment about confessing that she had not heard from Mrs Harrison for months. No. She could not. The letters were the one powerful thing she had in their eyes. Heather had her little bit of fame, Bennett had all that love to share, Jude – well, Jude was just Jude, a glittering, powerful presence. The letters were the only thing that made Cissie special. She stared out of the window. How could Mrs Harrison just abandon her? It was so cruel, so unfeeling.

'We should do this again,' Jude suddenly said in a decisive tone. They turned to look at her, white and gaunt, dark eyes staring out of tired skin.

'Go to London?'

'No, stupid. Beatles reunion.'

Heather brightened. 'I know! We could meet outside the school gates ten years from now – to the very day.'

Jude shook her head, causing her eyes to roll around a little. She was, apparently, not well. 'Flu, she had told them. 'We should meet on John Lennon's birthday,' she said.

'Why?' they chorused, indignant. 'Why John?'

Jude shrugged. 'Because he's the most important,' she said implacably. 'We should meet every year outside the school gates. John's birthday. Ninth of October.' Her words were slurring.

Heather was sitting upright, heated. 'Why John?' she repeated angrily. 'Why do we always have to do things the way you want?'

Jude looked at her coolly for a moment, the old Jude, in control. 'No reason. We'll put it to the vote, shall we?'

'Why is it you're allowed to show up here after all this time and take over –'

Jude sighed and blinked, squinting away from the light suddenly beaming in through the windows as the sun broke through the clouds for a moment. 'Because I make things happen.'

Bennett flashed a warning glance at Cissie, and obediently Cissie intervened. 'What year?' she asked.

Heather and Jude looked at her blankly. They were dappled in winking spots of light, as the sun flashed behind a passing copse of pines.

'What year was John born?'

'Don't know.' Jude said, weary.

'I do,' Heather said, always the one who collated the facts. '1940.'

'And Paul?'

'1942. Eighteenth of June.'

'God! Fancy knowing that!' Jude looked out of the window, affecting scornful indifference. It was clear her head was spinning, her brow furrowed as she tried to stay awake. 'Look like a poncy dolly bird . . .' she mumbled. 'More like a bloody accountant . . .'

Cissie was thoughtful. 'Let's have a compromise. 1940's easy to remember. Nice round number. We meet on John's fiftieth birthday. That'll be 1990.'

'I still don't see why it has to be –'

Bennett sat up, interested. '1990!' she repeated. 'Where? Surely not that bloody old school.'

'I liked it,' Heather said to no one in particular.

'Liverpool Street station,' Cissie said. 'Under the clock. Peggy told me that's where people meet.' *Where lovers meet*, she had said. *Sweethearts. Where you said good-bye to your husband or your fiancé when he went off to war. Where I said good-bye to Cecil for the last time.* Endings and beginnings. It was right.

'OK,' said Jude, dreamily, her head pressed against the window, her eyes sliding over the landscape.

'Right,' Bennett said, thwacking her drumsticks decisively on the table-top. '1990 it is. Let's make it midnight. Under the clock.'

Heather was the only one looking doubtful. 'What's wrong with 1992? Is that so hard to remember? And what if we've got children? Midnight's a very inconvenient –'

'Hey,' Bennett said suddenly, wanting to move on. 'Hey – remember the pigs?' She did a little drum-roll on the table. 'Who's your favourite group?' Drum roll. 'Pig Floyd.'

The others groaned.

'Favourite silent film star?' Drum-roll. 'Mary Pigford.'

With a united scream they descended on her, Jude and Heather piling across the table, mock-throttling the grinning offender, who sang, strangled, '*Have you seen the little piggies, crawling in the dirt . . .*'

The man sitting behind them, disapprovingly ensconced next to the sleeping Robbie, turned to glower at them, rising out of his seat. 'Do you mind?' he said.

They subsided, breathless and laughing.

'Yeah, we mind,' Jude said in her old mock-John Lennon voice. 'After all, it's his train, isn't it, mister?'

Bennett pulled on her arm. 'Hey – listen – Jude – joke.'

'No!'

'John Lennon was reading the paper one day –'

'I don't want to hear –'

269

'And Ringo says to him, "Are they thick lens glasses you're wear-ing?" and he says, "No, they're mine" . . .'

'That's a terrible joke, Bennett. It was terrible when you first told it and it's still terrible now.' Heather's pronunciation of the word 'terrible' had reached new heights of Edinburghian disap-proval.

Robbie's head appeared from the seat behind. 'Hey, man,' he said sleepily, 'are we there?'

The train was slowing down. Jude climbed across the table and scribbled a clearing in the glass. 'Colchester,' she said.

Bennett nudged Cissie, nodding in the direction of Robbie. 'He's got track marks in his arms,' she said in a low voice. 'Did you see?' Cissie looked at her, disconcerted.

'Oh my God,' Heather was saying. 'Oh my God. Oh no. Oh no. Oh my God.'

The train had stopped, this time easing gently into stillness. Once more there was the rustle and disruption of disembarkation. Heather was staring across the table at Bennett and Cissie, her face frozen, aghast. She slid suddenly downwards, her head disappearing under the table.

'Hey, Heather.' Jude attempted to crouch down, peering under the table after Heather, but the effort made her head spin and she crawled upward again, groaning.

'Heather?'

Someone had paused by the table. They looked up. 'Hamster alert,' Bennett said quietly, as Heather slid upwards again, sheep-ishly pink. 'Hamster alert.'

The train stood for an interminable time in Colchester station, rumbling and creaking. There seemed to be some kind of a delay, explained by an incoherent voice over the tannoy, something to do with points at Manningtree.

Heather stood in the corridor, her face blotched with tears, hidden from her husband's view by the protective arms of Cissie and Bennett.

'Why don't you sod off?' Bennett was saying angrily.

Ray, stiff in a striped suit, ignored her, his eyes never leaving the spot where he presumed Heather to be. 'I came in the car,' he said. 'I read your diary.' His wife's only reply was a muffled, choking sound.

'You did what?' Bennett's eyes had become circles of surprise. 'You *what?*'

Cissie looked out of the window, tense. 'Train's about to leave, Ray.'

Ray was still addressing a spot somewhere behind Bennett's angry chest. 'You know what it said for today? Of course you do. You wrote it.'

'Ray —' Heather's voice was tiny, desperate. 'Ray, I love you —'

'Apple,' he said, implacable. 'Apple. London. Paul McCartney. At last.'

'Ray —'

'Paul McCartney,' he repeated, a small note of astonishment entering his voice. 'At last.' He was breathing heavily, as if he had been running, his big hands hanging helplessly at his sides. 'Either you get off this train with me now,' he said, 'or the marriage is over.'

The train's belly rumbled beneath them and moved into a new chorus of mechanical groaning. 'Ray, don't be a prat,' Cissie said.

'You can shut up,' he said. His lower lip trembled and a sheen of sweat had slowly descended from his hairline, glazing his forehead. He turned back to the hidden Heather. 'Apple,' he repeated. 'That's where you're meeting him, is it?'

Bennett, perhaps for the first time, seemed suddenly to see the pain behind Ray's anger. She moved forward a little, about to speak, but Ray pushed her away, misunderstanding.

'Ray —'

'Don't!' His mouth was trembling ominously. 'You — you lot — you're all to blame. Filling her head full of thoughts. You should all grow up, that's what you should do.'

'Train's moving,' Cissie said. And indeed, they were slowly edging along the platform, the last doors slamming, the guard's whistle rising in a shriek.

At last Ray had his eyes fixed on Heather's face, partially revealed. 'Are you getting off?' he demanded.

She simply shook her head, gasping back a sob.

'Are you coming back with me?' he asked, as if to make sure she had understood the question.

She shook her head again, turning away. Bennett put out a hand, touching Ray's striped sleeve, but he misunderstood the gesture and reaching across her with a swift movement, he grabbed at Heather, pulling her towards the door. Cissie was pushed out of the way in a rough split second, hitting the wall with an uncomfortable thud as Ray struggled to pull his wife off the train, impeded by Bennett. Wincing, Cissie pulled herself upright, rubbing at her shoulder, about to speak, to try and remonstrate, when she saw in a muddled moment that Jude and Robbie had appeared in the corridor, returning from the buffet car laden with Smiths Crisps, Club biscuits and lemonade. She saw, in a terrible second, what was going to happen next.

'Hey!' Robbie shouted, crisps falling to the floor. 'Hey, man! You can't —' He lunged wildly at Ray and the pair hit the floor, falling silently in a tangle of legs as the train picked up speed and began to move out of the station.

'I'm getting off!' Ray shouted, his voice muffled under the pressure of Robbie's chest.

'Attacking women, you shit!' Robbie was transformed, a wild-eyed, gaunt-cheeked tiger, pounding at Ray's face in a flurry of feeble, bony fists. Heather screamed. Jude stood, uncomprehending. Bennett and Cissie struggled to intervene amid the flailing limbs, but stood back as Ray began to gain control, pulling Robbie back by his hair in a brutal movement and crawling round until at last he had his assailant pinioned to the floor, sitting astride him, triumphant. He looked down at Robbie.

'Do I know you?' he asked. His hand slid away from its iron grasp on Robbie's hair, as if knowing it should not have been there in the first place.

'I don't know, man,' Robbie said, confused. His head was spinning, the roots of his hair were screaming.

The two of them struggled to their feet. Ray registered the back gardens of Colchester moving past the window and groaned a small, helpless groan. 'I'll be prosecuted by British Rail,' he said, his voice deep with despair. He turned to Heather, bitterly, rubbing the side of his chin where Robbie's skull and crossbones ring had caught his flesh. 'You want to go to bed with Paul McCartney?' he said. 'Fine. You can have him.'

Heather sniffed, her mouth moving in anxious tics. 'I never said –'

'For Christ' sake, Ray!' Cissie suddenly exploded. 'Half the bloody country wants to go to bed with Paul McCartney.'

'Half?' Jude looked dubious, unwrapping a Penguin bar. Cissie quelled her with a look.

'I'm only her sodding husband, after all,' Ray said sulkily.

'Bloody hamster,' Bennett said.

'One more time,' Ray glared at her, 'one more time and I knock your block off.'

'She isn't going to sleep with Paul McCartney,' Cissie interjected desperately.

'She wants to, though, doesn't she. It's the wanting to, that's the thing.'

'Of course she wants to!' Cissie exploded. 'Of course she does! He's bloody Paul McCartney, of course she bloody does!'

'Doesn't mean your marriage is over,' Bennett said helpfully.

'You can shut up,' Ray said ferociously, blurting the words out in spite of himself, his cheeks blotched with two fierce spots of red. 'Susan bloody Bennett. We all know what you think about marriage.'

She looked at him. There was a strange, loaded moment between them, which Cissie did not comprehend. 'Do we?' Bennett had fixed her eyes on him, her face calm. 'And do we all know what you think about marriage, Ray?'

Heather stopped scrubbing at her face with a damp handkerchief and looked up. 'Leave him alone, Bennett,' she said. A look of surprise slid between Cissie and Bennett. 'Yes!' Heather said in a loud voice, and then, shockingly, began to shout. 'All of you! Leave him alone! Always picking on him, always taking the piss! He's my husband!'

'Lucky you!' said Bennett sarcastically. Heather turned, her face savage, her lips suddenly taut.

'And what's your fantasy, Bennett?' she asked, her voice sliding up an octave into its most prim and Scots-sounding. 'Still waiting for your mother to return from the planet Mars?'

With a strangled cry, Bennett lunged at Heather, with Cissie hauling her back and Ray placing his body between his wife and her attacker, who had produced a drumstick and was waving it threateningly at Heather's head.

'That's it!' Bennett cried. 'You smug little – you think your life's so perfect? You think your husband's so perfect? You want to know how perfect he is?'

They were facing each other, noses only a few inches apart. 'Yes!' said Heather. 'Yes, I want to know! Tell me!'

The air shimmered with expectation. There was a collective gulp of air, almost audible. Then Bennett drew back, lowering her arm, dropping her eyes.

'Forget it,' she said.

A small, static moment ensued, a tableau of reactions. Then Heather suddenly moved across the swaying corridor, a small determined figure in her voluminous coat, and took hold of Ray's arm. 'Come on, Ray,' she said. 'Let's go and sit somewhere else.'

'Right,' he said. They began to move away.

'Somewhere quiet,' she said.

'No hippies,' he said, casting a derogatory eye over Jude and Robbie.

'No spiteful, so-called friends,' she said.

'No junkies,' he embellished, beginning to enjoy himself as the distance between himself and his rivals increased.

'And no Beatles,' Bennett called after them. This only served to increase their speed, hurrying away as if the devil were after them. Robbie was watching their departure, thoughtful.

'Has he got money?' he asked Jude, studying Ray's receding back.

'She has,' Jude said. 'She's a famous TV personality, didn't you know?'

Cissie was picking up the fallen crisps packets. 'Leave them alone, Robbie,' she said. It was all going wrong. It had become ugly and petty and there was no magic now.

'I'm not going to rob them,' he said. 'Just give them the story of my life.'

Jude took another sleepy bite of her Penguin. 'You mean bore them into submission,' she said.

Robbie was looking at her significantly. 'You got any better ideas?' he asked. Cissie saw Jude lower her eyes and fall silent. Robbie headed off after Ray and Heather, weaving erratically with the movement of the train down the corridor, exhausted but determined. Jude slid down the wall, lost in some private nightmare, crouching on the dirty floor of the corridor, chocolate flaking in the corner of her mouth, eyes desolate. Bennett and Cissie looked out of the window, separated by their thoughts. Jude's head lolled forward, her mouth slack. The other two ignored her. The train rattled onwards.

Cissie watched the passing back gardens of Stratford, hypnotized by the glimpses of alien lives − chained dog barking, two small boys briefly whooping on top of a garden shed, young woman with a basket of washing, old West Indian in a porkpie hat standing bent-backed in a neat allotment, staring up at the passing train. She felt curiously empty, as if she had become a blank sheet of paper waiting to be written on. What had George said − or sung? '*The farther one travels, the less one knows . . .*'

She was sitting back in her seat, the contents of her George Box spread out on the table in front of her: the letters from Mrs Harrison, the note she had passed on from George, scribbled on the back of an envelope: '*Dear Mum, get me up at 3, love George*', the crumpled and smoothed picture cut by Mrs Harrison from the *Daily Mirror*, which the Beatles had all signed, and which one of them had adorned with a big, red, mocking, lipsticked kiss. Cissie had always imagined it was John who had done that. It seemed a

John sort of thing to do. The earrings from the concert. The poem from *Beatles Monthly* she had earnestly copied in 1963: '*A's for Appearing in a show, B is for Beatles, we all know, C is for Clamour (by the Fans) for more, D is for Dashing through a side door, E's for Escape to hotel from stage, F's for Fans, over you they rage, G's for George (whata lotta hair he's got!) H is for Hopeless, something you're NOT!*' The signed, glossy photograph of George, with 'Love Louise Harrison' written on the back. She fingered them all lovingly. They told her who she was.

Opposite her, Bennett was knitting something purple and green, frowning, concentrated. Jude leaned half out of the seat next to Bennett, her feet in the aisle, head craning round, looking for Robbie, her face taut.

'Nearly there,' Bennett said, for something to say. No one replied.

Jude picked up the end of the lurid length of knitting and fingered it. Bennett pulled it away.

'Your kids,' Jude asked, 'whose are they?'

Bennett finished a row and surveyed her handiwork without emotion. She shrugged a little. 'Doesn't really matter,' she said. 'I don't see their fathers.'

'Poor you,' said Jude, sitting upright, knees tucked up under her chin, her old face an odd contrast to her wiry girl's body.

Bennett looked at her, picking up the sliver of malice in Jude's tone. She shook her head. 'No,' she was decisive. She started another row, needles clacking efficiently. 'They may not be the most beautiful kids, or the most intelligent kids, or the most soulful or the most creative. But they're very lovable. You know. Like Ringo.'

'Don't you want a man?' Jude asked, genuinely puzzled.

Bennett looked up suddenly and caught Cissie's eye, smiling. 'You never know,' she said. 'One day Ringo might get a divorce.'

Jude had uncurled herself from her odd, foetal position. Robbie was weaving his way down the carriage, triumphantly waving a ten pound note. He stood swaying above Jude, looking down at her. 'Well?' he said, proud, waiting for praise.

'So go on, then,' Jude snapped. 'It's no use here, is it?'

Crestfallen, Robbie staggered away again. Bennett and Cissie exchanged a silent, grim glance but said nothing.

'Pointless, isn't it,' Jude said, looking at no one, picking at her nails, her body curled up again in the seat in a strange, uncomfortable contortion.

'What is?' Bennett did not look up from her knitting.

'This. The Beatles thing. I mean, it's over. The Beatles. It's over.'

She had their attention now. The needles had stopped clacking. Cissie sat holding a bubble-gum card picture of George Harrison, all lurid colours and white teeth, but her eyes were on Jude.

'They're always fighting,' Jude said. 'They're not a group any more, are they. Not a proper group.'

There was a silence, as Bennett and Cissie absorbed this heresy.

'That's just what the newspapers say,' Cissie said.

'They still play together,' Bennett said.

Jude looked out of the window, past Bennett, her eyes expressionless. 'It's all over,' she said. 'I'm telling you.'

Cissie and Bennett exchanged a glance. 'Not for us it isn't.'

Cissie discovered to her surprise that her heart was beating really fast, as if it would burst. Carefully, she laid the bubble-gum George picture back in its place, on top of the letter from Bettina Rose, Beatles fan club secretary, that she had received in 1964 when she had written asking if the Beatles would be coming to Norwich again. She knew the reply by heart. *Dear Cissie*, it said, with the word 'Cissie' written in by hand, *Dear Cissie, Thank you for your enquiry about the boys' next tour. The tour dates confirmed so far are as follows* . . .

'What about real men, then?' Jude was demanding, glaring at them, aggressive. 'Eh? What about real men?'

'How can you say it's over?' Cissie had hardly heard the question. 'What about John?'

'Yeah,' Jude said, her voice dry. 'Yoko – remember? And George has got Patti, and Ringo's got Maureen, and Paul's got Linda. Come on – what about real men?'

Bennett was looking at someone behind them, and Jude caught her eye and turned round. Robbie had reappeared at the end of the carriage and was leaning against the window, in furtive conversation with a strange, lean figure with long hair and a grubby Afghan coat, the hair round the sleeves matted and grey, the embroidery almost invisible under layers of dirt.

Bennett looked at Robbie and then back at Jude. 'Yeah,' she said. 'Real men. 'Nuff said.'

Jude got up suddenly and left them without a backward glance, stumbling down the carriage towards Robbie and the stranger. The three of them disappeared through the door at the end of the carriage.

Cissie looked at Bennett. 'Nearly there,' said Bennett. She banged her knitting needles on the table, a small, tinny, sad drum-roll.

Cissie finished re-packing her George Box, carefully placing everything where it always went. She felt Bennett's eyes on her, and looked up.

'You got a picture of your dad in there?' Bennett asked.

Cissie snapped the lid of the box shut. 'No,' she said, trying not to sound defensive. 'No, of course not.'

'I just wondered.' Bennett's head was bent over her knitting again. Cissie was silent. She ran her finger over the worn box lid, scored a hundred times with savage biro lettering. George. GEORGE. *George*. **George**. GEORGE.

'Only, I haven't got a picture of Freddy Lemon to give Gandy,' Bennett said. 'And I wouldn't want Doma to have a picture of her dad – might give her nightmares.'

Cissie listened, wondering what she was supposed to say. But Bennett carried on, still not raising her head, needles clicking. 'I always think your mum was a bit like me,' she said. 'Bit of a free spirit. You know.'

Cissie absorbed this, puzzled. 'Do you mean she was a tart?' she asked.

Bennett shifted in her seat, uncomfortable. Cissie looked at her, a little startled, for she had realized at last that Bennett was trying to tell her something important, and now the moment had come.

'Because I don't mind,' Cissie carried on hurriedly, her heart full of dread. 'I don't mind if she was. I know about the war. Mill was always going on about it, how they were all at it like rabbits down the underground when the Blitz was on.'

Bennett pulled at a ball of wool, winding some of the slack round her fist. 'It was only one bloke,' she said. She looked up, and Cissie saw she was embarrassed. 'It was your dad,' she said. 'It was Cecil.'

Cissie saw in her mind's eye the picture on the kitchen wall at Brigadoon, the twinkling face, the carefree stance, standing up to his thighs in the water, grinning at the camera, eyes screwed up against the sun. Cecil.

'Only she never married him,' Bennett said. 'She met him when he came to Norwich to help rebuild one of the shoe factories that got bombed in the war. He was only there for six months. Then she met him a few times in London. Then he just – disappeared.'

The train was edging its way along a narrow track, steep brick walls obliterating the sky on either side.

She met him a few times in London. *Liverpool Street. Where lovers meet.*

'He knew she was pregnant,' Bennett said, knitting. 'But one day she went to meet him at the station and he just never showed up.' Cissie was silent. Her hand rested on the George Box, her eyes focussed on the table, her brain spinning. 'Maybe he was married,' Bennett's voice went on, inexorably. 'Maybe he just didn't fancy the responsibility.'

'Maybe' – Cissie heard her voice, choked and faint, as if someone else were speaking the words – 'Maybe he was on his way to the station and he had an accident –'

'No.' Bennett was emphatic. 'No. She went to the address. It was a boarding house in Finsbury Park. The landlady said he'd just moved out. No forwarding address. Nothing.'

Cissie looked up, a strange sensation rushing into her head, making her ears hot. 'He could still be alive,' she said. 'He's probably still alive.'

Bennett paused for a moment and looked at her. 'Probably,' was all she said. Then she went back to her knitting, as London closed in around them.

★

279

They saw Ray and Heather on the platform at Liverpool Street station, glimpsing them ahead in the crowd, making for the barrier.

'No hurry,' Bennett said. 'We'll catch up with them. Ray's got to buy a ticket, remember? With a bit of luck they'll arrest him for evading his fare.'

But Ray was waving some kind of voucher at the ticket-collector and they passed through. 'Damn,' said Bennett, craning her neck desperately. 'He must have paid on the train. Now we'll have to find out which platform the Norwich train goes from, and get hold of Heather at the barrier.'

Cissie pulled at her arm. 'What's the point?' she asked. She had slowed down almost to a standstill, irritating the passengers crowding along the platform behind her, who jostled past, using suitcases as weapons. Bennett stopped, too. 'What's the point?' Cissie repeated. 'Heather doesn't want to come with us. She wants to go home with Ray.'

Bennett chewed her lip, absorbing this. 'You're right,' she said finally. They walked slowly along the platform, behind the crowd, staring at their feet. It was hard to accept. Heather was not coming. She had made her choice. 'Then there were three,' Bennett said.

'It's Jude we've got to keep hold of,' Cissie said. They avoided each other's eyes. Jude had told them she would meet them under the clock in five minutes – she had some business to attend to. They both had a fair idea of what the business was: it involved the furtive, long-haired figure from the train, it was about clandestine transactions, paranoid deals. It was about heavy drugs. It was outside their understanding. But they had no choice but to wait for Jude to do what she had to do and then follow her, as they had always done.

'I can see her,' Bennett said, pointing. 'Look – there – past the barrier.'

Jude was hurrying round to platform eleven, where the Norwich train was soon to depart. She began to murmur some complex, fabricated story to the man at the barrier, but he let her through, indifferent to the details. She began to weave gracelessly down the platform, peering in the carriage windows, occasionally darting a glance back to the station concourse where she had left Robbie involved in the deal. But she had to do this. She had to do this.

Finally she glimpsed her quarry. Their faces were very close, framed in the window, leaning across, ready for a conciliatory kiss. Grinning, Jude banged on the window, enjoying the start they gave as they leapt apart like guilty lovers.

'I just wanted to tell you something,' she mouthed at them. Inside the carriage, Ray said something to Heather, annoyed. She indicated that she wanted him to open the window. Frowning, he stood up and pulled the window down, glowering at Jude below, Heather at his shoulder.

'Just want to tell you,' Jude repeated, her eye fixed on Heather, her grin lop-sided, 'I slept with one of them.'

'Eh?'

'The Beatles. I slept with one of them. I thought you ought to know.'

Ray pulled at Heather's arm. 'Heather, don't –'

Behind Jude, a whistle blew. The train jerked forward.

'Which one?' Heather asked. The train moved once again. Heather pushed her head out of the window. Jude stood immobile on the platform. 'Which one?'

But it was too late. The train moved more swiftly now, sliding out under the great glass canopy with a deafening hiss, until its nose burst out into the winter light, its tail snaking round the last bend of the platform. Heather's face was still visible in the distance, a small white 'O' of desperation and surprise, and then it too disappeared into the exit tunnel and was gone.

Jude turned away, satisfied, and made her way back up the platform.

Bennett and Cissie were sitting on a bench trying not to panic. 'I can see Robbie,' Bennett said, craning her neck to catch a glimpse of his shambolic figure through the crowds of people criss-crossing the station. 'Look! He's over by the newspaper stand.'

Cissie turned, and at the same moment they saw Jude emerge from platform eleven. They stood up, relieved, watching as Jude hurried across to Robbie and said something urgently to him. He

281

pulled at her arm and murmured close to her ear, their eyes fixing on something at the far end of the station, near the exit for the taxi rank. It was then that Cissie and Bennett, following their gaze, saw the man from the train in the grubby Afghan coat, hovering in the shadows near the arched exit, his eyes sliding this way and that.

'What's happening?' Cissie asked, confused.

Bennett nodded towards the tall windows of the station snack bar, darkened with years of soot and grime. Standing below one of the grey panes was a policeman, who leaned back on his heels contemplating the passing travellers with a look of boredom. 'I don't know,' she said. 'But I don't think it's good.'

Jude had suddenly materialized before them, grey-faced and sweating. 'Got to go,' she said, her lips white and dry, 'Sorry – got to split –'

'You can't!'

Jude's eyes were on the policeman. 'Can't stay,' she said. 'Just mention my name at Apple. They'll let you in.' And she was gone, turning away, finding Robbie, the pair of them racing in a confused zigzag through the crowds, the echoing tannoy undulating above, until they joined forces with the man by the entrance, and the three of them disappeared through the dark arch into the blazing light of the bright January day.

CHAPTER TEN

Here Comes the Sun

'CENTRAL LINE,' BENNETT SAID, poking triumphantly at the map on the wall. 'See? Oxford Circus. Come on!'

She headed for the Underground ticket counter, pleased with herself. She had gritted her teeth and accosted the languid policeman outside the station snack bar, hoping that no one hip noticed her fraternization with the enemy; amazingly, he had not asked to search her pockets for dope, or arrested her for loitering – he had told her how to get to Savile Row. For Bennett, it was all falling into place. She joined Cissie, and handed her a ticket.

'What do we do when we get there?' Cissie asked, fearful.

Bennett was already at the turnstile, pushing through. 'Listen, we got this far,' she said over her shoulder. 'We'll think of something.' She waited as Cissie reluctantly followed her. They paused in a draughty tiled corridor, with the warm air blowing up from below, lifting Bennett's skirts and gusting through Cissie's long hair.

Bennett looked into her friend's eyes, and saw panic. 'We don't need them,' she said firmly. 'Heather and Jude. We don't need them.'

Cissie looked back at Bennett and saw the steadfastness and the determination, the survival of their shared teenage dream, and for a hopeful moment believed her. Her heart lifted. 'Did we ever need them?' she asked.

They hurried towards the escalator, both of them grinning suddenly, exhilarated by the loud rumble of the passing trains, the alien labyrinth of tunnels, the bustle of indifferent Londoners, the fact of their arrival once again in their city of a million fantasies, the city where the Beatles were.

She was looking out for him. She was standing in the doorway of Apple, dazzled by the bright colours of the paintwork, the psychedelic pyrotechnics of purple and green and yellow and pink looping over the brickwork. She was wearing the perfect outfit, designed by The Fool, the one she had seen in Vogue *magazine, with the velvet tunic, the drooping sleeves, the fluttering silk skirt in rainbow colours. And she was looking out for him.*

The tube train rolled and rumbled through the tunnels, passing under the dark, narrow streets of the City, under the dome of St Paul's, rushing onward to the centre.

Bennett was sitting some way down the crowded carriage, lost in some Ringo dream, smiling a little, hemmed in by men in damp mackintoshes.

He had come up behind her, from the interior of Apple, the last place she had expected him to be. She had been looking out into the street, searching for expensive cars, assuming he would drive up to the front door. He had touched her on the arm, gentle as a butterfly, and had said 'Hello.' She turned, and there he was at last, smiling that smile, that enigmatic look in his eye, being George. George.

They had come up out of the wrong exit at Oxford Circus, and found themselves somehow in front of the BBC building. Bennett peered up at the street signs. 'It definitely says Regent Street,' she said dubiously. 'But it also says Langham Place.' She made a decision. 'I'll ask that bloke in the uniform.' She crossed over to the commissionaire standing outside the revolving doors of the great grey building, and returned, beaming. 'Wrong way,' she said. 'We have to go back across Oxford Street.'

'Just think,' Cissie said, staring up at the bank of windows above. '*They*'ve been in there. Lots of times. All those *Saturday Clubs* and Christmas Specials.'

Bennett's gaze followed hers. '*Easy Beat* . . .' she said, remembering, '*Top Gear* . . .'

They stood for a moment, awed. This most definitely *was* the centre of the universe, for every way you turned, the Beatles had been there. A small plump man in spectacles emerged from the building and hurried past them in search of a taxi.

'Wasn't that Harry Secombe?' Cissie asked.

Bennett shook her head. 'He'd have a limousine waiting, wouldn't he. He wouldn't be walking about, Cissie.'

They made their way back the way they had come, past the tall, anonymous buildings, across the chaos of Oxford Street, hurrying past the fur coats in the windows of Dickins and Jones, the puppets in the windows of Hamleys, the shoe shops and the boutiques, both caught up in the moment, their excitement growing. They were here. It would happen.

Savile Row was a shock after the bustle of Regent Street. Here were sombre, restrained office buildings, men's outfitters, brass plaques and discreetly curtained windows. They found number three, and stood silent before its genteel façade, jaws dropping.

'Looks like a solicitor's office,' Bennett said, unable to keep the disappointment out of her voice. Like Cissie, she had imagined something wild, psychedelic, inappropriate, something shouting 'Beatles!' at the universe, an act of defiance in bricks and mortar. The last Apple building had been like that – she had seen it in magazines, the one in Baker Street with the giant Indian painted on the walls, standing out like a jewel amidst the pedantic brick palaces of commerce. But number three Savile Row was just an office building.

'I can't see it,' Cissie said.

'What?'

'Them. Going in and out of there.'

Bennett looked at her, a thought making her catch her breath. 'Do you think they're in there? Now?'

They stared across, their faces intent, as if concentration might make the walls dissolve.

'Come on,' said Bennett. Together they crossed the road, Bennett in front, Cissie a nervous step behind. They began to mount the steps towards the entrance. A man in a suit suddenly emerged from behind the shining glass door and stood on the steps in front of them, polite, impeding their progress.

'Can I help you?' he asked.

'Yeah,' Bennett said, her voice strong and confident. 'We're friends of Jude Reynolds. She said we could see the filming.'

His face was expressionless. 'Jude – sorry?'

'Reynolds,' Cissie said.

'*International Times,*' Bennett said.

The man looked at them, unsmiling. 'Just wait here a moment, would you?' he turned and disappeared inside. Cissie and Bennett exchanged a look, hardly daring to hope. No. This was too easy. They shuffled to one side of the steps to make way for a group of men in suits who had emerged from a taxi on the pavement below and who were now bounding up the steps in an authoritative way, clutching their briefcases and chatting. They too disappeared inside. A man in a strange, bright green jacket and velvet flared trousers emerged, blinking, into the light and descended the steps in front of them, his long fair hair streaming out behind him. They nudged each other, excited.

'Who is it?' hissed Bennett.

'Don't know . . .'

It did not matter. He had quite clearly been touched with the glister of fame, his whole demeanour said show business. He was one of those golden creatures you saw emerging from nightclubs with Jean Shrimpton on their arm, going off to eat at swanky French restaurants whose names you would not know how to pronounce, getting up at lunchtime and doing something arty and creative with their days. Men like that did not exist in Norfolk.

The man in the suit re-emerged. 'Sorry, ladies,' he said. 'No one of that name here.'

'No,' said Bennett patiently, 'She's not actually *here* –'

'She said we could give our names,' Cissie said.

The man looked at her. 'You'll have to leave,' he said. 'I'm sorry.'

Bennett took a deep breath. 'Could you check again?'

The man did not seem to have heard her. 'Off the steps, please,' he said, looming above them, impassive. 'Off the steps, ladies.'

They had been waiting more than an hour. Bennett was tapping on the railings with her drumsticks and whistling through her teeth.

Cissie sat cross-legged on the pavement, getting in the way of passers-by. She was too disappointed to care. Occasionally she would look up and see the man in the suit standing on the steps of the Apple building, hands behind his back. Sometimes his eye would catch hers and he would look away. She no longer knew why they were still there, except that there seemed nowhere else to go. A limousine with darkened windows passed.

'Look!' said Bennett.

Cissie looked. 'No,' she said. Bennett subsided. Cissie looked up at the windows of Apple. 'Do you think they're in there?' she asked. Bennett did not answer, the tapping of her sticks increasing in speed. 'Jude says she slept with one of them,' Cissie said. The drumming stopped. On the third floor of the building, a curtain moved. Someone was looking down into the street. *In there . . .*

'She's a bloody liar,' Bennett said.

'He's in there,' Cissie said, her certainty growing. 'George is in there.'

'Let's go home.'

Cissie looked up, surprised. Bennett was crying. She scrambled to her feet, shocked. She had never seen Bennett cry before – not when her mother had been taken away outside the library, not when she was pregnant, not when the Jermyns had forbidden her to wear kinky boots. Now here she was, her face creased and red and wet. 'I want to go home,' she said.

'Bennett –'

'I bet it was Ringo. I bet she slept with Ringo.' She was turning the drumsticks over and over in her hands, embarrassed by what she knew was an uncharacteristic display of emotion, yet incapable of stopping it.

'Come on, Bennett.' Not knowing what to do, Cissie touched her friend gently on the shoulder. 'Look,' she said, her voice brightening, desperate, 'we're going to get in there!'

Bennett shook her head, sniffing. 'No we're not,' she said. 'It's a mess. Just like before. Like all the other times.' There was a sudden, sharp, snapping sound. Cissie looked down and was startled to see one of the drumsticks in two pieces in Bennett's palm. She was crying in earnest now. 'Just like before,' she repeated.

Cissie was beginning to shiver. 'She didn't sleep with any of them,' she said. The waiting, the chill wind, the anxiety were all beginning to act on her. Her head buzzed, her limbs trembled. 'She's a liar. Jude's a liar. You know that.'

Bennett was silent, staring at the two pieces of drumstick in her hand as if she had surprised herself with her own vehemence. 'It's over,' she said, her voice almost inaudible above the rumble of passing traffic.

Cissie stood helplessly, trying to think of the right words to say, but none came.

'That's it,' Bennett said dully. 'No Ringo. No Mum –'

'Your mum'll get better.'

Bennett shook her head. 'No she won't.' She looked at Cissie with red-rimmed eyes. 'This is it. Me. The kids. Social Security. Hooray for the 1970s.' She stuffed the remains of the drumsticks into her bag and straightened up. 'Come on,' she said. 'Let's go home.'

They started walking slowly, almost unable to leave but not able to stay. Bennett was gulping back the last of her tears, wrenching herself back to normal. 'It's all Peggy's fault,' she murmured finally, sounding more like her old self, scrubbing at her face with a piece of shredded grey Kleenex.

Cissie looked at her, surprised. 'Is it?' They had reached the end of Savile Row and were about to turn into Conduit Street.

'Peggy said we had to come,' Bennett said. 'Had one of her psychic feelings, she said.'

Cissie stopped short, staring. Around them, office workers came and went and a queue was forming for mid-morning doughnuts at a nearby sandwich bar. On the pavement, interested pigeons were gathered, collecting crumbs. Cissie made a decision. She pulled at Bennett's sleeve. 'Come on,' she said. 'I'm going to get us in.'

She turned and started to walk rapidly back the way they had come. Bennett followed her. 'How?'

'Never mind how.' Cissie was walking vigorously now, come to life, her cheeks pink, hair flowing behind her. 'Ringo's in there, Bennett. George is in there. Come on!' And she began to run, her skirts flying out, a bright-haired creature among the besuited office workers, causing them to turn and stare after her, as if they had seen Boadicea suddenly striding into their midst.

She flew up the steps of the Apple building and slid through the grasp of the man in the suit, who had to make do with grappling with Bennett and holding her in a vice-like armlock on the pavement. To her astonishment, Cissie found herself inside.

A young woman with a sheen of perfect hair looked up from behind a mahogany reception desk.

'Hello,' Cissie said, breathless, speaking rapidly before her nerve failed her. 'I need to speak to Mr Harrison. George Harrison.'

The receptionist's expression did not alter. 'I'm sorry,' she said politely, 'he's not in the building today. Did you have an appointment?'

'I'll wait,' Cissie said, desperate.

The receptionist smiled at her, pressing a button on the desk as she did so. 'You can't wait in here,' she said. 'I'm sorry.'

Cissie looked around her frantically. Apart from a group of people chatting in the foyer, no one seemed to be taking any notice of her.

'Can I leave a message?' Cissie could feel time running out. A shout from outside told her that Bennett was still struggling with the security man. 'Please?'

The young woman picked up her pencil and said, 'If you like,' her expression kind.

'Will you try and pass it on?' Cissie asked urgently. 'To George?'

The receptionist's pencil was poised over a notepad. 'What's the message?'

She took a deep breath. 'Tell him – tell him the girl from Norfolk with the flying table is here and would like to speak to him.'

A man had materialized at her elbow. He took hold of her arm. 'All right, you,' he said. He began to lead her away. She went without a struggle.

'Norfolk!' she called to the young woman, over her shoulder, as they headed for the door, 'with the flying table. I'll be outside.'

'Flying table,' the receptionist repeated, writing it down. 'Right.'

They waited for a long time, but he did not come. They waited until it would have been ridiculous to wait any longer. The first wave of office workers was already emerging from cafes, shrugging into their coats and going back to work after lunch. A man had set up his stand at the end of the road and was shouting, '*Standard*! Get your early *Evening Standard*!'

Finally Bennett said, 'Maybe we should try and contact Jude.' The words hummed between them, loaded with meaning. They had lost. They could not do this on their own.

Cissie looked at her. 'How do we do that?'

Bennett shrugged. 'I dunno. We could try and phone *International Times*. They might know where she's supposed to be living.'

It seemed like a stupid idea, but at the same time there seemed little point in standing in the cold waiting for a miracle to happen.

'There's a phone box in the next road,' Bennett said. 'We passed it when we arrived.'

When we arrived. When the air was buzzing with anticipation and I could believe he was close enough to touch.

A girl at *International Times* told them she had never heard of Jude Reynolds. No, no one else in the office had, either. 'She might have come in and packed papers for us at some point,' the voice on the other end of the line said. 'Or she might have been a street seller. They come and go, you know. We don't keep a record of where they live.'

They stood shivering in the phone box.

'She probably never worked for *International Times*,' Cissie said into the disappointed silence.

'We should go home,' Bennett said.

Cissie picked up the receiver. 'I'm going to ring Mum,' she said. Bennett looked surprised, but said nothing. With cold fingers, Cissie dialled the code for Norfolk and the number. She stood listening to the telephone ringing, imagining the scruffy living room and the phone ringing on its scuffed table in the corner, Peggy running in from feeding the chickens, or Mike racing in from the shed. There was a click as someone picked up the receiver in Brigadoon.

'Hello?' It was Peggy.

'Mum – it's me –' Cissie was breathless, stuffing coins into the slot, not sure herself why she was phoning. 'Just to let you know – we're about to head home. Me and Bennett.'

There was a tiny pause at the other end. Cissie could imagine her mother, the slight frown of concentration on her face, eyes closed, a frond of red hair falling on to her cheek, standing by the fireplace, picking up the vibrations.

'And – Mum – Bennett told me about Cecil.'

The miles between them twanged with unspoken explanations, questions. Cissie waited for Peggy to respond. 'Did you see them?' her mother asked finally. 'The Beatles – did you see them?'

'Not yet,' Cissie said, her voice uncertain. She heard a distant, tinny laugh at the other end.

'In that case you're not to come back!' she heard her mother exclaim. 'Do you hear? I don't want to see you till you've met George. Now get on with it!' And then, astonishingly, she heard the line go dead. She stared at the receiver. Her mother had put the phone down.

'What is it?' Bennett asked.

'Nothing,' said Cissie, perturbed by what Peggy had said. Cissie had tried. The moment had passed. She would never meet George. How could she? 'Come on,' she said slowly. 'Let's just have one last look at Apple before we get the tube.'

They walked morosely, back towards Savile Row. It was time to go home. They had no words left to say, no emotions left.

Bennett stopped suddenly. 'Can you hear anything?' she asked.

'What?' Cissie looked at her. 'Yes. Cars. Buses. People.'

'No,' Bennett said. 'Listen.' Cissie listened. 'Do you hear it?'

Faintly, Cissie could hear music in the distance. She looked at Bennett. 'What is it?'

They stood, paralysed, straining to hear above the sound of the traffic. 'It's them,' Cissie said. She began to smile. 'It's them. Bennett. It's them.'

They began to walk again, more quickly, then gradually breaking into a run. Around them, others began to do the same. People had paused in the street and were listening, rooted to the spot, curious. A taxi pulled up near them with a screech of brakes and the driver looked out and upwards, pointing, saying something excitedly to his passenger. They ran on. The music was louder now. They could hear the throb of the bass, the crash of the drums, the voices. Those voices. They raced round the corner into Savile Row. Behind them, a girl screamed 'Paul!'

The street was crowded, transformed, no longer sedate and business-like, but with people jiggling up and down, grinning, amazed, excited. Groups of girls gazed upwards, their eyes fixed on the roof, straining for a glimpse of anything human, anything that might be one of the Beatles. For it really was them. Across the windy rooftops they could hear clearly now, Paul's voice, the words not clear enough, the music loud, distorted; but it was Paul. It was the Beatles, up on the roof of Apple, magically, mysteriously, singing. The crowd was silent, breathless. '*Get back, get back . . .*' People grinned at each other, delighted. Up on the rooftops across the street, little groups of office workers teetered precariously on precipices, straining to see. A man with a moustache, complaining about the noise outside a gentleman's outfitters, was rounded on and silenced by a group of indignant typists. More people were arriving, hurrying from Regent Street, where word had filtered through: running, excited, only to be hushed by the waiting listeners. Two old women danced a little jig. Near Cissie and Bennett, a young girl in school uniform wept a little, murmuring 'George . . .!' to herself.

They stood mesmerized as one song ended and another began; as songs were repeated, false starts gone over, impatient little guitar riffs filled the waiting moments, sudden bursts of music rose into the air. The Beatles were giving a concert – why, no one down in the street knew. What they were doing up on the roof, no one down in the street knew; but it was the Beatles and they were up there, singing, happy, united, harmonious. Occasionally, the listeners could hear laughter, or scattered applause, or some inaudible piece of sarcasm delivered in the unmistakable drawl of John Lennon. Then another song, more applause, more guitar tuning, a little drum-roll from Ringo, another song. It was the perfect concert: impromptu, unrehearsed, full of human error, four musicians having fun and mischievously stopping the traffic as they did it. To their admiring listeners, it was a perfect moment of Beatle anarchy. To the grumbling businessmen from nearby offices, it was a bloody cheek.

People were beginning to relax, over the initial shock, grinning round at strangers, enjoying the sense of significance, their part in the moment, when two policemen materialized and entered the building. A faint boo went up from the crowd, then its collective attention returned again, slightly more intense now, to the invisible giants on the roof, still playing, still singing.

Bennett was ecstatic. Eyes shining, she held Cissie's arm so tightly that it hurt. 'He's up there,' she whispered, breaking the silence. 'Ringo. It's magic.' Cissie hardly heard her, eyes fixed on some invisible spot beyond the edge of the rooftop, where he stood, even now. He stood. 'I'm going to get some more sticks,' Bennett was hissing in her ear. 'Keep practising, get the band going again.'

Cissie was still listening, frozen, betrayed, heartbroken. He had been there all the time. George had been in Apple, and he had not come out to see the girl from Norfolk. The music stopped, and again they heard the faint trickle of applause descend from the skies; then a more prolonged silence, and a glimpse of someone on the roof reeling in a cable. A confused moment, with people asking, 'Is that it?', 'Do you think that's it?' – and then a policeman appeared at Cissie's elbow. 'Show's over,' he said. 'Move along, girls.' Already the party atmosphere had evaporated. Almost sheepishly people returned to normal, hurrying off to catch buses, eat their lunch, finish their shopping. Cissie and Bennett shuffled obediently away with the crowd, too overcome to argue.

'Of course they reached their peak with *Sergeant Pepper*,' Cissie heard a boy in denims say knowledgeably to his companion. 'I mean the *White Album* was good, but it was erratic, too many out-side influences . . .'

They found a cafe, one of those ubiquitous Italian snack bars scattered about the streets of London, with a narrow eating area, a magnificent coffee machine, a clapped-out juke-box and a vast list of misspelt sandwiches scratched on to a board above the propri-etor's head. They were the only customers.

'We just heard a bit of history,' Bennett was prattling excitedly, her face flushed and animated, 'a bit of history! Remember what I said on the train about telling our grandchildren? We've done it, Cissie, we've done it. We've heard them give a concert. Do you realize they haven't done a live concert since – oh, I don't know – years and years . . . And we saw this one. Well, we heard it . . .'

Cissie listened, silent and tearless, staring at Bennett's pink face.

'So much for Jude's theory about it all being over,' Bennett con-tinued, her voice triumphant. 'They were there – I heard John's voice, I heard George doing the chorus on one song, and we know we heard Paul on that one about getting back. And it was definitely Ringo on the drums, I'd know his action anywhere.' She performed a jubilant drum-roll with her hands on the edge of the table.

'She stopped writing,' Cissie said abruptly.

Bennett looked up. 'Who?'

'Mrs Harrison. She just stopped. Never answered my letters.'

Bennett was staring at her, hands suspended above the table. She had stopped drumming. 'Didn't you know?' she said. 'She's ill. Mrs Harrison. In hospital. It was in the papers.'

Cissie's throat closed up. 'Why didn't you tell me?' She managed to say.

Bennett gripped the edge of the table guiltily. 'I didn't like to mention it. Thought you knew. Thought you were too upset to talk about it. They say she's very ill.'

The cafe proprietor, a thin man with a grubby apron and a sallow complexion, deposited two cups of strong, greasy-looking tea on the table. 'That'll be one and six,' he said.

Cissie stared at Bennett, still absorbing the news about Mrs Harrison. 'I wrote her a horrible letter,' she said.

Bennett's face softened in sympathy. 'She probably never got it,' she said.

'One and six,' the man said again.

'Can't we pay on the way out?' Cissie asked, irritated.

He stood, obstinate, arms folded. 'No money, no tea.' His accent was an odd mixture of Cockney and Italian. 'Bloody Apple scruffs. That's what you are, in't it? Apple scruffs, eh?'

Bennett began fishing in her bag for the money. Cissie watched her. She was ready to weep. 'George was in there all the time,' she managed to say, finally. 'He never came out to see me.'

'Probably never got the message,' Bennett said, searching for her purse.

'He was up there.'

'That John Lennon,' the man said. 'He comes in here.'

'Yeah.' Bennett eyed him cynically. 'Sure.'

'Bacon and eggs,' he said, and then began to elaborate, seeing their looks of disbelief. 'Breakfast. Always has two slice of fried bread. Yes. John Lennon.'

Bennett slammed some coins on to the table. Cissie felt suddenly a great hot wave of nausea rising up inside her. It was the man and his Brycleemed hair, it was the slap of the money on the stained table-top, it was the smell of fried onions, Bennett's triumphalism, the aftermath of quivering, gut-wrenching emotion, the loss of George, the loss of Mrs Harrison, the end of everything. Cissie pushed her chair back and stood up. 'I'm going to the loo,' she said.

'You won't find him in there!' The man called after her. He began to sing, in a mocking, nasal voice, '*She loves you, yeah, yeah, yeah . . .*'

The toilet was little more than a broom cupboard. Cissie crammed herself into the tiny space and locked the door. Outside, she could hear the cafe-owner still singing, loud and spiteful, and the sound of Bennett drumming on something, her spirits revived. Cissie leaned over the sink, wondering if she would vomit. She turned the tap, but the trickle of water that emerged was brown. She breathed in and out for a few moments, listening to the sound of air being inhaled and then expelled from her gullet. Gradually the heat in her head diminished, the spots before her eyes faded, the world spun back on its axis and righted itself. She straightened up and turned off the tap.

She pulled her George Box out from her bag, and balanced it carefully on the sink, looking at it for a moment. Then she delved back inside her bag and found an eyeliner pencil. Leaning towards the fly-blown mirror, she stared at her face. A pale, sad girl looked back, and mouthed the word 'George' wanly. She squinted a little, re-applying the eyeliner so that her eyes were big and dark again. Then she stood back a little, assessing her handiwork. She was about to leave, picking up the George Box ready to return it to her bag, when she suddenly changed her mind. She put the George Box back on the sink. She looked thoughtfully round the shabby toilet. Then she leaned forward and wrote 'GEORGE' in large letters across the mirror, frowning in concentration as she strove to get the lettering even. She had always been good at lettering in Mr Jarvis's art class at Crookfield Grammar. She finished the job and smiled at it, pleased. Then she turned to the wall on her right. Someone had scribbled 'Justin 4 Me' in nervous, tiny writing in one corner, and the remains of a heart containing the words 'JOE COCKER' were just visible. Someone had evidently tried to scrub the wall clean recently. Cissie looked in her bag and found a green eyeliner pencil. She reached up and began to write, but the wall surface was too slippery, and nothing happened. She peered in her bag again, and produced a nail file. Carefully, she began to scratch a large 'G' into the wall, scraping the paint away, letting the flakes fall to the floor as she concentrated on her task. She finished the letter and stood, admiring it. It was huge, an ugly, searing blight on the almost pristine wall. She had never done anything like this before. It gave her immense satisfaction. She began work on the next letter, humming a little to herself.

Back in the cafe, Bennett was in trouble. She was finishing the second cup of tea, sipping unconcernedly.

'I said no drumming,' the cafe-owner was saying. 'I said no drumming and I said one and six. Out.'

'Haven't finished my tea,' Bennett said.

'Out.'

Cissie returned, calm. 'Let's go,' she said. Bennett sipped her tea in an exaggeratedly ladylike manner, little finger crooked. Then, staring defiantly at the man, she replaced the cup in the saucer very deliberately and stood up.

'Sixpence more,' the man said.

'It was rotten tea.'

'Bennett –' Cissie's expression begged her to leave.

They began to make a dignified exit. 'Bloody Apple scruffs,' the man said. 'Bloody layabouts.'

They had reached the door. Cissie turned, and saw that the man was watching her, full of suspicion. He turned and headed for the toilet.

'Quick!' Cissie said. 'Quick, Bennett! Run!'

Bennett had paused outside the cafe and stared at her. 'Why? What did we do?'

Through the glass, Cissie could see the man emerging from the back of the cafe, scowling with anger.

'Run!' she shouted, and then she leapt away, racing along the grey street like someone possessed, screeching and laughing, her red hair flying, clutching her George Box under one arm, Bennett panting behind her, confused and breathless, calling her name as they turned yet another corner, still running, Cissie colliding with irritated passers-by, narrowly missing a car pulling out from the kerb, laughing in the face of its angry driver.

'Wait, Cissie!' Bennett yelled, thundering along behind, hampered by her skirts and her shoulder bag and her larger frame. 'Wait!'

Finally Cissie stopped. She had run out of breath and now collapsed against a wall in a narrow backstreet, speechless, hysterical, panting with laughter. Bennett rounded the corner, saw her and stopped running, puce and wheezing. She stopped in front of Cissie, doubled up, clutching, gasping, 'Stitch!'

Cissie, recovering, grinned at her. 'Hundred yards sprint champion of the third year, remember?'

'You're mad, you are,' Bennett panted. 'What did we do? Why

297

did we —' But Cissie was no longer listening. She was staring at someone beyond Bennett's heaving profile. Bennett turned.

He had stepped out of a door in the building opposite, a tall, blank establishment with few windows, the featureless rear of Savile Row.

She heard Bennett's sharp intake of breath. 'Isn't that —?'

Yes it is. He was more familiar to her than anyone else in the world. He was wearing a long black coat, green trousers, sneakers. Following him was a young woman in a hat, tall, slender, blonde. *I'm not looking right, my face is red, my hair all over the place.* His hair was longer than she expected, brushing his collar, thick and dark. *His hair. It's his hair. Yes it is.* He was reaching for the door of a Mercedes parked by the entrance, a bunch of keys in his hand. The girl in the hat had hurried round to the passenger door. *Those long white fingers, my fingers, my hand, my George.* For one frozen, infinitesimal second, he looked up and their eyes met. *Yes it is.* Aware he had been spotted, he quickly unlocked the car.

'Not now,' he said, his voice weary and polite. 'Please.' *George had spoken to her.*

He was climbing inside and slamming the door, disappearing abruptly behind a tinted screen of smoked glass. The blonde in the hat was inside the car now. The engine roared into life and the Mercedes reversed suddenly towards them and then lurched away in a half-turn, preparing to head off down the alleyway into the street beyond.

He was going. This was it. He was going and she was standing there, paralysed, as she always was, helpless in the face of an uncertain and unpredictable world, always reacting, never acting. She was standing there, and a few feet away was George Harrison. Suddenly Cissie leapt forward. She began to run, slowly at first, unsure of what she was doing, then gathering momentum, keeping up with the car, her heart pounding, her body alive and tingling. She could just see him beyond the opaque window, only a shape behind the wheel, but she knew it was him. *Yes it is, it's you.* She began to hammer on the window with her fists, hardly aware that she was on the passenger side of the car, pummelling at the glass until her knuckles hurt. She began to shout, hearing her voice, screaming, reverberating inside her own head, but somehow out there, a shrill screech in the empty street.

'I'm the girl from Norfolk with the flying table!' she yelled at him, a full-throated, red-bellied, gut-stirring triumph of a yell. 'I'm the girl from Norfolk, you bastard!'

She was losing ground. In desperation she hurled her George Box at the car with a great whoop, and heard as it smashed on to the pavement behind her as she ran, scattering pictures and letters and earrings and secrets and memories and passion and hope and despair all over the road, tumbling into the gutters, flying under parked cars, fluttering into the damp January puddles and mingling with the discarded sweet wrappers and cigarette packets of careless passers-by.

And in that same second there was the whirr of a descending electric window, a sudden glimpse of a white, frightened face framed by wisps of fair hair, large eyes, a moment of connection, and then the car accelerated away, screeching round the corner, a blur of shadowy shapes in the back window visible before it disappeared.

Cissie stood watching the space where the car had been, her shoulders shaking.

It had been Patti who had looked at her — Patti, gazing at her with pitying eyes. George's wife. Still Cissie stood there, staring into the distance. Patti Harrison. They were exactly the same age. Perhaps in another life they might have been friends. But Cissie had seen the look on Patti's face in that tiny moment when their eyes had locked, and in that look, like a great clap of thunder, she had understood everything; for those eyes — those big, round, dolly-bird eyes that she had envied and loathed and wept over and burned images of — those eyes had been full of pity. *She's got a life*, Cissie thought, *and I haven't.*

Patti had a husband, and a car full of shopping and a bungalow called Kinfauns. These things were real to her, they were her life, not Cissie's. *Not now*, George had said, *please.*

Bennett approached.

'Cissie . . .' she said, ready with words of comfort. But when she put her arm around her friend and pulled her close she saw that there was no threat of incipient tears. Cissie was calm, an expression of resignation on her face. Or was it realization?

Cissie pulled away from her, seeing something lying on the road near by. She went over and picked it up. It was a small piece of blue fabric, a neat square. *George. The Star Club. Hamburg.* She pressed it to her lips and closed her eyes, seeing for a moment a brief, incongruous vision of her mother, her face pleading, gazing at her with the full force of her love and saying, 'Go on!'

Cissie opened her eyes. Bennett was staring at her, confused, unsure what to do or say, standing clumsily in the road in her big, muddy skirt, silenced. Cissie stuffed the small square of cloth into her pocket. She turned her back on the space where George had been, and went to join her friend.

'Come on,' she said, putting her arm through Bennett's. 'The show's over.' Together, they walked away.

At Brigadoon, Peggy was spring cleaning. She had returned Mrs Bennett to the hospital, and the children were playing a noisy game of cowboys and Indians in the garden. A sudden desire to be busy had overcome her. She had scrubbed the mud-encrusted tiles of the kitchen, she had delved with rubber-gloved hands into the dusty recesses of the stove, pulling out handfuls of cat hair and dead earwigs, groaning to herself in disgust. Cleaning was not something Peggy did often, but today felt somehow like a day for change, for renewal.

Now she stood, bracing herself, in front of the cupboard under the stairs. Inside, she knew, was heaped ten years' accumulation of odd wellington boots, discarded socks, old dog leads and Christmas decorations, as well as a rich seam of cobwebs and assorted insect life. Stepping forward with her duster, she suddenly caught sight of the photograph of Cecil on the wall by the cupboard door. She looked at it for a moment, frowning a little. She had always fancied somehow that she could see the slant of Cecil's cheekbones in Cissie's small, pointed face; but perhaps it was an illusion. She stepped closer to the photograph, squinting a little at it, trying to focus it with her short-sighted eyes. Cecil himself sometimes seemed like an illusion. She thought of Cissie, standing in a phone box in London somewhere, saying again, 'Mum. Bennett told me about Cecil.' She frowned a little, private, anxious frown. At last the slow tide of lies had been stemmed. Peggy had not meant it to happen, the progressive, fictional killing-off of Cecil; she had been trying to be kind to a withdrawn and difficult daughter. As the years passed and the fantasy grew, she had known, finally, that it had to stop, but she could not bring herself to say the words, to look into Cissie's untrusting, pain-filled eyes and say, 'The one thing that gave you strength – it was a lie.' Bennett had been her saviour. She had a sudden picture of Mike, standing in the kitchen, saying, 'Susan Bennett, Angel of Mercy.' He had been right.

Outside, she could hear the shouts of the children and the reassuring sound of Mike's anvil, as he hammered steadily at something in his sheds. One of his lumps, she heard Mill say, disapprovingly, and smiled to herself. She reached up and lifted the photograph in its wooden frame down from the wall. She dusted it carefully, breathing on the glass and then rubbing it, smearing it a little. Cecil. It was all so long ago.

She headed out of the kitchen, still carrying the picture, humming to herself, remembering a darkened cinema, holding hands with a lover, *Seven Brides for Seven Brothers*.

She stepped carefully over the muddy puddles in the yard, scattering the hens as she went, until she reached the shed. Pushing open the door, she stepped inside. In the musty darkness, next to the bicycles, stood a large crate, waiting to receive the rejects from spring cleaning destined for the attic. She dropped the picture inside on top of some old curtains, and then turned and pushed open the door again, stepping out into the thin spring light, singing quietly to herself, a medley of songs from the time when she was young and the future beckoned. The lover she remembered was Mike. Just the cupboard to do, then she could stop and have a cup of tea . . .

★

'You're very quiet,' Bennett remarked. They had reached Liverpool Street station, and were sitting in the dingy cafe drinking tea and smoking cigarettes, waiting for the Norwich train.

Cissie looked up. She had been stirring her tea with undue intensity. 'What will you do when you get home?' she asked Bennett.

Bennett raised her eyebrows. It seemed an odd question. 'I dunno. Collect the kids from Brigadoon. Go and see Mum. Go back to the commune. What else would I do?'

Cissie was looking at her, an odd expression on her face. 'What would you do if you had the chance? I mean, what would you *really* like to do?'

Bennett thought for a moment, then decided. Her bright, honest face beamed at Cissie. 'Exactly what I just said, I think. I like my life. I love my kids. I want to help Mum. I like Norwich, I love the house, I like my friends.' She seemed embarrassed by this admission, and bit sheepishly into a Shortie biscuit. 'I suppose I'd quite like to be a famous girl drummer,' she added, dubiously, 'but only if I could take the kids with me on tour.' She stared at Cissie, who seemed uncharacteristically fidgety, her face a blur of confused emotion, far removed from her usual withdrawn calm. Gone was that quality of stillness that made people look at her and think about pre-Raphaelite women, replaced by a more feverish demeanour, a sense of excitement, of incipient chaos.

'What about you?' Bennett asked suspiciously. 'What would you really like to do?'

Cissie thought for a moment. 'I'd like to be called Margaret. I'm fed up with being called Cissie. Margaret. Maggie. It's my second name. More groovy, don't you think?'

Bennett grinned. 'The girl from Norfolk with the flying table. That's your name.'

Cissie shook her head. 'No. The flying table wasn't ever mine, was it? It was Mum's.' She stood up. 'We'd better get going,' she said. 'The train will be in by now.'

'You haven't answered my question,' Bennett said.

'I know.'

Cissie was thinking about Oliver. She and Oliver had some

302

unfinished business to resolve. She wasn't sure what it would lead to, but she knew she had to face him, to see if those peculiar, exciting moments of shared emotion in the past had any future.

Slowly, they made their way across the concourse towards platform eleven. It was the rush hour, and the station was buzzing with commuters racing for suburban trains to take them to their homes in Essex. Bennett paused under the station clock and looked up at it, causing a small knot of human congestion behind her.

'What did she say? John Lennon's birthday.'

'Midnight. October the ninth. His fiftieth.'

They walked on slowly. 'Will you be there?' Bennett asked.

'Of course. You?'

Bennett grinned. 'If only to see if Heather's still married to Ray.'

Cissie looked sad. 'And to see if Jude's still alive.'

Bennett laughed. 'To see if *any* of us are alive! Christ, we'll all be old women!'

They passed the barrier, showing their return tickets to the inspector at the gate.

'Let's get near the buffet car,' Bennett said, moving ahead. 'We can get drunk on the way home. I've still got ten bob.'

Cissie followed her, silent. The platform was busy with farewells and trolleyloads of luggage. A party of French schoolchildren noisily impeded the progress of passengers trying to get further up the train to the emptier carriages. Bennett jumped up occasionally, peering in the darkened train windows, until she found what she was looking for.

'Here,' she said. 'Completely empty. And a smoker. This'll do.' She opened the door and climbed up, bunching her skirts in one hand, bag slung over her shoulder, turning to hold the door for Cissie.

'I'm not coming,' Cissie said. She was rooted to the platform, surprised to hear the words issuing from her own mouth.

Bennett stood looking down at her.

'I'm dropping out of university,' Cissie said. 'I'm not coming back.'

Bennett absorbed this, the suspicion of a tremble about her mouth. 'What do I tell Peggy?' she asked, finally.

Cissie thought for a moment. 'Tell her Cissie went mad and decided to hitch-hike to Paraguay.'

'You're not. Not really.'

'I might be.'

Bennett struggled for a moment. 'Did George go to Paraguay?'

'No. He went to India.'

Bennett pondered. 'So. I tell Peggy you're going to Paraguay.'

Cissie's eyes shifted restlessly along the platform. The driver was approaching, intent on studying a football report on the back of the *Evening Standard* as he walked, taking his time, a cigarette dangling from his lips. She recognized him. He was the driver who had brought them to London this morning. Everyone was going back to Norfolk. Except her. She would no longer be the girl from Norfolk.

Slowly, Bennett pulled the carriage door closed. Doors slammed along the length of the train. To Cissie, standing small on the platform, Bennett seemed already distant.

She was hanging out of the window, seemingly at a loss for words. 'You can always come and stay with us,' she said, 'at the commune.'

'I know,' Cissie said.

Bennett laughed a little, uncomfortable. She was not good at good-byes, at scenes where there was the potential for visible emotion. 'Always plenty of bean stew.'

The train shuddered into life. The guard was peering down the platform, whistle at the ready.

'It wasn't because of me telling you about Cecil, was it?' Bennett asked, suddenly fearful. Cissie shook her head, smiling. Her heart was beginning to pound. She was going to have an adventure: it was the rest of her life. 'You're not going off to search for him or anything, are you?' Bennett was struggling not to weep. 'Because if I thought that —'

'I don't care about Cecil,' Cissie said.

The train rolled forward slowly. 'What will you do?' Bennett was leaning further out of the carriage window, her face still creased with anxiety. 'I mean — now, this minute? Where will you go?'

Cissie began to walk along next to the moving train. 'I think I'll go and see Oliver,' she said, and a pink blush spread across her cheeks. 'After that – who knows?' The train was beginning to speed up. Her eyes met Bennett's.

'Man had an ear transplant,' Bennett said. 'They gave him a pig's ear.'

Cissie was running now. 'Bennett. I don't want to hear this.'

'Years later the man goes back to the doctor's –'

In a moment Bennett would be gone. 'Yes –'

Cissie reached up her hand, racing to keep level with the window. Bennett was shouting now, above the increasing roar of the engine as the train picked up speed. 'Doctor says, how's the ear? Man says fine, but I still get a bit of crackling now and then –'

For a brief moment, her fingers touched Cissie's. Then the train jerked away, faster now, and Cissie stood alone on the platform, watching as the carriage bearing Bennett back to Norfolk disappeared out of sight, the rest of the train snaking behind. She stood there until the small, square window at the back of the train had disappeared into the darkness.

Then she turned, hurrying back along the platform, plunging into the crowded chaos of the station, and disappearing down the escalator to the underground.

EPILOGUE

Wednesday 9 October 1990

MUSIC CROSSED THE great space.
A whistle blew somewhere in the echoing vaults of
the railway station, and a train began slowly to pull away,
edging out into the sharp autumn night.

On the shiny station concourse, the warmth generated by a
myriad hurrying commuters had dissipated, and a chill descended,
clinging to the shoulders of the woman on the red metal bench. She
looked at the clock. Perhaps she had got it wrong.

A porter was passing, pushing a trolley piled high with parcels.

'What day is it?' she asked him.

'Ninth,' he said, not pausing, not even looking at her. 'Ninth of
October.'

She retrieved her plastic cup from the bench next to her,
and carefully poured in a small measure of Special Brew. The can
wobbled, clicking against the plastic rim as she delicately angled it
so that just a light, steady stream of liquid descended.

A shout startled her, and she looked up, shocked and hopeful. But
it was two young men, drunk in their city suits, racing across the
empty vastness of the station, skating on the polished tiles, trying in
vain to catch a train that had already departed. One of them kicked
savagely at a wastebin. 'Fucking trains,' he said. 'Fucking British
Rail.'

The woman watched them as they wandered, disconsolate, back
towards the exit, past the red benches where she sat alone with her
drink.

'You know what day it is?' she shouted suddenly, as they drew

306

near. They looked away. 'It's John Lennon's birthday! Fifty today!' she said and raised her plastic cup. 'Happy Birthday!'

One of the young men turned to grin at her. 'He's dead,' he said. 'Didn't you know?' And the two of them, suddenly galvanized into life by the sight of a taxi on the pavement outside with its yellow light glowing, ran shouting into the dark arches of Liverpool Street station and disappeared.

She stared at the clock. It was the right day, wasn't it? There had been some argument about the time, about midnight being inconvenient, but they had resolved it, she was sure.

Someone was standing over her. She looked up, a blaze of hope suffusing her face. But it was only one of the station cleaners in his bright red overalls, pulling on rubber gloves over his black hands. 'Come on, love,' he said. 'Better get moving. The polisher's coming this way soon.'

She blinked up at him, wondering who the polisher was. 'You look like Jimi Hendrix,' she said. But he did not seem to hear.

'That's right, love,' he said, soothingly. 'You get along.'

She stood up unsteadily. 'I've got an appointment,' she said in a loud, clear voice. 'I'm meeting someone off a train. From Norfolk.'

She had studied the arrivals board. A train had been due to arrive from Norwich at 11.55.

The man shook his head. 'No Norwich trains coming in for at least an hour,' he said. 'I worked here five years. I know these things. You wait outside, all right?'

He had an arm under her elbow, well-meaning. The floor polisher had appeared like a huge crab from under the archway leading to the shopping mall, its engine whirring, its mandible brushes sweeping the floor in brisk circular motions. The words 'Station Sanitation' were emblazoned on its gleaming white sides. The driver, also wearing red overalls, waved at the cleaner and began to head towards them. The woman watched, dazed, as the shining white creature bore down on them. The polisher. She quivered as it approached, the roar of its internal organs a terrible hubbub in her head, muddling her thoughts. She began to back away, but the man had hold of her, his black fingers strong round her bony forearm.

She was lost in the face of what was modern; the world seemed to be crowded with machines and equipment, electronics, buttons to press, beeping sounds.

The creature stopped in front of them and was suddenly silent. The driver jumped down and stood leaning against one of the giant wheels. He and the other cleaner began to converse in a language the woman did not understand. She stood, swaying, miserable. Then, as if to taunt her, the Muzak floating across the concourse became suddenly recognizable, a lush, violin-filled version of 'Across The Universe'.

One of the men turned to her. 'Come on, old love,' he said. 'Time to go.'

She tried to pull away, misunderstanding his touch. 'Don't you do that!' she said sharply. 'You men – all the same. Only want one thing. One thing . . .'

He sighed, patient. 'Time to go, my darling.'

He was right. 'OK,' she said. Then she paused again, remembering. 'I was in love once,' she said.

He grinned, displaying a gold tooth. 'Only once?' he teased.

She nodded. 'He was a true man. A real hero.' He could feel her quivering beneath his hand. 'He was a Beatle.'

He did not understand. He merely nodded, half-listening, grinning at the other man, his mind on his tea break. Her mouth had begun to tremble uncontrollably. 'I miss my friends,' she said.

'I know.' He squeezed her arm, sympathetic, pushing her gently away. 'Exit's that way.'

They watched her go, waiting until they saw her disappear into the great arch that marked the exit. Then they turned and climbed back on board the great machine, bringing it to life once more as it resumed its great purge of the new and gleaming station floor.

AUTHOR'S NOTE

Louise Harrison died in July, 1970.

ACKNOWLEDGEMENTS

The song and poem extracts in this book are quoted by permission of the copyright holders, as follows:

'Speedy Gonzales' (Lee/Kaye/Hess): lyric reproduced by kind permission of Carlin Music Corporation, UK, administrator in respect of Ethel Lee's 33.33% interest; copyright © 1961, renewed and assigned to David Hess Music Co., Mill Valley, California. Administered throughout the world except the United States and Canada by Memory Lane Music International Limited, London; Buddy Kaye.

'I Want To Hold Your Hand': words and music by John Lennon & Paul McCartney; copyright © 1963 Northern Songs. Used by permission of Music Sales Limited. All rights reserved. International copyright secured.

'Not A Second Time': words and music by John Lennon and Paul McCartney; copyright © 1963 Northern Songs. Used by permission of Music Sales Limited. All rights reserved. International copyright secured.

'I'll Get You': words and music by John Lennon and Paul McCartney; copyright © 1963 Northern Songs. Used by permission of Music Sales Limited. All rights reserved. International copyright secured.

'I'm Happy Just To Dance With You': words and music by John Lennon and Paul McCartney; copyright © 1964 Northern Songs. Used by permission of Music Sales Limited. All rights reserved. International copyright secured.

'Rocky Raccoon': words and music by John Lennon and

Paul McCartney; copyright © 1968 Northern Songs. Used by permission of Music Sales Limited. All rights reserved. International copyright secured.

'When I'm Sixty-Four': words and music by John Lennon and Paul McCartney; copyright © 1967 Northern Songs. Used by permission of Music Sales Limited. All rights reserved. International copyright secured.

'Friend' by Gregory Corso: from *Long Live Man*, New Directions Publishing Corporation, 1962.

'Piggies' by George Harrison: copyright © 1968, 1981 Harrisongs Ltd. All rights reserved. International copyright secured.

'The Inner Light': words and music by George Harrison; copyright © 1968 Northern Songs. Used by permission of Music Sales Limited. All rights reserved. International copyright secured.